TIMOTHY ZAHN

arrow books

Published by Arrow 2013

2 4 6 8 10 9 7 5 3 1

First published in Great Britain in 2013 by
Century
Random House, 20 Vauxhall Bridge Road,
London SW1V 2SA

www.starwars.com
www.randomhouse.co.uk

Addresses for companies within The Random House Group Limited
can be found at: www.randomhouse.co.uk

The Random House Group Limited Reg. No. 954009

A CIP catalogue record for this book
is available from the British Library

ISBN 9780099542926

The Random House Group Limited supports the Forest Stewardship
Council® (FSC®), the leading international forest-certification
organisation. Our books carrying the FSC label are printed on FSC®-
certified paper. FSC is the only forest-certification scheme supported
by the leading environmental organisations, including Greenpeace.
Our paper procurement policy can be found at:
www.randomhouse.co.uk/environment

Printed and bound by Clays Ltd, St Ives plc

THE STAR WARS NOVELS TIMELINE

BEFORE THE REPUBLIC
37,000-25,000 YEARS BEFORE
STAR WARS: A New Hope

c. 25,793 *YEARS BEFORE STAR WARS: A New Hope*

Dawn of the Jedi: Into the Void

OLD REPUBLIC
5000–67 YEARS BEFORE
STAR WARS: A New Hope

Lost Tribe of the Sith†
Precipice
Skyborn
Paragon
Savior
Purgatory
Sentinel

3954 *YEARS BEFORE STAR WARS: A New Hope*

The Old Republic: Revan

3650 *YEARS BEFORE STAR WARS: A New Hope*

The Old Republic: Deceived
Red Harvest
The Old Republic: Fatal Alliance
The Old Republic: Annihilation

Lost Tribe of the Sith†
Pantheon
Secrets

2975 *YEARS BEFORE STAR WARS: A New Hope*

Lost Tribe of the Sith†
Pandemonium

1032 *YEARS BEFORE STAR WARS: A New Hope*

Knight Errant
Darth Bane: Path of Destruction
Darth Bane: Rule of Two
Darth Bane: Dynasty of Evil

RISE OF THE EMPIRE
67–0 YEARS BEFORE
STAR WARS: A New Hope

67 *YEARS BEFORE STAR WARS: A New Hope*

Darth Plagueis

33 *YEARS BEFORE STAR WARS: A New Hope*

Darth Maul: Saboteur*
Cloak of Deception
Darth Maul: Shadow Hunter
Darth Maul: Lockdown**

32 *YEARS BEFORE STAR WARS: A New Hope*

STAR WARS: EPISODE I
THE PHANTOM MENACE

Rogue Planet
Outbound Flight
The Approaching Storm

22 *YEARS BEFORE STAR WARS: A New Hope*

STAR WARS: EPISODE II
ATTACK OF THE CLONES

22–19 *YEARS BEFORE STAR WARS: A New Hope*

The Clone Wars
The Clone Wars: Wild Space
The Clone Wars: No Prisoners

Clone Wars Gambit
Stealth
Siege

Republic Commando
Hard Contact
Triple Zero
True Colors
Order 66

Shatterpoint
The Cestus Deception
The Hive*
MedStar I: Battle Surgeons
MedStar II: Jedi Healer
Jedi Trial
Yoda: Dark Rendezvous
Labyrinth of Evil

*An eBook novella
**Forthcoming
† Lost Tribe of the Sith: The Collected Stories

THE STAR WARS NOVELS TIMELINE

19 *YEARS BEFORE STAR WARS: A New Hope*

STAR WARS: EPISODE III
REVENGE OF THE SITH

Kenobi
Dark Lord: The Rise of Darth Vader

Imperial Commando
501st

Coruscant Nights
Jedi Twilight
Street of Shadows
Patterns of Force

The Last Jedi

10 *YEARS BEFORE STAR WARS: A New Hope*

The Han Solo Trilogy
The Paradise Snare
The Hutt Gambit
Rebel Dawn

The Adventures of Lando Calrissian
The Force Unleashed
The Han Solo Adventures
Death Troopers
The Force Unleashed II

REBELLION
0–5 YEARS AFTER
STAR WARS: A New Hope

Death Star
Shadow Games

0

STAR WARS: EPISODE IV
A NEW HOPE

Tales from the Mos Eisley Cantina
Tales from the Empire
Tales from the New Republic
Winner Lose All*
Scoundrels
Allegiance
Choices of One
Empire and Rebellion: Honor Among Thieves**
Galaxies: The Ruins of Dantooine
Splinter of the Mind's Eye
Empire and Rebellion: Razor's Edge

3 *YEARS AFTER STAR WARS: A New Hope*

STAR WARS: EPISODE V
THE EMPIRE STRIKES BACK

Tales of the Bounty Hunters
Shadows of the Empire

4 *YEARS AFTER STAR WARS: A New Hope*

STAR WARS: EPISODE VI
THE RETURN OF THE JEDI

Tales from Jabba's Palace

The Bounty Hunter Wars
The Mandalorian Armor
Slave Ship
Hard Merchandise

The Truce at Bakura
Luke Skywalker and the Shadows of Mindor

NEW REPUBLIC
5–25 YEARS AFTER
STAR WARS: A New Hope

X-Wing
Rogue Squadron
Wedge's Gamble
The Krytos Trap
The Bacta War
Wraith Squadron
Iron Fist
Solo Command

The Courtship of Princess Leia
A Forest Apart*
Tatooine Ghost

The Thrawn Trilogy
Heir to the Empire
Dark Force Rising
The Last Command

X-Wing: Isard's Revenge

The Jedi Academy Trilogy
Jedi Search
Dark Apprentice
Champions of the Force

I, Jedi
Children of the Jedi
Darksaber
Planet of Twilight
X-Wing: Starfighters of Adumar
The Crystal Star

*An eBook novella
**Forthcoming

The Black Fleet Crisis Trilogy
Before the Storm
Shield of Lies
Tyrant's Test

The New Rebellion

The Corellian Trilogy
Ambush at Corellia
Assault at Selonia
Showdown at Centerpoint

The Hand of Thrawn Duology
Specter of the Past
Vision of the Future

Scourge

Fool's Bargain*
Survivor's Quest

NEW JEDI ORDER
25–40 YEARS AFTER
STAR WARS: A New Hope

Boba Fett: A Practical Man*

The New Jedi Order
Vector Prime
Dark Tide I: Onslaught
Dark Tide II: Ruin
Agents of Chaos I: Hero's Trial
Agents of Chaos II: Jedi Eclipse
Balance Point
Recovery*
Edge of Victory I: Conquest
Edge of Victory II: Rebirth
Star by Star
Dark Journey
Enemy Lines I: Rebel Dream
Enemy Lines II: Rebel Stand
Traitor
Destiny's Way
Ylesia*
Force Heretic I: Remnant
Force Heretic II: Refugee
Force Heretic III: Reunion
The Final Prophecy
The Unifying Force

35 *YEARS AFTER STAR WARS: A New Hope*

The Dark Nest Trilogy
The Joiner King
The Unseen Queen
The Swarm War

LEGACY
40+ YEARS AFTER
STAR WARS: A New Hope

Legacy of the Force
Betrayal
Bloodlines
Tempest
Exile
Sacrifice
Inferno
Fury
Revelation
Invincible

Crosscurrent
Riptide

Millennium Falcon

43 *YEARS AFTER STAR WARS: A New Hope*

Fate of the Jedi
Outcast
Omen
Abyss
Backlash
Allies
Vortex
Conviction
Ascension
Apocalypse

X-Wing: Mercy Kill

45 *YEARS AFTER STAR WARS: A New Hope*

Crucible

*An eBook novella

dramatis personae

Han Solo; smuggler (human male)
Chewbacca; smuggler (Wookiee male)
Lando Calrissian; gambler (human male)
Bink Kitik; ghost thief (human female)
Tavia Kitik; electronics expert, ghost thief assistant (human female)
Dozer Creed; ship thief (human male)
Zerba Cher'dak; pickpocket, sleight-of-hand expert (Balosar male)
Winter; living recording rod (human female)
Rachele Ree; acquisitions, intel (human female)
Kell Tainer; explosives, droid expert (human male)
Eanjer Kunarazti; robbery victim, funding (human male)
Avrak Villachor; Black Sun sector chief (human male)
Qazadi; Black Sun vigo (Falleen male)
Dayja; Imperial Intelligence agent (human male)

A long time ago in a galaxy far, far away. . . .

STAR WARS™
SCOUNDRELS

CHAPTER ONE

The starlines collapsed into stars, and the Imperial Star Destroyer *Dominator* had arrived. Standing on the command walkway, his hands clasped stiffly behind his back, Captain Worhven glared at the misty planet floating in the blackness directly ahead and wondered what in blazes he and his ship were doing here.

For these were not good times. The Emperor's sudden dissolution of the Imperial Senate had sent dangerous swells of uncertainty throughout the galaxy, which played into the hands of radical groups like the so-called Rebel Alliance. At the same time, criminal organizations like Black Sun and the Hutt syndicates openly flaunted the law, buying and selling spice, stolen merchandise, and local and regional officials alike.

Even worse, Palpatine's brand-new toy, the weapon that was supposed to finally convince both insurgents and lawbreakers that the Empire was deadly serious about taking them down, had inexplicably been destroyed at Yavin. Worhven still hadn't heard an official explanation for that incident.

Evil times indeed. And evil times called for a strong and massive response. The minute the word came in from Yavin, Imperial Center should have ordered a full Fleet deployment, concentrating its efforts on the most important, the most insubordinate, and the most jittery systems. It was the classic response to crisis, a method that dated back thousands of years, and by all rights and logic the *Dominator* should have been at the forefront of any such deployment.

Instead, Worhven and his ship had been pressed into mule cart duty.

"Ah—Captain," a cheery voice boomed behind him.

Worhven took a deep, calming breath. "Lord d'Ashewl," he replied, making sure to keep his back to the other while he forced his expression into something more politically proper for the occasion.

It was well he'd started rearranging his face when he did. Barely five seconds later d'Ashewl came to a stop beside him, right up at his side instead of stopping the two steps back that Worhven demanded of even senior officers until he gestured them forward.

But that was hardly a surprise. What would a fat, stupid, accidentally rich member of Imperial Center's upper court know of ship's protocol?

A rhetorical question. The answer, of course, was nothing.

But if d'Ashewl didn't understand basic courtesy, Worhven did. And he would treat his guest with the proper respect. Even if it killed him. "My lord," he said politely, turning to face the other. "I trust you slept well."

"I did," d'Ashewl said, his eyes on the planet ahead. "So that's Wukkar out there, is it?"

"Yes, my lord," Worhven said, resisting the urge to wonder aloud if d'Ashewl thought the *Dominator* might have somehow drifted off course during ship's night. "As per your orders."

"Yes, yes, of course," d'Ashewl said, craning his neck a little. "It's just so hard to tell from this distance. Most worlds out there look distressingly alike."

"Yes, my lord," Worhven repeated, again resisting the

words that so badly wanted to come out. That was the kind of comment made only by the inexperienced or blatantly stupid. With d'Ashewl, it was probably a toss-up.

"But if you say it's Wukkar, then I believe it," d'Ashewl continued. "Have you compiled the list of incoming yachts that I asked for?"

Worhven suppressed a sigh. Not just mule cart duty, but handmaiden duty as well. "The comm officer has it," he said, turning his head and gesturing toward the starboard crew pit. Out of the corner of his eye he saw now that he and d'Ashewl weren't alone: d'Ashewl's young manservant, Dayja, had accompanied his superior and was standing a respectful half dozen steps back along the walkway.

At least one of the pair knew something about proper protocol.

"Excellent, excellent," d'Ashewl said, rubbing his hands together. "There's a wager afoot, Captain, as to which of our group will arrive first and which will arrive last. Thanks to you and your magnificent ship, I stand to win a great deal of money."

Worhven felt his lip twist. A ludicrous and pointless wager, to match the *Dominator*'s ludicrous and pointless errand. It was nice to know that in a universe on the edge of going mad, there was still ironic symmetry to be found.

"You'll have your man relay the data to my floater," d'Ashewl continued. "My man and I shall leave as soon as the *Dominator* reaches orbit." He cocked his head. "Your orders *were* to remain in the region in the event that I needed further transport, were they not?"

The captain allowed his hands, safely out of d'Ashewl's sight at his sides, to curl into frustrated fists. "Yes, my lord."

"Good," d'Ashewl said cheerfully. "Lord Toorfi has been known to suddenly change his mind on where the games are to continue, and if he does, I need to be ready to once again beat him to the new destination. You'll be no more than three hours away at all times, correct?"

"Yes, my lord," Worhven said. Fat, stupid, and a cheat besides. Clearly, all the others involved in this vague high-stakes gaming tournament had arrived at Wukkar via their own ships. Only d'Ashewl had had the supreme gall to talk someone on Imperial Center into letting him borrow an Imperial Star Destroyer for the occasion.

"But for now, all I need is for your men to prepare to launch my floater," d'Ashewl continued. "After that, you may take the rest of the day off. Perhaps the rest of the month as well. One never knows how long old men's stamina and credits will last, eh?"

Without waiting for a reply—which was just as well, because Worhven didn't have any that he was willing to share—the rotund man turned and waddled back along the walkway toward the aft bridge. Dayja waited until he'd passed, then dropped into step the prescribed three paces behind him.

Worhven watched until the pair had passed beneath the archway and into the aft bridge turbolift, just to make sure they were truly gone. Then, unclenching his teeth, he turned to the comm officer. "Signal Hangar Command," he ordered. "Our passenger is ready to leave."

He threw a final glower at the aft bridge. Take the day off, indeed. Enough condescending idiocy like that from the Empire's ruling class, and Worhven would be sorely tempted to join the Rebellion himself. "And tell them to make it quick," he added. "I don't want Lord d'Ashewl or his ship aboard a single millisecond longer than necessary."

"I should probably have you whipped," d'Ashewl commented absently.

Dayja half turned in the floater's command chair to look over his shoulder. "Excuse me?" he asked.

"I said I should probably have you whipped," d'Ashewl repeated, gazing at his datapad as he lazed comfortably on the luxurious couch in the lounge just behind the cockpit.

"Any particular reason?"

"Not really," d'Ashewl said. "But it's becoming the big thing among the upper echelon of the court these days, and I'd hate to be left out of the truly important trends."

"Ah," Dayja said. "I trust these rituals aren't done in public?"

"Oh, no, the sessions are quite private and secretive," d'Ashewl assured him. "But that's a good point. Unless we happen to meet up with others of my same lofty stature, there really wouldn't be any purpose." He considered. "At least not until we get back to Imperial Center. We may want to try it then."

"Speaking only for myself, I'd be content to put it off," Dayja said. "It *does* sound rather pointless."

"That's because you have a lower-class attitude," d'Ashewl chided. "It's a conspicuous-consumption sort of thing. A demonstration that one has such an overabundance of servants and slaves that he can afford to put one out of commission for a few days merely on a whim."

"It still sounds pointless," Dayja said. "Ripping someone's flesh from his body is a great deal of work. I prefer to have a good reason if I'm going to go to that much effort." He nodded at the datapad. "Any luck?"

"Unfortunately, the chance cubes aren't falling in our favor," d'Ashewl said, tossing the instrument onto the couch beside him. "Our tip-off came just a bit too late. It looks like Qazadi is already here."

"You're sure?"

"There were only eight possibilities, and all eight have landed and their passengers dispersed."

Dayja turned back forward, eyeing the planet rushing up toward them and trying to estimate distances and times. If the yacht carrying their quarry had *just* landed, there might still be a chance of intercepting him before he went to ground.

"And the latest was over three hours ago," d'Ashewl added. "So you might as well ease back on the throttle and enjoy the ride."

Dayja suppressed a flicker of annoyance. "So in other words, we took the *Dominator* out of service for nothing."

"Not entirely," d'Ashewl said. "Captain Worhven had the opportunity to work on his patience level."

Despite his frustration, Dayja had to smile. "You *do* play the pompous-jay role very well."

"Thank you," d'Ashewl said. "I'm glad my talents are still of *some* use to the department. And don't be too annoyed that we missed him. It would have been nicely dramatic, snatching him out of the sky as we'd hoped. But such a triumph would have come with its own set of costs. For one thing, Captain Worhven would have had to be brought into your confidence, which would have cost you a perfectly good cover identity."

"And possibly yours?"

"Very likely," d'Ashewl agreed. "And while the Director has plenty of scoundrel and server identities to pass out, he can slip someone into the Imperial court only so often before the other members catch on. They may be arrogant and pompous, but they're not stupid. All things considered, it's probably just as well things have worked out this way."

"Perhaps," Dayja said, not entirely ready to concede the point. "Still, he's going to be harder to get out of

Villachor's mansion than he would have been if we'd caught him along the way."

"Even so, it will be easier than digging him out of one of Black Sun's complexes on Imperial Center," d'Ashewl countered. "Assuming we could find him in that rat hole in the first place." He gestured toward the viewport. "And don't think it would have been *that* easy to pluck him out of space. Think Xizor's *Virago,* only scaled up fifty or a hundred times, and you'll get an idea what kind of nut it would have been to crack."

"All nuts can be cracked," Dayja said with a shrug. "All it takes is the right application of pressure."

"Provided the nutcracker itself doesn't break in the process," d'Ashewl said, his voice going suddenly dark. "You've never tangled with Black Sun at this level, Dayja. I have. Qazadi is one of the worst, with every bit of Xizor's craftiness and manipulation."

"But without the prince's charm?"

"Joke if you wish," d'Ashewl rumbled. "But be careful. If not for yourself, for me. I have the ghosts of far too many lost agents swirling through my memory as it is."

"I understand," Dayja said quietly. "I'll be careful."

"Good." D'Ashewl huffed out a short puff of air, an affectation Dayja guessed he'd picked up from others of Imperial Center's elite. "All right. We still don't know why Qazadi is here: whether he's on assignment, lying low, or in some kind of disfavor with Xizor and the rest of the upper echelon. If it's the third, we're out of luck."

"As is Qazadi," Dayja murmured.

"Indeed," d'Ashewl agreed. "But if it's one of the first two . . ." He shook his head. "Those files could rock Imperial Center straight out of orbit."

Which was enough reason all by itself for them to play this whole thing very carefully, Dayja knew. "But we're sure he'll be staying at Villachor's?"

"I can't see him coming to Wukkar and staying anywhere but the sector chief's mansion," d'Ashewl said. "But there may be other possibilities, and it wouldn't hurt for you to poke around a bit. I've downloaded everything we've got on Villachor, his people, and the Marblewood Estate for you. Unfortunately, there isn't much."

"I guess I'll have to get inside and see the place for myself," Dayja said. "I'm thinking the upcoming Festival of Four Honorings will be my best bet."

"*If* Villachor follows his usual pattern of hosting one of Iltarr City's celebrations at Marblewood," d'Ashewl warned. "It's possible that with Qazadi visiting he'll pass that role to someone else."

"I don't think so," Dayja said. "High-level Black Sun operatives like to use social celebrations as cover for meetings with offworld contacts and to set up future opportunities. In fact, given the timing of Qazadi's visit, it's possible he's here to observe or assist with some particularly troublesome problem."

"You've done your homework," d'Ashewl said. "Excellent. Do bear in mind, though, that the influx of people also means Marblewood's security force will be on heightened alert."

"Don't worry," Dayja said calmly. "You can get through any door if you know the proper way to knock. I'll just keep knocking until I find the pattern."

According to Wukkar's largest and most influential fashion magazines, all of which were delighted to run extensive stories on Avrak Villachor whenever he paid them to do so, Villachor's famed Marblewood Estate was one of the true showcases of the galaxy. It was essentially a country manor in the midst of Iltarr City: a walled-off expanse of landscaped grounds surrounding a former governor's mansion built in classic High Empress Teta style.

The more breathless of the commentators liked to remind their readers of Villachor's many business and philanthropic achievements and awards, and predicted that there would be more such honors in the future. Other commentators, the unpaid ones, countered with more ominous suggestions that Villachor's most likely achievement would be to suffer an early and violent death.

Both predictions were probably right; the thought flicked through Villachor's mind as he stood at the main entrance to his mansion and watched the line of five ordinary-looking landspeeders float through the gate and into his courtyard. In fact, there was every chance that he was about to face one or the other of those events right now.

The only question was which one.

Proper etiquette on Wukkar dictated that a host be waiting beside the landspeeder door when a distinguished guest emerged. In this case, though, that would be impossible. All five landspeeders had dark-tint windows, and there was no way to know which one his mysterious visitor was riding in. If Villachor guessed wrong, not only would he have violated prescribed manners, but he would also look like a fool.

And so he paused on the bottom step until the landspeeders came to a well-practiced simultaneous halt. The doors of all but the second vehicle opened and began discharging the passengers, most of them hard-faced human men who would have fit in seamlessly with Villachor's own cadre of guards and enforcers. They spread out into a loose and casual-looking circle around the vehicles, and one of them murmured something into the small comlink clip on his collar. The final landspeeder's doors opened—

Villachor felt his throat tighten as he caught his first glimpse of gray-green scales above a colorful beaded tunic. This was no human. This was a *Falleen.*

And not just one, but an entire landspeeder full of them. Even as Villachor started forward, two Falleen emerged from each side of the vehicle, their hands on their holstered blasters, their eyes flicking to and past Villachor to the mansion towering behind him. Special bodyguards, which could only be for an equally special guest. Villachor picked up his pace, trying to hurry without looking like it, his heart thudding with unpleasant anticipation. If it was Prince Xizor in that landspeeder, this day was likely to end very badly. Unannounced visits from Black Sun's chief nearly always did.

It was indeed another Falleen who stepped out into the sunlight as Villachor reached his proper place at the vehicle's side. But to his quiet relief, it wasn't Xizor. It was merely Qazadi, one of Black Sun's nine vigos.

It was only as Villachor dropped to one knee and bowed his head in reverence to his guest that the significance of that thought belatedly struck him. *Only* one of the nine most powerful beings in Black Sun?

Just because the Falleen standing in front of him wasn't Xizor didn't mean the day might not still end in death.

"I greet you, Your Excellency," Villachor said, bowing even lower. If he was in trouble, an extra show of humility probably wouldn't save him, but it might at least buy him a less painful death. "I'm Avrak Villachor, chief of this sector's operations, and your humble servant."

"I greet you in turn, Sector Chief Villachor," Qazadi said. His voice was smooth and melodious, very much like Xizor's, but with a darker edge of menace lurking beneath it. "You may rise."

"Thank you, Your Excellency," Villachor said, getting back to his feet. "How may I serve you?"

"You may take me to a guest suite," Qazadi said. His eyes seemed to glitter with private amusement. "And then you may relax."

Villachor frowned. "Excuse me, Your Excellency?" he asked carefully.

"You fear that I've come to exact judgment upon you," Qazadi said, his voice still dark yet at the same time oddly conversational. The gray-green scales of his face were changing, too, showing just a hint of pink on his upper cheeks. "And such thoughts should never be simply dismissed," the Falleen added, "for I don't leave Imperial Center without great cause."

"Yes, Your Excellency," Villachor said. The sense of dark uncertainty still hung over the group like an early morning fog, but to his mild surprise he could feel his heartbeat slowing and an unexpected calm beginning to flow through him. Something about the Falleen's voice was more soothing than he'd realized.

"But in this case, the cause has nothing to do with you," Qazadi continued. "With Lord Vader's absence from Imperial Center leaving his spies temporarily leaderless, Prince Xizor has decided it would be wise to shuffle the cards a bit." He gave Villachor a thin smile. "In this case, a most appropriate metaphor."

Villachor felt his mouth go suddenly dry. Was Qazadi actually talking about—? "My vault is at your complete disposal, Your Excellency," he managed.

"Thank you," Qazadi said, as if Villachor actually had a choice in the matter. "While my guards bring in my belongings and arrange my suite, we will go investigate the security of your vault."

The breeze that had been drifting across Villachor's face shifted direction, and suddenly the calmness that had settled comfortably across his mind vanished. It hadn't been Qazadi's voice at all, Villachor realized acidly, but just another of those cursed body-chemical tricks Falleen liked to pull on people. "As you wish, Your Excellency," he said, bowing again and gesturing to the mansion door. "Please, follow me."

The hotel that d'Ashewl had arranged for was in the very center of Iltarr City's most exclusive district, and the Imperial Suite was the finest accommodation the hotel had to offer. More important, from Dayja's point of view, the humble servants' quarters tacked onto one edge of the suite had a private door that opened right beside one of the hotel's back stairwells.

An hour after d'Ashewl finished his grand midafternoon dinner and retired to his suite, Dayja had changed from servant's livery to more nondescript clothing and was on the streets. A few minutes' walk took him out of the enclave of the rich and powerful and into a poorer, nastier section of the city.

Modern Intelligence operations usually began at a field officer's desk, with a complete rundown of the target's communications, finances, and social webs. But in this case, Dayja knew, such an approach would be less than useless. Black Sun's top chiefs were exceptionally good at covering their tracks and burying all the connections and pings that could be used to ensnare lesser criminals. In addition, many of those hidden connections had built-in flags to alert the crime lord to the presence of an investigation. The last thing Dayja could afford would be to drive Qazadi deeper underground or, worse, send him scurrying back to Imperial Center, where he would once again be under the direct protection of Xizor and the vast Black Sun resources there.

And so Dayja would do this the old-fashioned way: poking and prodding at the edges of Black Sun's operations in Iltarr City, making a nuisance of himself until he drew the right person's attention.

He spent the rest of the evening just walking around, observing the people and absorbing the feel and rhythms of the city. As the sky darkened toward evening he went back to one of the three clandestine dealers he'd spotted earlier and bought two cubes of Nyriaan spice, commenting casually about the higher quality of the drug that he was used to.

By the time he was ready to head back to the hotel he had bought samples from two more dealers, making similar disparaging observations each time. Black Sun dealt heavily in Nyriaan spice, and there was a good chance that all three dealers were connected at least peripherally to Villachor. With any luck, news of this contemptuous stranger would begin filtering up the command chain.

He was within sight of the upper-class enclave's private security station when he was jumped by three young toughs.

For the first hopeful moment he thought that perhaps Black Sun's local intel web was better than he'd expected. But it was quickly clear that the thugs weren't working for Villachor or anyone else, but merely wanted to steal the cubes of spice he was carrying. All three of the youths carried knives, and one of them had a small blaster, and there was a burning fire in their eyes that said they would have the spice no matter what the cost.

Unfortunately for them, Dayja had a knife, too, one he'd taken off the body of a criminal who'd had similar plans. Thirty seconds later, he was once again walking toward home, leaving the three bodies dribbling blood into the drainage gutter alongside the walkway.

Tomorrow, he decided, he would suggest that d'Ashewl make a show of visiting some of the local cultural centers, where Dayja would have a chance to better size up the city's ruling class. Then it would be another solo excursion into the fringes, and more of this same kind of subtle troublemaking. Between the high classes and the low, sooner or later Villachor or his people were bound to take notice.

He was well past the security station, with visions of a soft bed dancing before his eyes, before the police finally arrived to collect the bodies he'd left behind.

CHAPTER TWO

Han Solo had never been in Reggilio's Cantina before. But he'd been in hundreds just like it, and he knew the type well. It was reasonably quiet, though from wariness rather than good manners; slightly boisterous, though with the restraint that came of the need to keep a low profile; and decorated in dilapidated scruffiness, with no apologies offered or expected.

It was, in short, the perfect place for a trap.

A meter away on the other half of the booth's wraparound seat, Chewbacca growled unhappily.

"No kidding," Han growled back, tapping his fingertips restlessly against the mug of Corellian spiced ale that he still hadn't touched. "But if there's even a chance this is legit, we have to take it."

Chewbacca rumbled a suggestion.

"No," Han said flatly. "They're running a rebellion, remember? They haven't got anything extra to spare."

Chewbacca growled again.

"Sure we're worth it," Han agreed. "Shooting those TIEs off Luke alone should have doubled the reward. But you saw the look on Dodonna's face—he wasn't all that happy about giving us the first batch. If Her Royal Highness hadn't been standing right there saying good-bye, I'm pretty sure he would have tried to talk us down."

He glared into his mug. Besides, he didn't add, asking Princess Leia for replacement reward credits would mean he'd have to tell her how he'd lost the first batch. Not in gambling or bad investments or even drinking, but to a kriffing pirate.

And then she would give him one of those looks.

There were, he decided, worse things than being on Jabba's hit list.

On the other hand, if this offer of a job he'd picked up at the Ord Mantell drop was for real, there was a good chance Leia would never have to know.

"Hello there, Solo." The raspy voice came from Han's right. "Eyes front, hands flat on the table. You too, Wookiee."

Han set his teeth firmly together as he let go of his mug and laid his hands palms down on the table. So much for the job offer being legit. "That you, Falsta?"

"Hey, good memory," Falsta said approvingly as he sidled around into Han's view and sat down on the chair across the table. He was just as Han remembered him: short and scrawny, wearing a four-day stubble and his usual wraparound leather jacket over yet another from his collection of flame-bird shirts. His blaster was even uglier than his shirt: a heavily modified Clone Wars–era DT-57.

Falsta liked to claim the weapon had once been owned by General Grievous himself. Han didn't believe that any more than anyone else did.

"I hear Jabba's mad at you," Falsta continued, resting his elbow on the table and leveling the barrel of his blaster squarely at Han's face. "Again."

"I hear *you've* branched out into assassinations," Han countered, eyeing the blaster and carefully repositioning his leg underneath the table. He would have just one shot at this.

Falsta shrugged. "Hey, if that's what the customer

wants, that's what the customer gets. I can tell you this much: Black Sun pays a whole lot better for a kill than Jabba does for a grab." He wiggled the barrel of his blaster a little. "Not that I don't mind picking up a few free credits. As long as I just happen to be here anyway."

"Sure, why not?" Han agreed, frowning. That was a strange comment. Was Falsta saying that he *wasn't* the one who'd sent Han that message?

No—ridiculous. The galaxy was a huge place. There was no possible way that a bounty hunter could have just *happened* to drop in on a random cantina in a random city on a random world at the same time Han was there. No, Falsta was just being cute.

That was fine. Han could be cute, too. "So you're saying that if I gave you double what Jabba's offering, you'd get up and walk away?" he asked.

Falsta smiled evilly. "You got it on you?"

Han inclined his head toward Chewbacca. "Third power pack down from the shoulder."

Falsta's eyes flicked to Chewbacca's bandoleer—

And in a single contorted motion Han banged his knee up, slamming the table into Falsta's elbow and knocking his blaster out of line as he grabbed his mug and hurled the Corellian spiced ale into Falsta's eyes. There was a brief flash of heat as the bounty hunter's reflexive shot sizzled past Han's left ear.

One shot was all Falsta got. An instant later his blaster was pointed harmlessly at the ceiling, frozen in place by Chewbacca's iron grip around both the weapon and the hand holding it.

That should have been the end of it. Falsta should have conceded defeat, surrendered his blaster, and walked out of the cantina, a little humiliated but still alive.

But Falsta had never been the type to concede anything. Even as he blinked furiously at the ale still running down into his eyes, his left hand jabbed like a knife inside his jacket and emerged with a small hold-out blaster.

He was in the process of lining up the weapon when Han shot him under the table. Falsta fell forward, his right arm still raised in Chewbacca's grip, his hold-out blaster clattering across the tabletop before it came to a halt. Chewbacca held that pose another moment, then lowered Falsta's arm to the table, deftly removing the blaster from the dead man's hand as he did so.

For a half dozen seconds Han didn't move, gripping his blaster under the table, his eyes darting around the cantina. The place had gone quiet, with practically every eye now focused on him. As far as he could tell no one had drawn a weapon, but most of the patrons at the nearest tables had their hands on or near their holsters.

Chewbacca rumbled a warning. "You all saw it," Han called, though he doubted more than a few of them actually had. "He shot first."

There was another moment of silence. Then, almost casually, hands lifted from blasters, heads turned away, and the low conversation resumed.

Maybe this sort of thing happened all the time in Reggilio's. Or maybe they all knew Falsta well enough that no one was going to miss him.

Still, it was definitely time to move on. "Come on," Han muttered, holstering his blaster and sliding around the side of the table. They would go back to the spaceport area, he decided, poke around the cantinas there, and see if they could snag a pickup cargo. It almost certainly wouldn't net them enough to pay off Jabba, but it would at least get them off Wukkar. He stood up, giving the cantina one final check—

"Excuse me?"

Han spun around, reflexively dropping his hand back to the grip of his blaster. But it was just an ordinary human man hurrying toward him.

Or rather, *most* of a man. Half of his face was covered in a flesh-colored medseal that had been stretched across the skin and hair, with a prosthetic eye bobbing along at the spot where his right eye would normally be.

It wasn't just any eye, either. It was something alien-designed, glittering like a smaller version of an Arconian multifaceted eye. Even in the cantina's dim light the effect was striking, unsettling, and strangely hypnotic.

With a jolt, Han realized he'd been staring and forced his gaze away. Not only was it rude, but a visual grab like that was exactly the sort of trick a clever assassin might use to draw his victim's attention at a critical moment.

But the man's hands were empty, with no blaster or blade in sight. In fact, his right hand wouldn't have been of any use anyway. Twisted and misshapen, it was wrapped tightly in the same medseal as his face. Either it had been seriously damaged or else there was a prosthetic under there that had come from the same aliens who'd supplied him with that eye. "You might want to see about getting a different eye," Han suggested, relaxing a bit.

"I need to see about a great many things," the man said, stopping a couple of meters back. His remaining eye flicked to Han's blaster, then rose with an effort back to his face. "Allow me to introduce myself," he continued. "My name is Eanjer—well, my surname isn't important. What *is* important is that I've been robbed of a great deal of money."

"Sorry to hear it," Han said, backing toward the door. "You need to talk to the Iltarr City police."

"They can't help me," Eanjer said, taking one step forward with each backward one Han took. "I want my credits back, and I need someone who can handle himself and doesn't mind working outside law or custom.

That's why I'm here. I was hoping I could find someone who fits both those criteria." His eye flicked to Falsta's body. "Having seen you in action, it's clear that you're exactly the type of person I'm looking for."

"It was self-defense," Han countered, picking up his pace. The man's problem was probably a petty gambling debt, and he had no intention of getting tangled up in something like that.

But whatever else Eanjer might be, the man was determined. He sped up to match Han's pace, staying right with him. "I don't want you to do it for free," he said. "I can pay. I can pay very, very well."

Han slowed to a reluctant halt. It was probably still something petty, and hearing the guy out would be a complete waste of time. But sitting around a spaceport cantina probably would be, too.

And if he *didn't* listen, there was a good chance the pest would follow him all the way to the spaceport. "How much are we talking about?" he asked.

"At a minimum, all your expenses," Eanjer said. "At a maximum—" He glanced around and lowered his voice to a whisper. "The criminals stole a hundred sixty-three million credits. If you get it back, I'll split it with you and whoever else you call in to help you."

Han felt his throat tighten. This could still be nothing. Eanjer might just be spinning cobwebs.

But if he was telling the truth . . .

"Fine," Han said. "Let's talk. But not here."

Eanjer looked back at Falsta's body, a shiver running through him. "No," he agreed softly. "Anyplace but here."

"The thief's name is Avrak Villachor," Eanjer said, his single eye darting around the diner Han had chosen, a more upscale place than the cantina and a prudent three blocks away. "More precisely, he's the leader of the particular group involved. I understand he's also affiliated with some larger criminal organization—I don't know which one."

Han looked across the table at Chewbacca and raised his eyebrows. The Wookiee gave a little shrug and shook his head. Apparently he'd never heard of Villachor, either. "Yeah, there are lots to choose from," he told Eanjer.

"Indeed." Eanjer looked down at his drink as if noticing it for the first time, then continued his nervous scanning of the room. "My father is—was—a very successful goods importer. Three weeks ago Villachor came to our home with a group of thugs and demanded he sign over his business to Villachor's organization. When he refused—" A shudder ran through his body. "They killed him," he said, his voice almost too low to hear. "They just . . . they didn't even use blasters. It was some kind of fragmentation grenade. It just tore him . . ." He trailed off.

"That what happened to your face?" Han asked.

Eanjer blinked and looked up. "What? Oh." He lifted his medsealed hand to gently touch his medsealed face. "Yes, I caught the edge of the blast. There was so much blood. They must have thought I was dead. . . ." He shivered, as if trying to shake away the memory. "Anyway, they took everything from his safe and left. All the corporate records, the data on our transport network, the lists of subcontractors—everything."

"Including a hundred sixty-three million credits?" Han asked. "Must have been a pretty big safe."

"Not really," Eanjer said. "Walk-in, but nothing special. The money was in credit tabs, one million per. A hip pouch would hold them all." He hitched his chair a little closer to the table. "But here's the thing. Credit tabs are keyed to the owner and the owner's designated agents. With my father now dead, I'm the only one who can get the full value out of them. For anyone else, they're worth no more than a quarter, maybe half a percent of the face value. And *that's* only if Villachor can find a slicer who can get through the security coding."

"That still leaves him eight hundred thousand," Han pointed out. "Not bad for a night's work."

"Which is why I have no doubt that he's currently hunting for a slicer to do the job." Eanjer took a deep breath. "Here's the thing. The business records Villachor stole don't matter. All the people who worked for us were there specifically and personally because of my father, and without him they're going to fade away into the mist. Especially since the credit tabs were on hand because we were preparing to pay out for services received. You don't pay a shipper, he doesn't work for you anymore."

Especially if that shipper was actually a smuggler, which was what Han strongly suspected was behind the family's so-called import business. He still wasn't sure if Eanjer himself knew that, suspected it, or was completely oblivious. "Let me get this straight," he said. "You want us to break into Villachor's place—you know where that is, by the way?"

"Oh, yes," Eanjer said, nodding. "It's right here in Iltarr City. It's an estate called Marblewood, nearly a square kilometer's worth of grounds surrounding a big mansion."

"Ah," Han said. Probably the big open space in the northern part of the city that he'd spotted as he was bringing the *Falcon* in. At the time, he'd guessed it was a park. "You want us to go there, break into wherever he's keeping the credit tabs, steal them, and get out again. That about cover it?"

"Yes," Eanjer said. "And I'm very grateful—"

"No."

Eanjer's single eye blinked. "Excuse me?"

"You've got the wrong man," Han told him. "We're shippers, like your father. We don't know the first thing about breaking into vaults."

"But surely you know people who do," Eanjer said. "You could call them. I'll split the credits with them, too. Everyone can have an equal share."

"You can call them yourself."

"But I don't *know* any such people," Eanjer protested, his voice pleading now. "I can't just pick up a comlink and ask for the nearest thief. And without you—" He broke off, visibly forcing himself back under control. "I saw how you handled that man in the cantina," he said. "You think fast and you act decisively. More important, you didn't kill him until you had no choice. That means I can trust you to get the job done, and to deal fairly with me when it's over."

Han sighed. "Look—"

"No, *you* look," Eanjer bit out, a hint of anger peeking through the frustration. "I've been sitting in cantinas for two solid weeks. You're the first person I've found who gives me any hope at all. Villachor's already had three weeks to find a slicer for those credit tabs. If I don't get them out before he does, he'll win. He'll win everything."

Han looked at Chewbacca. But the Wookiee was sitting quietly, with no hint as to what he was thinking or feeling. Clearly, he was leaving this one up to Han. "Is it the credits you really want?" he asked Eanjer. "Or are you looking for vengeance?"

Eanjer looked down at his hand. "A little of both," he admitted.

Han lifted his mug and took a long swallow. He was right, of course. He and Chewbacca really weren't the ones for this job.

But Eanjer was also right. They knew plenty of people who were.

And with 163 million credits on the line . . .

"I need to make a call," he said, lowering his mug and pulling out his comlink.

Eanjer nodded, making no move to leave. "Right."

Han paused. "A *private* call."

For another second Eanjer still didn't move. Then, abruptly, his eye widened. "Oh," he said, getting hastily to his feet. "Right. I'll, uh, I'll be back."

Chewbacca warbled a question. "It can't hurt to ask around," Han told him, keying in a number and trying to keep his voice calm. A hundred sixty-three million. Even a small slice of that would pay off Jabba a dozen times over. And not just Jabba, but everyone else who wanted a piece of Han's head surrounded by onions on a serving dish. He could pay them all off his back, and still have enough for him and Chewie to run free and clear wherever they wanted. Maybe for the rest of their lives. "I just hope Rachele Ree's not off on a trip somewhere."

To his mild surprise, she was indeed home.

"Well, hello, Han," she said cheerfully when Han had identified himself. "Nice to hear from you, for a change. Are you on Wukkar? Oh, yes—I see you are. Iltarr City, eh? Best Corellian food on the planet."

Chewbacca rumbled a comment under his breath. Han nodded sourly. His comlink was supposedly set up to prevent location backtracks, but electronic safeguards never seemed to even slow Rachele down. "Got a question," he said. "Two questions. First, have you heard anything about a high-level break-in and murder over the last month or so? It would have been at an import company."

"You talking about Polestar Imports?" Rachele asked. "Sure—it was the talk of the lounges about three weeks ago. The owner was killed, and his son apparently went underground."

"Well, he's bobbed back up again," Han said. "Is the son's name Eanjer, and was he hurt in the attack?"

"Let me check . . . yes—Eanjer Kunarazti. As to whether he was hurt . . . the article doesn't say. Let me check one of my other sources . . . yes, looks like it. His blood was found at the scene, anyway."

"Good enough," Han said. He hadn't really thought Eanjer was pulling a scam, but it never hurt to check. "I mean, not *good,* but—"

"I know what you mean," Rachele said, with what Han could imagine was a sly smile. "Second question?"

"Can you run a few names and see if any of them is in spitting distance of Wukkar right now?" Han asked. "Eanjer's offered me the job of getting back the credits that were stolen."

"Really," Rachele said, sounding bemused. "You been branching out since I saw you last?"

"Not really," Han said. Fighting a battle or two for the Rebel Alliance didn't qualify as branching out, he told himself firmly. "He just likes the way I do things."

"Doesn't everybody?" Rachele countered dryly. "No problem. Who are you looking for?"

Han ran down all the names he could think of, people who were both competent and reasonably trustworthy. Considering how many years he'd spent swimming through the galaxy's fringe, it was a surprisingly short list. He added three more names at Chewbacca's suggestion, and pointedly ignored the Wookiee's fourth offering. "That's it," he told Rachele. "If I think of anyone else, I'll call you back."

"Sure," Rachele said. "Did your new friend mention the potential take? Some of these people will want to know that up front."

Han smiled tightly, wishing he were there to see her

expression. "If we get it all, we'll be splitting a hundred sixty-three million."

There was a moment of stunned silence at the other end. "Really," Rachele said at last. "Wow. You could practically hire Jabba himself for that amount."

"Thanks, but we'll pass," Han said. "And that number assumes Eanjer lives through the whole thing. You should probably make *that* clear, too."

"I will," Rachele said. "So it's all in credit tabs, huh? Makes sense. Okay, I'll make some calls and get back to you. Does he have any idea where the credit tabs are?"

"He says they're with someone named Villachor," Han said. "You know him?"

There was another short pause. "Yes, I've heard of him," Rachele said, her voice subtly changed. "Okay, I'll get started on your list. Where are you staying?"

"Right now we're just bunking in the *Falcon.*"

"Well, you'll eventually need something in town," Rachele said. "Of course, everything in sight's already been booked for the upcoming Festival. But I'll see what I can come up with."

"Thanks, Rachele," Han said. "I owe you."

"Bet on it. Catch you later."

Han keyed off the comlink and put it away.

Chewbacca warbled a question.

"Because I don't want him, that's why," Han said. "I doubt he'd show up even if I asked."

Chewbacca growled again.

"Because he said he never wanted to see me again, remember?" Han said. "Lando *does* occasionally mean what he says, you know."

A motion caught the edge of his eye, and he looked up to see Eanjer moving hesitantly toward them. "Is everything all right?" Eanjer asked, his eye flicking back and forth between them.

"Sure," Han said. "I've got someone looking into getting a team together."

"Wonderful," Eanjer said, coming the rest of the way to the table and easing into his seat. He must have seen the end of that brief argument, Han decided, and probably thought it had been more serious than it actually had. "This person is someone you can trust?"

Han nodded. "She's a low-ranking member of the old Wukkar aristocracy. Knows everyone and everything, and isn't exactly thrilled with the people who are running the show right now."

"If you say so," Eanjer said. He didn't sound entirely convinced, but it was clear he wasn't ready to press the issue. "I think I've come up with a perfect time for the break-in. Two weeks from now is the Festival of Four Honorings."

Han looked at Chewbacca, got a shrug in return. "Never heard of it," he told Eanjer.

"It's Wukkar's version of Carnival Week," Eanjer said, his lip twisting. "Anything Imperial Center does, someone here has to do better. Anyway, it's a seven-day event with a day each devoted to stone, air, water, and fire, with a prep day in between each of the Honorings. It's the most important event on Wukkar, with people coming from as far away as Vuma and Imperial Center to attend."

"And probably pickpockets from as far away as Nal Hutta," Han murmured.

"I wouldn't know," Eanjer said. "My point is that Villachor hosts one of the city's biggest celebrations on his grounds."

Han sat up a little straighter. "On his *grounds*? You mean he lets people wander around right next to his house?"

"More a mansion than a house," Eanjer said. "Or perhaps more a fortress than a mansion. But yes, thousands of people come and go freely over those four days."

Chewbacca warbled the obvious point. "Of course he'll have beefed-up security," Han agreed. "But at least we won't have to get over any walls and through an outer sentry line. How do we get an invitation to this thing?"

"None needed," Eanjer said. "It's open to all." The half of his mouth that was visible curved upward in a bitter smile. "Villachor likes to style himself as a philanthropist and a friend of the city. He also likes to show off his wealth and style."

"That's okay," Han said. "Some of my best deals came from people who thought they were better and smarter than everyone else. This might actually work."

"Then you'll help me?" Eanjer asked hopefully.

"Let's first see what Rachele comes up with," Han said. "I've got some ideas, but like I said before, this isn't our specialty. But if we can get the people I need, we should at least have a shot."

"Make sure they know what's involved," Eanjer said. "A hundred and sixty-three million."

"Yeah, I got that part," Han said. "Give me your comlink number, and I'll call when we've got more to talk about."

"All right," Eanjer said a bit uncertainly as he dug out a data card and handed it over. "When will that be?"

"When," Han said with exaggerated patience, "we've got more to talk about."

They were back at the *Falcon* when Rachele's report came in.

As usual with life, the results were mixed. Many of the people Han had hoped to contact were out of touch, out of the immediate area, or temporarily out of circulation.

Others who might otherwise have been possibilities would take too long to get hold of, especially with the two-week countdown to the Festival that Eanjer was looking at.

And there were a couple who were unavailable themselves but had people they could recommend. Mazzic, in particular, had already grabbed the initiative and informed Rachele that he would be sending two new recruits who matched the skills of the ones Han had asked about.

Chewbacca wasn't at all sure he liked that. "Yeah, me neither," Han agreed, frowning at the note Rachele had sent. Still, Han had known Mazzic for a number of years, and he and Chewbacca had occasionally run cargoes for him and his small smuggling organization. Mazzic had shown himself both trustworthy and competent.

More to the point, he was notorious for not trusting anyone himself until he'd thoroughly checked out the candidate. If he was okay with these recruits, they were probably safe enough.

Unless he was trying to get back at Han for something. But that was unlikely. Han hadn't done anything to Mazzic, not that he could remember. Certainly not lately.

Chewbacca grunted a question.

"I guess we go hunting," Han told him, levering himself to his feet. "Go fire up the *Falcon*. I'll see about getting us a liftoff slot."

CHAPTER THREE

The rooftop defenses were intriguing.

The long slide down the syntherope was exhilarating.

The window security was a joke.

Bink Kitik shook her head as she focused the medical laser beam through the transparisteel onto the alarm connector. Most amateur thieves who got this far, she knew, would use the laser to slice all the way through the link, successfully disconnecting the primary alarm but at the same time activating the impedance circuit that would trigger the secondary. Bink's more subtle approach, burning the connector just enough to melt the wires into a short circuit, would leave all the warning bells intact but quickly and smoothly drain the alarm's power cell and render it useless.

She finished her cut and put away the laser, checking the time as she did so. Twenty seconds, no more, and the alarm should be deactivated.

"Sitch?" Her sister's strained voice came over the comlink clip on her shoulder.

Bink smiled fondly. Tavia hated Bink's work—hated every single minute, every single aspect, every single job. But even with all that, she was still far and away the best groundliner Bink had ever worked with.

Tavia also worried like a mother hen—this was her

fourth situation check since Bink had emerged onto the roof. "Sitch go," Bink assured her. "Twenty to pen."

She gave it thirty seconds, just to be on the safe side. Then, activating her vibroscalp, she began cutting gently through the transparisteel, wondering idly whether the people who designed such wonderful medical instruments ever realized how useful they would be to a resourceful ghost burglar. Probably not.

She finished her cut and exchanged the vibroscalp for a probe, easing it in through the new opening and tapping the window release. It slid open, nearly but not quite catching the probe as she hastily withdrew it, and she was in. She pulled herself up on the sill, making sure not to tangle her harness—

"Whoa! What the—?"

Reflexively, Bink grabbed for her hold-out blaster. "Tav?" she whispered urgently.

"It's okay," Tavia said, the startlement mostly gone from her voice. Mostly. "I was just—it's okay," she repeated. "Everything's crankapacky. Just keep going."

Bink frowned. *Crankapacky* was the correct private code word for *no problem*. But what in the galaxy could have made her normally cool if overly judgmental sister jump like that without being a problem? "Should I bail?"

"No, it's crankapacky," Tavia repeated. "Just hurry it up."

The safe was harder to crack than the window, but not seriously so. Bink had it open in two minutes flat, clucking disapprovingly under her breath the whole time. Some people just didn't deserve to be rich.

The plan had been to take a few minutes to size up the safe's contents, picking and choosing which gems were worth taking and which would be too easy for the governor's soon-to-be-outraged chief accountant to track down. But with Tavia's startled exclamation ringing through her mind, Bink decided she would just grab what she could inside of a twenty-count and then call it a night. Snapping open the gem boxes at random, mindful that such boxes were usually tagged and couldn't be taken as is, she started shoveling their contents into her hip pouch. One of the more interesting-looking boxes had a lock of its own, which the fingersnips attached to the undersides of her fingernails made quick work of.

Her twenty-count ran to zero. Closing the safe, she hurried back to the window and made her exit.

The plan had been for her to return to the roof and exit as she'd arrived, via the building's stairway. But the rooftop anchors were expendable, her syntherope dispenser had more than enough line to reach the street, and suddenly she wasn't feeling like hanging around this neighborhood any longer than she had to. Closing the window behind her, she released the lock on the dispenser and rappelled her way down the side of the building.

Halfway to the ground, she drew her blaster. Just in case.

Tavia, as expected, had spotted the unplanned descent and was waiting when Bink came to a smooth halt on the walkway. "What happened?" she asked anxiously. "I thought you were going back to the roof."

"You and your startled yelp happened," Bink said. "I thought I'd better expedite matters."

"I *said* crankapacky."

"I heard you say crankapacky," Bink agreed, looking around. A figure had appeared from the doorway where Tavia had been handling her groundliner sentry duty and was striding toward them. He was human and male, and even with the streetlight throwing his face into shadow he seemed familiar. He continued his approach, his swinging hand brushing past a holstered blaster with each step. Bink tightened her grip on her own weapon . . .

And then, as the man passed through the light of a home security lamp, she got a clear look at his face. She exhaled in a puff, feeling the tension drain into limp relief. No wonder Tavia had been startled. And no wonder she'd said *crankapacky.* "Hey, Solo," she greeted the newcomer. "What are you doing on Kailor?"

"Looking for you, Bink," Solo said calmly. "Nice to see you're keeping busy."

"We are," Bink said. "Only I'm Tavia, not Bink. We decided I finally needed to learn the dirty part of the job."

For a long second he looked like he was going to buy it. His eyes flicked between the women's faces, searching for a clue as to which face belonged to which twin.

He wouldn't find one, of course. Not even if they'd been standing in a brightly lit room instead of a nighttime city street. Bink and Tavia had pulled this same trick countless times over the years, and their past was strewn with the red faces of those who'd fallen for it.

But Solo was smarter than most. And if he couldn't find any visible proof that Bink was lying, he knew her well enough to make an educated guess. "Good idea," he said, looking her straight in the eye. "I need you and Tavia for a job on Wukkar. Interested?"

"Could be," Bink said. "Decent payoff?"

"Very decent," Solo confirmed. "Come on back to the *Falcon* and we'll talk about it."

"Let's meet at our ship instead," Bink suggested. "Docking bay twenty-two. Go on in and make yourselves comfortable. We'll be there soon—got a stop to make first."

"Make it quick," Solo warned. "We're on a tight schedule."

He turned and strode off into the night. As he approached the end of the block, another figure, this one taller and shaggier, stepped into view. Chewbacca, playing his usual backup.

Smuggling partnerships didn't always last, Bink knew, and when they ended they usually ended violently. It was nice to see that this one was still holding together.

"We should go," Tavia said, her voice even more disapproving than usual.

"Right." Bink used her fingersnips to cut the synth-erope free from her harness, and they headed for the spot where they'd parked their landspeeder.

"You going to take the job?" Tavia asked as they walked.

"Probably," Bink said. "We'll hear him out first, of course. But probably."

"You realize that the payoff's probably not nearly as big as he implied," Tavia warned. "Things like this practically beg to be exaggerated."

"I know," Bink said. "But we've got nothing else planned, and pickup jobs can be fun." She shrugged. "Besides, it's Solo. What could go wrong?"

Tavia snorted. "You want me to give you a list?"

"No need," Bink said ruefully. "I've got my own."

The grand market at Jho-kang'ma was known mainly for two things: the freshest produce and animal products on the planet—due to the army of indentured farmers and herdsmen held in thrall just beyond the hills bordering the market—and the number and quality of performers hired to stroll through the grounds for the shoppers' amusement.

There were a lot of them out today, Han noted as he and Chewbacca walked along the wide straw-covered corridors between the vending tents. There were jugglers, musicians, ribbon dancers, and one large being who seemed to be eating and then spitting low-power blaster bolts. That was one Han hadn't seen before.

But the most popular acts, certainly the ones that seemed to draw the biggest crowds of chattering children, were the magicians.

Some of them had little movable stands that they would set up in out-of-the-way corners for a five- or ten-minute performance. Others simply wandered around with their entire show in pocket or hip pouch, making coins appear and disappear, creating living plants that grew and flowered from pots that also appeared from thin air, creating and releasing small birds, or doing simple but bewildering tricks with decks of sabacc cards.

They found Zerba Cher'dak in the center of one of the largest crowds, dressed in a bright yellow clown-type suit with a brown vest over it, flipping small sticks between his hands and making them change color or length seemingly at will. Like most Balosars Han had seen on human-run worlds, Zerba had retracted his antennapalps and concealed them within the fluffed waves and heavy lacquering of his hair to blend in better with the dominant population.

Chewbacca rumbled a comment.

"One of the best," Han agreed as Zerba continued to play with the sticks, occasionally turning one of them into a glittering gemstone to the giggling delight of his audience. "At least, the best we could get."

Chewbacca rumbled again.

"No, I'm not going to tell him that," Han promised patiently. He *did* know how to use tact, despite what Chewbacca seemed to think.

The show ended, and with a final flourish of twin fistfuls of sticks Zerba waved the children back to their parents. The audience melted away, and Zerba stuck his hands in his vest pockets and strolled over to Han and Chewbacca.

"If it isn't the notorious Han Solo," Zerba said, inclining his head in greeting. "I was just thinking about you." He touched the spot on his petrified hair where his antennapalps were hidden. "We're very sensitive to evil and criminal thoughts, you know."

"I've heard that," Han said. "I figure your ears work pretty good, too. Let me guess: Jabba refreshed the bounty on me?"

"Basically," Zerba said, sounding a little deflated. "If you're looking for somewhere to hide out, this place is an excellent choice." He looked Han up and down. "Though without any entertainment skills, you'd probably be set to work with the herds. Still, I know at least three other Wookiees who help manage—"

"We're not here to hide," Han interrupted him. "We're here to offer you a job. A big one."

"Really?" Zerba asked, clearly surprised. "You want *me*?"

For half a second Han was tempted to go ahead and tell Zerba that he was actually number eight on his particular skill list, just to see how the other would react. But he pushed the thought aside. Zerba probably didn't have a ship of his own, and Han had no desire to have a depressed Balosar moping around underfoot the whole way back to Wukkar. "Absolutely," he said instead. "I've been working on a few different plans for this thing, and all of them will need sleight of hand, a quick-change artist, or something else in your bag of tricks. So. Interested?"

"Yes, of course." Zerba looked furtively around. "Is this job, ah, offworld?"

Han nodded. "Wukkar, to be exact."

"Ah." Zerba pursed his lips. "The thing is, as I may have implied earlier, I'm lying low at the moment. But that security comes at a bit of a cost."

Han rolled his eyes. "Let me guess. Your current employers won't let you leave."

"Let's just say they like keeping track of me." Zerba waved a hand over his yellow outfit. "Hence the chicken suit. They take the indentured nature of their performers very seriously."

Han looked at Chewbacca, saw his same thought reflected in the Wookiee's face. They'd already worked their way down to number eight on the list. They really couldn't afford to work it down any farther. "How much will it take?" he asked.

"Oh, it's not a matter of credits," Zerba said, slipping out of his vest. "But thank you for offering. Here, take this, will you? Any chance you could give me transport? I don't have a ship of my own."

"Sure," Han said, frowning as he took the vest. It was heavier than it looked. Probably filled to the top of each pocket with Zerba's magic stuff. "But you just said—"

"Wonderful," Zerba interrupted, taking off the multipocket belt that had been concealed under the vest and handing it to Chewbacca. "Let me collect my things and I'll meet you at the spaceport."

Chewbacca rumbled a question.

"Oh, don't worry," Zerba said. "They don't watch me *that* closely. And I've been prepared for this day for quite a while." He looked around. "I just need to make sure none of them is right here. . . ."

"One other thing," Han said. "The things you'll be collecting include that old lightsaber you used to have, right?"

Zerba's head snapped back, his eyes darting between Han and Chewbacca. "Wait a minute," he said suspiciously. "Is *that* what this is about? All you need is my lightsaber?"

"No, we need you, too," Han hastened to assure him.

"Besides, if I wanted a real lightsaber, I know another guy who's got one."

"What do you mean, a *real* lightsaber?" Zerba huffed. "Mine cuts as well as anything else you can find out there."

"I mean a lightsaber with a blade longer than *this*," Han said, holding his hands twenty centimeters apart. "Yours is more like a lightdagger. Or a light-breadknife."

"Yet it seems to be worth you coming all this way to get it," Zerba countered. "Why? What do you want with it?"

"To cut something," Han said, fighting back his impatience. This wasn't exactly the right time or place for this conversation. "I don't know what yet. But there's always something that needs cutting."

For a long moment Zerba stared at him in silence. Han stared back, trying to remember where exactly number nine on their list was at the moment.

Then, to his relief, Zerba nodded. "Of course," he said. "And yes, I still have it. Though the blade length's down to about fifteen centimeters now. I don't know why it keeps shrinking."

"That should be fine," Han assured him. So Zerba wouldn't be moping, but he'd probably be paranoid and suspicious the whole way back. Not much of a gain. "You with us or not?"

"I'm with you," Zerba said. He glanced around one final time, then reached into his pocket and pulled out something the size and shape of a small egg—

And in a single blink of an eye, his yellow suit turned into a long, dark red jacket, a patterned blue shirt, and baggy tan trousers.

Chewbacca barked a startled expletive.

Zerba smiled and cocked his head in an abbreviated nod. "Like I said, I've been ready," he said. Turning, he disappeared into the crowd of shoppers.

Chewbacca rumbled again.

"Hadn't seen that one before, huh?" Han asked as he headed off through the crowd in the opposite direction. "Someone told me once that it's just a silk outfit with tear-away seams and connecting threads that yank all the pieces off and into that egg thing he was holding."

Chewbacca seemed to think that one over a moment. Then he growled again.

"Well, yeah, I'm sure it sounds easier than it really is," Han said. "Boil it down, and all *we* do is move cargo from one place to another."

Chewbacca rumbled.

"Right," Han conceded. "Without getting caught."

The big, burly man was too far away across the spaceport landing field for Han to hear what he was saying. But from the way his arms were waving as he faced the Rodian half of the conversation, he wasn't very happy.

Judging by the way the Rodian's green-scaled hand was resting on the grip of his holstered blaster, it didn't look like he was very happy, either.

Beside Han, Chewbacca growled a question.

"Because we need a front man," Han told him. "Someone who can pitch a good story and make him believe it." He nodded toward the arguing duo. "Dozer's got the presence, the confidence, and even a hint of a Corellian accent."

Chewbacca rumbled an objection.

"Yeah, but *thug* is the look we're going for," Han reminded him. "He's a little rough, but he could pass as someone who's worked his way up through the ranks. Besides, none of my other choices was available."

Chewbacca rumbled again.

Han got a firm grip on his temper. Was Chewie *never* going to drop this subject? "Sure, Lando could probably do it better," he said with forced patience. "And no, we're not calling him. End of subject." He glared up at the Wookiee's stubborn expression. "And I *mean* end of subject. Got it?"

Glowering, Chewbacca rumbled a grouchy affirmative. Han turned his attention back to the distant and, from the looks of things, increasingly turbulent conversation.

The really irritating part was that Chewbacca was right. Lando Calrissian would be the perfect front man for the scheme he had in mind—no Corellian accent, but smoother and more urbane than Dozer Creed could manage on even his best day. But after the Ylesia incident, Lando had told Han in no uncertain terms that he never wanted to see him again. The fiasco with the Yavin Vassilika statue had done nothing but strengthen that animosity.

Maybe Lando would eventually cool off. Maybe he wouldn't. Only time would tell, and Han wasn't in any hurry to find out.

The conversation across the landing field was growing louder. Han watched Dozer's wildly waving arms, wondering if it was time for him and Chewbacca to step in. If either party decided to raise the stakes by drawing, this thing could run flat into a wall in record time.

And then, suddenly, it was over. The Rodian handed Dozer a small pouch, Dozer picked up the travel case beside him and handed it to the Rodian, and both turned and headed off their separate ways.

"See?" Han said, gesturing toward the big man. "No problem—just talked his way through it. Come on, let's see if he's free." He started toward Dozer—

And stopped in his tracks as something hard dug into his back.

"Don't turn around," a quiet voice came from behind

him, just in case the blaster barrel hadn't been enough of a message.

Han stopped, exhaling a little sigh. He should have guessed it wouldn't be this simple. "Take it easy," he soothed the man behind him as he slowly moved his hands away from his sides. "We're just passing through."

"Maybe," the man said. "Here's what we're going to do. We're going to wait, nice and quiet, until that thieving son of a Ranat comes over here. And don't even think about trying to warn him."

"Hey, no problem," Han assured him. Across the field, Dozer had spotted his visitors and changed direction toward them. "What happens then?"

"Then he gives me my ship back," the man said. "Or I kill him."

"Fair enough," Han said, studying Dozer's face. The other was watching Han and Chewbacca—mostly Chewbacca, really—with a slight frown on his face. But it was a curious frown, without any alarm or suspicion mixed in.

Which meant he hadn't noticed the gunman behind them. "You sure he's the one who did whatever it was that happened to your ship?" Han asked, listening carefully.

"If I were you, I wouldn't ask too many questions," the man advised. "If I get even a hint you're working with him, you might not walk away from this."

"Yeah, got it," Han growled. He'd been right: the voice was definitely coming from his left and a couple of centimeters above his ear. Which meant the man was too tall to be hiding behind him.

Which meant he was hiding behind Chewbacca.

"And go easy on the threats, okay?" he continued. "The Wookiee here has a bad heart, and excitement isn't good for him. Too much of it and he might have an attack."

"Yeah, right," the man said sarcastically. "I hear about Wookiees with heart trouble *all* the time."

"I'm not kidding," Han insisted. "He had seumadic fever when he was a kid." He reached up and touched Chewbacca's arm. "You okay?"

Chewbacca gave a plaintive trill and rocked a little on his feet. Good—he was on to the plan. "Hang on, buddy, hang on," Han urged. "Can I at least get him his medicine?" Without waiting for an answer he dug into his side vest pocket.

And froze as the blaster again jabbed into his back. "Hands at your sides," the man snapped. "You—Wookiee—stand still. Blast it, stand *still*!"

"He can't help it," Han said, gripping Chewbacca's arm tightly. The Wookiee was really getting into his role, weaving back and forth like a tent in a hurricane. If Han hadn't known better, he would have sworn his partner was on the verge of collapsing in a heap.

Their assailant thought so, too. Han could hear him swearing in anxious frustration as his walking shield threatened to move far enough to one side or the other that he would be exposed to Dozer's view. Han could hear the faint scuffling of boots on duracrete as he tried to match Chewbacca's movements.

And with the gunman's full attention focused on keeping himself hidden, Han half turned, swept his left arm backward to knock the blaster out of line, and rammed his right fist into the man's gut.

With an agonized cough, the gunman folded up and dropped to his knees. Chewbacca spun around and grabbed their assailant's other arm, steadying and pinning him while Han twisted the blaster out of his limp grip. He was a lot younger than Han had guessed, despite his height. Not much older than Luke, with a lot of the same air of wide-eyed gullibility. "You want to explain this?" Han asked mildly, hefting the blaster in front of the kid's eyes.

The kid glared but remained silent.

"Let's try it again," Han suggested, shifting his grip on the blaster to point the weapon at the kid's face. "You just pulled a blaster on two total strangers. I want to know why."

"Well, well." The bemused voice came from behind Han. He turned, tensing, then relaxed as he saw it was only Dozer, strolling almost casually toward them. The big man's hand was resting on the grip of his blaster, but he was making no move to draw. "What have we here?"

"We have someone who isn't very happy with you," Han told him. "He's too choked up to explain. You want to give it a shot?"

Dozer shook his head sadly. "Jephster, Jephster," he admonished the kid. "I already told you: your ship's over in the North Quadrant."

"I looked," the kid ground out, the words coming out with obvious effort. "Bay two-fifty, just like you said."

"Two-*fifty*?" Dozer sighed theatrically. "Jephster, I said two-fifteen. Two-*fifteen*."

The kid looked up, a stricken look on his face. "Two-*fifteen*?" he repeated weakly.

"Two-fifteen," Dozer said firmly. "I'm sorry—I really thought you'd heard it correctly. But no harm done, eh?" He pulled out his comlink. "Tell you what. I'll call over to the gate supervisor, tell him you got confused, and have him confirm it for you. All right?"

"No," the kid said hastily, struggling back to his feet. "No, that's okay. I'll just go over and . . . I can find it myself." He looked at Han. "Sorry," he added.

"Next time make sure you know what you're doing before you start waving your blaster around," Han warned as he reversed the weapon and dropped it back into the kid's holster. "Other people don't bother asking questions before they start shooting."

"Yeah," the kid wheezed. "Sorry." Nodding weakly, he turned and limped away.

Dozer waited until the kid was out of earshot. "Nice job," he murmured. "That could have been messy. It's Solo, right?"

"That's me," Han confirmed. "Forgotten us already?"

"Oh, I never forget a face," Dozer assured him. "I just have trouble matching them up with their proper names. What brings you to this corner of the galaxy?"

"I've got a job," Han said. "Not smuggling this time. More along the lines of a vault robbery."

"Really," Dozer said. "And what, you need a ship or two for the scheme?" He waved a hand at the field all around them. "Anything you see here, I can lift it for you."

"I was more thinking of having you play front man," Han said. "You've got the presence and smooth talk we need."

"Ah—so there's some con work involved, too?" Dozer said. "Interesting. I'm in."

Han frowned. "Don't you want to hear the take first?"

"You wouldn't have come all this way if it wasn't decent," Dozer pointed out. His eyes flicked to the kid. "Besides, getting off this rock for a while would probably be a good idea."

"Probably," Han agreed. "I take it you've already sold his ship?"

"Actually, it was never his in the first place," Dozer admitted. "I find my profit margins are so much more satisfactory when I can sell the same merchandise twice."

"Easier to do in your line than mine," Han said. "Just out of curiosity, what would you have done if he'd let you talk to the gate supervisor?"

"And have people know he'd been stupid enough to

draw on total strangers after he'd misheard a number?"

Dozer shook his head. "Not a chance. Young men of his age will go to extraordinary lengths to avoid being embarrassed."

"Lucky for you."

Dozer shrugged. "You *did* already have his blaster," he pointed out. "Still, as I believe a great poet once said, discretion is the foundation of continued existence. Ready whenever you are."

"Good," Han said, gesturing toward another part of the field. "The *Falcon*'s this way. Unless you'd rather bring your own ship."

"Never actually owned a ship of my own," Dozer said. "Maintenance costs are *way* too high."

"You said it," Han said ruefully. "Come on, let's get out of the sun before the kid comes back."

CHAPTER FOUR

Eanjer was waiting in the Iltarr City Spaceport docking bay as Han, Chewie, Zerba, and Dozer filed out of the *Falcon.* Han handled the introductions, and while Eanjer was polite enough, Han had the distinct feeling that he was a bit startled at the size of the group. Possibly he was starting to wonder how many times his pile of credits was going to be split before he got a piece of it for himself.

Fortunately, whether he'd expected a crowd or not, he'd come prepared. Instead of a standard four-seat landspeeder, he'd brought a ten-passenger speeder truck.

"Is everyone else here?" Han asked, wincing a little as Eanjer maneuvered them out of the parking area and onto the crowded street. He still didn't know how well Eanjer could see out of that prosthetic eye, and driving in city traffic with a single hand was tricky at the best of times. But he'd made a beeline straight for the driver's seat the moment they reached the vehicle, and Han hadn't yet figured out a diplomatic way to get him out of it.

"No idea," Eanjer said, "since I don't know who else you might have coming. So far we have three: Rachele, plus the young man and woman Mazzic sent. Oh, and the twins—Bink and somebody? They arrived just as I was leaving to pick you up."

"Bink's sister's named Tavia," Han said.

"Right—Tavia," Eanjer said, nodding. "So is that it?"

"That's it," Han assured him, looking around at all the traffic. Rachele had warned him that, with the city filling up ahead of the Festival of Four Honorings, she might have trouble finding them accommodations. "So was Rachele able to get us a room?"

"Yes." Eanjer smiled slyly. "And no."

Sure enough, she hadn't gotten them a room.

She'd gotten them a huge, two-floor suite.

"I'm impressed," Dozer commented, looking back and forth at the various furnishings as Rachele gave them the grand tour. One of the rooms was all shades of brown, with a hardwood floor and adjustable recline chairs around a glass-topped and holo-equipped table. Another room was done up in light blue, with a round game table, a stand-up bar, and floor-to-ceiling artwork. "And Han can tell you that's not easy to do. I can boost ships all day long. How in the Empire do you boost *real estate*?"

Rachele shrugged. "It's not hard when you know how."

"That doesn't tell me anything," Dozer said.

"It wasn't intended to," Rachele assured him.

Dozer inclined his head. "Fair enough."

"Bink and Tavia arrived about two hours ago," Rachele said as she led them to a wide spiral stairway leading to the floor above. "They're unpacking and setting up their gear in one of the bedrooms. Mazzic's people have been here since yesterday."

"Did Mazzic bring them himself?" Han asked.

"Actually, no one brought them—they flew in commercial." She smiled faintly. "We can throw chance cubes to see which of us gives them a ride when it's time to leave. Come on—they're in the upstairs conversation room. I'll introduce you."

She started up the stairs. Han followed, mentally shaking his head. Not only a suite, but even a suite with a view of Villachor's Marblewood Estate.

The really crazy thing was that this was just a hobby for Rachele, something she did as favors for friends or to amuse herself. If she ever decided to quit her regular life and turn to a career of crime, the Empire would never be the same.

Given the type of person Mazzic typically hired, the man and woman conversing quietly over a datapad were something of a surprise. For one thing, they were younger than Han had expected, no older than their early twenties and possibly younger. For another, neither had hardened, suspicious eyes and expressions, like the majority of the criminals Han had run into over the years. However it was they'd entered Mazzic's service, they probably hadn't been born or indentured into it.

"You must be Han," the woman said as the group filed up the stairway behind him and Rachele. Despite her youth, her hair was an almost shimmering pure white, and Han wondered briefly whether it was natural or some strange affectation. "My name is Winter."

"Winter what?" Zerba asked.

The woman flicked him a look. "Just Winter," she said.

"She's right," Han agreed before anyone else could speak. "We stick with first names from now on. Safer that way. This is Chewie and Rachele, Zerba, and Dozer. Rachele says you've already met Bink and Tavia."

"The ghost burglar and her sister," Winter said, nodding. "Yes, we have. An amazingly close set of identicals."

"They've also met our employer," Rachele added.

"Good." Han gestured to the kid sitting next to Winter. "And you?"

The kid had been staring at the rest of the group with

fascination or revulsion, Han couldn't tell which. Now, thrust suddenly into the center of attention, he seemed to snap himself back to reality. "I'm Kell," he said.

"And you do . . . ?" Dozer asked.

Kell frowned. "Do?" he echoed.

"What's your specialty?" Dozer said. "What do you do that makes you worthy to sit here among all this greatness?" He waved a hand around the room.

"Oh," Kell said, his face clearing. Easily bewildered, Han decided, but just as quick to get on track again. "I'm pretty good with explosives—make 'em, plant 'em, set 'em off. I know a lot about droids, too."

"Of course," Dozer said dryly. "A knowledge of droids is essential to any good caper."

"Actually, in this case, it is," Rachele told him. "Villachor's vault security includes a set of guard droids."

"Oh," Dozer said, sounding a bit off-stride. But like Kell, he recovered quickly. "Well, that's good to know. What about you, Winter?"

"I know a fair amount about security systems," Winter said. "I also have an eye for detail."

Kell snorted gently. "An eye, and a brain," he said. "She remembers everything she sees or hears. *Everything.*"

"That could come in handy," Han commented, eyeing Winter. He'd heard of people with that kind of memory, but they were few and far between.

"It already has," Rachele said. "We've been watching Villachor's mansion—" She broke off as a pleasant chime came from across the room. "Oh, good, he's here," she said, hurrying toward the door.

Han frowned, doing a mental count. Him and Chewbacca, Zerba and Dozer, Kell and Winter and Rachele, with Bink, Tavia, and Eanjer elsewhere in the suite. That was everyone he'd invited.

So who was Rachele expecting?

He turned, dropping his hand to his blaster. Rachele reached the door and opened it.

And striding in past her as if he owned the place came Lando Calrissian.

"Hello, everyone," he said, smiling that easy smile of his as he looked around the room. His gaze flicked to Han, turned quickly away. "So what is this job, exactly?"

It took Han a second to find his voice. "Rachele, can I see you a minute?" he asked, forcing his voice to stay casual.

A slight frown creased her forehead, but she nodded and headed toward an alcove off to the side that had been set up as a study. Han followed, listening with half an ear as Lando and the others began renewing acquaintances or making introductions as needed.

Rachele stopped just inside the study and turned around. "Yes?"

"What's he doing here?" Han demanded in a low voice.

Rachele's frown deepened. "You told me to invite him."

Han stared at her. "When?"

"I got a message three days ago," she said, her voice suddenly gone mechanical as she belatedly caught on. "Right after you messaged that you'd picked up Bink and Tavia." Her face screwed up in a wince. "You didn't send it, did you?"

Han sighed. Chewbacca. Or maybe Bink—she'd always had a thing for Lando. Maybe even Mazzic, figuring that loaning them Winter and Kell gave him the right to help with the rest of the guest list. "No, I didn't," he said. "Did I happen to mention that he hates me?"

"I don't think he does," Rachele said. "Not really. He told me he'd been thinking it over, that maybe what happened wasn't completely your fault."

"*Completely?*" Han retorted, feeling anger stirring inside him. Not a single microgram of either of those fiascos had been his fault. "Nice. Good thing we don't need him. You brought him, so you can go back in there and tell him—"

"He needs the credits," Rachele said quickly.

Han snorted. "Lando *always* needs credits."

"I'm serious," Rachele said. "I think this time he's genuinely desperate."

Desperate enough even to work with a man he hated? Han turned and looked back at the group, still in the midst of friendly chitchat. If Lando was desperate, it sure didn't show in his face.

But then, it never did. If there was one thing Lando was good at, it was hiding whatever dark secrets were churning around inside him. Which was what made him such a good—and annoying—gambler and con man.

And, he admitted reluctantly, why he would be such a good front man for this job. Far better than Dozer.

"You can take his payoff out of my share," Rachele offered. "Like you said, he's here because of me."

For a moment Han was tempted. But it really wasn't Rachele's fault.

Besides, if this worked, there would be plenty to go around. "No," he told her. "Whatever we get, we split it equally. That was the deal." He took a deep breath. "You were starting to say something about Villachor's mansion?"

"Yes," Rachele said, and he could hear the relief in her voice. That had been a very awkward position for her to be in. "He's been having visitors—"

"Don't tell *me,*" Han interrupted, putting his hand on her back and guiding her gently back toward the conversation room. "Tell everyone."

It took a minute to close down the conversations and get everyone seated, and two minutes more to collect

Bink, Tavia, and Eanjer from the other ends of the suite.

"As I started to say earlier," Rachele said when everyone was finally assembled, "Winter, Kell, and I have been watching the traffic in and out of Villachor's grounds, and we've spotted an interesting pattern. First, a group of three heavy landspeeders goes in through the western gate and they all park by the south wing's private entrance. One person gets out of one of the vehicles—which vehicle it is seems to be random—and goes inside."

"Could you tell who he is?" Dozer asked.

"Who, or what?" Bink added.

"He was humanoid, but that's all we could get," Kell said. "The entrance's awning was always deployed, and the landspeeder drove right up beneath it. All we could get from this angle were shadows, and they weren't clear enough for anything beyond basic shape."

"Can we use a punch sensor?" Tavia suggested. "If the awning's thin enough, that might get you a better view."

"Punch sensors are traceable," Dozer said. "We don't want Villachor backtracking us here."

"We're far enough away, and in the middle of a group of high-rise buildings," Tavia pointed out. "As long as you keep the punch short, odds are slim that he could find us."

"It doesn't matter, because punch sensors won't work," Winter said. "Marblewood has an umbrella shield that extends all the way down to just above the outer wall. If turbolasers can't get through, punch sensors certainly won't."

Dozer waved a hand. "Of course they won't," he said apologetically. "Sorry—I should have figured he'd have something like that in place." He nodded to Rachele. "Please, continue."

"Ten to thirty minutes after those landspeeders arrive,

another landspeeder comes in, a different one each time," Rachele said. "A single person gets out and goes in through the main entrance. *Those* visitors we've gotten clear looks at, and so far they've always been important officials connected to either the government, industry, or financials. About an hour later that visitor comes out and drives away. Ten to fifteen minutes later, the passenger from the other landspeeder comes out through the private entrance, and the convoy also leaves."

"It's been happening three to four times a day," Kell added. "There's usually an early morning visit, then one around midday, one in the evening, and one day there was also one just before midnight."

"The interesting point is that they're the same three landspeeders each time," Winter said. "The ID tags are different, but the landspeeders are the same."

"As are the passengers, we assume," Rachele said.

"How do you know they're the same landspeeders?" Zerba asked.

"They have the same small scratches, dents, and other marks," Winter said.

"You're sure?" Dozer asked.

"Very sure," Winter said. "Rachele has good electrobinoculars, and those details come through very clearly."

"Sounds like Villachor's playing host to some kind of ongoing meetings," Bink suggested.

"He's trying to find a slicer to steal my credits," Eanjer said blackly. "Probably brought in someone from offworld who's taken advantage of the Festival crowds to slip into the city. If we don't get in there quickly, we're going to lose everything."

"Steady," Bink soothed. "Rushing off before you're ready is a recipe for disaster. Besides, if this visitor is Villachor's personal slicer, why isn't he staying at Villachor's place instead of coming and going?"

"And why the parade of local officials coming in to see

him?" Tavia added. "No, there's something else going on."

"How do these officials look when they come out?" Lando asked. "Happy, angry, depressed?"

Winter and Kell looked at each other. "Nothing, really," Kell said. "They just look—I don't know. Normal."

"You say there's usually a midday visit?" Lando asked, standing up and walking over to the window. "Which direction do they come from?"

"Northwest, usually," Winter said, going over and standing beside him. "They come into view along one of those streets up there, then head down the wide avenue along the outer wall, then go in through that gate, the one in the southwest corner."

"And they leave the same way?"

"They leave through the same gate, but then take various routes back to wherever they're ultimately going."

"Have you tried following them?" Han asked.

"I didn't think it would be safe," Rachele said. "I'm guessing they have someone running high cover, and we need to have more than just a couple of trackers if we're going to tail them without being spotted."

"Well, we've got a decent-sized group now," Han said, crossing to the chair beside Bink and Tavia and sitting down. "Winter, keep an eye out—see if they run their usual schedule. The rest of you, come over here and let's see what Rachele's found out about Villachor's place."

"It's going to be a short demo, I'm afraid," Rachele said as the others came back to the conversation area and sat down. Lando, Han saw with private amusement, was heading toward the seat between Bink and Tavia until Tavia noticed and scooted just far enough toward her sister to close the gap. Lando didn't even hesitate, but smoothly changed direction and sat beside Zerba instead.

"Here's the basics," Rachele said when everyone was seated. She did something to her datapad, and a large multifloor schematic appeared in the air over the holoprojector. "Villachor's mansion was originally built a hundred fifty years ago as the sector governor's new home. You'll note the rough *aurek* shape of the building: straight-edged north and south wings facing west, with northeast and southeast wings branching off from the center section behind them."

"Let me guess," Dozer said. "The governor's name began with that letter?"

"His wife's name, actually," Rachele said. "The governorstead was moved again eighty years later, and the mansion went through a variety of owners until Villachor bought it eleven years ago."

"Are these schematics up to date?" Bink asked.

"Mostly," Rachele said. "As far as I can tell, none of the previous owners did anything drastic to the building. The biggest renovation was those skylights over the entry atria and the wings, which were installed about fifty years ago. But none of the basic structure or layout was changed until Villachor took over." She keyed her datapad again, and the view zoomed in on a large ground-floor room near the southern end of the building's south wing. "This is the junior ballroom. Villachor's first—and biggest—renovation was to turn it into his vault."

Lando whistled softly. "What does he keep in there, small starships?"

"I gather that most of it's still empty space," Rachele said. "We know he's armored the walls and ceiling somewhat. Not all that seriously—I looked at the old material requisitions, and I'm guessing there's no more than four or five centimeters of warship-class hull plate in place, with the door made of the same material. Nothing to sneer at, but not as bad as it could be. Unfortunately, the whole vault's also magnetically sealed, and there's probably a layer or two of sensor shielding in there, too."

"You said the armoring is just on the walls and ceiling?" Dozer said. "Nothing on the floor?"

"There might be some down there, too," Rachele said. "But given that the entire south wing sits on ten meters of solid stone, I doubt he bothered."

"The walls shouldn't be a problem," Zerba said, one finger prodding thoughtfully at his lower lip. "Even at your upper estimate it shouldn't take more than a couple of minutes for me to carve us our own door."

"Even with the magsealing?" Kell asked.

Zerba nodded. "Shouldn't be a problem."

"What *could* be a problem is if the plating is honey-trapped," Bink warned. "Even something that thin has plenty of depth to work with."

"What's a honey trap?" Eanjer asked.

"Honeycomb-style booby traps," Bink explained. "You put pockets of explosives, acid, or pressurized poison gas inside your walls so that whoever's behind the cutting torch gets a lethal surprise halfway in."

"It's all the rage among the better class of paranoid criminal bosses," Dozer added dryly. "What about it, Kell? You have any experience with those? Or do you just blow things up and leave the defusing to others?"

"No, I can do both," Kell said, his forehead wrinkled in thought. "I can probably handle any explosive traps we find, provided Zerba doesn't set them off before I can get there." He wrinkled his nose. "Not so sure about the acid and gas, though."

"Actually, I doubt the walls will be our biggest problem," Rachele said. "It looks like what he's got *inside* the room will be the real challenge."

"And what exactly would that be?" Lando asked.

Rachele made a face. "That's the problem," she admitted. "No one knows. At least, no one I can get to."

There was a moment of silence. "No problem," Han said. "Just means the first job is to get someone inside to take a look."

"Yes," Rachele said uncertainly. "Only no one's allowed in there. There are guards on duty at the vault doors around the clock—armed *and* armored—and Villachor's the only one they'll let in."

"Or Villachor and a friend," Han said. "It has to be set up so he can bring someone else in if he wants to."

"Only one way to find out," Dozer said. "Which of us gets to be Villachor's new best friend?"

"No contest," Lando said, smiling at the twins. "I nominate Bink."

"Why, thank you, sir," Bink said, smiling sweetly back at him. "I just *love* making new friends."

"You really think he'll fall for that?" Eanjer asked, sounding confused.

"I'm quite certain he won't," Tavia said stiffly, countering Lando's smile with a frosty look of her own. "May I suggest instead that we send in Zerba and his lightsaber to cut a peephole in the wall? We could set up a recorder and see what exactly goes on in there."

"How are you going to get him that far into the mansion?" Kell asked, pointing at the schematic. "I'm seeing the mansion's outer wall *and* another interior one before you even get to the vault."

Chewbacca rumbled.

"Chewie's right," Han agreed. "Even if the crowds Villachor's letting in for the Festival aren't supposed to go inside, his security's bound to be stretched thinner than usual. We'll find a hole."

"Or make one," Dozer said.

Han nodded. "Or make one."

"At least we'll know where to start looking for those holes," Rachele said. "Marblewood's been a Festival venue for the past six years, and it's had extensive coverage, official and unofficial both. I've taken a look at the various records, and there are a lot of things Villachor seems to do the same way every year."

"I thought the pattern and order of the Honorings were always the same anyway," Dozer pointed out.

"I'm talking about the details," Rachele said. "Like where he positions the food pavilions, or how he dresses all the service and maintenance droids in coordinated and themed overgarments for each day of the Festival. Little things like that."

"Patterns are good," Lando said. "Like in sabacc, when someone always bets the same—"

He broke off as, across the room, Winter suddenly snapped her fingers. "Here they come," she announced.

There was a mad scramble as everyone jumped out of their seats and rushed to the windows. "Where?" Zerba asked.

"Those three landspeeders two blocks away," Winter said, pointing. "No—don't," she added as Dozer started to open the door leading onto the long balcony. "If someone's watching, we'll be way too visible out there."

"Where are those electrobinoculars?" Lando asked.

"Here," Kell said, pressing a set of the oversized viewers into his hand. "Rachele?"

"I'll get the other one," Rachele said, and hurried away.

The room fell silent. Han watched the landspeeders maneuver to and through the gate onto Villachor's grounds, noting that the vehicles barely even slowed down before the guards waved them through.

"Here," Rachele murmured in his ear.

"Thanks," Han said, taking the electrobinoculars from her and pressing them to his eyes. The landspeeders were even more impressive close up than they were at a distance: black and heavy-looking, obviously armored, with tinted windows concealing the passengers.

"Boost-equipped, looks like," Lando murmured. "See the reinforced lower edge plates?"

"Yeah, I see 'em," Han confirmed. The vehicles might look like normal landspeeders, but with the hidden boosts they could instantly become airspeeders anytime they wanted.

"So why are they bothering with the streets?" Zerba asked. "Why not just fly in?"

"The airlanes in Iltarr City aren't much faster than the landlanes," Rachele said. "Besides, they'd have to come to ground to get in anyway. The umbrella shield, remember?"

"And if you're the paranoid type, you might like having one direction that you can't be shot at from," Lando added.

The vehicles tracked along the pathway between the hedges, bushes, and small trees and finally came to a halt by the covered entrance at the mansion's south wing. Han held his breath, holding the electrobinoculars as steady as he could, wondering if this would be the day the mysterious visitor made a mistake.

He didn't. The awning over the entrance completely blocked their view of him as he left the landspeeder and headed inside. And with the sunlight streaming down from nearly overhead, there weren't even any of the tantalizing shadows Kell had mentioned.

"They're slick, all right," Lando commented. "How soon did you say the next wave is due?"

"Ten to thirty minutes," Winter said.

"So just enough time for a snack," Lando concluded. "Do I smell carni chips and glaze sauce coming from somewhere?"

"Yes," Eanjer said, sounding a bit taken aback by the sudden change in subject. "And also some kamtro grassticks. But shouldn't we be watching Marblewood?"

"I'm watching it," Lando assured him, turning back to the window. "Winter, tell me when you see a likely landspeeder. Bink, would you do me a favor and get me a small plate of those carni chips?"

Bink sent Tavia a wry smile. They knew Lando all too well. "Sure," she said, and headed toward the kitchen.

Han started to turn away, stopping as a hand caught his arm. "A word?" Dozer said quietly.

They stepped a few meters away from the others. "Problem?" Han asked.

"More of a question." Dozer nodded toward Lando, who had pulled a chair over to the window and settled himself in it. "You told me that I was going to be front man on this scheme. Now that Calrissian's here, I assume that's changed?"

"Probably," Han said. "But don't worry—there'll be other stuff for you to do."

"Uh-huh," Dozer said. "And the split?"

"Same as before," Han assured him. "Everyone gets the same share."

Dozer pursed his lips, and it wasn't hard to read the calculation going on behind his eyes. The shares might be passed out equally, but an even split among eleven was still smaller than an even split among ten.

"That going to be a problem?" Han pressed.

Dozer's expression cleared. "No," he said. "Just wondering." With a little nod, he turned and headed over to where Tavia and Rachele were standing.

There was a rumble from behind him, and Han turned to see Chewbacca standing there. "You heard?"

The Wookiee rumbled again.

"He'll be all right," Han assured him. "Dozer wouldn't let hurt pride get in the way of a paying job. Besides, I'm pretty sure he knows Lando will do better as a front man than he will."

Chewbacca warbled one final time and moved away.

"He'll be fine," Han murmured to himself as he turned back toward Dozer. "Trust me."

Ten minutes later and halfway through Lando's first helping of chips, the expected visitor cruised through the gate and onto Marblewood's grounds. Han, having already turned his electrobinoculars back over to Winter, watched from the side as he munched mechanically on a plate of kamtro grassticks. Something big was going on here, something way bigger than Eanjer and a stash of stolen credit tabs.

The two big questions were whether they could figure out what Villachor was up to and whether it was going to affect their own operation.

He'd left the window and was off in the corner, discussing the finer points of lock-picking with Bink, when Lando gave a warning whistle. "He's coming out," he called.

Once again, there was a brief scramble as the group reassembled by the windows. Han strained his eyes, but at this distance all he could see was a human male stalking down the steps to the waiting landspeeder. The man climbed in, the door closed, and the vehicle turned and headed back down the pathway.

"Interesting," Lando murmured, lowering his electrobinoculars. "That man just lost something."

"What did he lose?" Dozer asked.

"I don't know," Lando said. "It could have been credits, prestige, or power. But the changes in his expression and body language were very clear. Whatever he lost, it was something he wanted to keep."

"Wasn't enough time for a high-stakes sabacc game," Zerba said thoughtfully.

"But plenty of time for a serious conversation," Han pointed out. "Especially if one side was doing most of the talking."

"You think Villachor threatened him?" Tavia asked.

"Or blackmailed or extorted," Dozer said. "Those are the main three ways of controlling someone without having to fork over credits to pay them off."

Chewbacca warbled a question.

"No idea," Winter said. "He wasn't in the group of holos Rachele gave me."

"I only gave her the top-level players in Iltarr City's power structure," Rachele explained.

"Maybe we should go down a tier or two," Zerba suggested.

"Agreed," Rachele said. "I'll see what I can pull together."

"And while you do that," Dozer said, "let's see if we can figure out who the other visitor is. I think we've got enough people now for a proper tail. Shall I go out and get us a few landspeeders?"

"No need," Rachele said. "Eanjer was able to scrape together enough credits to get us a few rentals. We have three of them downstairs, plus the speeder truck, plus two airspeeders in the rooftop lot."

"Good," Dozer said. "It's probably too late to get in position before he leaves, so we'll have to pick him up later tonight."

"Assuming the drama gets a repeat performance," Bink said.

"It will," Winter assured her. "These people like to think they're being clever, but they're very much into patterns."

"Great," Dozer said. "Who's up for a little drive?"

"You should ask Han," Eanjer said. "He's the one in charge."

Dozer blinked, then smiled wryly. "Of course he is,"

he acknowledged, turning to Han and inclining his head. "Sorry. Too many years of working for myself. So who's going?"

Han looked around, doing a quick assessment. "You, Bink, Zerba, and me in the landspeeders," he decided. "Lando and Chewie will coordinate from the airspeeder."

"Sounds good," Dozer said.

"I'd like to go along, too, if I may," Eanjer said. "I want to help." He looked down at his medsealed hand. "Though I'm not sure what I'd be able to do," he added ruefully.

Han hesitated. They had a lot of reasons to keep Eanjer happy. A hundred sixty-three million of them, to be exact.

But he was an unknown quantity, and Han had no idea how he would react in a crisis situation. If something went wrong, one panicked person could easily run the whole thing straight into a wall.

To his relief, Chewbacca had followed the same line of thought and was already on it with a tactful suggestion.

"Good idea," Han said. "Chewie says an extra pair of eyes would be handy in the airspeeder."

Dozer gave a small snort. "A *pair* of eyes?"

"I meant an extra observer," Han corrected, glaring at the ship thief. Eanjer was aware enough of his handicap without someone drawing attention to it. "You can go with him and Lando, Eanjer."

"Thank you," Eanjer said. He looked at Dozer, a hint of fire in his single eye. "And my current prosthetic works well enough, thank you," he added icily. "I plan to get something more aesthetically pleasing when I get my stolen credits back and can afford to fix the rest of the injuries Villachor caused me."

"That's settled, then," Lando said cheerfully into what could have been the start of a long and awkward silence. "Chewie will fly, you and I will watch, and by the time we settle in for the night we'll have gotten to the bottom of this little mystery." He beamed a smile around the room. "While we wait, anyone for a game of sabacc?"

The man's name was Crovendif, and he thought of himself as an up-and-coming crime lord.

He wasn't, of course, and never would be. True, he had the clothing and style down, and had even made an effort to get the rhythm and pitch of his voice to match those of prominent holodrama criminals. But what he *didn't* have was the empty eyes and utter soullessness that Dayja had seen far too often in the humans and aliens he'd dedicated his life to bringing down.

No, Crovendif was just a lost kid who'd fallen in love with the idea of being a crime lord, or maybe had seen that as his path to contentment, security, and respect. Sooner or later those half-formed dreams would fade, and he would accept the fact that a crime lord's street manager was all he would ever be.

All of that assuming, of course, that he survived the next few minutes.

"You've been dancing a challenge through my territory for nearly two weeks," the would-be crime boss said, his voice low and menacing, his head raised slightly so that he could stare down his nose at his prisoner. He even had the holodrama stance down cold, Dayja noted. "Give me a reason why I shouldn't have you killed right here and now."

"I'm not looking to take over your territory," Dayja said mildly. "I'm sorry if I gave you that impression."

Crovendif's expression slipped, just noticeably. Expecting bluster and defiance from his prisoner, he wasn't prepared for a quiet, conciliatory response. "Really," he said sarcastically. "And what impression *should* I have gotten?"

"I'm looking for a partner," Dayja said. "I have some product that's worth a lot of credits. But I don't have the time or resources to set up the distribution end of the business."

"And what makes you think I'd be interested in such a deal?" Crovendif scoffed.

"Not you," Dayja corrected. "Your boss. I have far more product than your six or seven blocks can deal with."

Crovendif's face darkened. Maybe he'd had a brief hope that this was his ticket to greatness. "If you think I'm going to bother anyone else with such a ridiculous story—"

"He'll want a sample, of course," Dayja continued smoothly. "May I?"

Crovendif hesitated, then nodded to the two men currently pinioning Dayja's arms. "Left," he ordered.

Silently, the thug on Dayja's left side released his grip on that arm. Dayja slipped two fingers into his side pocket, pulled out a small vial, and tossed it across to Crovendif. The other caught it with a nimble quickness that suggested he'd started as a blade fighter before joining up with Black Sun. Yet another reason he'd probably never get any higher than he was already. "Glitterstim, obviously," he said as Crovendif looked closely at the vial. "But with a difference. Mine is artificial."

"Then it's not glitterstim," Crovendif said.

"You're right," Dayja conceded, inclining his head. "I misspoke. What I should have said was that it's genuine glitterstim, created by genuine Kessel spiders. But *not* spiders currently living on Kessel."

There was a pause as Crovendif apparently worked that through. "You have spiders here on Wukkar?"

"Let's just say they're nearby and creating glitterstim as we speak," Dayja said. "Bottom line is that I can make the product for a fraction of what it costs to make it on Kessel, and that doesn't even take the lower transportation costs into account."

"And you expect me to just take your word for all this?"

"Not at all," Dayja said. "Take the vial to your boss, give him my offer, and ask him to run some tests. If he's interested, great. If he's not, no harm done—there are lots of other fish in the river. Either way, he can keep the sample with my compliments."

"And if I refuse?"

"You mean if you decide to keep the vial for yourself, sell the product, and make yourself a bit of extra cash?" Dayja asked. "If that's what you want to do, I certainly can't stop you. All I can say is that you're not your boss's only street manager. If you don't want to bring this opportunity to him, I'm sure someone else will."

For a few seconds Crovendif continued to stare at his prisoner, frowning as if weighing the possibilities and coming to a decision. But it was all for show. Dayja had him, and they both knew it.

"Very well," Crovendif said at last, making it official. "How do I find you with his answer?"

"I'll be in touch." Dayja nodded to the thug on his right. "Now, if you don't mind . . ."

Crovendif gestured again, and the man holding Dayja's right arm released it. "Thank you," Dayja said. "I'll be seeing you."

He was sitting in his nondescript landspeeder half a block away when Crovendif and two of his men slipped out of their warehouse headquarters and climbed into their own vehicle. Dayja gave them a one-block head start, then settled in to follow. He was 90 percent sure that Crovendif was taking the vial to his boss, and he was another 90 percent sure that that boss was Villachor. But it never hurt to make sure.

Sure enough, Crovendif drove straight across Iltarr

City to the Marblewood southwestern gate. Not the brightest move if he was trying to conceal his affiliations, but Dayja had already concluded Crovendif wasn't the brightest star in the sky.

Still, the purpose was to pique Villachor's interest, and as long as Villachor got the vial of glitterstim, the details of the delivery weren't important. All Dayja had to do now was sit back, wait for Black Sun's chemists to analyze his gift, and then accept Villachor's inevitable invitation for a meeting.

Once inside the mansion, of course, the real challenges would begin. But he would deal with those as they arose.

Crovendif was still sitting at the gate, probably trying to convince the guards that he was one of Villachor's people and that his errand was important enough to pass up the line. Dayja drove casually by, glancing back and forth among the various landspeeders as he passed them.

He paused, his eyes flicking a second time to a dark blue landspeeder parked just inside one of the cross streets. Unlike most of the parked vehicles in the area, this one wasn't empty. A man was sitting in the driver's seat, attempting to look casual.

And he was watching the southwestern gate. Very closely.

Dayja continued on without slowing, turning at the next corner. Odds were that the man was another of Villachor's guards, stationed there as backstop in case there was trouble.

But he hadn't seemed the Black Sun type. And the last thing Dayja wanted was for someone else to grab Villachor's attention. Especially someone from a rival gang.

And so, instead of heading back to the hotel as he'd planned, he found a parking space within view of the mysterious watcher and settled down to wait. If the man was a guard, there would probably be a shift change somewhere in the next few hours.

If he wasn't, Dayja had no intention of letting a gang war start. Not here, and certainly not now.

Pulling out the thermajug of Karlini tea he always brought with him on drives like this, just in case, he poured himself a cup and settled down to wait.

CHAPTER FIVE

Eight minutes after the early evening visitor left Marblewood, the now-familiar three-landspeeder convoy also headed out.

Han and his blue landspeeder were right behind them.

Beside Lando, Chewbacca rumbled under his breath.

"I'm sure he knows," Lando assured him, studying the map of the area he'd pulled up on his datapad. The convoy had headed south, which meant they were traveling along Packrist Avenue . . .

"What does he know?" Eanjer asked from the backseat. "What did Chewie say?"

"He was warning Han not to get too close," Lando said. "I told him Han already knew that."

"Oh," Eanjer said, sounding nervous. "Shouldn't we be going?"

"Going where?"

"Following the landspeeders," Eanjer said. "I thought that was why we were up here."

"No, we're up here to watch for their backup," Lando said, listening with half an ear to the running commentary going on through his comlink. Han had broken off the chase now, just as he was supposed to, and Bink had the convoy in sight and was preparing to pick it up.

"Oh. Right." There was a soft hiss as Eanjer shifted in his seat. "Sorry. I'm afraid this isn't my area of expertise."

"That's why you hired us," Lando reminded him patiently.

Still, if the man had to be somewhere, he might as well be parked up here with them and out of the way.

The convoy turned, and Bink picked up the tail, moving in ahead of them and alerting Zerba to the change of direction. "May I ask you a question?" Eanjer asked.

Lando suppressed a sigh. Maybe he should send Eanjer across to the edge of the roof and tell him to watch for the convoy from there. "Go ahead."

"Why do you hate Han?"

Lando wrinkled his nose as the obvious answer popped into his mind. But obvious didn't necessarily mean correct. "I don't hate him," he said, picking his words carefully, painfully aware that Chewbacca was listening closely from half a meter away. "Not exactly. There was a deal—a couple of deals—where he ended up stiffing me out of what he'd promised."

"Doesn't sound right," Eanjer murmured. "No wonder you hate him."

"I *don't* hate him," Lando said, irritated. "I already said that. Besides, the more I've thought about it, the more I think it probably wasn't all his fault. That he was stiffed along with the rest of us. But that doesn't change the fact that he was the one who pulled us in and made all the big promises." He looked sideways at Chewbacca, wondering how he was taking this. But the Wookiee was gazing out the side window, his face turned away. "I don't hate him, but I don't want to work with him anymore," he concluded. "If he hadn't specifically asked for me on this job, I wouldn't have come."

"I see," Eanjer said. "Well, I for one am glad you came. I know you'll be a great help to the team. And for whatever it's worth, your share of the proceeds should make it possible for you to never have to work with him again."

"I'll keep that in mind," Lando said. Shaking away thoughts of Han, broken promises, and future riches, he focused his attention back on the running comlink conversation.

"They've turned *again,*" Zerba reported, his voice uneasy. "Same direction."

"Break off," Han ordered.

"Already done," Zerba said. "I don't know, Han—there's something's screwy here. If they're on to us, shouldn't one of the chase cars have broken off to check us out?"

"Maybe they're stalling," Dozer suggested darkly. "Stringing us along while they bring in extra backup."

Chewbacca rumbled, tapping Lando's arm with one hand and pointing with the other.

Lando looked along the straightened finger to another rooftop parking area three blocks away. "Let's find out," he said, pulling out his electrobinoculars and training them on the vehicle Chewbacca had marked, a landspeeder parked right at the edge of the roof.

The Wookiee was right—it was the same type as the ones in the convoy Han and the others were currently tailing. There were two human men sitting inside this one, both with electrobinoculars pressed to their faces, their heads moving back and forth as they scanned the airspeeder traffic moving past above them. A few meters away, a third man was crouched at the edge of the roof, his electrobinoculars focused on the streets below.

Lando smiled tightly as he keyed his comlink for transmission. Earlier he'd considered sending Eanjer to watch the street. The pair out there had apparently had exactly the same idea. "Everyone, break off," he ordered. "Repeat, break off."

"What is it?" Han demanded.

"We've found their spotter," Lando said, eyeing the men in the landspeeder. They looked to be just as comfortably settled as he, Chewbacca, and Eanjer were. And if they weren't expecting to have to take off into the air on a moment's notice . . .

"New positions," Lando continued, dropping the electrobinoculars into his lap and picking up his datapad. The parking area was . . . right there. Which meant—"Han, go to *resh*-seven on the map. Bink, take the side street one block north of him. Zerba: *senth*-seven. Dozer: *senth*-eight. Find parking places and wait."

"On my way," Bink acknowledged.

"Me too," Zerba added. "Hope you're not in a hurry—the traffic down here is horrendous."

"What's the plan?" Han asked.

"The spotters are sitting about three blocks away, not moving and not looking like they're about to," Lando said. "I'm guessing they're watching the end point of the drive, making sure no one's hanging around waiting to ambush their boss."

"You sure they're part of this team and not someone else's?" Bink asked.

"Pretty sure," Lando said. "They're in the same model landspeeder, with the same style boost system installed."

"Worth a shot," Han said. "If it doesn't work, we can always try again tomorrow."

"Unless they're already on to us," Dozer warned. "In which case, they'll have some nasty countermeasures ready."

"So let's make sure we get this right," Lando said.

The minutes ticked by. Han and the others reported their individual arrivals at their designated spots, then went silent.

Chewbacca rumbled a suggestion.

"Good idea," Lando agreed, sliding down in his seat so that his head was below the level of the windows.

"What did he say?" Eanjer asked.

"He said we should slouch down out of sight," Lando

translated, propping his electrobinoculars on his seat's shoulder support. Using the reflection from one of the building windows a block away, he should be able to keep track of what the spotters were doing. "So far it doesn't look like they've checked this direction, but if they do, we don't want them seeing us."

"Ah," Eanjer said, and Lando heard the soft hiss of cloth on leather as the other also slid out of sight. "Yes. Good idea."

Lando craned his neck around to where he could see Eanjer out of the corner of his eye. "Don't you have any Wookiees on Wukkar?"

"Of course we do," Eanjer said, sounding a little defensive. "But most of them are laborers, bodyguards, or hired muscle. I've never—" He broke off.

"Thought it was worth learning how to understand them?" Lando suggested.

The half of Eanjer's mouth that wasn't hidden by medseal twisted in an uncomfortable grimace. "I suppose," he said reluctantly. "Not that I didn't . . . well, no. I guess I just . . . I guess I should have."

Lando looked at Chewbacca, whose taller frame had forced him to slouch down even farther and more uncomfortably than Lando and Eanjer. There was some annoyance simmering in his eyes, but mostly he just looked resigned. It was all too common these days for his people to be treated as little more than convenient labor or expendable fighters.

Or as forgettable and throwaway slaves.

More minutes ticked by. Lando was starting to wonder if he'd guessed wrong, and was working on an alternative plan in case the convoy's boss was onto them, when the spotter's vehicle suddenly activated its boosts and rose into the air.

"Got 'em," Han said. "Convoy just pulled into view."

"Spotter's on the move," Lando said, easing his head

up for a clearer look. The man who'd been at the edge of the roof was still in position, watching the street below. "Everyone, stay put—spotter's on the alert."

"I've lost them," Han growled. "Around a corner, heading north. Anyone else?"

"Not here," Bink reported.

"Or here," Zerba said.

"Same," Dozer said. "Lando? Looks like it's up to you."

"Right," Lando said, wincing as he sat up straight in his seat and motioned Chewbacca and Eanjer to do likewise. If those spotters over there were worth their pay, the minute Chewbacca lifted off and headed that direction, they would be instantly in the center of unfriendly attention.

But if there was no other way, there was no other way. "Okay, Chewie—"

"Wait a second—I've got them," Bink said suddenly. "Heading straight up—*blast,* those are good boosts—looks like the service alley between Twentieth and Twenty-first, western end."

The words were barely out of her mouth when Lando had to grab for his datapad as Chewbacca kicked the airspeeder to power and shot toward the flow of traffic above them. The Wookiee twisted the vehicle to the right—

"Hold it—that's the wrong way," Eanjer warned. "The alley is two blocks to the *left.*"

"And the spotters will be watching for anyone heading that direction," Lando told him. "He's doing it right." Twisting around in his seat, he brought up his electrobinoculars.

There they were: three black landspeeders, rising swiftly alongside a tall, blocky building. "I see them," he said. "What's that building, a hotel?"

"Yes—the Lulina Crown," Bink confirmed.

"There's a covered airspeeder parking garage on the top floor," Rachele put in. "Secure entrance, residents and guests only. Let me see if I can pull up their current occupant list."

"Bink, can you see the front?" Han asked. "Maybe we'll get lucky and they'll turn on their lights when they hit their rooms."

"What if their rooms are in the back?" Eanjer asked. "She won't be able to see those from the street."

Again, Lando grabbed for his datapad as Chewbacca warbled a suggestion and made a sharp climbing turn, slipping the airspeeder deftly between two other vehicles in the next lane up.

"Chewie says we'll watch the back," Lando said, looking down and trying to orient himself after too many rapid changes of direction. The Lulina Crown . . . there it was. "Rachele, is there any way to boost the range on these things?" he asked, lowering the electro-binoculars for a quick look at the zoom control.

"Try turning the clarity control all the way up and raising the contrast," Rachele suggested. "That should help."

"Thanks." Lando made the adjustments. It wasn't perfect, but it was better than what he'd started with. "Bink?"

"Looks like they've landed," Bink reported.

"I think I see your spotters now, too," Zerba added. "They've left their roof and are heading across toward the hotel."

"I see them," Bink confirmed. "Those are *really* nice boosts."

"Easy, kiddo," Dozer said. "You be a good girl, and when all this is over you can pick out one of them for your very own."

"Like we've got room for one of those aboard our

ship," Bink muttered. "Though I guess I could store it in Tavia's cabin."

There was a faint and unintelligible comment from somewhere in the background. "Tavia says there's already too much of your stuff in her cabin," Rachele relayed. "She says if you want to bring a boosted landspeeder aboard, you should start by cleaning out your wardrobe closet."

"I need every one of those outfits," Bink said primly. "Just because *she* never goes out on the town—"

"Hold it," Lando put in. In the distance behind and beneath them, a group of windows at the rear of the Lulina Crown had just brightened. "I've got fresh lights in the windows. About a third of the way up, midway from either end."

"Can you tell which floor?" Rachele asked.

Lando squinted, trying to count as the airspeeder moved steadily farther from the hotel. "Looks like the sixth," he said. "It's a little hard to tell—there are a bunch of trees in the way."

"Probably a WilderNest garden," Eanjer said. "That's a small park with various types of trees and other plants, often wild ones that you don't usually see inside cities, the whole thing ringed by tall crescent or twistbark trees. Hotels with multiple buildings like to put them in the centers of their complexes."

"Checking the sixth floor now," Rachele said. "Let's see . . . yes, that entire center section is an eight-room suite. Bink, you seeing anything?"

"Nope," Bink reported. "Not on the sixth or anywhere else. If they've got any rooms on this side, they're being coy about it."

"They must really like parks," Dozer commented. "I'd think the outside rooms would have a better view."

"I don't think a view is what they have in mind," Bink

said thoughtfully. "Rachele, any chance of getting us a room somewhere near that suite?"

"I'll try," Rachele said. "No promises, though—with the Festival coming up, pretty much every room in the city was snatched up weeks ago."

"Are we done out here?" Lando asked.

"Yeah, we're done," Han confirmed. "Everyone head on back. Time to figure out our next move."

To the complete lack of surprise of everyone—except possibly Rachele herself—Rachele did indeed get them a room.

Though it wasn't exactly what Bink had hoped for when she'd turned Rachele loose on the job. She'd envisioned a room she could use as a base of operations for breaking into the place. Something right next door or, even better, something directly above or below. But even Rachele's computer wizardry and network of high-level connections could only do so much.

Still, if the place wasn't perfect, it could have been a lot worse.

"Is that it?" Tavia asked, stepping up to the window beside her and brushing a stray lock of her black hair behind her ear.

"That's it," Bink confirmed, gazing across the little pocket park at the other building. Two of the suite's windows were blocked by the trunks of the big trees lining the greenery, but the rest were clear and visible.

"At least you're not going to be rappelling down to it," Tavia said. "Not from here."

"You're right on that one," Bink agreed. Of all the aspects of Bink's job that Tavia hated, watching her sister slide down the side of a building on a thin synth-erope line was probably the part she hated the most.

Not that this would be a whole lot better, at least not

from Tavia's point of view. Still, swinging from tree to tree on a grappling harness wasn't as bad as that long, barely controlled fall from a rooftop.

"Wow," Kell said under his breath from somewhere behind the two women. "And you just moved us in here?"

"It wasn't that hard," Rachele assured him. "I noticed the couple who were supposed to move in here tonight are registered with the Wilderness Order, so I arranged for them to be offered a free safari in the Megrast Preserve down in Ancill Province. Simple, really."

Kell shook his head in amazement. "I still say wow."

Bink felt her lip twitch. Kell could be as impressed as he liked, but he really should stop being so vocal about it. There were enough swelled egos in this business as it was.

She sent a casual look over her shoulder at the others milling around the room. Maybe Winter would be willing to give him a few lessons on playing things cool. The white-haired woman was clearly just as impressed at Rachele's achievement as Kell was, but was hiding it a lot better.

"Trouble?" Tavia murmured.

"No, it's fine," Bink murmured back.

Theoretically, it was. Solo was a pretty good judge of character, mostly. So was Mazzic, even if Bink didn't always see eye to eye with him. If Mazzic said Winter and Kell were okay and Solo accepted that judgment, then they probably were.

But there was something about the two recruits that bothered her. Kell struck her as way too young, not just in age but also in experience and mental toughness. At the same time, she could see unnamed ghosts lurking behind his eyes. Something unpleasant in his past was driving him, maybe farther than he was really equipped to go.

Winter, oddly enough, was almost the exact opposite. She wasn't much older than Kell, but her eyes held a startling depth of age and maturity. She had a natural poise, too, the kind of grace and self-assurance that Bink could also see in Rachele. Did that mean Winter, like Rachele, was a member of some world's aristocracy? And if so, what in the Empire was she doing with a gang of thieves? Was she in it for revenge?

"Here," Solo's voice brushed into Bink's musings. She blinked the thoughts away and found him holding out one of Rachele's fancy electrobinoculars. "Rachele says we've got until tomorrow afternoon to get out of here. You think you can get us in by then?"

"Of course," she said, taking the electrobinoculars from him. If there was one thing she'd learned in this business, it was to never tell a client you couldn't do something.

Turning back to the window, pressing the electrobinoculars to her eyes, she got to work.

There wasn't a lot to see over there. And what there was wasn't very encouraging.

But it would be possible. Not easy, but possible.

She lowered the electrobinoculars and turned back around. In the intervening minutes, the rest of the group had found chairs or couches to sit on and were talking in low voices among themselves. "Here's the deal," she announced, walking over to the empty seat beside Rachele and sitting down.

The room went suddenly quiet.

"The hotel's windows have built-in security systems, but the occupants seem to have disabled them," she continued. "That means—"

"They *disabled* the security systems?" Kell asked, frowning.

"Central security systems are way too easy to slice into," Tavia told him. "Especially hotel systems, which aren't exactly known for sophistication. Our friends over there were probably afraid someone would take over the systems and use them to spy on them."

"Which we absolutely would have," Bink agreed. "You'll also note they picked a sixth-floor suite on the garden side of the building, with big trees that would hamper any attempt to get to their windows via airspeeder. Both of those bespeak a certain paranoia."

"Sounds about right for people who deal with Villachor," Eanjer muttered. He was sitting a few meters away from the others, staring broodingly across the park, his left hand absentmindedly massaging his misshapen right hand through the medseal wrapping.

"And having disabled the hotel's version of security," Bink continued, "what could be more natural than that they would set up their own?" She waved toward the suite. "Their first line of defense was to bolt a set of transparisteel plates onto the inside of the normal glass of the windows. The good news on that is that the plates aren't very thick, so I should be able to use a mono-edge wheel to cut through whichever one I want."

"Or you could just use Zerba's lightsaber," Dozer suggested. "Be a lot faster."

"Well, there's just one teeny little problem with that," Bink said. "Their second line of defense is a set of power sensors."

"You sure?" Lando asked. "Usually power sensors are set up out of sight."

"I'm positive," Bink said. "The ripple pulse in the glass is unmistakable. You bring anything with a power cell within five meters of any of the windows and you'll trigger alarms from one end of the suite to the other."

"Cute," Dozer grunted. "No way to disable them, I suppose?"

"Not from out here," Bink said. "But I think we've

got a manual crank drive for the mono-edge." She looked at Tavia. "Right?"

"Yes," her sister said, her mouth set in a thin, unhappy line. "How exactly were you planning to get close enough to use it?"

Bink braced herself. Tavia was not going to like this. "It's going to have to be tree to tree," she said. "Harness and manual grapples."

Tavia's thin lips compressed a little tighter. "Manual grapples don't set as solidly as powered ones."

"It'll be okay," Bink assured her. "I'll just make sure I have a good anchor on whichever tree I'm swinging from. If the grapple fails, I can just pull myself back and try again."

"How about using powered ones halfway across and then switching to manual?" Rachele suggested. "You should be able to use power along this building and at least halfway along the side set of trees. As long as you switch to unpowered before you get close to the suite you should be all right."

"Not worth the effort," Bink said. "Powered grapples are an integrated system. I'd have to strip off the harness, leave it draped over a branch or something, and pick it up on my way back. Besides, that five-meter range I quoted on the power detectors is only a guess. They may have focused detectors aimed in random directions that have two or even three times that range. I'd look pretty stupid if I reached the window to find half a dozen men with blasters waiting patiently for me to get there. Don't worry—the manual system will work just fine."

"Let's say it does," Lando said. "Once you're there, then what?"

"Ah," Bink said, lifting a finger. "That's actually the easy part." She lowered the upraised finger to point over her shoulder out the window. "Smack in the middle of that room over there is a Jaervin-Daklow floor safe. Probably bought here in the city—it looks new. They're big, heavy, nearly impossible to break into, and have a touch-pad coder that's virtually impossible to slice."

"Unless?" Solo prompted.

"Unless you can see the pad while the code's being entered," Bink said, feeling a mischievous smile tugging at her lips. "Our friends over there were smart enough to set up the safe facing away from the window so no one could watch from, oh, say, right here." She flicked a finger against her forehead. "What they *weren't* smart enough to realize was that the room's inside wall is facing the safe from less than three meters away. And said wall has a fresh gloss-white coat of paint."

For a moment the room was silent. "You're joking," Zerba said.

Bink shrugged. "You turn sticks into butterflies and change clothes faster than people can blink," she reminded him. "Jedi could supposedly lift rocks with their minds and make people forget their own names. We all have our specialties. This one's mine."

"The individual button lights on a keypad are never exactly the same," Tavia said. "Differences in the emitters, plus bits of dust and finger oils, all shift the color and optical texture a bit. When one of the buttons is pushed, that light is blocked and the pattern on the wall behind is changed."

"What do you need to work it?" Solo asked.

"I need to be at the window when they start keying in the code," Bink said. "The rest is just reading reflections."

"And shadows," Tavia added. "If we can figure out whether the operator is left- or right-handed—and we usually can—the way the shadows shift when he hits individual keys can also be read."

Bink rolled her eyes. "Tavia, you're not supposed to

tell people how the trick works," she said mock-severely. "They'll lose all respect if they know how simple it is."

"Yeah, *that'll* happen," Solo said dryly. "When can you be ready?"

Bink looked at Tavia. "Two hours?"

Her sister didn't look happy, but she gave a little nod.

"Two hours," Bink confirmed, turning back to Solo. "If Villachor has another late-night visitor, and if our friends across the way are invited, I can be by the window when they get back. After that, maybe half an hour to get in and crack the safe, see what's inside that'll tell us who they are and what they want with Villachor, then ten more minutes to seal up again."

"What if Villachor's already closed shop for the night?" Zerba asked. "If he sticks to schedule, he won't have another meeting until tomorrow morning."

Bink shrugged. "Then we do it tomorrow morning."

"In broad daylight?"

"Not a problem," Bink assured him. "There's enough foliage out there to hide me from most people."

"It's the ones who aren't *most people* I'm worried about," Zerba muttered.

"I may be able to buy us another night here if we really need it," Rachele said doubtfully. "It'll be tricky, though."

"Hold it," Lando said, straightening suddenly in his seat, his eyes on the window. "Looks like they're on the move."

Bink turned around, craning her neck. The room's light was on, with enough of a shifting shadow on the far wall to show that someone was over there opening the safe. She lifted the electrobinoculars to her eyes and focused in on the shadow.

Yes, it would work, she decided. She would have to be right up against the window to read the movements and decipher the keystrokes, but she was planning to be there anyway. The light and shadows shifted, marking the opening and closing of the safe door. The man back there emerged into view—

She stiffened. Only it wasn't a man. The face that passed briefly through her field of view was green-scaled, with a mass of black hair tied and flowing down his back.

From somewhere in the area where Kell and Zerba were sitting came a sharp gasp. "Is that—"

"It's a Falleen," Eanjer confirmed, his voice grim. "What in the Empire is a Falleen doing *here*?"

"Take it easy," Solo advised. But he didn't sound any more thrilled than Eanjer did.

Or any more thrilled than Bink felt, for that matter. There were Falleen all over the Empire, of course, just like there were Rodians and Duros and even Wookiees. But this close to Imperial Center, the odds were unpleasantly high that any given Falleen would be working for—

"Take it *easy*?" Kell demanded. "Falleen mean *Black Sun.*"

"Not necessarily," Winter said. Of all of them, she seemed to be maintaining the best semblance of calm. "Besides, Prince Xizor isn't the only Falleen voice in the galaxy these days. Most of them have nothing to do with Black Sun. In fact, there are groups who are actively trying to restore honor to the Falleen name by bringing him down."

Chewbacca rumbled.

"Well, sure, most of those groups are probably on Vader's payroll," Solo agreed. "Doesn't mean they're not out there."

"And I'll bet they've got Xizor really worried," Kell muttered.

"You're welcome to bail if you want," Zerba offered.

Kell set his jaw. "No," he said. "Thanks."

"If it helps any, I think there's just the one Falleen in the suite," Rachele offered, peering at her datapad. "Looking at the room-service records, I see only a single order per mealtime that a Falleen would be likely to choose. The rest of the food is more suited to humans."

"How many humans?" Lando asked. "What kind of numbers are we dealing with?"

Rachele's lips moved as she did a silent count. "I'd say ten to twelve, plus our Falleen."

"Maybe the Falleen isn't the one in charge," Tavia suggested.

"Don't kid yourself," Dozer said. "If it's Black Sun, the Falleen is definitely in charge."

"From what I've heard, Black Sun has plenty of humans in its ranks, too," Eanjer pointed out. "So if it *is* Black Sun, what does that mean for our plan?"

"Right now, nothing," Han said. "We still have to figure out what his connection is with Villachor, and for that we still need a look into that safe. Bink?"

"I'm game," Bink assured him, standing up. "And now, you're all invited to take yourselves and your conversation elsewhere."

"We're not going anywhere," Kell insisted.

"Oh, yes, you are," Bink said firmly. "I need to lay out and test my equipment, and I don't want a bunch of big nervous feet walking all over it."

"Besides, we all have jobs of our own to do," Solo added, getting to his feet. "Rachele, what's the hotel's security like?"

"Not too bad," Rachele said, again manipulating her datapad. "Looks like all you need to get up from the lobby is a keycard. There don't seem to be any security holocams except in the lobby and meeting areas, either."

"That's handy." Solo looked at Zerba. "You think you can get us a keycard?"

Zerba puffed contemptuously. "With guests walking in and out all the time? In my sleep."

"Good," Solo said. "Rachele, I want you to go back to the suite and watch Villachor's compound. Let us know when the Falleen and his convoy arrive and when they leave."

"Sounds like I get the boring duty," Rachele said.

"Don't worry, I've got another job that should keep you busy," Solo assured her. "Winter, Eanjer, you go with her. Chewie, you and Lando stay here with Bink and Tavia. Zerba, Kell, Dozer—you're with me."

"I'd like to stay here instead of going with Rachele, if I may," Winter spoke up.

"Any particular reason?" Solo asked.

"As I said earlier, I know a fair amount about security systems." Winter inclined her head toward Bink. "Not as much as Bink and Tavia do, of course. But three sets of eyes are better than two, and I might spot something they missed."

Solo looked at Bink and raised his eyebrows in silent question.

"It's fine with me," Bink said, eyeing Winter. The white-haired woman was right about the correlation between success and the number of knowledgeable eyes on the scene.

Besides, Bink didn't like working with enigmatic people. Keeping Winter here might give her an opportunity to get a better feel for her.

"Okay, then," Solo said. "Chewie, Lando—keep an eye out for trouble. Everyone else, we've got places to go. Let's get to them."

CHAPTER SIX

The sky had darkened to full night, though the streets and buildings of Iltarr City were as bright as ever.

Which, Winter thought as she stood well back from the window, could be a problem.

Not that Bink in full camo gear was particularly easy to see. In fact, even knowing where she was, Winter had a hard time keeping track of her position. Most of the time she was pressed close to one of the tall trees out there, the outfit she'd chosen blending almost perfectly with the spots and shadows of the city's lighting. It was only when she was swinging between the trees that she was really noticeable, and those moments passed quickly.

But the moments were still there. And there was something about the brightness of city lights combined with the instinctive fear of the night that made that combination particularly dangerous.

"Seems to be doing all right," Tavia murmured from her side.

Winter nodded. Outwardly Tavia was as cool as Bink had been as she slipped out the window and began her trek around the edges of the park. But beneath the calm exterior, Tavia was worried about her sister. Winter could see it in the other woman's anxious glances out the window, in the silent drumming of her fingers, and in her slight back-and-forth rocking even when she was trying to stand still.

The others could see it, too. Across the room, Chewie rumbled soothingly, and Lando looked up from his datapad. "She'll be fine," he assured Tavia. "She's done this a thousand times."

"I know," Tavia said tightly. "But usually I'm right there with her. Not *with* her, but—you know what I mean. Wired in and watching to make sure it goes all right." She shook her head. "I feel helpless just watching. Helpless and useless."

"You two been doing this long?" Winter asked.

"Since we were ten," Tavia said. "Not the ghost burglar stuff, not at first. But the whole life-on-the-fringe thing." She looked sideways at Winter. "We didn't have a choice," she added, a defensive edge in her voice. "Our father was killed in the Clone Wars, and Mom died a few years later. We had no other relatives and no friends. It was this or starve to death."

"Luckily, Bink proved to have some hidden talents in the field," Lando murmured.

Winter eyed Tavia, noting the tightness around her mouth. "And she also discovered she liked it?"

Tavia lowered her gaze. "Why shouldn't she?" she said. "Everyone likes doing the things they're good at." She smiled wanly at Winter. "I'm sure you do, too."

"I suppose," Winter said, looking back toward the window. There was a flicker of movement, and Bink had made it one more tree toward her goal.

Yes, Winter enjoyed her job. Or at least she had once. But there was enjoyment, and there was passion, and there was duty. Right now, all Winter had left was duty. Duty, and a simmering hatred she didn't want and couldn't afford to feel.

Alderaan. Her home, her friends, a lifetime of memories. All of it, all of them, gone.

A haze of red flowed across her vision, flickering with a thousand faces she couldn't forget and a million memories that would now forever be stained with fire and blood. Princess Leia and the other leaders of the Rebel Alliance had always been in awe of Winter's perfect memory, of her ability to memorize shipping manifests with a glance and reproduce details of the most complex schematics or transfer operations without effort. None of them had truly grasped the horrible downside of being unable to forget anything.

Long ago, Winter had occasionally tried explaining the reality of her gift to some of the people around her. Now she no longer even made the effort.

The one exception to that rule was Leia. The Princess had enough troubling memories of her own that she might actually understand and appreciate Winter's burden.

If she was still alive.

More images flicked across Winter's indelible memory, pictures and events of all the times she and Leia had worked or played or gotten into trouble with Leia's father, Bail, while they were growing up together.

Had Leia been on Alderaan when that insane monster Tarkin had destroyed it? That was the crucial, horrible question. Leia had been in the area around that time, but she might have been sent on some other mission before her world was destroyed. Winter desperately needed to know the truth, one way or the other, so that she could either get some relief or else add Leia's face to the collection of bloodstained images in her mind. For her, uncertainty was a killer, an enemy that sapped focus, strength, and determination.

Only Winter had no way of finding the truth. All she knew was that Alderaan was gone, that there were rumors the Death Star was gone, and that neither the Imperials nor the Alliance had quite figured out how they should react to the doubly unexpected situation.

But who had died and who had lived, Winter had no way of knowing. The people she worked with in Procurement had been deliberately isolated from the Alliance command structure and all direct lines of communication. Until some kind of official word came down from Imperial Center, or until she received the less official but usually more accurate information from Alliance HQ, all Winter could do was hope, worry, and pray.

And continue to do the job she'd been given. For now, that meant maintaining her cover as a smuggler's assistant and doing whatever Mazzic told her to do. Even if the task had nothing to do with bringing down the Empire she had learned to despise.

By the time Rachele reported that the three-landspeeder convoy had once again left Marblewood, Bink had reached the far corner of the park. By the time Han reported from outside the Lulina Crown that the convoy had arrived, she was two trees away from her target window.

She was resting more or less comfortably in her chosen tree, three meters back from the window, when the lights in the suite came on and the Falleen they'd seen earlier strode back into the room.

"Don't worry, she'll pull it off." Lando's voice came softly from behind her.

Winter looked around. He'd come up from the other end of the room and was standing between her and Tavia. Closer than he needed to be, far closer than Winter liked strangers getting.

But his eyes weren't on her. They were on the windows across the park. "I've seen her pull off crazier stunts than this," he continued. "Like I said before, she has talent." He pulled his gaze back long enough to flash Winter a charming, slightly roguish smile. "Both of them do," he amended, resting his hand on Tavia's shoulder.

"Yes," Winter said, turning her own gaze back to the window. It was annoying, though hardly surprising, that Han had been smart enough to insist on the group sticking to first names. There were no fewer than fifteen Landos in the criminal databases she'd memorized over the years, most of those files unfortunately without any decent holos in them. Briefly, she wondered if this Lando was one of those fifteen or someone who hadn't yet caught the Imperials' attention.

The Falleen across the way had taken off his coat, revealing an expensive-looking thigh-length tunic beneath it. Winter studied his neck, hoping there would be a clan or loyalty tattoo somewhere that might give some clue to his identity or affiliation. Some groups of Falleen went in for that sort of thing.

But there was nothing, at least nothing she could see from her distance. The Falleen dropped his coat on a low table beside the room door, then reached into a hip pouch and pulled out an odd-looking datapad, setting it beside the coat. Hunching his shoulders once, as if shaking away the residual weight of the coat, he stepped to the safe and disappeared around its side.

Winter frowned at the datapad. Something about it seemed familiar.

Abruptly she stiffened. "Electrobinoculars," she snapped, tearing her gaze from the datapad and looking wildly around. Where had the devices gotten to?

"Here," Tavia said, pressing a set into her hand.

Winter jammed them to her eyes, her fingers keying in the focus control. The image settled down; then an alien hand appeared from the side and snatched the datapad out of her field of view. Before she could refocus, the

Falleen had again disappeared around the side of the safe, taking the datapad with him.

"What is it?" Tavia asked tightly. "What's wrong?"

"That datapad," Winter said, lowering the electrobinoculars and looking over at the section of floor where Bink and Tavia had laid out their equipment. "I need a closer look to be sure. But if it's what I think it is, we've got trouble."

"But Bink can't bring it here," Tavia objected. "The power sensors—"

"I know," Winter cut her off, thrusting the electrobinoculars back at her and hurrying over to the equipment. "I'll have to go to her."

"How?" Lando asked. "Bink has the only unpowered harness."

"So I'll have to improvise." Winter picked up the powered grapple harness and gave it a quick assessment. If she removed the central framework, then unplugged the shoulder-mounted targeting rangefinder . . .

The Wookiee growled a question.

"It's more than just important," Winter said. "It's absolutely vital." She got a grip on the framework and glanced around for a knife—

And twitched back, startled, as the Wookiee stepped to her side and plucked the harness from her hands. Three seconds later, he'd pulled off the framework, the rangefinder, and a section of trim that she hadn't realized was powered. He thrust it at her, gestured for her to put it on, and unlooped the bandoleer from his shoulder.

"You sure you know what you're doing?" Lando asked. "That's a long way."

Chewie gave an impatient roar.

"Okay, okay," Lando said hastily, holding up his hands, palms outward. "Tavia, get the window open."

The light had gone out in the room across the way by the time they were ready. Chewie and Winter stood facing each other in the open window, Winter secured in her harness with the harness's outer anchor straps wrapped securely around the Wookiee's massive shoulders.

He looked down at her, murmured a last-chance question.

"I'm ready," she said, nodding. He nodded back.

And an instant later, he leapt out of the window into the night air.

Winter gasped despite herself, her hands clutching reflexively at the hair around Chewie's ribs. An elongated second later her grip was nearly jerked loose as his hands and feet slammed into the nearest tree. For another instant it felt like they were going to slide off and plummet to the park below. Then there was another jerk as the Wookiee somehow caught them. Winter started to take a deep, shuddering breath—

And with a shove and violent twist of his body, the Wookiee flung them away toward the next tree in line.

Winter had been wrong. She was not in any way ready for this.

But one of the side effects of a perfect memory was that she could quickly adjust to new experiences, especially repetitive ones. By the time they reached the end of their building and turned the corner she knew when to brace herself, when to grip her harness, and when to let herself go limp. She also knew exactly how many trees stood between them and Bink, which meant she was able to count down the number until the ordeal was over. Psychologically, knowing the end point helped immensely.

Even so, for most of the trip she kept her eyes tightly closed.

Bink saw them coming, of course. And it was quickly clear that she wasn't happy about it. "What are you doing?" she demanded in a loud whisper as Chewie settled onto the final tree.

"The datapad in there," Winter said, struggling to turn around in the strictures of the harness. Bink, she saw, had the outer window open and was in the process of cutting a small circular hole in the transparisteel barrier behind it. It was hard to tell from her angle, but it looked like she was most of the way through. "Did you see it?"

"Yeah, I saw it," Bink said. "So what?"

"I need a closer look," Winter said. "It's important."

Bink's lip twisted, but she nodded reluctantly. "It better be," she warned. "Okay. Give me two minutes after I'm inside, then you can come in. You can get her to the window, Chewie?"

The Wookiee growled an affirmative. "Fine," Bink said. "Just don't make any noise once you're in there. And *don't* break anything." Turning around again, she got back to work on the window.

Winter had done a fair amount of breaking and entering during her years with the Rebel Alliance. But most of those sorties had been into low-security areas like foodstuff or spare-parts warehouses, and most of the time she'd had someone more experienced along to help. Never had she tried to break into a place with this kind of security.

Lando had been right. Bink definitely had a talent.

Carving a hole in the transparisteel barrier was only the first step. After that came the use of some gummy substance to get the circle out of its place. A pair of long probes slipped through the opening tweaked aside a pair of trackers, while a jumper cable on the end of an even longer probe bypassed some kind of detector Winter didn't recognize.

Finally, when all the backup sensors and detectors had been stifled, confused, or distracted, one final probe tripped the release and swung the transparisteel plate out of the way. Getting a grip on the sill, Bink unhooked her harness from the adhesive anchors she'd fastened to the outside wall and climbed nimbly through the opening and into the room. She closed the window and transparisteel plate most of the way, flashed Winter a look, and slipped around the side of the big floor safe.

"How do we work this?" Winter murmured to Chewie.

In answer, he motioned toward the nearest branch. "I was afraid of that," Winter said, wincing as she got a firm grip on the branch. Chewie waited until she was ready, then slipped the harness straps one at a time off his shoulders. Moving carefully and, for her, unusually awkwardly, she moved around and climbed onto his back, reaching over his shoulders and catching hold of the clumps of hair over his collarbones.

She'd read once that those were the safest and least painful ways to hold on to a Wookiee. Fervently, she hoped the author of that particular article hadn't gotten it wrong.

Bink's two-minute countdown ran down. Chewie rumbled a warning, then threw himself away from the tree toward the window. His hands caught the lower edge, and his body slammed into the side of the building with a jolt that nearly broke Winter's grip.

Luckily, the Wookiee had already anticipated that danger. Even as she struggled to hold on, he bent his knees and brought his feet up beneath her, giving her something to brace her own feet against. Waiting until she had resettled her grip, he bent his elbows and pulled them both face-level with the lower edge of the window.

Winter had a grip on the window and was starting to open it when, across the room, the door opened and a big, rough-looking man strode in.

She froze, knowing how horribly exposed she was, but also knowing that any movement would instantly catch the man's eye. Chewie apparently knew that, too, and also froze. The man walked past the back of the safe to a pair of chairs flanking a small table, pulling out a datapad as he did so. He started to sit down, turning his back briefly to the window—

An instant later, Winter's view was cut off as Chewie took advantage of the man's turned back to drop them back down to a hanging position, where everything but his fingertips would be out of sight.

But she'd seen enough. The good news was that the man had clearly not been suspicious. The bad news was that he'd had the look of someone about to settle in for a while, either to read, do some work, or maybe just take a nap.

All of which would leave Bink trapped on the far side of the safe.

Winter craned her neck to look behind her. At this distance, and with the trees partially blocking her view, she couldn't tell whether or not Tavia and Lando had spotted the problem. She could only hope fervently that they had.

And that they could come up with something to do about it.

"Got it," Dozer acknowledged. Clicking off his comlink, he pulled open the stairwell door, exchanged nods with Zerba, and strode out onto the plush carpet and into the delicate scent pattern drifting through the Lulina Crown's sixth-floor hallway.

And as he walked, he smiled tightly to himself. Calrissian might have the looks and the smile and the easy charm, and maybe that was all Solo wanted for this job. Or at least all he *thought* he wanted.

But Calrissian was nothing more than a smuggler and

occasionally lucky gambler. Boosting ships was the job that took *real* con artist skills.

Time to show them how a professional did it.

The doors at the Lulina Crown Hotel had nice little bell buttons beside them for visitors to use, buttons that no doubt created nice little chirping or twittering sounds inside the suite. Dozer bypassed the button in favor of pounding on the door with the edge of his fist. "Hello?" he called. "Delivery."

Nothing. Dozer pounded again, hoping the lack of response didn't mean Bink had been caught and everyone in there was too busy to answer the door. "Hello?" he called again, putting some serious volume into it this time. "You want to get the door? I haven't got all night." He raised his fist again—

With a suddenness that caught him by surprise, the door was yanked open and he found himself staring into the muzzles of a pair of large, mean-looking blasters.

"Hey, hey, hey—take it easy," he said quickly, opening his hand to show it was empty. The men behind the blasters, he noted, were every bit as large and mean-looking as their weapons.

"What do you want?" one of them demanded.

"Quickline Courier Service," Dozer said, nodding toward the gold nameplate fastened to his jacket. "I've got a delivery for Mencho Tallboy." Carefully, he lifted the small security case in his left hand. "Is he here?"

The man's eyes narrowed, and with an effort Dozer kept his breathing steady. *Tallboy* was the name Rachele had pulled from the room service orders, but she'd had no way of knowing whether it was a real person or simply a convenient alias the Falleen and his troop used for such mundane matters. A supposed delivery to a nonexistent person would do nothing to ease anyone's suspicions, and that was the exact wrong direction Dozer wanted this conversation to go.

"Yeah, he's here," the man said, drawing his blaster back a few centimeters and reaching out his other hand. "I'll take it."

"Are you Master Tallboy?" Dozer asked, wincing back like a man who knows he's about to deliver unwelcome news to an armed man. "I'm really sorry, but the order was very specific. I need to deliver the package personally to Master Mencho Tallboy."

"Whose order?" the man asked, his hand still outstretched.

"The sender's," Dozer said, letting more nervousness and a little confusion creep into his voice. "I'm just a courier. I just do what I'm told."

For a couple of heartbeats the two men continued to stare. Then the one with his hand outstretched twitched his fingers. "Datapad," he ordered.

"Yes, sir," Dozer said, fumbling the security case to his right hand and pulling out his datapad with the other. The second man holstered his blaster and took the datapad, frowning intently as he began punching keys.

Out of the corner of his eye, Dozer saw a small black sphere appear through the half-open stairway door and roll down the corridor toward him at a far better clip than an object that size had any business doing on carpet this thick. It bounced off the far wall and angled back in his direction.

And a second later exploded in a brilliant blast of fire and a cloud of roiling black smoke.

Bink was nearly through the safe's combination when the door across the room opened.

Her first thought was the obvious and horrifying one: that the gig had just come to a crashing halt, and she was about to be in a fight for her life. Pressing herself against the safe, she slipped her right hand into her hip pouch and got a grip on the mono-edge cutting wheel. It wasn't much of a weapon, but it was the best she had.

To her relief, the opening door was accompanied by only one set of footsteps, and leisurely ones at that. Someone just wandering into the room for some other purpose than hammering an unwelcome ghost burglar?

A fresh jolt of tension washed over her as she suddenly realized that Winter should be climbing in the window just about now. But the footsteps showed no indication that the other woman had been spotted. The visitor strolled casually past the other side of the safe, and Bink heard the faint sound of cloth on leather as he sat down in one of the reading chairs.

Which now left her officially trapped.

She licked some moisture onto suddenly dry lips. Getting caught in the act was one of the ever-present dangers of this job, but so far she'd managed to mostly avoid such unpleasantries. With a Falleen and possibly Black Sun involved, a confrontation here was to be avoided at all costs.

She hoped Tavia had something extra-special up her sleeve.

Eighty seconds went by. Bink counted and examined every single one of them, her mind tumbling as she tried desperately to come up with an escape plan of her own in case Tavia didn't come through.

Then, across the room's silence, came the faint murmur of a distant voice, as if coming over a comlink clip. Bink couldn't make out any of the words, but suddenly there was a second cloth-on-leather creak as the visitor got abruptly to his feet. Bink squeezed the mono-edge wheel tightly, but the footsteps merely tracked briskly back across the room to the door. Another opening and closing . . .

Cautiously, she peeked around the edge of the safe. There was a motion at the edge of her vision, but it was only Chewie hoisting himself back into view and Winter pulling the cracked window the rest of the way open. Breathing a quiet sigh of temporary relief, acutely aware that whatever was going on elsewhere in the suite wouldn't hold the thug's attention forever, Bink ducked back to the front of the safe and returned to work.

She was nearly done when Winter appeared at her side. "Almost," Bink whispered, mildly surprised that the other woman had made it through the window and across the room without making any noise. Maybe Winter was more experienced in criminal activity than Bink had thought.

She keyed in the final number, and there was a soft click from the mechanism. Mentally crossing her fingers, hoping there wasn't some hidden alarm she hadn't spotted, she rotated the lever—

From somewhere in the distance came the faint sound of an explosion. She twisted her head toward the door—

"That must be our diversion," Winter whispered. "Hurry."

Clenching her teeth, Bink leaned back, throwing her full weight on the lever. The heavy door swung ponderously open.

Bink felt her eyes widen. The safe was empty.

No; not quite. On the middle shelf was an odd-looking datapad. "What the—"

She broke off as Winter reached past her and picked up the device. She took a step to the side, moving into the light, and briefly turned the datapad over in her hands. Then, stepping back again, she returned it to the safe. "Time to go," she whispered, and headed back toward the window.

"No kidding," Bink whispered sourly to herself. A datapad. She'd risked her life for a kriffing *datapad.*

Closing the safe, she resealed it and followed Winter back across the room.

A long minute later she was safely outside, the transparisteel plate back in position, the window closed, and the plugs she'd cut out of both of them back in place. For the moment the plugs would be visible, but three more minutes and the adhesive she'd used to glue them in would have everything melded back together, leaving not even a hint that either plate had ever been cut. The rock putty anchors she'd fastened to the side of the building for her harness were the last to go, their adhesive melting away with a few blasts from her solvent spray bottle.

And with that she was on her way back, following Chewie and Winter, firing her grapples and swinging to each tree as quickly as she could. She'd lived through yet another operation, and the sooner she was safely back inside their room, the happier she would be.

She could only hope that whichever of Solo's people had provided the explosive diversion back there would likewise make it back in one piece.

The bomb was a tiny one, a little squeaker charge that Kell had put together for the occasion, all smoke and sound and very little actual fury. It wasn't nearly powerful enough to knock Dozer over.

The man with the blaster, on the other hand, was. Dozer landed flat on his back on the thick carpet, the man's left palm pressed hard against his chest the whole way down, his blaster pressed equally hard against Dozer's left cheek. Somewhere along the way, the sound of the blast was echoed by the sound of the suite door being slammed shut.

Dozer had intended to yelp something terrified-sounding, something that would fit in with his innocent-bystander persona. But the impact with the floor left him barely enough air for a choking gasp. Out of the corner of his eye, beneath the tendrils of smoke and past the knees of the man now kneeling beside him, he saw two more armed men charging toward the stairway, their blasters drawn and ready.

Mentally Dozer shook his head. Brave men, and undoubtedly very tough. Also very stupid. They had no idea whether there was one man or twenty lurking in the stairway they were heading toward. If he'd been in charge, he'd have sent either a five-man squad or no one at all.

But it was a Falleen calling the shots in there, and Falleen weren't known for caring about any species other than their own.

Down the corridor, the stairway door thudded open as the two men charged in, prepared to kill or die at their master's command. Luckily for them, this time they had nothing to worry about either way. Between Kell's squeaker and Zerba's spring-loaded timed kick launcher, those stairs had been long since deserted.

"Don't worry, we're going to get your friend," the man leaning over Dozer said. "It'll go a lot easier for you if you talk now."

"I'm just a courier," Dozer managed, putting a good healthy shaking into his voice, as a truly terrified man would. "I'm just here to deliver a package."

"And get us to open the door so your friend could roll a bomb in at us?"

"I don't know anything about any bomb," Dozer protested, putting a little more trembling into his voice. It wasn't all that difficult, not with that blaster grinding into his cheek. "Look, I was standing right there with you. You think I *want* to get blown up?"

The man grunted. "Gorkskin? Talk to me."

"Looks legit," someone outside Dozer's field of view said reluctantly. "Got a businessmark here that checks out with the Iltarr City data lists. *And* there's a delivery order here for Mencho, tagged with time and place."

Dozer's guard grunted again. "Open it." He raised his eyebrows. "Any objections, courier?"

Dozer considered reminding him that the box could legally be opened only by the proper recipient. Under the circumstances, he decided that would be extremely out of character. Not to mention dangerously stupid. "No," he said.

"Good. Gorkskin?"

"It's locked," Gorkskin said.

"You sure?"

There was a quick double snap-and-flash of blaster shots, and Dozer winced as the heat washed over his face. "I guess not," Gorkskin said sarcastically. There was another crunch as he broke open the damaged security case. "Well, well. You're going to love this, Wivi. The box is filled with cash. Five or six hundred credits at least."

The blaster at Dozer's cheek dug in a little deeper. "Well, well," Wivi said, his voice deceptively casual. "I wonder who likes Mencho enough to send him credits."

"All coinage, too," Gorkskin said. "Not some nice, easily traceable credit tab."

"Of course not," Wivi said. "Let's try this again, courier. Who sent you?"

"I told you," Dozer said, throwing as much fear and confusion into his voice as he could, wondering uneasily if he'd bitten off more than he could swallow. They'd seen the whole fake backdrop Rachele had planted in the datapad and city records, and they still weren't buying it. If Solo had more evidence, he'd better get busy and trot it out. "I'm just a delivery man—"

"For Quickline Courier Service," a new voice put in calmly.

Dozer felt his stomach tighten. On the surface, the

voice was quiet, peaceful, and quite civilized. But that air of civilization was molecule-thin . . . and beneath it was something cold and dark and very, very evil.

"With all respect, Lord Aziel, you shouldn't be out here," Wivi said, his voice suddenly deferential. "Not until we've secured the area."

"There's no danger," the voice said. There was a hint of something different in the corridor's scent flow, Dozer noticed.

And then, to his surprise, he felt his heartbeat slowing and a new calmness flowing into him. Maybe the newcomer, this Lord Aziel, could do something about his predicament.

"The attacker, whatever his purpose or plan, is long gone," the voice continued. "And this man is as he claims: a mere courier."

"Sir, we haven't yet confirmed that," Gorkskin said.

"Then let us do so," the voice said. "Allow him to stand."

Wivi gave Dozer one final frustrated scowl. Then, reluctantly, he pulled the blaster away from Dozer's cheek and got to his feet. After another second's hesitation, he reached down and stretched out his hand. Dozer hesitated, too, just the fraction of a second that a still-terrified bystander should hesitate, then reached up to the proffered hand and allowed Wivi to haul him upright.

And as he started to straighten his jacket, Wivi half turned him around and he found himself face-to-face with the Falleen they'd seen earlier from across the park.

Only the alien wasn't nearly as threatening as he'd seemed back then. In fact, as Dozer gazed into his green-scaled face and dark blue eyes he couldn't even remember why Solo and the others had thought he was someone they had to worry about in the first place. This was a gentleman of the highest order, hardly someone who would engage in anything as vulgar as criminal activities.

"Are you indeed a courier?" Aziel asked.

Dozer swallowed, a flood of guilt and regret washing over him. The Falleen standing before him was honorable and caring. To even *think* about lying to such a person felt like a betrayal of all that was right and proper about the universe.

And yet a small, nagging part of his mind remembered that there *was* a reason that Dozer was here. Something about all this that was vital he keep secret from even this splendid Falleen. Vital to other people's lives as well as Dozer's own.

Maybe he could have it both ways. Dozer had certainly brought the security case in here at Solo's request. So . . . "Yes," he said. "I'm a courier."

"For Quickline Courier Service?"

Given that Quickline didn't really exist and Dozer was literally its only employee: "Yes."

"Did you have anything to do with that explosion?"

The squeaker had been Kell's handiwork, the delivery system had been Zerba's, and the plan had been Solo's. "No," Dozer said.

"Very well," Aziel said. He looked at the two glowering thugs—for that was all they were, Dozer realized now: low-living creatures who barely even qualified as sentient compared to the nobility of their master—and gave a small gesture. "Return his case, and allow him to go his way."

"And the credits?" Wivi asked.

"The delivery order says they're to go to Mencho Tallboy," Aziel reminded him. "So shall they be delivered." His eyes glittered. "And he can then explain the source and purpose. At any rate, the courier may go his way."

Dozer felt a rush of gratitude as Wivi silently handed him the damaged case. There were so few true gentles in the Empire these days. It was an honor to have met one of them.

It wasn't until he was in the turbolift heading back to street level that the feeling began to fade, and he slowly began to realize what had just happened to him.

And how with just a hair less care on his part he might have given the whole thing away.

He was still shaking when Han pulled their landspeeder back into the flow of late-night traffic.

CHAPTER SEVEN

"It's called a cryodex," Winter said when the group was once again assembled in their suite overlooking the Marblewood Estate. "It was an old Alderaanian encryption device, built into a specially modified datapad. Unlike normal encryption methods, which use software and overlays, the rotating single-spark patterns here were built directly into the machine."

"Sounds tricky," Lando commented.

"Not to mention inefficient," Tavia added. "If the encryption becomes obsolete, you'd have to scrap the whole device and build a new one."

"In theory, yes," Winter said. "But the system had two advantages. First, a message encrypted by one cryodex could be read on any other cryodex. That meant you could have one device at each end of your diplomatic channel without worrying about transmitting the encryption pattern back and forth or trusting a courier to deliver it."

"A thief could still intercept the message itself," Tavia pointed out.

"True," Winter agreed. "But it wouldn't do him any good . . . because the second advantage is that a cryodex-encrypted message can't be decrypted. By anyone. Ever."

"Really," Lando said, a hint of polite skepticism in his voice.

"Really," Winter said, with an edge Han hadn't heard from her before. "In over two hundred years of use, no cryodex encryption was ever broken."

Han nodded to himself as part of her aura of mystery came clear, and he suddenly understood the air of tension and sadness about her. "You know this from personal experience?" he asked.

Winter turned to face him, and for a moment they locked eyes. He watched as she fought a brief battle within herself and came to a reluctant decision. "Yes," she said quietly. The brief moment of edge was gone, leaving only the sadness. "I was connected with the royal palace on Alderaan."

There was a moment of silence as the others digested that. The official details surrounding the Death Star's single tour of duty were still sketchy, Han knew, but Alderaan's destruction was all over the HoloNet. "I'm so sorry," Rachele murmured at last.

"Thank you," Winter said, back on balance again. Briefly, Han wondered how she could put it out of her mind so quickly. He'd seen how deeply Princess Leia and the others at Yavin had been affected, and even though Han himself hadn't lost a bunch of friends or family, it had still been a severe gut punch to fly through a swarm of rocks that had once been a thriving world. Either Winter had terrific self-control or she was really good at suppressing memories. "I didn't tell you that to elicit sympathy," she continued. "I told you, as Han said, so that you'd understand that I know firsthand what I'm talking about."

"So where did this particular cryodex come from?" Zerba asked. "Any idea?"

Winter's lips compressed briefly. "There were a hundred thirty-seven cryodexes known to be in existence as of—" She broke off. "All but eight of them were on Alderaan," she continued. "Of those eight, seven were in upper-level diplomatic hands." She hesitated. "The eighth went missing four years ago, presumed stolen."

"Three guesses as to which of the eight this is," Kell murmured.

"You have any idea who stole it?" Bink asked.

"A possible thief was identified," Winter said. "But we never found out whether he did in fact steal it, and if he did, who he then delivered it to."

"I assume that the others were shut down when that one went missing?" Lando asked.

Winter nodded. "They were still occasionally used for minor purposes, but all top-level diplomatic encryption was immediately shifted to other methods."

"Wait a minute," Tavia said, frowning suddenly. "You said only *one* cryodex was stolen?"

"She's right," Zerba said, sitting up a little straighter. "You just said you need two to send a message. What use could anyone have for just one?"

"Maybe he already had access to one of the diplomatic instruments," Bink suggested doubtfully. "No, that doesn't work. If he already had one, why bother stealing another? He could just decrypt whatever diplomatic dirt he wanted to read and send the message to whoever else wanted it."

"I don't know the motivation behind its disappearance," Winter said. "The reason we never learned what happened was that the presumed thief died shortly after being arrested."

Kell shivered. "Lovely."

"What did you expect?" Dozer muttered. His voice was dark, his brooding eyes locked on the tall glass of ale he'd poured himself the minute they'd arrived back at the suite. As near as Han could remember, those were the first words the man had spoken since they'd all driven away from the Lulina Crown Hotel.

"What do you mean?" Tavia asked.

"I mean of *course* he died in custody," Dozer growled, glaring at her. "I'm surprised he didn't die on the way *to* custody. These people are evil, Tavia—pure, unstrained evil. They'll kill anyone who gets in their way." He dropped his gaze back to his drink. "Including us."

"Whoa," Bink said, peering closely at him. "Is that Dozer the formerly nerveless ship booster I'm hearing?"

Dozer shook his head. "You weren't there, Bink," he said. "You didn't face him. Didn't hear him. Do you know that I came within a sabacc wheel of giving the whole thing away? And for no reason other than that he asked nicely."

"You *didn't* give us away, did you?" Zerba asked anxiously.

"You think we'd all be sitting here if I had?" Dozer bit out. "But I came close. Way too close. And I'll tell you something else." His gaze flicked around the room, settling at last on Eanjer. "I'm not sure this is worth it anymore. If they figure out who we are and what we're up to, we're dead. We're just dead."

"They're not Jedi, Dozer," Eanjer said soothingly. "You ran into Falleen pheromones, that's all. They use them to manipulate you into—" He waved his good hand. "I don't know. Their best friend, their slave—whatever. The point is that you didn't break, and now that you know what you're facing you can fight it."

"What if I can't?" Dozer shot back. "Or what if one of the rest of you gets picked up and *you* can't?"

"We're still talking a hundred sixty-three million credits," Bink reminded him. "For that kind of score, I, for one, am perfectly capable of resisting a whole roomful of Falleen."

"Are you sure about that?" Dozer countered. "Because I'm not."

Chewbacca rumbled.

"Yeah, let's not jump off any roofs here," Han agreed. "Dozer's right—having a Falleen involved could mean trouble. But Bink's also right—there're a lot of credits on the line. Enough for all of us to make brand-new lives for ourselves if we want."

"It's like when that perfect hand comes along," Lando murmured. "You have to see it, recognize it, and bet big."

Han frowned, wondering if that was some sort of dig at him. But Lando was merely gazing thoughtfully down at the center table.

Anyway, Lando was the least of his worries right now. All of Dozer's ranting about his newly minted nervousness was starting to seep into the rest of the group. If the man didn't shut up, he might unravel the whole thing.

And if the group fell apart, so did the job. They would all scatter back to their own lives, and any chance for Han and Chewbacca to get free of Jabba would be gone.

He wasn't going to let that happen. Not just because a Falleen was involved. Absolutely not because Dozer had taken delivery of a case of cold feet.

"Let's take a few minutes," he suggested. "Go wander around the suite, stare out at the city, get a drink, do whatever you want. Think about it, and we'll meet back here in an hour. Okay?"

"Sounds good to me," Lando said, standing up.

"And if anyone has a contact in law enforcement, you might try calling them," Rachele suggested as the rest of the group rose from their chairs and couches. "Now that we know we're dealing with a Falleen, there may be some official information out there as to who and what we're up against."

"Good idea," Han agreed. "You'll be calling some people, too?"

She gave him a tight smile. "I already have a list."

Dayja's plan, once he reached the balcony, had been to attach a probe link to the window, listen to whatever the people inside were saying, and try to figure out who and what they were.

He wasn't expecting to arrive at his destination just as the party was breaking up.

But breaking up it was. The whole group—nine humans, one Wookiee, and one near-human, probably a Balosar—were on their feet, wandering off in different directions across the conversation room, apparently heading for different corners of the suite.

Dayja muttered a curse as he backed to the side of the balcony, out of view from the windows. The car he'd spotted had been watching Marblewood, all right, and had followed an unidentified convoy from there to the Lulina Crown Hotel. The tracker had then returned here, after which he and most, if not all, of his gang had left and reassembled in the hotel across the park from the Lulina Crown. Some had then left, others had gone around to the front of the hotel, and finally the whole group had returned here to the suite, which Dayja had tentatively identified as their main headquarters.

That was a lot of running around for one day, especially given that it hadn't produced any results that Dayja had spotted. And if it hadn't been for that late evening explosion at the Lulina Crown, Dayja might have decided he had better things to do and left the group and their activities for the local police to deal with.

But the explosion had taken that decision off the table. Bombings were typically associated with theft, kidnapping, murder, or serious property damage. But this blast hadn't been connected with anything on that list. That fact pushed the odds inexorably toward the conclusion that the incident had been a diversion.

But a diversion for what? D'Ashewl was currently sitting in their hotel suite sifting through the police data, but so far he hadn't spotted any crime that the blast might have been intended to confuse, distract from, or cover up.

Still, Dayja had no doubt that these people were involved. So he'd tracked down their suite, found a currently empty room three floors above them, and rappelled down to their balcony.

Only to find his would-be unsuspecting informants closing down for the night.

He was still trying to decide what to do next when he noticed one of the suite's occupants, the one with the medsealed hand and half-medsealed face, heading toward the balcony door.

Dayja dropped his hand to his hidden knife, his mind racing. He could run, he could hide, or he could attack.

Or he could do what he'd come here to do.

He waited until the other man had come all the way out onto the balcony and settled down with his elbows on the railing, gazing at the lights of Marblewood across the way. Then, keeping an eye on the window beside him to make sure they weren't interrupted, Dayja took a couple of steps toward the newcomer. "Good evening," he said quietly.

For a fraction of a second the man didn't react, as if his ears were having trouble sending a warning to his brain. Then, like a sudden gust of wind, a shiver ran through the man's body. He twisted half around toward Dayja, his single good eye going wide. Either the man had the slowest reactions in the galaxy, or else he had so much pain medication in him that he was living in a permanent fog. Given the sheer area of medseal involved, Dayja guessed it was probably the latter.

"Who are you?" the man demanded, his voice tight. "No—stay there."

"Relax—I'm not going to hurt you," Dayja soothed, taking another couple of steps forward. "I just want to talk."

The man's single eye flicked a glance toward the glass, the prosthetic eye implanted in the medseal glittering hypnotically in the haze of city lights. "About what?"

"You." Dayja gestured toward the empty conversation room. "Them. Your interest in Avrak Villachor. That sort of thing." He raised his eyebrows. "You *are* interested in Villachor, aren't you?"

The man's tongue flicked briefly across his upper lip. "Are you one of his men?"

"Hardly," Dayja assured him dryly. "My name is Dayja. What's yours?"

The man's eye flicked to the window again. "Eanjer."

"A local name, I see," Dayja commented. "Interesting. How about your friends? Most of them are from out of town, aren't they?"

Eanjer frowned, his eye darting around the balcony as if he'd suddenly remembered where they were standing. "Where did you come from?" he asked. "How did you get up here?"

"Oh, let's not talk about me," Dayja chided. "Let's talk about you and your friends. What are you all doing in Iltarr City?"

Eanjer's face hardened. "Looking for justice."

"That's good," Dayja said encouragingly. "That's very good. You see, I'm also a seeker of justice." He focused on the pupil of Eanjer's remaining eye, knowing that the first and most honest response would come there. "I'm with Imperial Intelligence."

Again Eanjer's eye widened. This time, Dayja was close enough to see the pupil widen along with it.

Widen, but then quickly return to its former size. The revelation had startled the man, but he'd recovered quickly. "Can you prove it?" he asked.

"Yes," Dayja said, throwing a look of his own through the glass. Sooner or later, one of the others was bound to wander back in. It wouldn't do for him and Eanjer to be standing here chatting when that happened. "Tell me, are you confined to this suite? Or can you come and go as you like?"

Eanjer snorted under his breath. "The latter, of course," he said. "Did you think I was a prisoner?"

Dayja shrugged noncommittally. "Do you play pool?"

Once again Eanjer's single pupil widened briefly before returning to normal. "Yes. Why?"

"There's a table in the library downstairs: second floor, just off the tapcaf," Dayja told him. "It'll be a nice, private place to talk."

"I'm sure it will," Eanjer said, a hint of nervousness in his voice.

"Don't worry, I just want to talk," Dayja assured him. "Maybe compare notes a little. I have the feeling you have information I could use." He smiled slyly. "I *know* I have information *you* can use."

Eanjer took a deep breath and straightened to a decision. "All right," he said. "I've got an hour before we're supposed to reconvene."

"Good," Dayja said, backing toward the end of the balcony and the ghost burglar harness waiting for him there. "I'll meet you in five minutes. If you get there before I do, rack up the balls and choose yourself a cue."

Over the years, Dayja had spent a fair amount of time in pool and five-pocket rooms like the one off the hotel tapcaf. But given the fact that most of those visits had been to gain information or do surveillance on a suspect instead of actually trying to master the game, he'd never gotten especially good at it.

Still, against a man with a medsealed and possibly alien prosthetic arm, he figured he had a pretty fair chance.

To his mild surprise, he didn't. Not even with Eanjer playing left-handed and having to balance the end of the cue awkwardly across his bandaged wrist.

But that was okay. In fact, it was more than okay. Dayja had long since learned that competitive sportsmen talked more freely when they were winning.

And Eanjer's talk was well worth listening to.

"A hundred sixty-three million, eh?" Dayja commented as he watched Eanjer set up for another shot. "That's an awful lot of credits. And you said it was going to be split eleven ways?"

"I said it was going to be split evenly," Eanjer corrected. He tapped the cue gently against the chaser, and Dayja watched as the white ball bounced into the stripe-three and sent it dropping neatly into the corner pocket. "I never said there were eleven of us."

"My mistake," Dayja said. "Still, it seems to me that you should get more than just a single share, given that they were your credit tabs to begin with."

Eanjer shrugged. "A hundred percent of nothing is nothing," he said as he walked around the end of the table. He lined up the cue against the chaser, aiming for the stripe-six this time. He drew the cue back to shoot, but before he could do so there was a flicker and the stripe-six abruptly went black. Simultaneously, at the other end of the table, the blackball flickered and became the stripe-six.

Eanjer swore beneath his breath. "Too bad," Dayja commiserated. "But it could have been worse. I've seen the blackball turn just as the shooter was about to hit the chaser, with no way he could stop in time. At that point, all the shooter can do is curse as he follows through and watches his own shot lose him the game."

"And then listen to the cackling of his opponent, I suppose," Eanjer said, giving Dayja a baleful look as he repositioned his shot. "Let's slice to the end, shall we? Are you looking to make the deal a twelve-way split?"

"Not at all," Dayja assured him. "I'm not interested in Villachor and his ill-gotten credits. All I'm interested in is his visitor . . . and his visitor's own little treasure."

"And what exactly might this mysterious treasure be?"

Dayja pursed his lips. This would be risky, but not as risky as taking on Villachor and Qazadi all by himself. "I'll make you a deal," he offered. "I'll tell you all about the prize, and lend you any quiet support I can, provided you bring it to me once you've raided Villachor's vault. In return, you'll promise not to tell the others where you got the information, and you'll keep me informed of your progress."

Eanjer eyed him closely. "And you'll let us stay with our plan? You, a law officer, are going to just let us walk in there and rob him?"

"Yes, because I was planning on doing the exact same thing," Dayja said. "This way, we can pool our resources and information and hopefully help each other."

"With my group taking all the risks."

"*And* getting most of the rewards," Dayja pointed out. "Besides, after that stunt you pulled at the Lulina Crown this evening, I could run you all in right now if I wanted. As you said, a hundred percent of nothing is nothing."

For a moment they gazed at each other in silence. "All right," Eanjer said at last. "Let's hear it."

"Certainly," Dayja said, laying his cue on the edge of the table and gesturing toward a row of seats off to the side. "Let's sit down, and I'll tell you about a criminal organization known as Black Sun.

"And about their secret and highly lucrative collection of blackmail files."

CHAPTER EIGHT

Han stared, feeling his stomach tighten into a hard knot. "You're joking," he said flatly.

"Does it *look* like I'm joking?" Eanjer countered. "I know it sounds incredible, and I admit right now that I don't really know if it's true. But my informant definitely believes it, and he's never been wrong yet."

"And your informant's name is . . . ?" Tavia prompted.

"Sorry," Eanjer said. "For the moment I have to keep that confidential."

"And he's really sure Villachor's working with Black Sun?" Dozer asked, his voice dark.

"He is," Eanjer said. "Though again, I can't prove that."

"You don't have to," Rachele said quietly. "It's true."

Han turned to her, aware that everyone else in the room was doing the same. "You *knew*?" he demanded. "And didn't tell us?"

"I didn't *know*," she said, a little defensively. "But like everyone else in the Wukkar upper strata, I've suspected the connection for several years. When you came to me with Eanjer's problem—" She hunched her shoulders. "I hoped we were all wrong, I guess. That Villachor was just an ordinary, local criminal slime."

"Actually, this makes a lot of sense," Lando said thoughtfully. "Not who Villachor is, but that the core of

Black Sun's political power comes from blackmailing high-level officials. Much easier and cheaper than having to buy them off."

"And keeping those files in a set of portable data cards is just perfect," Bink agreed. "Even if one of Xizor's enemies managed to get through all the scared officials running interference for him and tried to grab them, he wouldn't even know where to start looking."

"Any idea how many cards there are in the set?" Han asked.

"My contact says there are supposed to be five, tucked away in some kind of fancy hand-enameled wooden box that no one outside Black Sun has ever seen," Eanjer said. "The whole thing should be small enough to fit in a satchel or even a hip pouch. Like Bink says, easily portable."

"It explains the cryodex, too," Winter said. "Perfect, unreadable encryption, and the only time you need to bring the two together is when you want to show someone the specific dirt you have on them."

"So why keep the cryodex in a downtown hotel instead of in Villachor's vault with the files themselves?" Zerba asked. "Bink just proved how much less secure it is there."

"Like I said: keeping them apart means no one knows where to go looking," Bink said. "You always want to keep the key and the lock away from each other if you can."

"And in this case, no one even knows what they're looking for," Eanjer added. "I'm pretty sure even my informant doesn't have the slightest idea there's a cryodex involved."

"There may be another reason for keeping the cryodex there," Han said, a new and interesting idea starting to form in the back of his mind. If the cryodex was being kept away from Villachor's place because the Falleen didn't trust him, an entirely different angle might be opening up in front of them. "Winter, could you make us a cryodex of our own? Not one that works, just something that looks right?"

"Certainly," Winter said, eyeing him thoughtfully. "It would be a relatively simple modification of an old Comp600 datapad, assuming we can find one."

"Bound to be a few around town somewhere," Rachele said. "I'll hunt one down for you."

"Wait a second," Tavia spoke up warningly. "If you're thinking what I *think* you're thinking, the answer is no. Bink's not going back in there. Not after Kell and Zerba's little bouncy-ball game out in the hallway."

"Too bad she didn't grab it when she could," Kell murmured.

"She couldn't," Tavia said. "The power sensors, remember?"

"She could have pulled out the power cell."

"We didn't know, it's too late now, and we're not going to talk about it," Han said firmly.

"And it wouldn't have mattered if she had," Lando said. "Half an hour after the cryodex disappeared, the files would have been off Wukkar and heading back to Imperial Center."

"At least they wouldn't have been able to use the files against anyone else," Kell pointed out.

"Of course they would," Lando scoffed. "You think Xizor's dumb enough to keep all his barks in one kennel? He's bound to have a backup cryodex squirreled away somewhere."

"There was only one reported stolen," Winter reminded him.

Lando shrugged. "So?"

"Which is why we're going to concentrate on the files and not the cryodex," Han said. "Tavia, how fast could you put together a full-spec spit-mitter, and how small could you make it?"

Tavia shrugged. "Couple of days. How small do you need it?"

"The size of a data card," Han said.

"That's pretty small," Tavia said, frowning off into space. "But I think I can make it work. Of course, for something that size the receiver will have to be pretty close. A hundred meters, maybe less."

"Shouldn't be a problem," Han assured her. "Now—"

"What's a full-spec spit-mitter?" Eanjer asked.

"Full-spectrum sensor cluster with integrated recorder and burst transmitter," Bink told him. "You slip one inside the place you want to burgle, and it spits you out the relevant details about security, guard stations, and everything else. If you pick your frequency right, the signal will slip right through the target's sensor-block fields."

"And by sending it in a short burst you don't have to worry about a transmission net catching it," Tavia added, her eyes steady on Han. "Of course, it *does* have to be inside the vault to do any good. You got some idea how to pull that off?"

"I'm working on it," Han assured her. "Okay. First job is to find out what these data cards look like. Rachele, you said you knew some of the people who've been going in and out of Marblewood over the past few days. Anyone there you might be able to get talking?"

"I don't think so," Rachele said, wrinkling her nose. "Most of them I only know by sight."

"I may know one of them," Eanjer offered. "What were some of the names?"

"Well, there was Tark Kisima," Rachele said, her eyes defocusing slightly as she thought back. "He was one of the first. I also saw Alu Cymmuj, Donnal Cuciv—"

"Donnal Cuciv—I know him," Eanjer interrupted.

"Who is he?" Dozer asked.

"The man in overall charge of incoming passenger and shipping lists at the Iltarr City Spaceport," Rachele said. "Supposed to be a pretty upright citizen. I wonder what Villachor has on him."

"Doesn't matter," Eanjer said. "I know him, and I'm sure I can get him to talk to me."

"Can you get him to talk about the data cards without tipping him off?" Han asked.

"*Especially* without him going straight to Villachor about it?" Lando added.

"Leave it to me," Eanjer said, standing up.

"Sure," Han said, frowning. It couldn't possibly be this easy. Could it? "Chewie, Dozer—you go with him."

"No," Eanjer said, shaking his head. "Sorry, but I need to do this alone. Donnal's a very private person. He's not going to say a single word if there's anyone there except me."

"You should at least have someone along for the ride," Rachele said. "You're probably still on Villachor's hunt list."

"Don't worry, I know how to stay out of Villachor's way," Eanjer said, his voice edged with bitterness. "I'll be fine."

Han looked at Chewbacca, but the Wookiee just rumbled a reluctant agreement. "Just make sure you keep your comlink on," Han said. "And call if you even *think* there might be a problem. You said this informant of yours doesn't know about the cryodex?"

"Correct," Eanjer said. "Actually, I don't think he's got the slightest idea how the system works. All he knows is that the files are probably here, and if they are, then Qazadi's got them."

"Good," Han said. "Let's keep it that way."

"Right." Eanjer turned and headed toward the door.

"Just a minute," Dozer said suddenly. "Before he goes, I want to get something straight."

"Sure," Han said, motioning for Eanjer to stop. "What?"

Dozer's lips compressed. "I want to make sure we're all still in this together," he said. "I mean, we're talking *Black Sun*. That's not what any of us signed up for."

"Fair enough," Han agreed, looking around the room. And here was where it all either held together or fell apart. "Anyone want to say something?"

There was a brief silence. "There's still a hundred sixty-three million in the vault, right?" Bink asked at last.

"Of course," Eanjer said.

"Then we're still in," Bink said. She nudged her sister. "Right?"

Tavia didn't look very happy, but she gave a dutiful nod. "Right."

"Plus whatever the blackmail files are worth," Winter spoke up. "Depending on who we can attract as a buyer, that could easily triple our final take."

"That's good enough for me," Zerba said.

"Me too," Kell seconded.

Han looked at Lando, who nodded silently. "That just leaves you, Dozer," he said. "If you're having trouble with this, now's the time to say so."

Dozer's gaze flicked around the room. Then, lowering his eyes, he hissed a breath out between his teeth. "No," he said reluctantly. "If everyone else is on board, I guess I am, too."

"You don't have to be," Han said. "You want to bail, no one's stopping you."

"No," Dozer said, more firmly this time. "Besides, I need the credits."

"So we're settled?" Eanjer said impatiently. "Wonderful. Can I go now?"

Han waved permission. Eanjer turned back to the door, and a moment later was gone.

"We'd better get to work on that spit-mitter," Bink said, standing up and motioning Tavia to follow. "Chewie, you want to give us a hand?"

The Wookiee warbled assent, and the three of them headed to the twins' room for Tavia's gear. As if their departure had been the signal for the party to break up, Winter, Kell, Rachele, and Zerba also rose from their seats, said a mutual round of good-nights, and headed toward their own rooms. Dozer followed behind them, not speaking to anyone as he made his brooding exit.

Leaving Han and Lando alone.

"He didn't sound convinced," Lando commented.

"He'll be okay," Han said, peering off in the direction Dozer had gone. But Lando was right. Dozer was running shaky—shakier than Han had ever seen him. "That thing with the Falleen has him a little rattled, that's all."

"You know him pretty well?"

"Well enough," Han said, looking back at Lando. "I thought you knew him, too."

Lando shrugged, gently swirling the remains of his drink. "We've crossed paths a couple of times, but that's about it. Zerba I only worked with once, on that Tchine thing. Winter and Kell I don't know at all."

"Mazzic recommends them."

"Mazzic's been wrong before."

"They're okay," Han insisted. "You don't have to stay if you don't want to."

"I like it here." Lando smiled faintly. "Besides, you need me."

Han thought about denying it. But unfortunately, it was the truth. "So what have you been up to lately?"

"Not much," Lando said, waving a hand vaguely. "Winning some, losing some. You?"

Han shrugged. *I picked up some crazy passengers, res-*

cued a princess, fought stormtroopers and TIE fighters, helped save the galaxy, and got my reward snatched right off my ship by pirates. "Not much," he said aloud. "Why are you here?"

"Rachele said you invited me."

"Yeah. Why are you here?"

Lando pursed his lips. "To be honest, I've been thinking about . . . you know. All the stuff that went down between us. I've been thinking that maybe it wasn't as much your fault as I thought at the time. That it wasn't so much you deliberately stiffing us, but more like you just being rotten at picking the people you could trust."

Han grimaced. "Yeah. I have that problem sometimes," he admitted.

"I've noticed." Lando nodded toward the door. "How well do you know this Eanjer character?"

"Met him for the first time eight days ago. But Rachele looked into his story. Seems solid enough."

"Did he ever mention that Villachor was Black Sun?" Lando asked pointedly. "Or did that part somehow get forgotten?"

"He didn't say anything about it," Han said. "But you heard Rachele. Even the top locals didn't know. He probably didn't, either."

"Maybe," Lando said. "But we know now. You still want to do this?"

"It'd be nice to have Jabba off my back for a change," Han said. "Credits are the only thing that'll do that."

"So you're going to trade angry Hutts for angry Falleen." Lando shook his head. "Not sure how good a deal that is."

"You play the hand you've got the best you can," Han said, frowning. "You trying to get me to bail on the job?"

"I'm trying to make sure you're not in over your head," Lando said. "You're a smuggler, Han. I'm a gambler. We're not con artists or thieves." He jerked his thumb toward the other end of the suite. "As far as I know, none of *them* has ever done anything on this scale, either."

He was right, Han knew. This whole thing was rapidly climbing to heights he'd never dreamed of when he'd gotten it rolling. The fact that he was having to trust this many other people to know what they were doing just made it worse.

Still, it wasn't the first time he'd had to trust people. Usually it worked out all right.

Usually.

"Maybe not," he conceded. "But together we've got all the skills we need to pull it off. All we need is the right plan, and a little confidence."

"Both of which you're going to supply?"

"With help from Chewie and Rachele and Bink," Han said. "And you, if you want to put in your half credit's worth."

"Of course," Lando said with one of those innocent looks he did so well. "We're old friends here to do a job together, right?" He lifted a finger. "One other thing, before I forget. Assuming everything goes according to plan, I want the blackmail files as my share."

Han stared. "You want *what*?"

"You heard me," Lando said. "I know a guy who'll pay good money for them."

"We won't have a cryodex to toss in with the deal," Han warned.

"He won't care," Lando assured him. "But the guy's a little touchy. It'd be better for me to approach him alone than for us to do it as a group."

"Uh-huh," Han said, nodding as the pieces fell together. "So which Hutt is it?"

Lando made a face. "Durga, if you must know," he

said reluctantly. "He's still pretty steamed at Xizor and Black Sun over the whole Ylesia thing."

"That happened a lot at Ylesia."

"So I've heard," Lando said with only a hint of sarcasm. "Deal?"

Han thought it over. Even given Durga's humiliation at Ylesia, he seriously doubted the Hutt would pay more than a few thousand credits for a set of unreadable data cards.

But it was entirely possible that Lando knew more about Durga's current situation and mood than he did. If he thought his chances were worth giving up his share of Eanjer's millions, he was welcome to give it a shot. Han certainly had no interest in adding another Hutt to his own list of potentially unsatisfied customers. "Sure, why not?" he said. "Cards instead of credits."

"Thanks," Lando said. He took a last swallow from his mug and leaned back. "So. Tell me about this plan."

It had been a long day, and as was his custom, Villachor had gone outside onto the balcony of his private suite for a few minutes of quiet and relaxation.

It was a cool, calm night, with no clouds and only a fitful breeze. The lights of Iltarr City glittered around him—around *and* above, since most of the buildings at the edges of his estate were much taller than his own modest four-story mansion. On most nights he reveled in the view, imagining himself to be on the dais in some Old Republic fortress, giving orders to an army of retainers standing around him in their humble silence.

Tonight, though, the dark light-flecked towers seemed to brood down on him. And instead of a lordly master, he felt like a target in the center of the practice range.

Something was going on out there. Something was lurking in the city streets, perhaps gazing at one of his gates at this very moment. Something that could potentially bring down everything he'd bribed and blackmailed and murdered to create on this world and in this sector.

And he had no idea what it was.

The indicator panel on his railing blinked a request: Sheqoa, his head of security, was at the door to his suite, requesting admittance. Flipping up the top of his armrest, Villachor keyed him in, making his usual private bet with himself that *this* time he would hear the man's entry onto the balcony behind him.

Once again he lost the bet. Former Imperial shock troopers, after all, weren't known for making unnecessary noise.

"I have a report from Riston, sir," Sheqoa said, his voice coming from barely two meters away. He'd reached the balcony, and then some. "He says Crovendif's glitterstim is the genuine article, and he's pretty sure it didn't come from Kessel."

"*Pretty* sure?" Villachor countered. "What is this *pretty sure* Sith-spit?"

"I'm sorry, sir," Sheqoa said, his voice respectful but firm. "But Riston says there's no way to be a hundred percent sure, not with something grown organically. Too much variation in the spiders themselves. All he can get is an eighty-five-percent certainty."

Villachor scowled, his first impulse to get up, march down to Riston's precious little lab, and shake the analyst's thin neck until he came up with something more useful.

But that wouldn't gain him anything more than momentary satisfaction. Sheqoa's primary job was Villachor's protection, but over the years the big ex-commando had also taken on the unofficial task of acting as buffer between his boss and the rest of the staff.

Which was probably a good thing. When there was

something to be gained by threats or violence, Sheqoa was right there at Villachor's side, handing him weapons or doing the job himself. But when there wasn't, he would likewise be there to keep his boss from wasting people. Especially competent people.

If Riston said there was nothing more to be gleaned from Crovendif's sample, he was probably right.

With an effort, Villachor forced away his reflexive thoughts of murder. "What about Crovendif himself?" he asked instead.

"He's worked for us for ten years, eight as a seller, two as a street manager," Sheqoa said. "Decent record. Nothing spectacular."

"Smart enough to pull a scam like this by himself?"

He could feel Sheqoa's frown. "He's barely bright enough to pull his correct percentage," the big man said. "You think this is a scam?"

"I think the timing is highly suspicious," Villachor growled. "Vigo Qazadi shows up; and then, barely nine days later, someone pops up and offers to sell us glitterstim below Black Sun's rates?"

Sheqoa was silent a moment, apparently trying to digest that. "Got to be the galaxy's unluckiest scammer," he said slowly. "Odds of that happening are . . . really low."

Villachor glared out at the city lights around him, once again forcing down the urge to strangle. He hadn't expected Sheqoa to understand the subtleties of the situation, and the security chief had lived right down to his expectations.

This wasn't coincidence. Not a chance. Either someone was tweaking Qazadi and Black Sun, which was an extraordinarily foolish thing to do . . . or else the mysterious stranger was one of Qazadi's people, and the glitterstim offer was a test.

A shiver ran up Villachor's back. A test. But a test of

what? Villachor's loyalty? Fine—Villachor could pass any such test.

But which direction was he expected to jump? Was he supposed to tell Qazadi about the glitterstim peddler and wait for the vigo to tell him what to do? That might show weakness and indecision on Villachor's part, hardly qualities Prince Xizor wanted in one of his sector chiefs. Should he instead look into the matter privately, bringing it to Qazadi's attention only after the investigation was complete? But if Qazadi caught him midway through the process, it could look as if he were planning to make a deal behind Black Sun's back. That would be the path to a quick, anonymous grave.

What if there *was* no right answer? What if Xizor had already passed judgment on him and this glitterstim test was nothing more than a way of letting Villachor choose the path of his own entrapment? Xizor hardly needed an excuse to eliminate one of his subordinates, but he might do it like this purely for the entertainment of watching the doomed man squirm in a net from which there was no escape.

Such thoughts should never be simply dismissed, Qazadi had said about Villachor's qualms at their first meeting, *for I do not leave Imperial Center without great cause.*

Villachor scowled. Qazadi had explained that the reasons for his visit were threefold: to remove the blackmail files from Imperial Center, thereby throwing off Vader and Xizor's other enemies; to get Qazadi himself out of range of various intrigues those same enemies were preparing to launch; and to use the files to generate a few more reluctant slaves from among Iltarr City's elite and the dignitaries who would soon be arriving on Wukkar for the Festival of Four Honorings.

Three reasons to make the trip from Imperial Center.

If there were three, why not four? Could the fourth reason be to engineer Villachor's destruction?

And then there was the incident at the Lulina Crown Hotel, where Qazadi's assistant Aziel had been at the center of some strange semi-attack. "Is there anything new on the Lulina Crown incident?" he asked.

"No, sir," Sheqoa said, his tone oddly reluctant. "Not really."

"Not *really*?" Villachor echoed sharply. "What does *not really* mean?"

"The police have closed the file," Sheqoa said, sounding pained. "They've written it off as a prank."

Villachor shifted halfway around in his chair and glared up at the other. "A *prank*?" he demanded. "A bomb goes off in a hotel hallway and it's a *prank*?" He turned back around, glaring at the city lights as he pulled out his comlink. Apparently it was time to remind Police Commissioner Hildebron of the level of service that Black Sun's bribe credits had bought from him.

"It was Commissioner Hildebron's order," Sheqoa said doggedly. "After he received a call from Master Qazadi."

Villachor froze, the comlink halfway to his lips. "Master *Qazadi* called off the investigation?"

"So it appears."

Slowly, Villachor returned the comlink to his belt. But that was insane. Why in the galaxy would Qazadi call off the investigators? Aziel was a fellow Black Sun official, a close colleague, and—as far as Villachor had been able to tell—as close to a friend as Falleen ever got. By all logic, Qazadi should be down at police HQ right now, pumping Hildebron's office full of pheromones and insisting that the threat against his colleague and the cryodex key codes be neutralized—

Villachor's throat tightened. Of course. The cryodex codes.

Because being a Black Sun boughtman didn't mean Hildebron wasn't good at his job. He was. And a truly proper investigation might easily expose the fact that Aziel was in Iltarr City as guardian of half of the key codes that activated the cryodex Qazadi had locked up in his suite.

Of course, an *im*proper investigation might lead to the theft of those same codes if whoever was trying to steal them decided to give it another try. But apparently Qazadi was willing to risk that.

Maybe he was right to do so. Aziel had to come to Marblewood to assist Qazadi in activating the cryodex before each of Villachor's blackmail sessions, but the cryodex and the files themselves were never at any risk. If Aziel's codes were stolen or destroyed, it would simply mean Villachor couldn't use the files against potential targets. An inconvenience, but hardly a serious problem.

But whether the attack had failed or been a prank, the fact of the matter was that a Black Sun official had had his evening ruined in the middle of Villachor's territory. That wasn't something that could simply be ignored or swept away.

And if the glitterstim was a test, maybe this was, too. "Do we have anyone over at the hotel?" he asked.

"No," Sheqoa said. "I thought Master Qazadi ordered us to stay away."

"That was before his people were attacked," Villachor growled. "I want a squad in place over there by midnight. Put at least two men on that same floor and the others in whatever rooms they can get above and below Lord Aziel's suite."

"Yes, sir," Sheqoa said hesitantly. "May I remind you, sir, that we're going to be stretched thin as it is for Festival crowd control? Removing a full squad from our roster will make it worse."

"I don't care," Villachor said tartly. "As long as we

keep a full quota on the vault, that's all that matters. If someone wants to use the Festival as cover to sneak into the house and steal a few spoons, he's welcome to try. Anything like that can be dealt with later."

"Understood," Sheqoa said, clearly still not happy but knowing not to argue the point further. "I don't suppose you could persuade Master Qazadi to bring Aziel and the others here instead? It would make security a lot easier."

Villachor felt his stomach tighten. Yes, it certainly would. Villachor had in fact pointed out that very fact to Qazadi at their first meeting.

But Qazadi had brushed off the suggestion, invoking a Black Sun policy of keeping the blackmail files and the cryodex coding separated unless one of the files was in the process of being read. Villachor had listened to that reasoning, nodded politely, and pretended to accept it, even though he wasn't any more satisfied than Sheqoa was. It had always struck him as less an explanation than a thinly plated excuse.

Maybe there was another reason for Qazadi to keep Aziel away from Marblewood. Maybe Aziel wasn't just here to handle the key codes, but was also waiting in the wings to move in and take over as Villachor's successor once Villachor failed Qazadi's test.

If that was the case, it would hardly be in Villachor's best interests to knock himself out stretching his resources to protect Aziel.

Tests within tests within tests. And Villachor still didn't know which way Qazadi wanted him to jump.

But there was one thing he *was* sure of: if Qazadi was hoping for a quiet and civilized transfer of power, he could forget it. "Go back to Riston," he ordered Sheqoa. "Tell him I want him to keep running tests until he can tell me with certainty where that glitterstim came from."

"I don't think there are any more tests he can run, sir," Sheqoa said.

"Then he'd better invent a few," Villachor shot back. "Go."

"Yes, sir," Sheqoa said. He didn't look happy, but he knew an order when he heard it.

"And you're not to tell Master Qazadi or his people about any of this," Villachor added. "Not until we're sure."

"Yes, sir," the big man said. "Good night, sir."

He turned and slipped away as silently as he'd arrived. Villachor turned around again, watching until Sheqoa's shadow had crossed to the door at the far end of the suite. Then, with a thoughtful hiss, he turned back to the cityscape.

Of course Riston wouldn't glean anything new. But ordering more tests would buy Villachor some time—enough, he hoped, to sort through the possible traps that had been laid so tantalizingly in front of him.

Meanwhile, the Festival of Four Honorings would begin in three days, and with it crowds of the great and small of Iltarr City would descend on his grounds and courtyard. Villachor had displays to build, entertainment to prepare, food and drink to coordinate, and a large number of officials to be quietly taken inside his mansion and bribed, threatened, or blackmailed.

By the time the Festival was over, he promised himself, even Xizor would have to concede that Villachor, and Villachor alone, knew best how to run Black Sun's operations in this sector. If Qazadi's plan was still to take him down, he would find Villachor a much more difficult target than he'd thought.

And if the glitterstim lure was someone else trying to move in on his territory . . .

Villachor bared his teeth at the towering lights. If

someone out there was really foolish enough to take him on, that someone would regret it. Very, very badly.

The lock clicked and the door opened, and with a weariness Dayja hadn't permitted himself to feel until that precise moment, he walked into the suite.

D'Ashewl was waiting up for him, sitting at the desk in the office. "How did it go?"

"It worked," Dayja said, wading through the thick carpet to the closest comfortable chair and dropping gratefully into it. It had been a long, long day. "Master Cuciv never saw me coming, and is currently sleeping off the Speakeasy drug."

D'Ashewl grunted. "I hope you know the chance you were taking with that," he warned. "An eighty-percent heart failure rate is not something to be taken lightly."

"I know," Dayja said, wincing at the memory of watching the elderly spaceport official fight his way through the drug's initial surge before his heart finally stabilized. "But there was no choice. We needed to know about the blackmail file data cards, and we couldn't leave Cuciv with any memory that he'd been questioned about it. That meant interrogation droids were out, along with Bavo Six, OV 600, or any of our other repertoire of drugs."

"And if he'd died?"

Dayja shrugged. "Eanjer had two other names. One of them probably would have survived the procedure."

D'Ashewl grunted again. "But you did get it?"

"Yes," Dayja said. "Standard data card size, matte black, with the Black Sun logo emblazoned across the front in a shiny black."

"Subtle," d'Ashewl said wryly. "Artistic, too. Not what you'd expect of Xizor's thugs. How big is the logo?"

"Well, that's the one small speck of gree in the grease," Dayja conceded. "Cuciv was just a hair vague on that point. Eanjer's going to have his team make up two or three versions and hope one of them is close enough to pass."

"Not ideal," d'Ashewl said. "But you can probably make it work."

For a moment the room was silent. Dayja unloaded his knife, comlink, and hold-out blaster from his pockets onto the low table beside the chair, trying to decide whether he was too tired to eat or too hungry to sleep. The latter, he concluded. Getting back to his feet, he headed toward the food station beside the entertainment cluster at the other end of the office. "Any luck tracking down my new best friends from the holos I sent you?" he asked over his shoulder.

"Not really," d'Ashewl said. "I never cease to be amazed at how few criminals have anything more than just their names in their police files. Even the ISB records don't have much."

"The high-level ones apparently employ slicers with way too much time on their hands," Dayja agreed.

"So it would seem," d'Ashewl said. "Has he asked the obvious question yet?"

"Why I don't just whistle up a legion of stormtroopers and descend on Marblewood in force?" Dayja asked sourly. "Not in so many words, but he's hinted at it. I've tried to give the impression that we're being required to stick to proper legal procedures. The whole civil liberties and warrants thing."

D'Ashewl snorted. "Liberties and warrants. Right." He sighed, the sound audible all the way over at the food station. "I hope you realize how very thin the ice is that we're walking on, Dayja. The Director is having serious problems with the court right now, and may be on his way out whether we get him the blackmail files or not. If we're tied to him when he goes over the edge—and as of nine days ago, we are—it won't be pleasant for any of us."

"There's still time," Dayja said firmly. "If he can find out which of his enemies are on Black Sun's payroll, he can turn that association against them."

"Maybe," d'Ashewl said, not sounding convinced. "But whether he pulls out of his dive or not, our futures are still balanced on the edge. If we get the files, we'll be heroes. If we can't, it may not matter whether the Director goes or not. Xizor will be furious that an attempt was even made, and with his blackmail capabilities intact he'll be a formidable enemy."

"Life's a gamble," Dayja reminded him, keying for something that would be quick to prepare and equally quick to eat. "Intel work even more so. Don't worry, this will work."

"I hope you're right," d'Ashewl said. "What are you going to do with the glitterstim gambit? That's already in the works, isn't it?"

"Yes, but it can be put on pause for a few days," Dayja said. "No one but that street manager, Crovendif, knows what I look like. As long as I stay off his streets I'll be fine."

"So you're letting Eanjer and his team take point?"

"For now," Dayja said. "I assume Qazadi will be here for the entire festival. If Eanjer isn't able to get the blackmail files, I should have time to go back to my original plan."

"This is an extremely dirty group of hands to be placing our lives into," d'Ashewl warned.

"It'll be all right," Dayja assured him, permitting himself a tight smile.

D'Ashewl's concern was touching and certainly not misplaced. But they both knew that his choice of pronouns was merely a courtesy. D'Ashewl had been in service long enough and had amassed enough friends and allies that even Xizor would hesitate to take him on. Certainly not over an espionage effort that had ultimately failed.

No, d'Ashewl's life wasn't in Eanjer's hands. But Dayja had no such high-powered backing. What happened over the next few days would make his career or would end it. Permanently.

But the risk had to be taken. Black Sun was an evil that had been gnawing at the roots of the galaxy for a long, long time, and it had to be stopped. If the Emperor wasn't inclined to take action and Lord Vader was too preoccupied, then the job would fall to lesser men.

And if those lesser men also fell . . . still, as he'd said, life was a gamble.

The dice had been rolled. He would just have to wait to see how they landed.

For a few minutes after Lando trudged off to his room, Han remained where he was, gazing out the window at the clump of lights of Villachor's mansion. With the relative darkness of the Marblewood grounds surrounding it, the mansion almost looked like a small star cluster drifting all alone in space.

And every pilot in the galaxy knew how dangerous star clusters were.

Lando was right, of course. Han was a pilot and a smuggler. What did he know about con artistry?

Nothing, really. But he knew people. He knew how people thought and reacted, especially people driven by greed and the lust for power. He'd seen it with Jabba and Batross, he'd watched it happen with Imperial officials, and he'd felt a twinge of it himself on occasion.

Maybe that was what he liked most about Leia. As a princess of Alderaan, she'd had plenty of power, more than most people could ever dream of. Yet she'd tossed it aside for what she considered to be a higher and nobler cause.

Whether it *was* a higher cause, of course, or whether it was just a fancy way of committing mass suicide still remained to be seen. But that wasn't Han's problem. His problem was that he'd more or less promised justice for Eanjer, and shares of 163 million credits for everyone else.

And Lando was right about another thing. Sometimes Han's trust in people turned out to be badly misplaced.

He thought about it a while longer. Then, prying himself out of the chair, he went in search of Dozer. Considering how the other had been acting when he'd left the conversation room earlier, there was only one likely place to start looking. He found Dozer in the kitchen, munching on an enormous sandwich.

"Am I interrupting?" Han asked as he walked in and sat down.

"No," Dozer said. "Is this about Lando being front man? Because if it is, forget everything I said before. Far as I'm concerned, he can have the job."

"Glad to hear it," Han said. "Because there's another job I want you to do for me. Something that might take you a few days."

Dozer's eyes narrowed. "You trying to get rid of me?"

"Course not," Han assured him.

"Because if this is about me being worried about Black Sun earlier, I'm okay with that now," Dozer persisted.

"I know," Han said. "This is just something I've thought of that we're going to need, that's all."

"Uh-huh," Dozer said, still looking suspicious. "Does it involve facing that Falleen again?"

"No Falleen," Han said. "It'll be a little tricky, but it should be safe enough."

For another few seconds Dozer continued to study his face. Then he carefully set his sandwich down on the plate and brushed the crumbs off his hands. "Okay," he said, leaning back in his seat. "Tell me all about it."

CHAPTER NINE

For the next three days the team stayed close to home. The twins' room quickly became an electronics shop as Bink, Tavia, Chewbacca, and Winter worked to build spit-mitters that would fit into the limited space inside a data card. Unfortunately, Eanjer's friend Donnal Cuciv hadn't been able to give them the correct size of the Black Sun logo on the data card that Villachor had showed him, which meant they were going to need at least three and possibly as many as five to safely cover the range of possibilities. With Winter and Chewbacca also building the fake cryodex, the timing was going to be tight.

Still, Chewbacca was on it, and the Wookiee had never let Han down yet. Han wasn't expecting this to be the first time.

The others had plenty of work of their own to do. Kell set up an explosives shop in the room next door to the twins' and spent the three days creating charges of various sizes and shapes. Zerba busied himself with the quick-change tear-away outfits Han had commissioned from him, with frequent breaks to rest his eyes and practice his sleight of hand. Eanjer, in contrast, had little to do but wander around the suite, ask questions, and otherwise make a nuisance of himself.

Lando and Han spent most of their time in the conversation room, staying out of everyone else's way and reading through the ever-increasing volume of material Rachele was able to pull up on Villachor, his staff, his mansion, and the people he most often dealt with, many of whom were probably also associated with Black Sun.

At times Han found the sheer amount of data a little overwhelming. Villachor had his fingers in practically every aspect of life in Iltarr City, with half the police and probably more than half the governmental officials apparently ready to drop everything at his command. It was a sobering confirmation that the team had set up shop in the middle of seriously hostile territory.

Lando, typically, didn't seem bothered by that. Possibly, as a gambler, he was more used to facing tables full of enemies. Possibly he was just better at hiding his uneasiness. He went through Rachele's data quickly and methodically, occasionally making comments about some particularly insightful or useful bit of information. Sometimes he experimented with various accents he thought might serve him when he finally met Villachor face-to-face.

It was a little irritating to see him so calm, but Han had to admit that maybe Lando had the better take on things. Jabba and the other Hutts weren't all that different from Villachor and Black Sun, except that their influence was more or less open and obvious instead of being buried in a maze of underground roots. Han had survived Hutt intrigues and animosity. He could get through whatever Villachor threw at him, too.

Dozer was the main exception to the others' general stay-at-home pattern. From the first time Tavia sent him out for some fresh power cells, he settled into the role of unofficial messenger boy, fetching everything from detonator components to fresh medseal bandages for Eanjer to Rodian carryout one evening when Zerba suddenly had an overpowering craving.

Rachele joked once that he was spending more time outside the suite than inside, and wondered aloud if she could get a discount for his part of the rental fee. It was an exaggeration, of course, but everyone had noticed that Dozer was often gone for hours at a time, tracking down his current objective.

Han just hoped none of them suspected the real reason for the man's lengthy absences.

And as they worked, Villachor's grounds far below were in the process of being turned into something that was half street fair and half exhibition grounds. From the sky, the displays and pavilions beckoned with the promise of a return to Old Republic magnificence.

From the ground, they more than delivered.

"This is amazing," Bink commented as the group walked along the drive toward the mansion. "I've never seen anything like it. And I've been *everywhere.*"

"This is just the first day, too," Kell reminded her, sounding even more awestruck than she was. "Who knew there were so many ways to move rock and dirt?"

"Stone," Dozer corrected dourly. "It's the Honoring of Moving Stone."

"Rock, stone—same difference," Kell said, still looking around.

"No, one is correct and the other isn't," Dozer insisted. "You want to sound like a wide-eyed tourist?"

"We *are* wide-eyed tourists," Lando pointed out calmly. "So are probably half the people here."

"If not this bunch, then the ones who'll be here later," Han agreed, looking at the streams of people on both sides of them. It was barely midday, with the event not even officially supposed to open for another two hours, and already hundreds or even thousands of people were here, with more streaming through the gates, all of them staring and oohing with the same amazement as Bink and Kell.

To be honest, Han couldn't blame them. Overhead, miniature solar systems drifted through the air, their planets, moons, and asteroids moving swiftly or lazily around their glowing suns. Some of the systems had tiny, sparkling ships moving through them, and occasionally one would flicker as if jumping to lightspeed and reappear in a different system dozens of meters away. Alongside the road, tethered near clumps of sculpted trees, were twisting sand tornadoes, their tall funnel shapes spinning with carefully confined fury. Farther away, he could see the cones of something Rachele had called cold-lava volcanoes, which seemed to erupt randomly, with even more violence and harmless ferocity than the tornadoes.

Han had seen more impressive sights in his travels around the galaxy. But seldom had he seen a display delivered with this kind of flair. It was easy to get caught up in the glitz and the carnival atmosphere.

It was a lot easier to resist the pull when he remembered that the whole thing was funded by blood credits.

"Fine," Dozer growled. He, at least, was in no danger of getting caught up in the spirit of the Festival. "Whatever. I just want him to show a little dignity. You know—*dignity*?"

"Sorry," Kell said, his earlier excitement noticeably muted.

Han looked sideways at Lando. The other looked back and gave a small shrug. Dozer hadn't wanted to come to Marblewood with them this morning. But at the same time he'd refused to be left behind.

"There's one," Bink said, nodding to the side.

Han looked in that direction and saw a droid standing motionlessly beside the road, probably put there to give directions or advice to first-timers. Unlike pretty much every other droid Han had ever seen, this one was wearing clothing: a long, stone-patterned gown with leggings down to its feet and sleeves and even loose gloves on its hands. Its head was covered with a draped cowl that had holes for the eyes and mouth and no other openings. It looked for all the world like a pile of rocks that just happened to be stacked in the shape of a droid, which presumably was the whole idea.

"Impressive," Lando murmured. "Slightly ridiculous, but still impressive."

"I can't wait to see the outfits for the Honoring of Moving Air," Bink commented. "Something flimsy and airy, no doubt. Rachele's right—there's not a chance of figuring out what kind of droid that is through all that."

"From the shape, I'd guess it's either an SE 4 or SE 6," Kell said. "Its voice might give us a clue. You want me to try that?"

Dozer snorted. "Yeah, good luck," he said, craning his head to peer over the crowd. "I can see at least a dozen droids right from here, and that doesn't even count the servers at the pavilions and whoever's stoking the volcanoes and geysers. You want to play question-the-Quarran with all of them?"

"Let's just stick to the plan," Han said.

"So what's our timing here?" Lando asked. "I assume we'll want to mill around a little and take in the sights before we make our respective moves?"

"Sounds good," Han agreed. "The minute you move on Villachor you'll be at the center of attention. Might as well use our anonymity while we've still got it. Let's take an hour, get the lay of the land, and then get to work. And remember that some of those floating planets up there are probably cam droids. Play everything like you've got an audience, because you probably do."

"And keep an eye out for Villachor," Lando added.

"There's no guarantee he'll be out and about this early. If he doesn't show, this whole trip will be for nothing."

"I don't know that I'd call it *nothing,*" Bink said, sniffing at the air. "There *are* still the food pavilions."

"Mind on the job, Bink," Han admonished. "One hour. And watch yourselves."

Marblewood's guest suite complex took up nearly a third of the top floor of the mansion's northeast wing and was equipped with all the finest amenities and décor that the Empire had to offer. In many ways, it was more magnificent even than Villachor's own suite, since Villachor's was intended merely for comfort while the guest suite was designed for comfort *and* to impress its occupants. The suite had played host to dozens of officials and Black Sun colleagues over the past eleven years, and by all accounts it had succeeded admirably in both goals.

But up to now, none of Villachor's guests had been so impressed by the suite that they'd refused to leave it.

As usual, there were two Falleen guards flanking the suite door when Villachor arrived. "Sector Chief Villachor, requesting an audience with His Excellency," he announced formally as he came to a halt a couple of meters away.

"The purpose of the audience?" one of the guards asked.

Villachor suppressed a snarl. It was the same arrogant and demeaning challenge he'd put up with for three straight days now. *Yes*, Qazadi was a vigo, but there was still no call for a simple bodyguard to talk to a Black Sun sector chief with such obvious lack of respect. Not even when the bodyguard was one of Prince Xizor's precious Falleen. "I want to invite His Excellency to the presentation balcony for the Festival's grand opening ceremonies later," he said between clenched teeth. "He'll have a much better view of the geyser eruptions from there."

The guard pulled a comlink from his belt and spoke briefly into it. There was a reply, and he returned the device to its loop. "His Excellency thanks you for your offer," he relayed. "He believes he can observe the events of the Honoring of Moving Stone quite adequately from his own balcony."

"I see," Villachor said, managing with a supreme effort to keep his voice civil. "Please thank him for his time and consideration."

Sheqoa was waiting by the turbolift where Villachor had left him. "Will he be coming, sir?" the security chief asked.

"No, he will not," Villachor bit out. "He apparently has no interest in anything except his own room and his own people."

Sheqoa gave a small grunt. "Maybe *he* doesn't have any interests," he said, "but his people sure do. Dorston and his patrol caught two more of them last night, this pair in the kitchen."

Villachor swallowed a curse. Qazadi's guards had been all over his mansion in the past three days, poking their noses and fingers everywhere. There'd already been several tense confrontations between them and Sheqoa's people, one of those altercations nearly reaching the point of drawn blasters.

And like Qazadi's self-imposed isolation, the skulking and prying had started the same night Crovendif had brought in that mysterious glitterstim sample.

"Did they say what they were doing?"

"Just that they wanted to look around," Sheqoa said. "But I think there was more to it than that. He said they were in the east-central end, near the dumbwaiter, and that one of them had a sensor probe with him."

Villachor scowled. The dumbwaiter was a leftover of the previous owner's time in the house, a narrow vertical lift shaft for carrying food or other items from the first-floor kitchen level to the fourth floor, where the basket or tray could be transferred to one of two horizontal conduits that led to either the main guest suite or Villachor's own master suite in the southeast wing. Apparently the owner had wanted a way to have meals delivered without having to open his door to servants or droids. "What were they doing with the probe?"

"I don't think they'd actually started anything yet," Sheqoa said. "As usual, they claimed that the freedom of movement you gave Qazadi also applied to them."

"Of course they did," Villachor said. It was a molecule-thin excuse, and he and Sheqoa both knew it.

But there wasn't anything they could do about it. Qazadi *had* to be given the run of the mansion—he was a vigo, after all. And once he'd been granted that autonomy, there was no way Villachor could restrict his bodyguards without looking petty or suspicious.

If there was one thing Villachor knew for certain, it was that *petty* and *suspicious* weren't labels he could afford to have attached to his name right now.

"I want the nighttime patrols doubled," he ordered Sheqoa. "And put an extra guard in the kitchen, somewhere where he can watch both the pantry and the dumbwaiter. With all the food prep we're doing for the Festival, we should have another man down there anyway."

"Yes, sir," Sheqoa said. He didn't sound any happier about the situation than Villachor felt, but it was obvious he didn't have any better ideas or suggestions.

"After you do that, I want you to get in contact with that street manager, Crovendif," Villachor continued. "I want him here, every day of the Festival, wandering around and keeping his eyes open. If the glitterstim peddler shows up, I want him."

"Yes, sir," Sheqoa said again. "Whenever you're ready to go outside, Tawb and Manning are waiting at the west portico."

Villachor glanced up through one of the skylights as one of the floating solar systems drifted past. He wasn't all that excited about going out there right now, out among the simple and stupid, forced to smile and chat with hundreds of his fellow Iltarr City citizens and pretend he actually cared that they existed. Especially not in his current mood.

But the new Minister for Trade Relations would be dropping by in less than half an hour. Villachor needed to be on hand to greet him, casually invite him into a more quiet, more private room inside the mansion, and explain to him the true realities of government service on Wukkar.

"I'm ready," he told Sheqoa. "You'd better get out there, too. This is one year we don't want any problems or incidents."

"Understood, sir," Sheqoa said grimly. "Don't worry. There won't be."

As usual, the crowds had already started streaming onto the grounds, even though most of the other Festival venues around the city and the planet weren't even open yet. But despite the numbers and the fact that the food service was really only now beginning, the crowd seemed happy and polite. As each visitor or group spotted their host approaching they stopped their activities or conversation, offered nods of respect or gestures of thanks and good cheer, then courteously moved aside to make way.

Sheep, every single one of them. But at least they were polite and friendly as Villachor and Black Sun stripped the wool and flesh from their bones.

He'd made his first circuit around the inner yard and was following the fresh stream of people heading toward the food pavilions when Tawb stepped close and touched his arm. "Sir?"

"What is it?" Villachor asked, exchanging nods with a Koorivar wearing a merchant's cowl and making a mental note to have someone check on the alien's status and travel plans. Many Koorivar traders also engaged in weapons smuggling, and Villachor could always use another such pipeline.

"I just had a report from one of Master Qazadi's guards," Tawb said, lowering his voice. "He thinks he's spotted the man from Quickline Courier Service who was at Lord Aziel's suite during the Lulina Crown incident."

"Really," Villachor said, frowning. The morning after the incident Aziel had told him that he was convinced the courier had been an innocent bystander. So why were Qazadi's people watching for him? "Where is he?"

"Near the northwest pavilion and volcano."

Which was also the closest public display to the mansion's north wing entrance. Coincidence?

Actually, it probably was. The cold-lava volcanoes were already proving to be a crowd-pleaser, and that particular pavilion was the one serving white sausage, a favorite of many of the locals. Certainly a common courier's presence here was nothing to raise eyebrows—one of the grand traditions of the Festival was that it was open to royal family and lowly worker alike.

Still, Villachor had no intention of taking any chances. "Have security keep an eye on him," he told Tawb. "No approach or detain, just observation."

"Yes, sir," Tawb said, and as he drifted back toward his guard flank position, he was already speaking quietly into his comlink clip.

With an effort, Villachor put his smile back in place. Qazadi and Aziel were playing some kind of game under the table—that much he was sure of. Whatever that game was, he was determined to cut himself in. Whether they wanted him in or not.

Dozer was eyeing the white sausage at the blue-topped food pavilion, wondering if Solo's orders to look around could be stretched to include a proper tasting tour of the grounds, when he realized he was being watched.

The first signs were subtle, as such things usually were. There was a glance from a hard-faced man that lingered just a bit too long. Another hard-faced man loitering near the pavilion looked in Dozer's direction, then turned away, his lips moving as if he were talking to himself. One of the two uniformed security men standing by the mansion's main entrance, who were probably there just for show, nudged his partner and nodded in Dozer's direction.

Dozer had been spotted.

With an effort, he forced himself to continue his casual wandering, his heartbeat thudding suddenly in his ears. He'd been spotted, but what did that mean? Were Villachor's men looking for an opportunity to sneak him out of the crowd and haul him inside for interrogation? Maybe even to face Lord Aziel again? He'd survived Aziel's last questioning purely through luck, Rachele's skill at creating cover stories, and the fact that Aziel had already been convinced of his innocence before they began their little chat. There were no guarantees that he'd get off so easily the next time around.

Steady, he cautioned himself. For starters, there was no reason a lowly courier company employee *shouldn't* be here. In fact, there were probably dozens or hundreds of Iltarr City citizens Villachor and his men knew by name or sight or reputation on the Marblewood grounds right now.

For another, this was a happy, cheerful planet-wide festival. Surely Villachor wouldn't do anything to wreck the mood until and unless he had some solid evidence that Dozer was up to mischief.

And if they had such evidence, surely they would have moved on him already.

He took a deep breath, feeling the tension draining away. So they knew he was here, they knew he was someone who'd interacted with Aziel under unusual circumstances, and they were going to keep an eye on him just in case.

That was fine. Dozer wasn't planning on making any mischief. At least not here and now.

But as long as they were watching him anyway . . .

Midway between Dozer and the guarded door were a couple of youngish men wearing the neat but plain tunic-and-trouser outfits that pegged them as working-class types who'd put on their finest clothing for their visit to Villachor's party. Both were holding cups, and from the way they were chattering and gesturing, it was likely that they'd had more than a couple of samples from the drink pavilions. Watching as much of the area around him as he could, Dozer headed toward the door.

The response was instant, nicely subtle, and extremely revealing. Both uniformed door guards and all three of the plainclothes ones he'd tagged suddenly seemed to have eyes only for him. Dozer saw one of the door guards say something, either to his partner or into a collar-clip comlink, but none of the others so much as moved their lips.

Which wasn't to say they weren't communicating. On the contrary, as Dozer kept walking toward the door, he saw the three men slipping through the crowd in a well-coordinated move that would put two of them between him and the door and one directly behind him in backup position. At that point, they would have several options on how to deal with him, none of which would likely be pleasant.

They were nearly to their chosen positions when Dozer reached the two men. "Hey!" he said affably, stopping beside them and raising a hand in greeting. "Thought I recognized you. You're friends with Cadger, aren't you?"

The men turned to him, their alcohol-creased grins taking on a slight edge of puzzlement. "Cadger?" one of them asked.

"Yeah," Dozer said. Out of the corner of his eye he saw the two security men pause, one of them holding position while the other edged a little closer to the conversation. "Well, *we* call him Cadger. Always borrowing stuff, never remembers to return it—you practically have to call out the Tweenriver garrison to get it back."

One of the men's faces cleared. "Oh," he said knowingly. "You mean Esmon."

"Yeah, Esmon," Dozer confirmed. "We always just call him Cadger. Listen, this is my first time in this venue. You guys know when those pavilions stop serving? I can't get close enough to ask anyone."

"Don't worry about that," the man assured him. "You'll scrap out long before they do."

"Just make sure you don't bleep so much that it'll take you more than a day to dry out," the other man added, raising his cup for emphasis. "'Cause the day after tomorrow is the Honoring of Moving Air, and Villachor serves the best whipped liqueurs on Wukkar. You'll want to be here bright and early for that."

"You bet," Dozer agreed, slapping the other genially on the shoulder. "Thanks. When you see Cadger—Esmon—tell him Blather said hi."

Turning, Dozer headed away from both the men and the door. Glancing casually around, he saw that the security men were likewise moving back to their earlier positions, the alert apparently having been rebranded as a false alarm.

Still, he had no doubt they would continue to watch him as long as he was here.

Which was fine. In fact, it was perfect.

Dozer had never been entirely comfortable with the thought of being front man on this job. A certain level of con work was necessary in any branch of thievery, of course, and ship boosting was no exception. If necessary, he could have done a fair job with this one, too.

But it would have been a fair job, not a spectacular one. Going up against a man like Villachor, Dozer knew, would require something better than just fair. Though he would never admit it, especially not to Solo, he'd secretly been relieved when Calrissian unexpectedly showed up at the suite door.

So let Calrissian grab the glory and the danger that went with being front man. Dozer had his own set of skills, skills none of the rest of them could match on their best day.

Turning south, he headed toward another of the pavilions, beyond which, not so coincidentally, was another of the mansion's doors. By the time the team reassembled at the suite, he promised himself, he would have a complete handle on Villachor's Festival security setup, their encirclement system, and their alert ripple paths.

Let Calrissian and his fancy smile top *that*.

There was an art and a science to bumping into people. Fortunately, Bink had long since mastered both.

"Oh!" she exclaimed, darting her hands up and letting her eyes widen with embarrassment and chagrin as she spun around to face the man whose chest she'd just gently bounced off. "I'm so sorry. Are you all right?"

"I'm fine," he assured her, giving her a small and slightly frosty smile.

"I'm so sorry," Bink said again, looking him up and down as if she were somehow expecting that whatever massive bruises her nudge had caused would be visible through his clothing. "Did I hurt you? I didn't spill your drink, did I? Please let me not have spilled your drink."

"Not a drop," he assured her, some of his stiffness easing. As well it should—this was Bink's best dippy-girl act, guaranteed to spark feelings of amusement, sympathy, or protectiveness in the majority of the male population. "See?" he added, holding his cup out for her inspection.

"Thank heavens," she breathed. The cup was about half full of Carlem brandy, she saw, about the right level for someone who'd been slowly savoring it for the past half hour or so. "That looks really good. I'd hate for someone to waste it. Especially me being that someone."

"It is, and you didn't," he again assured her.

"I'm so glad," she said. He was lying, of course, at least about the first part. The cup might be only half full, but there were no drops or other traces of liquid on the cup's rim or inner sides. It had been half full right from the start, and he hadn't taken so much as a sip.

He also had a collar-clip comlink, the slight bulge of a concealed blaster beneath the right side of his tunic, and the equally subtle bulge of a knife strapped to his left forearm beneath the sleeve. The lack of drinking alone would have tagged him as one of Villachor's people. The hard eyes and the weapons clinched it.

Of course, so did the fact that his face matched the holo Rachele had pulled up of Lapis Sheqoa, the head of Villachor's household security force.

Holos really did take the fun out of this game.

"Just try to be more careful," he said, offering a slightly more genuine smile this time. "Looking behind you when you're walking is a bad idea, especially in a crowd like this." He leveled a warning finger. "Besides, next time you might walk into someone's seafood fork."

"And it would serve me right," Bink declared mock seriously, matching the tone with a wry smile as she backed away from him. "See you."

She spent the next half hour strolling around the grounds, admiring the displays, striking up casual chatter with a couple of the other women in the crowd, getting herself a cup of something fruity to drink, and making sure not to keep the slightest track of where Sheqoa was. He would almost certainly be watching her, at least off and on, and it couldn't look like she was doing the same.

When it was time, she didn't expect to have any trouble finding him again.

She judged she'd waited long enough, and gave it ten minutes more. Then, joining the celebrants at one of the serving tables, she loaded up a small plate with a sampling of the snacks, carefully creating just enough imbalance to make the plate difficult to handle without making the imbalance obvious. With the plate in one hand and her cup in the other, she headed out to find Sheqoa.

As she'd predicted, there was nothing to it. Barely two minutes after leaving the pavilion she spotted him through the crowd, still doing his casual wandering act as he watched for trouble.

Time to kick things up a level.

The first step was to come to a sudden and awkward halt, her eyes on her plate and the suddenly tottering stack of glazed pental crackers there. Next came her requests to passersby for help, all of her increasingly frustrated entreaties completely ignored by everyone as they walked by.

Of course, the reason for that was that she was moving her lips but not making any actual sound, which meant none of the people passing by had the slightest notion that she was having any difficulty. But Sheqoa had no way of knowing that, not at his distance and with the low roar of the crowd and the moving stone displays all around them.

She kept up her pantomimed calls for help for several seconds, until her gut told her that that part of the charade had run its course. Still dodging passersby, she began studying the ground at her feet, as if trying to figure out if there was any safe place where she could set down her cup—

Abruptly, and a couple of seconds sooner than she'd expected, a hand appeared from the edge of her vision and plucked the cup from her hand. "Here—let me help," Sheqoa offered.

"Oh, thank you," Bink said, letting her pretended anxiety and frustration roll out in a flood of relief as she rearranged the pental crackers into a more stable configuration. "Thank you," she repeated, looking up. "I was—oh. You."

"We do seem to keep running into each other, don't we?" he said, offering a more genuine smile this time.

But it was still a guarded smile, with a thick layer of vigilance behind it. "At least this time I didn't try to turn your whatever-it-was into one of those volcano things," she said. "Thank you so much for your help. Those pental crackers are just too good to waste as ground clutter. I'm Katrin, by the way."

"Lapis," Sheqoa said. "This your first Festival?"

"First one here," she told him. "I did the Barrange venue twice when I was living in Opolisti."

"I've heard that one's pretty nice," he said.

"Not as nice as this one," she said ruefully. "Not that

I got much chance to enjoy it. I had the same kind of boss back then that you do."

"What do you mean?" he asked, frowning.

"Your comlink," she said, pointing to his collar. "You're on call, right? Off duty, but still on call, and he could yank you away on half a second's notice."

"Something like that," he said. "So how come you know that setup? Are you police? Military? Med tech?"

Bink snorted out a laugh. "This'll kill you. I'm an accountant."

"An *accountant*?"

"Isn't that just insane?" she agreed. "Come on—when was the last time someone called an accountant after working hours and said"—she dropped the pitch of her voice into a caricature of a stern, humorless boss—" 'We need you to rush in and examine some numbers *right this very minute*'?"

He chuckled, some of his reserve fading away. "Most of the numbers I know are perfectly happy to wait until business hours," he agreed.

"And the crazy thing is he actually *did* it," Bink told him. "He actually hauled me in *twice* for things that could have been left until the next day without anyone in the universe except him caring. One of those times I got the call right in the middle of an opera." She shook her head in reminiscence. "The *looks* on people's faces as I stumbled past them. If the Empire wants to kill Rebels, they should talk to those folks. Some of those looks could fry banthas at fifty meters."

"The opera, huh?" Sheqoa said. "I would never have tagged you as that sort."

"Oh, I'm not," Bink said. "But the guy I was with at the time really liked them. I'm more the three-stroke glitz type. What about you? I assume you're not an accountant, unless my ex-boss has opened an Iltarr City branch."

"No, no, I'm something far less interesting," Sheqoa said. "I'm with Master Villachor's household security."

Bink let her eyes widen. "Oh. Wow. Did I—I didn't say anything bad about anything, did I?"

"You said Master Villachor runs a better Festival than Master Barrange, that my drink looked good, and you didn't want to spill pental crackers all over the ground," Sheqoa said. "The cleaning staff will be especially pleased about that last one."

"Oh, good," she said. "Because I really am enjoying this. I'd hate to be banned from the rest of it."

"Just try not to run over anyone else and you should be fine." He held out her cup. "And now I need to get back to my duties."

"Oh, yes, of course," Bink said, accepting the cup back. "Thank you again. Quick question: someone told me once that Master Villachor has the original Sunright Feinhomm glitz instruments. Is that true?"

"It is," Sheqoa confirmed. "Maybe I can show them to you someday."

"That would be *so* great," Bink said, giving him her most dazzling smile. "Well, it was nice meeting you, Lapis. I'll probably see you around."

"I'll be here," Sheqoa said, smiling and giving her a sort of abbreviated wave. He was still smiling as he turned and wandered away into the crowd.

Taking a sip from her drink, Bink headed toward one of the seating areas. Yes, that had gone well. He was totally into her.

He was also totally on to her.

She smiled to herself. Perfect.

The crowds were already substantial, and it seemed like every third person who spotted Villachor wanted to come over to greet him, thank him for his hospitality, or chat a moment with him as if he were an actual friend.

But if there was one thing Lando had learned at the sabacc table, it was patience. He cultivated that patience now, strolling around the edge of Villachor's entourage, studying the man and his bodyguards. The locals used particular words and gestures in their greetings, all of which he noted while at the same time trying to sort out Villachor's own telltales for signs of interest, impatience, or boredom.

Finally there was a lull. Villachor paused, looking around as he murmured something to one of his bodyguards. Slipping around a pair of hammer-headed Ithorians, Lando moved toward the group.

Villachor spotted his approach, and Lando caught a brief twitch of his lip before his face broke into yet another of his counterfeit smiles. "Good afternoon," he said, probably hoping that by getting in the first word he would be able to control the duration of the conversation. "Enjoying the Festival?"

"Very much," Lando said, giving one of the polite nods that seemed to be associated with the upper-class Iltarr City citizens. "I imagine something like this is extremely expensive to run."

Villachor's smile slipped, just a bit. Apparently, most of the people he'd talked to had known better than to bring up such a crass subject. "It's well worth the cost," he said evenly. "The pleasure the Festival brings to the average citizen is something that can't be measured."

"Indeed," Lando said. "And of course, I expect the Festival provides unique opportunities to meet with people. Some of whom may bring you interesting offers."

Villachor's smile broadened even as it cooled a few degrees. "I'm sorry, but all new business discussions are paused during the Festival," he said. "But feel free to contact my office after the Honoring of Fire is over." He inclined his head and started to turn away.

"I understand," Lando said, taking a long step closer, aware that the two bodyguards were already moving to intercept. "Let me just say one word. Cryo—"

He broke off as both bodyguards grabbed him, one of them throwing a warning forearm across his throat as they started to pull him away from Villachor.

"A moment," Villachor said, stopping them with an uplifted finger. "Very well," he continued, his voice studiously casual. "One word."

The guard lifted his arm fractionally from Lando's throat, ready to clamp down again if necessary. Lando cleared his throat. "Cryodex," he said.

He counted out six heartbeats before Villachor spoke again. "Bring him," he said shortly. Spinning around, he strode back toward the mansion, heading in the direction of one of the smaller service doors. The bodyguards released their grips, one of them nudging a silent order into Lando's back.

Not that he needed any prompting. He set off briskly after Villachor, adjusting his pace to slowly catch up to the other. There were dozens or possibly hundreds of extra people and droids moving in and out of the mansion today, he knew, resupplying the pavilions with food and drink and handling other chores. It would be instructive to see exactly how Villachor had arranged the door locks to allow for such traffic while at the same time preventing random strangers from wandering inside.

It was, as it turned out, distinctly anticlimactic. Villachor merely marched up the flagstone walkway to the door, gripped and turned the handle, and pushed open the door without any fuss, bother, or challenge.

Lando suppressed a smile as he and the two bodyguards followed him in. Like one of Zerba's magic tricks, there was more to this one than it appeared. Villachor had gripped the handle, but right before he'd turned it, he'd bowed just slightly at the waist. Some kind of electronic trigger, then, with the receiver in the handle mechanism and the activator concealed somewhere in Villachor's shoulder or neck area. Possibly the fingertip-sized rectangular glazed-stone pendant he'd noticed riding a small choker chain around Villachor's neck.

And, he noted now, riding his bodyguards' necks as well.

They had their way inside. Maybe.

Villachor had stopped a few steps inside the door and was waiting for them beside two more guards. "And now," he said, even the false warmth gone from his voice, "let's go someplace quiet and have a little talk."

CHAPTER TEN

The various displays that Villachor had put together for the Honoring of Moving Stone were uniformly impressive, Han had decided early on during his private walking tour of the grounds. But for him, the sand tornadoes were the most interesting, the most photogenic, and, ultimately, the most potentially useful. He went from one tornado to the next, standing for a couple of minutes at each, admiring the twisting shapes and pretending to take endless pictures with the fake holocamera Chewbacca had built for him the previous night.

He wasn't alone in his activities, either. Lots of others were doing exactly the same thing, and Han usually found himself in the middle of a small crowd as he snapped his pretend holos. Most of those crowds involved families with younglings, all of whom treated the miniature storms with a combination of amazement, delight, and solemnity that only very young children could pull off. The more adventurous of the younglings dared to step closer, a few recklessly, the rest cautiously, reaching out to touch the edge of the swirling sand and then rushing, giggling, back to their parents. The parents, for their part, seemed to trust Villachor's engineering, assuming that the tornadoes' designers had made sure the tethering and repulsor-field encasing would keep the sand from leaking out and endangering their offspring.

They were mostly right. The first four tornadoes Han checked out were as isolated and protected as if they were just holos floating above the ground. The children could still get to the spinning sand, but each touch released only a few grains from the fields, which dropped harmlessly to scatter across the ground. Han spent as little time at each of those as he figured he could get away with, considering his role as holo-crazy tourist, before moving on to the next.

It was at the fifth tornado that he finally hit pay dirt. Literally.

Something had gone wrong with that display's confinement field. Not seriously wrong, not even all that obviously wrong. But whereas the ground by each of the others showed only the light scattering of sand released by the probing of small human and alien fingers, this one had an obvious ring of escaped material that had gathered about a meter away from the tornado's edge.

The ring wouldn't be there long, he knew, not with cam droids floating past overhead and security men roaming the grounds. Sooner or later, someone would spot the problem and call it in, and maintenance droids dressed in those ridiculous moving-stone outfits would hurry out to fix the leak and clean up the sand.

But the ring was here now, and that was all Han needed.

He'd made sure to keep track of the time he'd spent at the other displays, and had no intention of drawing attention by spending significantly more or less at this one. But this time he eased his way a little closer to the tornado as he took his pretend holos, listening closely to the chatter of conversation around him.

Just to his left was a middle-grade child asking her parents for permission to touch the tornado. Still snapping away with his holocamera, Han edged closer to the child. The parents discussed the matter briefly, then gave their permission. The girl scampered adventurously forward—

And as she brushed past Han's elbow, he jerked his hands as if she'd slammed into his arm, losing his grip on the holocamera and sending it arcing right into the middle of the ring of sand.

"Meelee!" the girl's mother gasped. "Look what you did!"

"It's okay," Han hastened to assure her as he stepped forward and knelt down by the holocamera. The girl, for her part, had already stopped and turned around, clearly confused by the outlandish result of what she knew had been barely a sleeve-on-sleeve touch, and equally confused by the grief she was getting for it. "Don't worry—these things hold together real good," he added. He reached down and got his hand on the holocamera.

And as he closed his fingers around it, he surreptitiously pressed the hidden button.

He'd told Chewbacca to make the vacuum pump quiet, and as usual the Wookiee had taken him at his word. Even kneeling directly above the device Han could barely hear the scratching noise of the sand being sucked in through the baffle vent, and the pump itself was completely inaudible. The rest of the crowd, three meters or more away, couldn't have heard a thing.

"See?" he said, picking up the device and turning back to the anxious parents. As he did so, he moved one foot casually across the sand, erasing all signs of the small crater the pump had made in the neat ring. "No problem. It's fine."

And with a friendly smile at the still confused girl, he slipped through the crowd and strode casually away.

He visited two more of the volcanoes, just to clear his backtrail, then headed off for his rendezvous with Kell.

He found the kid waiting in a seating area between two of the pavilions near the northern end of the mansion and

Villachor's oversized landspeeder and airspeeder garage. "Any trouble?" Kell asked as Han came up and sat down across the table from him.

"Nope," Han said, patting the vest pocket where he'd stashed the holocamera. "You ready?"

In his opinion, Kell still didn't look ready to knock over a child's coin bank, let alone a crime lord's private vault. But his nod was firm enough. "Let's do it."

"Okay," Han said, reminding himself yet again that Mazzic had vouched for the kid. He looked around and spotted a pair of droids busily collecting discarded plates and cups from one of the nearby tables. "Give me a five-count lead," he instructed. "And watch your timing."

The droids were still clearing the table when he got there. "Hey," he said, coming up to one of them. "Can you tell me when they stop serving lunch stuff and switch to a dinner menu?"

"There is no set time for food exchange," the droid said, turning its hooded face toward Han as it continued to gather the tableware. The cowl covering its face fluttered in the breeze, giving an unsettling masquerade-type atmosphere to the conversation. "The various dishes change at different times throughout the day. If you wish, the servers in the pavilions can provide you with a schedule for each switchover."

"Yeah, well, I'm mostly looking to see if you're going to have braised kiemple," Han said. Out of the corner of his eye he saw Kell approaching the table from his right. "You know what that is? Never mind," he said before the droid could answer. "I've got a holo here somewhere from last year's Festival," he went on, pulling out his holocamera and fighting back a sudden surge of doubt.

I can do this, he told himself firmly. The timing was going to be close, but he and Chewbacca ran close timing every time they flew the *Falcon*. This would be like a normal smuggling day. "Here it is," he continued, thrusting the holocamera in front of the droid's mask. Beside him, Kell stepped up to the table.

And as the kid reached past the plate the droid was aiming for, Han tapped the holocamera's release and dumped the sand he'd collected straight down the droid's glove. As the hand closed around the plate and Kell's wrist there was a soft crunching noise—

"Hey!" Kell protested. "Let go." He grabbed the hand, as if trying to pull it off, but instead squeezed the mechanical fingers tighter together around his wrist. He yanked his arm back, jerking the droid along with him. "Let *go*."

"Oh, dear," the droid said in a pained voice. "I'm terribly sorry, but I appear to be stuck."

"Great," Kell growled. "Hey—you."

"What? Me?" Han asked.

"Yes, you," Kell said. "Go find someone to get this thing off me, will you?"

"Is there a problem here?" a new voice put in.

Han turned. One of Villachor's security types was striding toward them, his eyes flicking over the scene.

"*Yes*, there's a problem," Kell bit out. "I was trying to get to my cup there and this thing grabbed me and won't let go."

"I'm terribly sorry," the droid said again. "My gears appear to be jammed."

"Yeah," the security man said, gingerly pulling the edge of the droid's glove away from the arm and peering down it. "Probably got sand in there—there's sure enough of it flying around."

"Great," Kell muttered. "So what do we do?"

"We get it off," the guard said calmly, gesturing toward the mansion. "Come on—there's a droid repair room right off the garage."

They headed off, Kell grumping, the droid apologizing, and the guard probably wishing his shift had ended half an hour earlier. Han watched them go, a glow of satisfaction running through him.

Like he always said, it was all in the timing.

The room Villachor led Lando to was small and windowless, and contained possibly the most intimidating working desk Lando had ever seen. Two more guards were waiting just inside the door, bringing the grand total of armed men up to six. "Sit down," Villachor said, pointing Lando toward a large padded chair in front of the desk as he walked around behind it. "Perhaps you'd like a little refreshment?"

It was probably a genuine offer, Lando knew. But it was also a test. Villachor was prodding at him, trying to get a feel for his speech, reactions, manners, and patterns. It was the same genteel dance that also accompanied every game of sabacc, and Lando was used to it.

It was just that the stakes usually weren't this high.

"No, thank you," he said, easing down into the chair. It was even more comfortable than it looked, the soft arms and cushions yielding to his weight and settling in around him. If he'd been planning a quick, unexpected exit, he would have been out of luck. Probably the reason for the chair's design in the first place. "I know your time is valuable."

"Indeed it is," Villachor said, settling into his own chair.

"But more valuable even than time is information," Lando continued. "And I'm fairly certain you don't want what I'm about to tell you to be heard by anyone except your closest, most trusted people."

Villachor smiled thinly. "If I didn't trust these men, they'd have been gone long ago."

"Of course," Lando said. "But there's trust, and then there's *trust*."

For a moment Villachor eyed him thoughtfully. Across the room the door opened, and the man Rachele's data pulls had identified as the security chief, Sheqoa, entered. Villachor glanced at him, looked back at Lando. "Fine," he said. "Tawb, Manning—wait outside. The rest of you, return to your duties. Sheqoa, you're with me."

As silently as Sheqoa had entered, the rest of the guards filed out. Villachor waited until the door was again closed, then gestured for Sheqoa to go stand behind Lando. "All right, you have your privacy," he said. "Rest assured that if this is some kind of bad joke, my face will be the last thing your eyes will ever see."

"No joke," Lando assured him. He was used to being threatened, but there was something in Villachor's voice that sent a chill up his back. "Let me begin by telling you a few things you already know. You're a high-ranking member of Black Sun, you're playing host to an even higher-ranking member, a vigo named Qazadi, and Master Qazadi has a set of blackmail files you're using to gain or cement leverage on various Wukkar citizens and probably some of the offworld visitors to the Festival." He paused for air.

"You're at the very least an amusing storyteller," Villachor commented, his face giving nothing away. "Please, continue."

"The blackmail files are, of course, heavily encrypted," Lando said. "The device used to decrypt them is called a cryodex. Alderaanian by design, and only a few still exist."

"Or possibly none at all," Villachor suggested.

"No, there are at least two," Lando assured him. "Master Qazadi has one." He cocked his head. "I have another."

Villachor's eyes flicked to Sheqoa, then back to Lando.

"I gather from your overly dramatic tone that you expect that to mean something to me."

"I do," Lando agreed. "And since we've both agreed that time is valuable, let me set my cards on the table. I represent a group of people who've taken on the task of scouring the Empire for those of like mind whose talents and ambitions are being underused or, in some cases, completely wasted. When such people are found, this group offers them better situations. Sometimes this involves a position with a different organization, one that values them more. Other times it means assisting them to strike out on their own. Sometimes a middle road is indicated, an indentureship or perhaps chartered autonomy."

"And if the person is perfectly happy where he is?" Villachor asked.

Lando gave a small shrug. "In my experience, no one who's working beneath his abilities is ever perfectly happy."

"Unless he knows that his current situation is the best he's ever likely to have."

"There's always something better," Lando said. "It's simply a matter of recognizing the opportunity when it comes along."

"You make it sound so easy," Villachor said dryly. "And so lacking in potential danger. Tell me about this supposed cryodex of yours."

"As I said, the cryodex is the key to reading the blackmail files currently stored in your vault," Lando said, keeping his voice steady. Han's whole plan depended on him selling this. "Those files would be of immeasurable value to the people I represent."

Villachor's smile was dark, brittle. "And all I have to do is hand over the files and wonderful opportunities will descend on me from the sky?"

"Wonderful opportunities, indeed," Lando confirmed.

"You'd literally be able to command your own chosen price." He shook his head. "But we both know it wouldn't be just opportunities that would descend. Prince Xizor himself would likely lead the expedition that came for your head."

"*And* yours," Villachor pointed out. "Because they would certainly pull every name, face, and memory from me before I was permitted to die."

"Oh, I have no doubt," Lando agreed grimly. "Which is why you'd be a fool to steal the files, and why *I* would be a fool to suggest it."

A slight frown creased Villachor's forehead. "In that case, why exactly are you here?"

"To offer a safer alternative," Lando said. "Not to steal the files, but to copy them."

Again Villachor's eyes flicked to Sheqoa. "Copy them," he repeated flatly.

"Exactly," Lando said. "You have the files; I have the cryodex. We meet in your vault, decrypt the files, and copy them onto standard data cards, perhaps overlaid with our own chosen encryptions."

"*Our* encryptions?"

Lando held up a hand. "A slip of the tongue. *Your* encryptions, of course."

"That's good," Villachor said, in a voice that once again sent a chill up Lando's back. "Because any attempt by you to make a copy for yourself would require me to kill you on the spot. For the sake of argument, suppose I had copies of the files. What then?"

"I'd introduce you to the gentlemen of whom I spoke," Lando managed, his throat suddenly dry. "You'll work out a mutually satisfactory deal, and your rise to your full potential will have begun."

"Yes," Villachor said thoughtfully. "Let me tell you what *I* think. I think you've never even seen a cryodex, let alone possess one. I think you have no organization behind you, certainly no one with any power. I think you're here purely as a test to see if my loyalty to Black Sun can be swayed by such a ridiculous and simple-minded story. And I think that, just to be on the safe side, I'm going to have you killed."

He leaned back in his chair. "Let's try it again. Who are you, and who do you work for?"

"There's no need for threats," Lando protested mildly, some of the tension draining from him. The threat was real; but oddly enough, that was actually a good sign. If Villachor hadn't been interested or at least intrigued by the offer, he would simply have had Sheqoa throw him out. "My name is unimportant, but you can call me Kwerve. As for my employers—" He shrugged. "For the moment they must remain anonymous."

"Too bad," Villachor said. There might have been a twitch of his eyebrow at the name, but it was small enough that Lando might have simply imagined it. "It would have been useful to know where to ship your body."

"Of course you don't wish to make any commitments now," Lando continued. "I wouldn't expect that. Let me make a suggestion and an offer. Two days from now is the Honoring of Moving Air. At that time I'll bring my cryodex to show you. You can select one of the blackmail data cards, and I'll decrypt *one* of the files for you. After that, we'll talk further."

"Assuming we're both still able to converse?"

"Why shouldn't we be?" Lando countered reasonably. "You've made no statements and taken no action that's in any way disloyal to your Black Sun masters. All you've agreed to do is see if a stranger claiming to have a valuable artifact does indeed have it. If I do, it could easily be that your intent is to purchase the artifact and send it to Imperial Center as a gift for Prince Xizor's collection of rarities."

"Perhaps," Villachor said, his eyes probing Lando's face. Lando sat quietly, waiting for him to work it through.

When it happened, it happened suddenly. "The day after tomorrow, fifth hour past midday," Villachor said abruptly. "The bound tempest will be presented at that time, drawing the visitors' attention to the northwest part of the grounds. You'll come to the door you're about to leave through and wait until it's opened to you. You will, of course, bring the cryodex."

"Of course," Lando said. He started to stand up, wiggling his hips to extricate himself from the overstuffed chair arms.

And abruptly dropped back as Sheqoa's hand pushed down hard on his shoulder. "If you plan betrayal," Villachor continued, his voice low and deadly, "I strongly urge you to instead leave Wukkar by the earliest transport."

"Understood," Lando said. "I'll see you the day after tomorrow at five hours past mid." He craned his neck to look up at Sheqoa. "May I?"

For a moment the big man just stared down at him, his expression wooden. Then he released his grip on Lando's shoulder. With more effort and wiggling, Lando finally got free of the chair.

"The men outside will see you out," Villachor said, remaining seated. "Until then, Master Kwerve."

"Until then," Lando confirmed. "One final observation, if I may. Nothing in this universe lasts forever. Not power, or position, or allies." He inclined his head. "Not even Black Sun." He turned the incline into a polite nod. "Good day, Master Villachor."

Sheqoa walked him to the door and murmured a few

words to the bodyguards waiting outside. One of them gestured silently to Lando, and without a word they escorted him along a wide corridor, through a pair of hand-carved doors, and to an unassuming door set in a thick but otherwise unassuming wall. Lando was ushered through it and found himself at the southern end of the mansion's south wing.

The very door, in fact, where Aziel always made his entrance.

Which meant that, assuming Rachele's schematic had been correct, he'd walked right past the junior ballroom and Villachor's vault.

Maybe in two days he'd get to see inside that vault, where even Rachele and her incredible spiderweb of contacts and sources hadn't yet been able to go.

Maybe in two days he'd be dead.

"Yeah, it's the sand," the tech said disgustedly as he led Kell and the droid still clamped to his wrist through a maze of workbenches and waist-high tool cabinets toward an uncluttered bench seat near the back. "Third one today, and the Honoring's barely even started." He turned Kell around and sat him down. "You—bend over," he ordered the droid.

Obediently, the droid bent forward at the waist, putting Kell's wrist and arm at a more comfortable angle. "At least it's only one day," Kell pointed out. "The rest of the Honorings should be easier on them."

"Don't you believe it," the tech grumbled. He peeled away the top of the droid's glove and peered down at the frozen joint. "The moving air stirs up dirt and dust and whatever sand the EGs didn't get swept up, the moving water gets places even the sand doesn't, and don't even get me started on the fire and the fireworks."

He clucked his tongue. "Yeah, I see it. Hang on—I'll have you out of there in a jiff."

He walked over to an open tool cabinet and peered into it, muttering under his breath. As he did so, Kell looked casually around the room.

It was an impressive place, better equipped even than most of the professional droid repair facilities he'd been in and out of over the years. One of the side walls was nothing but high-end Cybot Galactica maintenance equipment, the machines interspersed with spare part bins and tool racks. Hooked into the machines or laid out on the nearby workbenches were partially dismantled sections of 434-FPC personal chefs, EG labor droids, and PD- and 3PO-series protocol droids. The equipment on the other side wall seemed to be dedicated to Industrial Automaton, SoroSuub, Changli, and GlimNova products, with a couple of SE4 servant droids and ASP-15 laborers on the tables. Tucked to one side, looking rather forlorn, was a WA-7 service unit that was probably a leftover from Republic days, most likely awaiting spare parts that Kell guessed were long since out of stock.

More ominously, a whole section of the back wall was devoted to 501-Z police droid equipment. A partially disassembled Zed was stretched out on one of the tables, and Kell took special note of its unusual upper arm, thigh, and waist sheathings.

"Here we go," the tech said as he plucked a long, thin probe from the cabinet. Returning to Kell, he slipped the probe down the droid's glove. A few seconds of silent fiddling, and suddenly the grip on Kell's wrist loosened. The tech pried the mechanical fingers a few centimeters apart, and Kell slipped his hand free.

"Wonderful," Kell said, massaging his wrist. "Thanks so much—I was afraid I was going to have to spend the whole Honoring stuck in here."

"No, that would be me," the tech said sourly. "Next

time you see a droid grabbing for something, do me a favor and stay out of its way, okay?"

"You got it," Kell promised. "That way out, right?"

"Right," the tech said. "The guard outside will take you back out to the courtyard."

The grand geyser eruption was the climax of the entire day, and it was as spectacular as the designers and techs had promised it would be. A multiple-stream spewing of sand and small pebbles burst from the largest of the cold-lava volcanoes, the various streams rotating and intermixing, with lights, sparklers, and glowings blazing among them, all to the accompaniment of music specially commissioned for the event. The crowd was as animated as the geyser itself, cheering and clapping and hooting their appreciation for every fresh nuance and unexpected switch-up. It was the crowning glory of the Honoring of Moving Stone, seen by thousands and sure to be talked about by thousands more in the days and months to come.

Standing alone on the presentation balcony, Villachor barely noticed the show.

Kwerve, the mysterious visitor had called himself. An innocuous name, certainly. A name that the vast majority of people wouldn't find the least bit unusual or interesting.

But Villachor wasn't most people. He was a Black Sun sector chief, and people in his dark line of work kept close tabs on one another. Bidlo Kwerve had been one of Jabba the Hutt's top people, until Jabba decided to make him the first official victim of his new rancor pet. A creature, if the stories were true, that Kwerve himself had found and helped present to the corpulent gangster.

So why had Villachor's visitor chosen that name? Was he saying he was working for the Hutts? That he *wasn't* working for the Hutts? That the ultimate goal of this operation was to bring down the Hutts?

If so, was part of that goal to set Villachor up in the organizational vacuum that Jabba's death would leave?

The insane part was that it would actually be possible. Xizor's blackmail files were hardly Black Sun's only weapon, but they were certainly one of the most potent. Being able to tag that population of Xizor's silent army could give a rival immense leverage, whether that rival chose to draw some of the hapless victims away or merely to expose them and thereby eliminate their usefulness to Black Sun.

Kwerve was right about another thing, too. At the moment, Black Sun was at the height of its power, but that position wouldn't last forever. Crime lords and organizations rose and fell like the tides, either destroyed by hungry rivals or corrupted and imploded by their own greed. That same chaos and death had brought down Sise Fromm, Alexi Garyn, Jorj Car'das, and countless others. Someday Jabba would fall, too.

As would Prince Xizor himself. Probably even sooner than Jabba, Villachor guessed, given his bitter rivalry with Lord Vader. Many crime lords underestimated Vader, or dismissed him as merely Palpatine's lapdog. Villachor knew better.

And when Xizor fell, where would Villachor be?

Alive, well, and someplace safe, he promised himself firmly. He would make sure of that. He would survive Black Sun, and if possible even prosper in the process.

Was Kwerve's offer the doorway to that freedom? Or was it simply another sadistic test, and its supposed doorway leading nowhere but sudden death?

He didn't yet know. But he was going to find out.

One way or another, he would end the Festival in a better position than when it began. Either he would have power and freedom or he would have a spare cryodex to offer to his master on Imperial Center. A cryodex, and very likely a freshly severed head.

Let Qazadi *dare* to test him then.

In the distance, the grand finale of Villachor's Honoring of Moving Stone was little more than a slightly blurry cloud of twinkling lights. "It's probably more impressive at ground level," Eanjer offered.

"Probably," Han agreed. "You ever been to one?"

"One of Villachor's?" Eanjer shook his head. "No. Just assuming. I have a question."

"Go ahead."

Eanjer paused, as if choosing his words carefully. "I realize that you and the others know more about these things than I do. But it appears to me that there are some serious problems with this plan that you seem to be ignoring."

"Such as?"

"Such as the fact that this Sheqoa fellow seems to be on to Bink," he said. "She as much as admitted that he'd seen through her act."

"He's a security chief," Han reminded him. "He wouldn't be very good at his job if he fell for something that obvious."

"Yes, but—"

"Don't worry, it's covered," Han said. "Whether he falls for the scam or not, he's still going to play along. That's all we need."

"But *why*?" Eanjer objected. "Why would he do that?"

"Because so far she hasn't done anything illegal or even threatening," Han explained patiently. "He'll want to give her enough line to trip herself up, and hopefully tag whoever she's working with while she's at it."

Eanjer shook his head. "Seems risky."

"Sure, but that's how men like that think," Han said. "Next?"

"Next what?"

"Next problem. You said there were several."

"Oh. Right." Eanjer paused again, apparently re-collecting his thoughts. "There's also the droids. I don't see why Kell's so happy about knowing how to disable all the simple ones when he admits we can't touch the police droids. I mean, it's not like we're going to have to fight our way through a phalanx of Three-pee-ohs or something."

"I hope not," Han said dryly, thinking back to that first ride with Luke and his two droids. "Three-pee-ohs can be really annoying."

"I'm serious," Eanjer growled. "Those Zeds are bound to be Villachor's first line of defense at his vault. How are we going to get the files and credit tabs with them standing in the way?"

"Easy," Han soothed. "We're still in the opening moves, remember? In two days we should have a better idea what we're up against. *Then* if you want to panic, you can go ahead."

Eanjer turned to face him, a baleful look in his eye. "You're incredibly confident," he bit out. "You know that? Especially for a small-time smuggler who's never pulled off a heist like this in his life."

"Who says I've never done this before?" Han countered. He hadn't, of course, but that was beside the point. "Besides, it's not about me. It's about getting the right people for the job." He gave Eanjer a lopsided smile. "And then giving them good leadership."

"Joke all you want," Eanjer growled. "You're not going to crack Villachor's vault with charm. Yours *or* Bink's."

"It's not about charm, either," Han said, gazing at the half-bandaged face as Lando's doubts about the man flashed to mind. Eanjer was seeking information and assurances. How much should he give him?

None, he decided. "It's about information," he continued. "Dozer and Kell got us some this afternoon. Lando and Zerba will get more in a couple of days. Let's just hang loose, and not panic, until we see the whole picture. Okay?"

For a long moment Eanjer continued to stare. Then, slowly, he turned back to the window. "I'm not convinced," he muttered. "But it's your show. We'll see if you can pull it off."

"I appreciate the vote of confidence," Han said, trying to keep most of the sarcasm out of his voice.

Eanjer nodded toward Marblewood. "Looks like they're done."

Han turned to look. Sure enough, the distant light show had ended, and the visitors were starting to flow out through the gates. "Yeah," he agreed. "So tomorrow is breakdown and reset, and then we get the Honoring of Moving Air?"

"*And* the moment of truth," Eanjer said grimly. "I just hope Winter and the others will be ready in time."

"They will," Han promised. "Like I said, the right people for the job."

CHAPTER ELEVEN

The Honoring of Moving Stone had been impressive. The Honoring of Moving Air, in Lando's slightly surprised opinion, was even more so.

By all sense and logic, it shouldn't have been. The Festival's first Honoring had included a lot of different materials for Villachor to work with: dust, sand, rocks, cold lava, and several motion sculptures that Lando had eventually concluded were stone-layered droids. It was hard to envision how simply moving air around could compete with a hand like that.

But Villachor's engineers had pulled it off. Part of the trick was to make the air visible, with tiny, glowing particles light enough to be suspended in the forced breezes of the air geysers, twist fountains, and cascaderies. Several of the basic geyser and volcano setups were being reused for those, resources Lando guessed would also be utilized for the other two Honorings.

But the main approach the engineers had used was to also bring the other senses into play. Delectable aromas wafted on the breezes, drifting across the grounds or spinning off the geysers and twist fountains, the mixtures continually changing and always complementary. Sounds had also been added: high-pitched bird calls accompanying the forced-jet cascaderies, complex music compilations from the various air geysers, with the volume and instrument balance shifting depending on where one stood. The sense of touch wasn't forgotten, and as Lando walked with Zerba toward the house, unexpected puffs of air occasionally tickled the hairs on the back of his neck or played gently across his cheeks and hands.

The droid outfits didn't look nearly as impressive as the moving-stone ones they'd worn two days earlier. But they made up for that with small air jets and aroma waftings of their own.

The whole show was so obviously designed for humans that Lando found himself wondering how the different aliens in the milling crowd were perceiving it. But as far as he could tell, they were enjoying it as much as he was. The handful of Wookiees towering over everyone else, in particular, seemed to revel in the air jets that ruffled through their fur.

Only later did it occur to him that there were probably color patterns and aromas in the mix designed specifically for aliens, embellishments his human senses were completely unaware of.

Rachele's data on Villachor had warned that he prized punctuality in his associates and demanded it in his subordinates, and Lando had carefully timed their arrival to be precisely on the five-hour mark that Villachor had specified. They were nearly there, and the crowd at the far end of the mansion had suddenly erupted into excited cheers, when the door swung open to reveal a silently glowering Sheqoa.

He didn't remain silent for long. "Who's this?" the big man demanded, his eyes on Zerba as he stepped into the doorway to block Lando's entrance.

"My assistant," Lando explained, gesturing behind him. "He carries the item for me."

Sheqoa's eyes flicked to the heavy-looking case hanging from Zerba's hand. "I'll carry it," he said, starting forward.

Lando took a quick step to the side, blocking him in turn. "*He* carries it," he said firmly. "I'll explain why once we're inside."

For a long moment the two of them locked eyes. Then, reluctantly, Sheqoa moved to the side. "Fine," he said, gesturing them forward. "For now."

Lando looked back at Zerba and nodded him forward, and the two of them walked through the doorway. Sheqoa closed the door behind them, cutting off the distant cheers, then brushed past them and led the way along the corridor the other guards had escorted Lando through two days earlier. This time, though, they got barely twenty meters before Sheqoa turned to the right, pushed open another door, and motioned them through.

It was a large room, of the type Lando had seen a thousand times before: wide and open, with curved and exquisitely decorated walls, chandeliers hung from high ceilings, and a hardwood mosaic floor. It was a gathering anteroom, the sort of place the rich and powerful built outside their ballrooms. It was the ideal place for guests to take a break from the music and dancing to chat with friends, renew acquaintances, or perhaps drift off to one of the side rooms for private talks and whispered deals. Virtually every large-scale sabacc tournament Lando had participated in had taken place in someone's version of a ballroom, and 90 percent of them had included an anteroom like this.

Most of those anterooms, however, hadn't included a phalanx of ten armored 501-Z police droids standing shoulder to shoulder, two rows deep, directly in front of the single door leading inward from the anteroom. In fact, now that Lando thought about it, none of them had.

"Who are you?" Villachor's voice came sharply from the side.

Lando looked over to see the crime lord striding toward them from another door at the north end of the anteroom, Lando's two guides from his previous visit striding along at his sides. "Master Villachor," he said, bowing his head. "Your timing is—"

"Who is this?" Villachor cut him off, glaring at Zerba. "You were ordered to come alone."

"Your pardon, Master Villachor, but I wasn't," Lando said, respectful but firm. "And my associate is an important part of the demonstration." He raised a warning finger. "And I wouldn't get too close to him if I were you."

"This is *my* house," Villachor retorted. "*I* make the rules and give the orders, not you."

"Of course," Lando said, noting that, despite his bluster, Villachor and his escort chose to stop a cautious five meters away. "My point is simply that I want to make sure my case doesn't leave here without me. At least, not in one piece."

In retrospect, he decided, he probably should have eased into the subject in a more diplomatic way. The words were barely out of his mouth when Sheqoa and Villachor's two bodyguards had their blasters out and pointed at the visitors.

"Easy," Lando said hastily. "It's only a small charge, just enough detonite to destroy the case and its contents. Nothing more." He pursed his lips. "At least, that's the theory," he added. "That's why I have someone else carrying it."

For a moment he gazed into Villachor's eyes, trying to ignore the blasters pointing at him. Then Villachor stirred. "Also why you're not standing too close to him, I assume?"

"Exactly," Lando said. "There are advantages to rising through the ranks."

"Indeed," Villachor murmured. He lifted a finger, and to Lando's relief the blasters were reluctantly lowered. "Open the case. I want to see it."

Lando turned to Zerba and nodded. Zerba nodded back and set the case gingerly down on the mosaic floor. He did something complicated-looking with the fasteners, then swung open the top and turned the case around toward Lando and Villachor.

There, in all its quiet glory, was their counterfeit cryodex.

Lando held his breath, forcing his expression to stay calm. He'd never seen a cryodex before—even Rachele hadn't been able to find any holos of them. He only had Winter's assurances that their version was even close, let alone a perfect copy.

To his relief, it apparently was. "Very nice," Villachor said, taking a couple of cautious steps forward and craning his neck for a closer look. "Of course, anyone can fake a casing. What matters is what's inside."

"Which we're ready to demonstrate," Lando said, gesturing to the door behind the Zeds. "Shall we?"

"Not *we,* Master Kwerve," Villachor corrected. "I'll get the card. You'll wait out here."

"My instructions are to never let the cryodex out of my sight," Lando said.

"You'll wait out here," Villachor continued with strained patience, "while I retrieve one of the cards and bring it to you."

He headed for the door, leaving his two bodyguards behind. "It would be simpler for all of us to go in there together," Lando offered. "I think it highly unlikely that either of us would try to steal anything."

"You can wait out here alive, or you can wait out here *not* alive," Villachor said. "Your choice."

"Point taken," Lando said, feeling a twinge of annoyance. Dozer and Bink had insisted that a really good con artist should have no trouble talking his way into Villachor's vault, especially with the cryodex as bait. Bink had gone so far as to offer to bet Lando fifty credits that he could do it, with Zerba acting as judge as to how hard he'd tried.

Lando had turned down the bet. Now he wished he'd taken it.

Still, while a look inside the vault would have been helpful, it wasn't necessary. Han had assumed that Villachor would keep them out, and the plan took that into account. At least he and Zerba were going to get a look at Villachor's entry procedure.

Most vault owners used some combination of keypads, voiceprints, and visual recognition to gain access to their property. But Villachor had come up with an added twist. He walked up to the nearest of the Zeds, held his hand directly in front of the droid's face, and waited. The droid stared at the hand a moment, then gave a short bow and stepped out of the way. Taking the cue, the rest of the droids similarly moved to the sides, leaving the entryway clear. Villachor walked through the group to the door, folded down a keypad from the wall beside it, and punched in a series of numbers. An almost inaudible background hum faded away as the magnetic seal cut off, and with a deep thud the door swung inward. Villachor walked through the opening, tapping something on the wall as he passed, and the door reversed direction and thudded closed behind him.

Lando eyed the guards, wondering if a casual question or two might give him a clue as to what the Zed had been looking for with his scan. But none of them seemed like the small-talk type.

He obviously couldn't ask the Zeds themselves, either. In fact, at this point even approaching the droids was out of the question. Along with heavy blasters holstered at their right hips, each of them also carried a coiled neuronic whip lashed to its belt with quick-release straps.

Lando winced as memories flickered back. He'd run into neuronic whips before—sometimes quite literally—and while they were primarily used as interrogation and slave-control devices, they also made terrific close-range weapons. This particular model, he knew, had a primitive droid brain of its own built into the handle, which would take a quick electronic echo sample from whatever skin or hide the whip was touching and instantly adjust the electric discharge to the precise frequency and pulse pattern for maximum pain to that particular being's nervous system.

He wasn't sure what the whips' maximum setting was. He wasn't anxious to find out.

They'd been standing there for about five minutes, and Lando was visually tracing a complex knot mirror on the wall to see if it had indeed been woven from a single thread, when Villachor returned, a black data card in his hand.

"Excellent," Lando said, walking toward him and holding out a hand. "As we agreed, I'll decrypt *one* file, drawn at random—"

He stopped as Villachor twitched the data card out of his reach. "Something you should bear in mind," the other said quietly. "I know the sound the cryodex makes when it's simply reading and decrypting a file. I also know the sound it makes when it's copying an entire data card. If I hear that latter sound, I'll kill both of you. Do you understand?"

"Of course," Lando said. Winter had implied that she'd seen cryodexes in operation back when she'd worked the royal palace on Alderaan. But he had no idea whether it had occurred to her to add the proper sound effects to her tricked-out datapad. "I have no intention of copying the card or trying any other tricks," he said as sincerely as he could manage. "Why would I take such a foolish risk when there are much higher profits waiting down the line?"

"*If* I agree to work with you."

"You will," Lando assured him. "Those higher profits are there for you, too."

For another moment Villachor stared at him. Then he held out the data card. "One file," he instructed. "And I want to see the readout. Do you have to enter an access code first?"

"I do, and it's already in place," Lando said, wondering uneasily if that had been a test. Winter hadn't mentioned anything about an access code.

Of course, she hadn't said there *wasn't* any coding, either. Presumably that was something a diplomatic tool would have as a matter of course.

He headed back to Zerba, glancing casually at the card as he walked. Matte black, with the proper-sized Black Sun logo in shiny black in the center. Perfect. "Any particular item number you want?" he asked as he handed Zerba the card and then stepped back away from him.

"Surprise me," Villachor said dryly.

Lando gestured to Zerba. "Surprise him."

Zerba nodded and keyed the cryodex. There was a soft, almost chuckling sound, and with a small flicker the display came on to show the bony-ridged head and flabby jowls of a Houk. Lifting the cryodex from the case, Zerba held it out toward Lando. "Here we go," Lando said, peering at the display. The guards' blasters were still pointed at the floor; Winter must have gotten the sound effects right. "A Houk named Morg Nar. He's currently employed by a crime lord named Wonn Ionstrike who runs an operation out of Cloud City on Bespin."

"What about him?" Villachor asked.

"Ionstrike seems to have it in for Jabba," Lando said, trying to ignore the warning bells going off in the back of his mind. There'd been something odd in Villachor's voice just then. "He's paralyzed—moves around in a hoverchair—and has apparently dedicated himself to putting Jabba out of business. Nar is the strongbeing who gets to do all his heavy lifting."

"And?"

"And it seems that Nar is actually on Jabba's payroll," Lando said, mentally crossing his fingers as he scrolled through the file the fake cryodex was pretending to read from the unreadable data card. Han had supplied the pointer toward Nar, keying off a few bits of gossip he'd picked up in Jabba's place on Tatooine, and Rachele had used her sources to fill in some of the gaps. But there was no way to know if the gossip or Han's assessment of it had been accurate. "He's supposedly helping Ionstrike throw out the Hutts, but behind the scenes he's helping Jabba close down some of his operations in an orderly way, while shifting the rest to other venues that Ionstrike doesn't know about."

"And Black Sun's interest in all this?"

"It doesn't say, but they're obviously looking to play the third hand in the game," Lando said. "It looks like Prince Xizor hasn't made a move on Nar yet, but he's probably just waiting for the right moment."

"Interesting," Villachor said. "There's only one problem."

Steeling himself, Lando turned around. "Which is?"

"There's no possible reason that particular file should be on that particular data card," Villachor said calmly. "That one is *osk* through *usk,* and neither Nar, Ionstrike, Jabba, Hutt, Bespin, nor Cloud City begins with that letter."

And suddenly the blasters were no longer pointed

at the floor. "And now," Villachor continued quietly, "you'll tell me what's *really* going on."

From the whistling and churning sounds coming from the northern end of Marblewood's grounds, Dayja surmised that the Grand Tempest spectacle that was supposed to be the early evening highlight was in full swing. From the approving roars coming from the crowd, it seemed to be fully living up to Villachor's promises and the audience's expectations.

For Dayja, though, the far more interesting show was going on somewhere past the mansion's southwest door fifty meters away.

Only he had no idea how that show was going. Or even exactly what it was.

He scowled to himself, taking a sip of the sour-tang drink he'd been nursing for the past hour. Eanjer had been remarkably cagey about the identities of his co-conspirators in this little con game they were running. He'd refused to give Dayja any names or even the participants' areas of expertise.

But Dayja had seen all of them the night he'd dropped onto their balcony, so he at least had their faces.

And two of the group had gone through that door fifteen minutes ago. Under escort from Villachor's head security man.

He eyed the door, wondering if there was some way he could talk or hotwire his way through it, or whether he should even try. The last thing he wanted was to find that he'd been scammed himself, that Eanjer and his gang were actually working for or with Villachor and Black Sun.

The second-to-last thing he wanted was for the gang to get themselves killed. Especially if they mentioned Dayja and his interest in Qazadi before they died.

"Hey," a voice came from behind him. "You."

Dayja turned. The two men walking up to him had the look of hired muscle, with the suspicious expressions and solid, confident strides he'd long since come to associate with men on a mission who were carrying concealed blasters.

But neither of them was wearing the glazed-stone key pendants he'd spotted on all of the official Marblewood security men. Extra thugs Villachor had hired for the occasion? Or something else entirely?

He had a fraction of a second to decide on his persona. Under the circumstances, he decided, slightly oblivious visitor would be his best approach. "Me?" he asked, putting on a blandly cheerful expression.

"Yes, you," one of the men said. He took a couple more steps forward, leaving his partner standing backup behind him. If they were thugs, at least they were well-trained ones. "What are you doing here? You're missing the big show." He pointed toward the sounds of the crowd.

"I know," Dayja said with a sigh. "But my lady friend needed to use the 'fresher. I'm waiting for her to come out."

The man glanced around. "What 'fresher?"

"There," Dayja said, pointing to the mansion door. "The 'fresher's in there, right?"

The man stared at him, probably wondering how anyone could be this stupid. "The 'freshers are over by the west courtyard," he said, again pointing toward the distant noise. "North and south of the main food pavilions."

Dayja dropped his mouth open a couple of millimeters. He threw a startled look at the mansion, then turned back. "But she said the south—" He broke off and sent another look at the door. "At the Covv'ter venue, the 'freshers were always inside."

"This isn't the Covv'ter estate," the man reminded Dayja patiently. "South 'fresher's about a hundred fifty meters that direction."

"You'd better get there before she gives up and finds someone else to enjoy the Honoring with," the second man added.

"Oh, no," Dayja breathed, letting his eyes go wide. "No. She wouldn't—oh, blast it all. Excuse me."

He turned and hurried away toward the crowd and the refresher stations, making sure to use the most inept shambling trot in his repertoire. A carefully controlled stumble gave him the chance to glance behind and see if they were following.

They weren't. They weren't interested in Dayja. They were interested in that door.

And whatever the reason for that interest, he suspected Eanjer's team wasn't going to like it.

A couple of security types had chased a lone visitor away from the area around the otherwise deserted garden area by the southwest door, but aside from that there hadn't been any activity south of the twist fountains since Lando and Zerba had gone into the mansion twenty minutes ago. Readjusting the electrobinoculars pressed against her face, Winter refocused on the nearest of the building's skylights—where there was nothing to be seen—shifted her view to the massive crowd watching the Grand Tempest—where there was way too much to be seen—and then returned to the door.

"Did you spot Bink?" Tavia asked, coming up to the window beside her.

"Sorry—I lost her in the crowd," Winter apologized. "But she seemed fine half an hour ago when Sheqoa left her for the meeting with Lando and Zerba."

"You're sure?" Tavia asked. "You remember her distress signals, right?"

"Yes," Winter assured her, passing up the obvious reminder that she would carry that list of subtle hand signals to her grave. "There were no signals. In fact, as near as I could tell from the body language, they seemed to be getting along quite well together."

"Of course they were," Tavia said with a sigh. "Another of Bink's many talents is getting people to do what she wants."

Including you? "It's a useful skill in your line of work," Winter said instead.

"I know," Tavia said. "And I don't mean to be prickly. I'm just . . . people say you can get used to anything. But I've never gotten used to this. I don't think I ever will."

"Maybe this is the last time you'll have to," Winter suggested. "The credits from this job should let you quit the business for good."

"It should," Tavia said tiredly. "But it won't. Bink's promised a hundred times to quit, practically every time she thinks she's looking at the big score. But somehow the credits are never as good as they looked going in, or the fence steals them, or we have to abandon most of the take, or there are other complications. There are always complications."

"Sometimes life itself seems to be nothing more than a series of interlinked complications," Winter agreed, forcing her mind away from the horrible complications that Palpatine and his Empire had forced on her and Leia and so many, many others. "All of them doing their best to get in the way of what you expected or wanted." She lowered the electrobinoculars, giving her eyes a moment to rest. "What were you expecting to get out of life, Tavia?"

"To be honest, just more of the same," Tavia said. "More poverty, more living hand to mouth, more of the two of us running and fighting the universe and trying to make it through one more day. What I *wanted* . . ." She smiled suddenly. "Remember I said that Bink liked what she does because she's good at it? That's what it is for me and electronics work."

"You can make a good living that way," Winter murmured.

"And I've tried," Tavia said, her smile fading. "I've tried, and tried, and tried. But every time I get a foothold somewhere, Bink manages to find something wrong with the job. Either it doesn't pay like it should, or the boss is rude, or the jobs I'm getting are menial or insulting, or my co-workers drink their soup too loudly. There's always something."

"Life's also sometimes a series of compromises."

"And I'm willing," Tavia said. "I try to tell Bink it'll be all right, that I can work through the problem. But you know Bink. Before I know it, we're back out on the street and she's breaking into someone's private office looking for that next big score."

Winter nodded ruefully. She knew people like that, many of them, men and women who could feel alive only when they were risking everything and defying the odds.

They had their place, certainly. In fact, without them the Rebellion would probably have come to a screeching, bloody halt long ago. But at the same time, she couldn't help but feel intensely sorry for them.

One day this war would be over. Maybe one day all wars would end. Distantly, she wondered what such people would do then.

"But at least we don't have to live one day at a time anymore," Tavia continued with a touch of wry humor. "Now it's more like month to month. Definitely an improvement. Maybe after this it'll be decade to decade."

"We can only hope," Winter agreed, turning back to

the window and raising the electrobinoculars back to her eyes. Still nothing.

She could also only hope that, whatever was going on in there, Lando was on top of it.

There were times, Lando reflected, when you were outnumbered, outgunned, with all exits blocked, and holding a losing hand. In situations like that, there was only one option.

Bluff.

"Interesting," he said calmly. "Are you sure?"

"Are you calling me a liar?" Villachor demanded.

"Am I?" Lando countered, putting an edge on his voice. He was a high-ranking member of a shadowy criminal organization, after all. Men like that didn't intimidate easily. "I saw that card, Master Villachor. I don't remember seeing any letters on it."

"They're not on the card itself," Villachor said. "And you're stalling."

"Then what makes you think this card has anything to do with those letters?"

"Master Villachor is asking the questions," Sheqoa growled.

"Master Villachor is angling for a second free sample," Lando said bluntly. "First of all, there's no reason for Prince Xizor to organize his blackmail files according to such an obvious system. In fact, I can think of a dozen reasons for him *not* to do so. An unauthorized person searching for a specific file could search until Imperial Center goes dark without finding it."

He let his face harden. "And second, I happen to know that one of the Falleen slang terms for Hutt is *slivki*. Which starts with the letter *senth*, which *does* fall in the *osk* to *usk* range."

Villachor's eyes flicked to Zerba, back to Lando.

There was still suspicion in his eyes, but there was also a growing uncertainty. *"Slivki,"* he repeated. "You're certain of that?"

"Quite certain," Lando said frostily. "I was there when a Falleen called a Hutt that to his face. It took the owner of the place three days to clear out the wreckage." He gestured toward the door. "Go ahead and look it up if you want. I'll wait."

Villachor looked at Zerba again. "Perhaps later," he said. "Morg Nar, you say."

"Yes," Lando said. "And that's *all* I'll say. You've had the sample I promised. You're welcome to check that out as well. But the moment of decision has come."

For another moment Villachor gazed at him, his face expressionless. It seemed to be the man's favorite pose, probably designed to keep the recipient off-balance while he thought something through. "*One* decision, at least, is at hand," he amended. He lifted his finger, and once again the three blasters were lowered toward the floor. "I'm no longer ready to kill you where you stand."

"I think that's a decision we can all get behind," Lando agreed.

"But the decision of whether or not to deal further with you is still in the future," Villachor continued. "Before I take any such step, I need to know more about your operation and how I would fit into it." His eyes narrowed. "For one thing, I need to know what *you* get out of any such deal."

"I'm what you might call a talent scout," Lando said with an offhanded wave. "I study the field and find those I think could do better elsewhere. If I'm right and the person joins the group, I'm paid a small fee."

"That fee being dependent on the value of the client?"

"Something like that," Lando said.

"And that value would be enhanced if the client brought valuable objects or knowledge to your superiors?"

"Most likely."

"Good," Villachor said briskly. "Then you won't mind if I speak directly to your superior. After all, who can better define the value of these files?"

Lando suppressed a grimace. Han had warned him that the conversation would probably end up here. "My superior usually doesn't like to make direct contact this early in the negotiations," he said. "I assure you that I have full authority to answer any questions and make any deals."

"I'm sure you do," Villachor said. "You'll nevertheless bring him to me."

Lando pretended to consider, then gave a little shrug. "Very well. I'll contact him tonight with your request and bring you his answer tomorrow."

"That answer had better be *yes*."

"I'll bring you his answer tomorrow," Lando repeated.

Villachor's lip twitched. "Not tomorrow," he said. "Bring the answer in two days, during the Festival of Moving Water. Your visit will be less conspicuous that way."

"Again, whatever you want," Lando said, inclining his head in a bow. So Villachor wanted Lando's visits to get lost in the Festival crowds, did he? Maybe he was genuinely starting to consider defecting from Black Sun.

Or else he was just trying to make Lando think that. Mind games, unfortunately, were a multidirectional spacelane. "One last question, if I may," he said. "Simply for my own curiosity. If the data card wasn't marked, how did you know which one it was?"

"It came from that slot in the file box," Villachor said.

"Ah," Lando said, nodding. And a spread of seven letters per card also implied there were five of them, just as Eanjer's contact had said. So far, this mysterious informer had been dead-on with everything he'd said.

"Again, that makes perfect sense. Your other invited visitors presumably see the card as their rather bleak futures are being read to them, and you don't want them knowing how the information is organized. Speaking of which . . ." He half turned and held out his hand. "Bib?"

Obediently, Zerba pulled out the data card and stepped forward. He handed the card to Lando, then immediately backed up again and carefully lowered the cryodex back into its case. "Your property, Master Villachor," Lando said formally, offering Villachor the card.

Silently, Villachor took it, the bulk of his attention on Zerba as he manipulated the booby-rigged case. "You call him Bib?" he asked.

Lando shrugged. "A small joke. Recognizable only to those who are already familiar with Jabba's history."

"Yes," Villachor said. "Kwerve and Bib, together again."

"Indeed," Lando said. Bib Fortuna and Bidlo Kwerve had been two of Jabba's highest-ranking servants, always jockeying for power and position until Kwerve's death and Fortuna's subsequent promotion to majordomo. Han had suggested that bringing Hutt history into their aliases would add an extra layer to Lando's story that Villachor might find intriguing. From the expression on Villachor's face, it looked like Han had been right. "I'm glad you appreciate it."

"I do," Villachor said. "Two days, Master Kwerve."

"Two days," Lando promised, giving another small bow.

Ninety seconds later they were once again out in the clean air, with the rumbling of the Festival crowd refreshingly welcome after the dangerously tense silence of the vault anteroom. "Well?" he asked quietly.

"Well what?" Zerba answered. "Did I switch the cards, or have the data come through yet?"

"The first," Lando growled, annoyed in spite of himself at the other's flippancy. Zerba's neck had been as much on the line in there as Lando's had, after all.

Or maybe not. It was possible that the extra senses Balosars claimed to have had given Zerba some insight into that face-off that Lando hadn't picked up on. Could Villachor's threat have been pure bluff, nothing more than a probe to see if Lando would bend under unexpected pressure?

"Yes, I switched the card," Zerba said calmly. "Actually, the answer to the other one is yes, too. Whether Bink and Rachele will be able to get anything useful out of it is a different question."

Lando shrugged. "We'll find out soon enough."

"So is *slivki* really an insulting term for Hutt?"

"Not that I know of," Lando said. "But that's the great thing about slang. There are so many versions and varieties—in *anyone's* language—that you can never be sure you've gotten all of it. Villachor can search the archives for the rest of the month without ever being able to prove I was bluffing."

"Nice," Zerba said. "I'll have to remember that one. Ready to head back?"

Lando nodded. "Let's go."

"I think not," a deep voice muttered in his ear as a set of strong fingers locked unexpectedly around Lando's right arm. "Nice and quiet."

Lando twisted his head around and found himself looking up at a pock-marked human face half a head above his own, a floppy-brim hat pulled down almost to the eyebrows. "Who are you?" he demanded. "What in the—"

"He said *quiet,*" another voice cut him off.

Lando turned in the other direction, to see that a second man had similarly taken hold of Zerba's arm. "Whoever you are, I suggest you let go of us immediately," Lando said coldly. "We're special guests of Master Villachor himself. One shout from me to any of the security men roaming the grounds—"

"Oh, you wouldn't want to do that," the first man admonished. "My little friend hates loud noises."

Lando winced as the hard muzzle of a blaster pressed into his ribs beneath his right arm. "I suppose we should try to keep him happy," he murmured.

"That's the spirit," the first man said encouragingly. "We'll be heading around the south end of the house and going out the southeastern service entrance. Much quieter over that way. Folx, be a good man and relieve your friend of that heavy-looking case, will you?"

"I wouldn't do that," Lando said quickly as the second man reached for the cryodex case. "Especially since your little friend hates loud noises."

The second man paused, his hand touching the case's handle. "Wolv?" he asked.

Wolv hesitated, and Lando could sense his shrug. "He can keep it," he said. "We'll figure out something at the other end of the ride." He dug his blaster a little harder into Lando's side. "Come on, step it up. We haven't got all night."

"We're going on a ride, then?" Lando asked as the group picked up their pace.

"A nice little ride to a nice quiet room," Wolv said. "Where we'll have a nice little talk."

"And after that?" Lando asked.

"After that—" Wolv shrugged again. "Well, that'll be up to you."

"Yes," Folx agreed, his voice dark and ominous. "Mostly."

"They're heading for the southeast gate," Rachele's tense voice came over Han's comlink. "They've already started around the end of the mansion."

"Yeah, got it," Han said, striding along the edge of the crowd watching the Grand Tempest, ducking past the people gathered around the food pavilions and trying desperately to strike the balance between speed and caution. If this was a genuine kidnapping attempt, he needed to get there as fast as he could.

But if it *wasn't* genuine—if it was a trick of Villachor's to draw out any allies Lando and Zerba had hidden in the crowd—then rushing full throttle to the rescue would do nothing but play perfectly into his hands.

"They're opening up the distance," Winter warned from her observation spot in the suite. "If you don't hurry, you're never going to catch them before they hit the gate."

"We can't go any faster," Dozer's voice snarled over Han's comlink. The ship thief sounded even more frustrated than Han felt. "We do, and they'll tag us for sure."

"What a wonderful idea," Bink cooed over the comlink, her voice still perfectly matched to her air-brained persona despite the tense danger facing them at the moment. "I haven't been shopping there in *ages*. When do you want me to meet you?"

"Just stay where you are," Han ordered her. "You're too far away to help, and we can't have you blowing your cover. Is Sheqoa there?"

"No, no," Bink said, still cooing. "I can hardly *wait* to tell you about this new guy I've met."

"Yeah, we can't wait, either," Dozer growled. "Come on, kid—we need to know whether he and the rest of Villachor's people are in on this."

"Ooh—got to go," Bink said, pumping some extra excitement into her voice. "Here he comes now. You're going to love him, Jessie—he is *so* hot. *And* so cool."

Han snarled an old curse under his breath. Bink's impromptu verbal code was hard to wade through, but *so hot and so cool* had to mean that she couldn't tell whether Sheqoa had any of the tension telltales that would indicate the abduction was Villachor's idea.

More delay and more uncertainty. And all the while Lando and Zerba were getting farther and farther out of range.

And then, suddenly, it was too late. "Dial it back," Rachele's tense voice came over the comlink. "You'll never get there in time now. Not without sprinting across open ground where they'll be bound to tag you."

Reluctantly, Han slowed from his fast walk to a slower one and shifted direction instead toward the southwest gate. "At least tell me Chewie's on it."

"He's on it," Rachele confirmed. "He headed for the roof the minute they were grabbed. Maybe he can get one of the airspeeders in the sky fast enough to follow them."

"There they go," Winter cut in. "Looks like an Incom PT-81 airspeeder—dark red, with yellow pinstripes around the front and canopy."

"Heading?"

"East," Winter said. "They're lifting . . . they're in the lower airlane. Lifting again . . ."

"Chewie?" Han demanded.

Even someone like Eanjer who didn't understand Shyriiwook would have had no trouble recognizing the anger and frustration in Chewie's roar. He was in the air, but the kidnappers were already gone.

"Too late," Rachele said, sounding close to tears. "We've lost them."

CHAPTER TWELVE

"Well?" Han demanded.

"Nothing," Rachele said, her head almost touching Winter's as the two of them peered together at Rachele's computer display. "There are just too many dark red PT-81s in the city's records."

"And the pinstripes are probably aftermarket add-ons," Dozer muttered. He was sunk deeply in one of the chairs, staring morosely at the tips of his boots.

Han looked around the room. Tavia was peering at another computer display, her face grim. Kell was sitting across from Dozer, tapping the fingers of his left hand soundlessly on the padded arm of his chair and fiddling with a blaster power pack with his right. Eanjer was standing at the window, framed against the lights of the city, staring out into the night as if his prosthetic alien eye could pierce the darkness and spot the missing airspeeder.

"I'll know it when I see it," Winter offered hesitantly. "For whatever that's worth. I could see some scratches and dents in the sides."

"But that kind of minor damage won't be in any official records," Rachele said.

Like Han hadn't already known that. "Tavia?"

"Sorry," Tavia said, shaking her head. "Those hats were blocking most of their faces. The bits I could see just weren't definitive enough for a search. And the ID tag had some kind of sparkledust on it that made it impossible to read from this distance."

Han nodded heavily as he keyed his comlink. Dead ends, all the way across the board. Whoever these guys were, they knew what they were doing. "Chewie? Anything?"

The Wookiee's report was short, frustrated, and as negative as everyone else's.

"Well, keep at it," Han told him. "It's sure as Kessel that none of the rest of us are going to spot him from here."

Chewbacca acknowledged and keyed off.

"Maybe we *should* go out," Rachele suggested hesitantly. "We've got another airspeeder on the roof, and Dozer could probably boost a few more off the street."

"And then what?" Han demanded. "Zoom around at random and hope we spot them?"

"It would beat hanging around here waiting for them to come get us," Dozer muttered.

"For who to come get us?" Kell asked.

"That's the point, isn't it?" Dozer bit out. "We don't have the slightest idea who they are. And until we do, we haven't got a hope of tracking them down." He jabbed a finger at Han. "You ask me, the thing to do now is get out of here. And I mean *right* now. Sooner or later, one of them will break. We need to be somewhere else when that happens."

"No," Han said firmly before anyone else could voice an opinion. "If they get loose, they'll be coming back here. We stay."

"*If* they get loose?" Dozer retorted. "Don't be ridiculous. Who do you think they are, Revan and Malak? I'm telling you, they're hammer squash. And so are we if we stay here."

"So go," Han said, waving at the door. "But you walk through that door and you're out."

"Oh, really?" Dozer snarled. He bounded to his feet and grabbed for his blaster—

And froze, the weapon halfway out of its holster, his eyes wide as he found himself staring down the barrel of Han's fully drawn blaster.

"Really," Han assured him quietly.

Dozer flashed a look around the room. Whatever he saw in the others' expressions apparently wasn't very encouraging. "Fine," he muttered, lowering his weapon back into its holster and flopping back down into his chair. "So what's our next move?"

That was, Han knew, a damn good question. In a single heartbeat this whole grand scheme had gone sideways, and suddenly he was flying blind. How this would end he couldn't even begin to guess.

Except for one thing: they were going to get Lando and Zerba out alive. Guaranteed. Han had lost enough people for one lifetime. He would see Villachor in hell before he lost anyone else.

"We change course," he said, putting away his own blaster. "Rachele, forget the airspeeder. Lando and Zerba were talking to Villachor. Start making a list of people who might not like that."

"Got it," Rachele said, and turned back to her computer.

Han threw a look outside at the deceptively cheerful lights of the city. Somewhere, somehow, they needed to catch a break.

And they had better catch it soon.

"You've certainly been busy little banthas," Wolv commented as the airspeeder wove its way through the nighttime traffic. "I understand this was your second audience with Master Villachor." He cocked his head. "Or was it your third? That glitterstim peddler *was* one of yours, wasn't he?"

"I didn't realize Master Villachor's guest list was under such scrutiny," Lando said, feeling his forehead creasing. A *glitterstim* peddler? When had a glitterstim peddler come into any of this?

"Everything Master Villachor does is under scrutiny," Wolv said. "Especially when it interferes with his proper business activities." He pointed to the case on Zerba's lap. "So is that the fancy glitterstim? Or is that the payout?"

"I have no idea what you're talking about," Lando said with as much haughtiness as he could manage. "But I promise you that when Master Villachor learns about this, he is *not* going to be pleased."

"Oh, I agree," Wolv said, an evil smile flicking briefly across his face. "The only question is whether or not you two are going to go down with him."

"I wouldn't count him out just yet if I were you," Lando warned.

"And I wouldn't count on him digging you out of this," Wolv shot back. "Your best bet right now is to open that case and hand over whatever's inside. You do that, and I promise you'll walk away."

Lando shook his head. "I have my orders."

The other snorted. "Fine—have it your way. But I'll tell you right now that when we get where we're going we'll be meeting someone who can get that thing open without scattering it over the downwind half of the city. My offer lasts until then, and *only* until then. Think about it." He looked pointedly at Zerba. "Both of you."

He held his pose another few seconds. When it was clear that neither of his prisoners was going to say anything, he shook his head in disgust and turned back around to face forward.

Lando looked sideways at Zerba. Zerba twitched an eyebrow and looked down at his binders. Lando followed his eyes and saw the small gap at the binders' connection.

So Zerba had already gotten his restraints open. No surprise there.

Unfortunately, with the binders connected to chains anchored to the airspeeder's floor, there was no way for Zerba to get to Lando's without their kidnappers noticing.

Zerba had obviously figured that out, too. He opened his hand slightly, giving Lando a glimpse of a small three-prong lockpick he'd been hiding somewhere, and twitched his eyebrow again in silent question.

Lando sighed. Equally unfortunately, he'd never mastered that particular school of lock picking. He shook his head, following it up with a short hunching of his shoulders. Zerba wrinkled his nose in sympathy and closed his hand again around the lockpick.

Still, the day wasn't lost yet. If Zerba could take advantage of his freedom to jump out of the airspeeder the second they touched down and manage to get himself and the cryodex to safety, Lando might be able to bluff or bargain his way to at least a temporary reprieve. Any breathing space he could buy would give him time to come up with something more permanent.

Or would give that same time to Han and the others.

He hoped they were working on a rescue plan. He hoped it very much.

"Can they be traced back to you?" d'Ashewl's voice came from Dayja's comlink.

"I don't know," Dayja said, scowling at the PT-81 zooming along eight vehicles ahead. Something about the way it was moving warned him that they were about to turn again. "I don't think so. But that's not the point. The point is that if Eanjer and his team slide off the edge, this whole operation is likely to slide down with them. I may not be able to restart my own game in time to get into Marblewood before the Festival ends."

"There's no indication that Qazadi intends to leave immediately after that," d'Ashewl reminded him.

"There's also no indication that he doesn't," Dayja countered. Ahead, sure enough, the airspeeder turned right and dropped into a lower, slower airlane. Dayja matched the maneuver, then dropped one level more. He still didn't know whether they'd spotted him or whether all this weaving in and out and around the city was just their idea of being cautious. Either way, it wouldn't hurt to let them get a little more distance on him.

"If it slides, it slides," d'Ashewl said with a hint of impatience. "I'm sorry, but I can't let you move in on this. And I *absolutely* can't let you call in any Imperial authorities."

Dayja ground his teeth. But d'Ashewl was right. If Qazadi got even a hint that Imperial Intelligence was on his back trail, the whole group would scramble, and he and d'Ashewl would be going back to Imperial Center empty-handed.

But if Dayja couldn't interfere directly . . .

"Got an idea," he told d'Ashewl. "I'll get back to you."

He broke the connection before d'Ashewl could reply. The airspeeder's tag had a subtle coating of sparkledust that was highly effective at disguising the letters and numbers from ordinary electrobinoculars. But Dayja's electrobinoculars were hardly ordinary.

If he and d'Ashewl were the only two Intelligence agents in Iltarr City, that didn't mean they were all alone. Not exactly.

Steering with one hand, trying to judge the best moment to climb back into the kidnappers' airlane, he keyed his comlink.

"*Onith* three *besh,*" Eanjer repeated, gesturing toward Rachele. "Anything else? . . . All right. Thanks." He keyed off.

"That was your contact?" Han asked.

"Yes," Eanjer said, his eye holding Han's gaze for only a second before he turned back to Rachele.

Turned with what looked suspiciously like a flicker of guilt or discomfort on his face.

Han wasn't the only one who noticed it, either. "Funny how he just happened to witness that airspeeder taking off," Dozer commented, his voice thick with suspicion. "*And* was close enough to see the tag with his own unaided eyes."

"Because there's no other way he got that number," Tavia agreed. "Not with sparkledust all over it."

"He has access to certain resources," Eanjer said. "What are you complaining about? We got the ID, didn't we?"

"That's not the point, is it?" Dozer countered. "Call me paranoid, but I like to know a little something about the people I'm working with. Especially since free information usually has hooks in it."

"Oh, we didn't get it for free," Eanjer said ruefully. "Trust me. I'll be paying through the nose for this little gem."

"Here it is," Rachele spoke up. "Well, well. It seems our kidnappers are running around in an unmarked Iltarr City police car."

"The *police* are on to us?" Kell asked, sounding stunned. "Oh, that's just great."

"Maybe not," Tavia said. "Remember how many local officials are on Black Sun's payroll. This could be some ploy of Villachor's to get more information out of Lando."

"But why snatch him from the grounds instead of just keeping him inside and squeezing him there?" Winter asked. "Unless Han was right about him trying to see who else Lando might have with him."

"I don't know," Rachele cut in, her fingers still dancing over her keyboard. "But here's the interesting part. I've heard whispers about a quiet and *very* unofficial police interrogation setup in an abandoned factory in the industrial area about ten kilometers east of the spaceport. Ten to one that's where they're headed."

"I don't know," Eanjer said doubtfully. "My contact said they're just flying around. If they have a place to go, why not just go there?"

"Because they need to make sure they're not being followed," Tavia told him.

"It's better than that," Han said, an idea starting to take shape in his mind. If they really knew where the kidnappers were going, and if he and the others had time to prepare before they got there . . . "They need to whistle up a bomb expert to get that case open."

"You're right," Kell said, a hint of growing excitement in his voice. "If they're waiting for him before they land, maybe we can beat them to the factory."

"Makes sense," Rachele said. "As soon as they land, they're vulnerable. This way, they're in motion all the way until they're ready to slice the case."

"I don't know," Dozer warned, looking around at the others in the room. "No offense, but even at seven-to-two odds, I don't like our chances."

"It's more like three to two," Han told him. "You, me, and Chewie."

"Hold on," Rachele warned. "If you think the rest of us are just going to sit this one out, you're badly mistaken."

"She's right," Winter said firmly.

"Not about herself she isn't," Han said, just as firmly. "Rachele's way too well known around this city. Anyone sees her, and she's under the hammer for sure." He gestured. "That goes for Eanjer, too. And with Bink still over at Villachor's, we can't risk anyone finding out she's got a twin, Tavia, so that lets you out."

"Which still leaves Kell and me," Winter pointed out.

"Right," Dozer said sarcastically. "And your areas of combat expertise are?"

"I know enough to know we could use some airpower," Kell said. "If you can get me some kind of atmo-fighter, I can fly it."

Dozer shot a frown at Han, then looked back at Kell. "You're kidding."

"Not at all," Kell said.

"He can," Winter seconded. "I've seen him fly."

"Unless you don't think you can boost something like that in time," Han said. The nebulous plan was starting to coalesce . . .

Dozer squared his shoulders. "Where do you want it delivered?"

"Just boost it and then keep it somewhere at the spaceport until I call for you." Han keyed his comlink. "Chewie? I need you back here. You're picking up Dozer and Kell and heading to the spaceport. We've got a plan."

He got an acknowledgment and keyed off. "Rachele, I need you to find me some heavy automatic weapons. Tavia, I need you to rig up some remote triggers for them."

"No problem—I already have a bunch of remotes," Tavia said, getting up and hurrying toward her room.

"Good," Han said. "Rachele, can you track down some weapons?"

"No need," Winter said. "I already know where there's a cache."

Han stared at her. "Really? How?"

She shrugged. "I *did* get here a full day before you did," she reminded him. "I wasn't just sitting around doing nothing."

"I guess not," Han conceded. "What kind of security has it got?"

"Nothing we can't handle," Winter said. "It's the demo stockpile of a Rodian who fancies himself an up-and-coming weapons dealer. It's small, but we should be able to find what we need."

Tavia reappeared, a black belt bag in hand. "Here are eight of them," she said, handing the bag to Han. "I hope that'll be enough."

"Thanks," Han said, peering into the bag. Standard trigger-switch type, comlink-enabled. "Winter?"

"Eight should do fine," she confirmed.

"Good," Han said, closing the bag again. "Come on—we'll take the other airspeeder. Rachele, see if you can pull up some floor plans for that factory. If you can, shoot them to me and Chewie."

"Got it." Rachele bent again over her computer.

"You've all got your jobs," Han told the others. "Get busy."

The factory was old and dilapidated, three stories tall, with peeling paint and windows layered with decades' worth of dust and wind scratches. It was the kind of place that no one would look at twice, no one would want to go into, and absolutely no one would ever put down good credits to rent.

Which made it the perfect place for a police force to set up an off-the-line interrogation room.

"You realize you're going to have to fire these things

blind," Winter warned as they set up the fifth of the six E-Web heavy repeating blasters they'd appropriated from the arms dealer's supply shed. "You try linking those triggers into electrobinoculars and cross targeting, and the data stream will be way too obvious for the other side to miss. They'll chase it straight back to you, and that'll be it."

"I know," Han said. "Good thing I don't care if we actually hit anything."

She paused long enough to flash him a look. "You aren't planning on *hitting* anything? Then what in space did we bring them for?"

"'Cause they're great little noisemakers," Han said, crouching down and hooking one of Tavia's triggers onto the firing mechanism. "Something to get everyone looking in all the wrong directions. Chewie and Kell will be doing all the real damage."

"Hopefully only where they're supposed to," Winter murmured.

"Chewie can handle it." Han eyed her over the E-Web's barrel. "Question is, can Kell?"

"I told you, I've seen him fly."

"Yeah, but you didn't say you'd seen him fly combat," Han reminded her. "How well do you know him, anyway?"

Winter shrugged as she finished anchoring the E-Web's tripod and climbed back into the airspeeder. "He joined up with Mazzic about six months ago, two months after I did. He seems competent and loyal enough, but I get the feeling he's got some history. Family stuff, probably."

"Yeah, well, who doesn't?" Han growled as he got into the airspeeder beside her. Keying the repulsorlifts, he lifted and headed for the spot he'd picked for their final emplacement.

"And he hasn't specifically said so," Winter added hesitantly, "but I think he's also Alderaanian."

Han felt his lip twist. Leia had put up a good front, both during the Death Star escape and afterward. But through it all, even when she'd been cheering him and Luke for their victory at Yavin, he had seen the deep and lasting pain behind her eyes.

He'd recognized the same pain in Winter. And now that he thought about it, he realized that she was right. Kell was carrying that same burden of memory.

Han had tasted that same pain, though not nearly to the extent Leia and Winter and Kell had, and he knew all too well that it did things to people. Sometimes it made them depressed, uncaring, and lethargic. Sometimes it made them permanently angry and unable to care about anyone or anything for a long, long time.

Sometimes it made them recklessly suicidal.

"Don't worry, he'll be all right," Winter reassured him. "He knows what's at stake, and he understands his duty. Whatever you told him to do, he'll do it."

"Well, if he doesn't, he'll answer to Lando," Han said. His comlink signaled, and he slipped it from his belt. "Chewie? What've you got?"

For once, the news was good. "Great," Han said, scanning the sky. The main city airspeeder traffic to the south and west was as thick as ever, and there were steady lines of intercity traffic flying back and forth across the less populated areas north and east of them. But nothing seemed to be heading in their immediate direction. "You and Kell wait for my call. And send Dozer out here right now—he might as well help with the E-Webs."

He got an acknowledgment and keyed off.

"Dozer would probably rather hang back at the spaceport," Winter pointed out.

"I wasn't giving him a choice."

"Maybe you should," Winter said. "Of everyone in the group, he's the one I worry about the most."

"He's okay," Han said. "He's just feeling a little out of his expertise, that's all."

"A ship thief who hasn't had any ships to steal until now," Winter said, nodding. "So why did you bring him in?"

"He was going to be front man until Lando showed up," Han said, swinging the airspeeder around and setting down beside a broken and rust-covered conveyer belt motor.

"Does that mean he resents Lando?" Winter pressed as she hopped out and got a grip on the last E-Web's barrel.

"Not Dozer," Han assured her as he grabbed the other end and helped her lift the weapon out of the airspeeder's cargo bay. "You give him the same credits for half the work and he'll laugh all the way home. We'll set this one up on the other side of that regulator."

They were halfway through the E-Web setup when Han spotted an airspeeder dropping out of the night sky toward them. For a bad moment he thought they'd run out of time, but as the vehicle came closer he saw it was one of theirs.

It settled to the ground, and Dozer climbed out. "How we doing here?" he asked as he strode over to them.

"Almost done," Han told him. "Chewie said you got Kell something?"

"Better than just *something,*" Dozer said, shading his eyes from the mass of city lights to the west as he looked at the factory. "I found him a Z-95 Headhunter. AF-4 version, even, with all the bells and toots you need to turn old buildings into piles of dust." He gestured. "Though if *that's* the target, I probably could have given him a couple of sonic pistols and called it a night. Where do you want me?"

"There," Han said, pointing toward a half-collapsed shed. "Should be enough room for you and the airspeeder in there. You'll be handling the two E-Webs on this side. Winter and I will be on the other side with the other four."

"Okay," Dozer said hesitantly. "So we're attacking as they're coming in?"

"Nope," Han said. "We wait for them to get inside."

"Ah," Dozer said, even more hesitantly. "And once we open fire, we keep the whole thing from collapsing on top of them *how*?"

"Actually," Han said, "we don't."

"There," Wolv said, pointing out to their right. "That must be them now."

Lando followed the other's finger. In the distance, two airspeeders had left the main traffic airlanes and were headed downward, aiming somewhere off to the left.

"About time," Folx grumbled. He turned the airspeeder into a tight curve, shifting around toward the others' projected grounding point.

Leaning toward the middle of the seat, Lando craned his neck to look between their two captors. They were flying over an industrial area, only about half of which seemed to be still in use. Directly ahead, their most likely destination was a three-story monstrosity of a building, standing all alone amid piles of rubble, that looked like it had been abandoned on day one of the Clone Wars.

"You watch that kind of talk," Wolv warned darkly, slapping his partner with the back of his hand for emphasis. "When the *chief* sounds scared, we're talking someone you don't want to mess with."

Folx snorted. "The chief's an old Ugnaught," he said scornfully. "One crime boss is pretty much like the next."

"You want to say the wrong thing and get your brains fried, go right ahead," Wolv countered. "Just do me a favor and save it for when you're with Cran or Baar instead of me, okay?"

Folx snorted again. "You're an old Ugnaught, too."

"Maybe," Wolv said. "But the way an Ugnaught gets to be an old Ugnaught is by being smart. So do me a favor. Be smart."

Folx shook his head, and Lando could imagine him rolling his eyes. "Fine. If it'll make you feel better."

Aside from a couple of holes in the factory's upper windows, the place didn't seem to have any openings at all, and for a moment Lando dared to hope that the rendezvous would take place outside. There weren't a lot of places to run to out there, but at least running would be an option.

But as they approached the building, a wide door behind a partially collapsed loading dock began to ponderously roll up. The other two airspeeders were already heading in, the first barely even waiting until the opening was big enough before threading the gap with a nonchalance that bordered on the arrogant. The second airspeeder gave the door an extra couple of seconds, then followed.

Lando looked at Zerba. *First airspeeder has the bodyguards,* he mouthed silently.

Zerba nodded and hunched his shoulders. *Where are they?* he mouthed back.

Lando gave him a wink and turned away. There was, after all, no reason why Zerba should worry, too.

Because he was right. Han and the others *should* be here by now. Chewie should be crouched by one of those collapsed equipment sheds with his bowcaster, carefully picking off segments of their repulsorlift cluster to drive Folx into a rapid but still controlled landing. Han should be somewhere closer to the docking bay, firing away with that overrated BlasTech DL-44 of his and keeping the other two airspeeders busy. Another of their group, maybe Dozer or Kell, should be pumping out cover fire for both of them, while someone else—*anyone* else—should be roaring up in an airspeeder for a fast grab and a faster getaway.

But there was nothing. No one was out there shooting. No one was even visible. No vehicles of any sort, anywhere. Plenty of sheds and hiding places where someone could lurk, but none of them with the kind of quick hit-and-fade capabilities a rescue like this required.

Because a hit-and-fade was the only way this would work. Once he and Zerba were inside the building, all bets were off. Lando was no structural engineer, but even from out here it was painfully clear that launching a firefight in that place would have an even chance of bringing the whole thing crashing down on whoever was inside.

Lando looked ahead at the door still grinding its laborious way open. Was it possible that there would be no rescue because the team didn't know where he and Zerba were?

Ridiculous. Winter and Tavia surely had witnessed the kidnapping from the suite, and Rachele surely must have been able to track the airspeeder somehow. Folx had been flying them around town for over an hour, more than enough time for Han to put together something clever.

Unless there would be no rescue because Han had decided not to bother.

Lando took a careful breath. No—that was crazy. Han wouldn't do something like that. *Yes,* Lando had told him off good the last time they'd parted company; and *yes,* he'd mentioned something about never wanting to see Han again. But Han *had* invited him into this job, and Lando had already backed off of that whole never-meeting-again thing. And Han certainly had seemed to accept Lando's apology.

Besides, even if Han wasn't ready to forgive him, surely Chewie wouldn't turn his back on two teammates in trouble. That wasn't like him.

At the very least, someone in the group ought to care enough about *Zerba* to try for a rescue.

So where were they?

"Take a good look," Wolv advised, waving a hand around. Lando snapped out of his dark thoughts to see that they were nearly to the open door. "It may be the last view of the outside world you ever see."

"Don't worry," Lando said as calmly as he could. Men like him, he reminded himself firmly, didn't intimidate easily. "We'll be coming out again just fine. The question is, will *you*?"

Wolv just snorted.

And then they were through the doorway, heading across an impressive expanse of dimly lit open floor, the sound of the airspeeder's engines echoing off the high ceiling. Ahead, the other two airspeeders had landed, and a half dozen large men were standing around them, blaster rifles held at the ready. Folx brought the airspeeder smoothly to the floor at a respectful fifty-meter distance, and he and Wolv climbed out, leaving Lando and Zerba alone.

"Now?" Zerba murmured. He twitched his fingers, bringing his three-prong lockpick into view.

"Not yet," Lando murmured back as their captors strode over to the waiting group. "The other guards are watching us."

"Right," Zerba said, his voice shaking just a little. "We're going to need a distraction, aren't we?" He gave the case in his lap a significant tap. "I figure we've only got one. But it's a doozy."

"Easy," Lando cautioned. "I'm not ready to cash in on the game just yet."

One of the guards gestured to the second airspeeder. The door opened, and a short elderly man climbed out. The bomb expert, probably. He moved aside to make room for a second figure—

Lando stiffened. Climbing out of the airspeeder behind the old man was a Falleen.

"Lando?" Zerba asked urgently.

"Not yet," Lando said, wondering why he was even bothering. He didn't know if that was the same Falleen that Dozer had tangled with at the Lulina Crown, but it almost didn't matter. He was a Falleen, he was almost certainly Black Sun, and suddenly a quick death by detonite didn't seem all that unreasonable anymore.

But Lando was a gambler. A true gambler never folded when he still had cards left to play. "Not yet," he repeated. "Han may still come through."

Behind them came a sudden dull thud. Lando looked over his shoulder to see that the roll-top door had slammed shut, sealing the factory away from the rest of the universe.

Han hadn't come through.

He and Zerba were on their own.

Across the field came the faint boom as the factory door closed. "Now?" Winter asked.

Han clicked his comlink. "Chewie? Kell? Dozer? *"Now."*

CHAPTER THIRTEEN

Finally, *finally,* the order came.

Practically before that single long-awaited syllable had finished coming through his comlink, Kell had the Z-95 in the air, the combination of repulsorlifts and main engines jamming him back into his seat, the indicator lights on his control board looking like a bleed-through of the stars above and the city lights to both sides.

The waiting was over. He was going into battle. Maybe not the intense combat that haunted both his dreams and his nightmares, but combat nonetheless.

And with the end of the waiting came the end of at least some of the doubts.

He'd worried that he would hesitate or, worse, freeze. He hadn't. He'd worried that he might not be able to handle a ship that, for all his earlier confident assurances, he'd had little experience with outside of game simulators. It seemed to be working fine. He'd worried that he might turn tail and abandon the mission. So far that hadn't happened, either.

He'd worried that he might not be able to face death for the sake of his teammates. That one, unfortunately, still lay ahead. And if and when it came down to that, he still had no idea how he would react.

But he didn't have to know. Not yet. Courage wasn't

a matter of taking the whole mountain in a single massive leap. Courage was taking it one step at a time, doing what was necessary now, preparing for the next step, and refusing to worry about whether some step in the future would be the one that would break him.

He was in the air, flying his fighter with adequate skill, and heading in the right direction. Three steps down. One at a time to go.

He keyed the Z-95's comm. "Chewie?"

There was an acknowledging roar, wordless confirmation that the Wookiee was in position behind him.

And maybe *that* was the real secret to courage, Kell realized suddenly: someone at your back, and the assurance that you weren't facing the mountain alone.

He straightened his shoulders. Enough philosophy. He had a fighter beneath him, a set of weapons at his fingertips, and teammates who needed rescuing. "Stay with me," he told Chewie. An order or a plea, he wasn't sure which. "I'm going in."

Wolv and Folx had been cleared by the Falleen's men, and the conversation had shifted over to the Falleen himself, when a group of ground-floor windows exploded inward, and the whole factory lit up with a multiple blaze of sustained blasterfire.

"No, no, no," Zerba moaned, hunching down as if trying to disappear into his seat. "Lando, what's he doing?"

"Getting us out of here," Lando said between clenched teeth. "Here—get these off me."

"Get us out of here *how*?" Zerba demanded, twisting his hands free of his binders and leaning over to work on Lando's restraints. "In body sacks? He's going to bring the whole place down on us."

"He's got a plan," Lando insisted, peering up at the

ceiling. So far the blasterfire was just tearing up the windows and flying harmlessly over everyone's heads. Was all the noise and fury supposed to be a diversion, with Han expecting them to grab their airspeeder and make a run for it?

Because if that was the plan, it was a rotten one. None of the broken windows was nearly big enough for their airspeeder to get through. Even if it was, this particular vehicle's design meant he or Zerba would have to get out of the backseat and go around to the driver's-side door to get to the controls, and he doubted that Wolv or Folx or the Falleen would just sit by and let that happen.

Speaking of whom . . .

"Hurry it up," Lando bit out, craning his neck to look through the airspeeder's canopy. At the first salvo, the bomb expert and the Falleen had dived back inside their vehicle, with the rest of the group taking up defensive positions. Wolv and Folx had joined them, but now both were looking back toward their own vehicle.

And even fifty meters away, with all those flashes glinting off the airspeeder's canopy obscuring their vision, Lando could see that they'd spotted the fact that one of their prisoners was free of his binders and the second soon would be.

"Why?" Zerba countered. "You got someplace else you want to be?"

"Yeah—anywhere but here," Lando shot back. Wolv was looking back and forth between the different vectors of blasterfire sizzling the air above his head, probably looking for a pattern. The minute he figured out the safe timing, Lando suspected, he would be heading their way.

Across the factory, one of the building's mid-wall supports abruptly snapped as the fire through the adjacent window sliced across its edge. The section of roof directly overhead slumped a couple of meters, the sudden change in pressure snapping two smaller supports and sending pieces of metal shrapnel arcing across the open space to rain down bare meters from the three airspeeders.

"Anywhere but here sounds great," Zerba snarled. "Only how are we supposed to get there? This place is—" He broke off as another support snapped and scattered itself across the landscape. "Is a deathtrap," he finished. "What's Han trying to do, kill us?"

Lando was still trying to come up with an answer to that one when, with a deafening crash, a group of windows below the ceiling blew in. The place was coming down, all right, and while the Falleen's airspeeders were probably armored, his and Zerba's definitely wasn't. He looked up toward the blast, wondering if any of the debris was coming toward them, wondering if he would see the chunk of wall or girder that would end up killing him.

The fireball of the explosion was still swirling through the cloud of smoke when a Z-95 Headhunter shot through the opening into the factory.

Kell winced as bits and pieces of the wall he'd just blown open slammed and rattled against the Z-95's canopy. He'd definitely cut that one a bit too close. Something to remember for the next time.

Assuming there *was* a next time. He'd barely cleared the blast debris when he was suddenly being hammered by heavy blasterfire raking across his underside. His first reflexive assumption was that Han or Dozer had glitched their targeting, but a second later he realized that the attack was coming from the men crouched beside the other two airspeeders down there.

A *heavy* attack, too. Those were seriously high-powered blasters they were firing, way too powerful for civilian equipment. Even the Z-95's armor, designed for full-bore space combat, was creaking and popping under the onslaught.

It would have been highly satisfying to zoom to the other end of the factory, spin his fighter around, and nail them all with a counterbarrage from his KX5 laser cannons. But he didn't dare. The E-Web attack had showed how dangerously unstable the factory was. The engine backblast and flash heating required to pull off that kind of attack could bring the whole place down. It would be a pretty pathetic rescue if Lando and Zerba ended up crushed to death because they were stuck in that eggshell of an airspeeder.

Fortunately, that problem was about to be fixed.

"Bogies at sixty-five and seventy-six," he called out, pitching the fighter a few degrees as he shot past for a better view of the factory floor. He took a moment to glance at his display, at the factory schematic that Rachele had sent and the targeting grid Chewbacca had overlaid on it. "Friendlies at fifty-eight. Drop target: sixty-seven. Repeat: drop target, sixty-seven."

The far wall was coming up fast. The plan was for him to fire another burst, make a new hole, and get out before he got himself shot down. Instead, he pulled back on the throttle, doing a quick skid turn to kill his forward momentum and coast to a stop. It was risky, and Chewie probably would have something to say about it later if they all survived.

But Han's plan was so insane, and the execution so impossible, that he just had to stick around and see for himself if it actually worked.

Some things in life really *were* worth risking everything for. The rest . . . well, it was always a judgment call.

Kell had blown through the wall and disappeared inside, he'd called out the targeting zone to Chewie, and the E-Web covering fire hadn't yet brought down the whole factory. So far, things were going according to plan.

And now, from out of the gloom, blazing its way across the night sky, was the *Falcon*.

Han clenched his hand into a fist. Chewie was one of the best pilots he'd ever seen, but this was the sort of gamble even Han would normally dismiss out of hand.

But when you had no other choice, you had to go with it. "Come on, Chewie," he muttered under his breath as the ship shot toward the hole in the wall Kell had made. The opening was way too small for the *Falcon* to fit through, of course, and there was no way any of them was going to try enlarging it, not with the shape the building was in. Even letting Kell in and out had been a calculated risk.

But Chewie didn't need to make the hole any bigger. All he needed to do was to play a single round of the galaxy's biggest game of hit-the-Hutt.

And he had exactly one chance to get it right.

The *Falcon* was gaining a little altitude now, and Han could hear Chewbacca easing back on the throttle as he fine-tuned his run. A quick surge of frustration and guilt washed through Han as he watched—by all rights, that should be him up there. He should be the one flying his ship and making this work.

But if he'd taken that job, who would he have left to organize the ground action? Dozer? Winter?

No. For better or worse, whether it made sense or not, he was the leader of this group. Down here, where the blaster bolts were flying the thickest, was where he needed to be.

Nearly there. A little more altitude . . . a bit less . . . slowing just a fraction more . . . shifting the approach vector just a shade . . .

And then Chewbacca was there, yanking up the bow

with a fraction of a second to spare, the ship angling up and over the edge of the building and shooting off toward space.

And only because Han was specifically looking for it did he spot the squat metal cylinder that popped out of the rear of the ship and arced neatly through the smoking hole into the factory.

Lando's first horrible thought was that the rumble approaching from outside was a missile, heading in to level the building and disintegrate every shred of evidence of what had happened here. But at the last millisecond the dark bulk flashed past the ragged opening the Z-95 had made, angling upward and roaring over the roof. He felt the whole place shake with the backwash, and a fresh rain of debris began falling on them. An extra-big piece of ceiling tile hit Lando's side of the canopy, shattering it and sending bits of transparisteel flying.

Without warning, something big and solid slammed into the floor directly between their airspeeder and the Falleen's men, the impact sending up a huge cloud of dust and duracrete chips. Lando winced back, wondering if it was in fact the missile nose cone he'd been anticipating a few seconds earlier.

It wasn't a missile. It was a CEC Class 1 escape pod.

The kind carried aboard the *Falcon*.

And with that, he finally got it. "Come on!" he snapped to Zerba, forcing open the airspeeder door and rushing out into the dust and falling tiles and metal shards. Running bent over at the waist to stay out of the blasterfire still pouring through the windows, he headed for the escape pod.

He was halfway there when Zerba caught up, the cryodex case clutched tightly to his chest. "Where are we going?" he panted.

"Inside," Lando told him. He dropped to one knee beside the pod and cycled the hatch. "It's Han's idea of armored sanctuary."

"But it's only a one-passenger pod."

"It'll be tight," Lando agreed as the hatch popped open. "You can stay out here if you'd rather."

Zerba didn't bother to reply.

"They're in!" Kell shouted toward the comm. "Hatch is sealed."

"Great," Han called back, and for the first time in hours Kell could hear some actual relief in his voice. "Kell, Dozer—take it down."

With a suddenness that caught Dayja completely by surprise, the multiple E-Web blasterfire hammering the factory shifted from covering to demolition.

His comlink signaled. "Dayja, what's going on out there?" d'Ashewl demanded. "Police nets are lighting up from here to Grackleton with reports of a firefight in your area."

"Oh, it's definitely a firefight," Dayja confirmed, peering at the factory from what he hoped would continue to be a safe distance. "But at the moment, it's seriously one-sided. E-Webs on the outside, a Z-95 Headhunter on the inside."

And some variety of Corellian light freighter, he didn't add, frowning as he searched the sky. The freighter had made a single run at the place and done nothing except veer off at the last second, then had headed off and hadn't been back. Either he was on some really wide return circle or he'd turned tail and made a run for it.

The first didn't make much sense. The second seemed way out of sync with what he'd seen of Eanjer's group.

And then he got it. The freighter pilot hadn't gotten cold feet. He'd done whatever he was supposed to do for the operation—distraction, reconnaissance, whatever—and then had taken off because he was hurrying to get back to the spaceport before the police and port authorities reacted to all the noise and started paying attention to what was happening in the sky above them.

Which meant the freighter was the one item Eanjer's team had brought out here that they weren't intending to abandon after the rescue.

Interesting. He wished now that he'd gotten a better look at it.

With a distant *whoof* a section of factory roof caved in, followed immediately by a partial collapse of the north wall. The attackers seemed to be deliberately bringing down the building, which begged the question of how they expected their kidnapped teammates to survive.

Maybe they were already dead. Maybe that was what the freighter and the Z-95 had been sent in to confirm.

Another section of the roof went, this piece apparently hitting some old tank on the way down and sending up a plume of gas that looked green and vaguely evil in the reflected light from the blasterfire. A second part of the northern wall collapsed.

And with that, the kidnappers had apparently had enough. Even as the blasterfire continued to wreak havoc, Dayja saw the three airspeeders shoot out from the freshly gaping holes and claw for altitude.

This time he was ready and got some good image captures with his electrobinoculars. Whoever they were, he should be able to track them down.

"Dayja? What's happening?"

"Looks like it's mostly over," Dayja said as the E-Web fire came to a halt. The Z-95 had now emerged and was settling to the ground nearby, and he could see three figures hurrying toward the wrecked building from different directions. "But it wouldn't hurt to keep the police away from the area for a few more minutes. Can you manage that without showing your hand?"

"*My* hand, yes," d'Ashewl rumbled. "But your team's hand may already be dead. If the kidnappers were indeed corrupt police, I don't know how they're going to spin this incident without Villachor and Qazadi concluding that Eanjer is connected with someone official."

"I don't know, either," Dayja said. "But I'm looking forward to finding out."

Lando already had the hatch open and was working his way out of the escape pod when Han and the others reached them. "You okay?" Han asked, offering a hand.

It seemed to him that Lando hesitated a fraction of a second longer than he needed to before taking the proffered hand. But his grip was solid enough. "Thanks," he grunted as Han helped him out. "Nice move, by the way. I gather that was Chewie in the *Falcon*?"

"Yeah," Han said, looking around. The devastation looked even worse in here than it had from the outside. "Figured if you got winged by the pod, you wouldn't be as mad at him as you would have been at me."

"Probably not." Lando half turned. "Zerba?"

"I'm here." A thin hand popped into view through the hatch. "A little help, please?"

"Hand me the case," Dozer instructed, crouching down beside the pod.

The hand disappeared and reemerged with the cryodex case. Dozer took it and handed it behind him to Winter, then helped Zerba out.

"Thanks," Zerba puffed. He turned a baleful eye on Han. "Don't *ever* do that again."

"Which part?" Han asked. "Shooting the bad guys off your back, or saving your life?"

Zerba considered. "Okay, good point," he conceded, sounding marginally mollified. "Can we get out of here now?"

"Sure," Han said. "Dozer, take them to your airspeeder and get them back to the suite. Kell can go with you, too."

"We leave the gear?" Dozer asked.

"All of it," Han confirmed. "Winter and me'll go to the spaceport and wait for Chewie."

Some orders, he reflected, only had to be given once. Dozer was already picking his way through the debris, Lando and Zerba right behind him.

"Interesting tactic," Winter commented.

Han turned. She was staring at the dented escape pod, an odd expression on her face. "They're designed to handle deep space, atmo penetration, and bumpy landings," he reminded her. "I figured they could hold off anything the kidnappers had with them." He waved a hand upward at the stars showing through the wrecked roof. "And that, too."

"It did seem to do the job," Winter agreed. "I was thinking more of what would have happened if Chewbacca had missed."

"Lando would probably never want to see me again," Han said. "Come on, let's go see if Chewie's made it back down yet."

"So you have no idea who they were?" Tavia asked as she handed Lando a drink.

"Only that there was a Falleen in the group," Lando said, taking a careful sip. Cognac was a notoriously unpredictable drink, the taste and quality varying widely between systems and often even across different regions of the same world. Thankfully, Tavia had picked a good, smooth one. "No idea whether it was Dozer's friend

Lord Aziel, or this Qazadi person Eanjer's contact claims is hiding in Marblewood."

"Not sure it matters which it was," Kell said. "They're both on the same team, aren't they?"

"He wasn't either of them," Zerba said. He was gripping his own cognac glass with both hands, clearly still shaken by the evening's events. "He was probably someone's bodyguard."

"How do you know?" Lando asked, thinking back. He hadn't noticed any weapons or body armor that might have led Zerba to that conclusion.

"He was young," Zerba said. "Way too young to be anyone with that kind of prominence."

"He ran back inside the airspeeder when the firing started," Lando pointed out.

"He got the bomb guy into the airspeeder when the firing started," Zerba corrected. "*Then* he got in. But he left the door open."

"So that he could direct their return fire," Winter murmured. "He did a decent job of it, too. Even firing blind, they were able to take out one of the E-Webs before Kell got inside."

"Well, whoever they were, they weren't with Villachor," Bink said positively. "Neither Sheqoa nor any of the other security guys I saw showed the slightest indication that they knew something big was going on."

"They must not have been monitoring the police comms, then," Tavia pointed out. "The whole network was going crazy with all the reports. I'm kind of surprised that they didn't drop the hammer on you before you got out of there."

"What, charge in on a Black Sun interrogation?" Lando countered. "Not likely."

"So what does all this mean for the mission?" Eanjer asked. He sounded calm, but the restless twitching of his fingers betrayed his tension.

"Nothing, really," Han said. "Whoever was behind it, all he knows is that Lando's got an impressive organization behind him. That's the story we were pitching in the first place."

"Except now that Lando's been tagged he needs to lie low," Bink said. "I guess Dozer's up next. Or you, Han."

It seemed to Lando that Han's lip twitched, just a bit. "Probably," Han conceded. "We can talk about that later." He turned to Rachele. "You ready?"

"Yes," Rachele said, her eyes looking troubled. "But I don't think you're going to like it."

"Ready with what?" Zerba asked.

"The analysis of the sensor data from the card you planted," Han told him, looking around. "Dozer?"

"Right here," Dozer said, emerging from the kitchen hallway with a sandwich in his hand. "Rescue work makes me hungry." He dropped onto the couch beside Tavia, forcing her to scoot to the side to make room. "Ready."

Han gestured to Rachele. She tapped her datapad, and the image of a mostly rectangular room appeared in the air above the holoprojector. "Villachor's vault," she identified it. "As we've already noted, it was built into the junior ballroom—note the curved corners and conversation alcoves."

"Which are probably guard posts now," Lando murmured.

"Mostly," Rachele confirmed. "Also note the high, undulating ceiling. That's the ballroom's original glitter coat up there, by the way, with the layer of armor plate we discussed earlier set into the between-floors gap above it."

"Glitter coat, huh?" Bink asked sourly. "Terrific."

"What's glitter coat?" Kell asked.

"The fancy man's interior décor of choice," Bink told him. "Nice, smooth, resilient, glitters in every type of lighting—you get the idea. Problem is, it's impossible to cut through without scattering clouds of white sparkly flakes all over the place."

"Which means no popping in, grabbing the loot, and popping back out without anyone noticing," Tavia added. "Once we start the operation, our footprints will be all over it."

"What kind of security has he got inside the vault?" Bink asked.

"Oh, you're going to love this," Rachele said. She keyed her datapad again, and a dozen figures appeared around the edges of the vault. "Remember those Zed police droids Kell said Villachor's got? Here's where they hang out."

"Plus the ten on guard outside the door," Lando said. "Armed with blasters and TholCorp OT-7 neuronic whips, just to make things interesting. Getting past that group is the first step in the entry procedure."

Chewbacca turned to Han and warbled a question.

"I don't know," Han said. "Kell? You know any way to knock out a Zed?"

"I'd have to look into it, but I'm sure it's possible." Kell waved a hand. "Of course, *anything's* possible. It's in the execution where you get hung up."

"A high-power jab in the motivator or memory core will do it for most droids," Bink pointed out.

"Hard to do through the kind of armor Zeds have, though," Kell said.

"And don't forget the whips," Lando added. "Those things pack a serious punch, and Villachor would hardly give them to his guards if they could be used against them. That implies extra electrical shielding."

"Actually, it's worse than that," Kell said. "Remember I told you the Zeds I saw had sheathings on their upper arms, thighs, and waists? Those limb parts are where the droids have thin parallel cylinders instead of a single wider limb part, and the waist is where the torso also gets extra narrow."

"So?" Bink asked.

"So with those sheathings in place, you can't tell whether they've got the original parallels and torso tube, or something wider," Kell said. "In other words, you can't tell whether or not that's really a Zed."

"Whoa," Dozer said, his sandwich momentarily forgotten. "Are you saying some of those Zeds might actually be armored *human* guards?"

"Exactly," Kell said. "It's really pretty clever. You go in with a tight-spectrum motivator punch like Bink said, all set to knock out a droid. Only the human inside the armor isn't bothered in the slightest and knocks you on your butt."

"While something designed to stun or paralyze a human won't work on a droid," Han said.

"And only Villachor will know which are which," Kell said.

"Speaking of droids, is there any way to deal with those floating cam droids outside?" Dozer asked. "I don't like the idea of someone in a monitor room watching everything we do in there."

"Not a problem," Tavia assured him. "We've got a gadget designed to fog their view. Not enough to trigger any alarms or self-diagnostic sequences, but enough to wipe out facial recognition. With all the dust, extra body heat, and repulsor containment fields they'll have out there, they should assume that's all that's bollixing their holocams."

"Is that going to be good enough?" Dozer asked, looking at Han.

"It should be," Han said. "We'll just have to make sure we don't stand out of the crowd."

"Until we need to," Lando murmured.

"Right," Han nodded.

"So how do we get it into the grounds?" Kell asked.

"Already done," Bink said calmly. "I planted it two days ago, on our first trip in."

"You could have told us," Dozer growled.

Bink shrugged. "I assumed it would be obvious."

"Let's get back to the Zeds," Zerba said. "Do we have any idea whether those were droids or humans outside the vault? More important, do we have any idea what kind of entry code they were running? There wasn't anything obvious I could see."

"You're right, it wasn't obvious," Rachele agreed. "Turns out there was a scent on Villachor's fingers that the Zed was sniffing."

"A *scent*?" Lando echoed, feeling his mouth drop open. "You mean like perfume?"

"Cologne, actually," Rachele said. "Either Rezi Eight or Rezi Ten—the two formulas are very similar."

Kell looked at Tavia. "You've got to be kidding. You put in a *scent sniffer*?"

Tavia shrugged. "Han said full-spectrum," she reminded him. "We gave him full-spectrum."

"Though we were mostly looking for airborne material cues," Winter added. "We didn't expect to pick up Villachor's preferences in vanity adornments."

"Just as well you did," Rachele said. "Unfortunately, I'm guessing the scent cue changes every day, and unless we can get into his private 'fresher cabinet I don't know how we're going to figure out which one we need."

Kell shook his head. "This just gets better and better."

"We haven't even started," Rachele warned. She keyed her datapad, and a large sphere connected by a short pillar to a wide, flat platform appeared in the center of the room. "Here's the safe itself," she said. "It's a six-meter-diameter sphere, the outer part made of duracrete poured over a hullmetal mesh."

"A *sphere*?" Winter asked. "Sounds a little crazy."

"Crazy like a Twi'lek," Zerba said sourly. "A square or rectangle has corners you can cut off for quick entry. A sphere doesn't. Even with a full-length lightsaber it'd take you forever to whittle off enough to get inside."

"And you'd probably run into honey traps along the way," Tavia added. "Poured duracrete is perfect for tucking in hidden gas pockets and shaped detonite charges."

"You said the outer part was duracrete," Han said. "What about the inner part?"

"That's even worse," Rachele said. "At the center of the sphere is the actual safe: a rectangular, closet-sized cabinet made entirely of Hijarna stone."

Lando looked around. From the puzzled looks on the rest of the faces, the others weren't any more familiar with the term than he was. "Which is?" Dozer prompted.

"A hard, black stone that's exceptionally hard to cut and absorbs blasterfire without even noticing it," Rachele said. "The most prominent example is a partially ruined fortress on the planet Hijarna. The point is that even Zerba's lightsaber isn't going to get through that. Not in the amount of time we'll have."

"Well, *Villachor* doesn't cut his way in each time," Bink pointed out. "Why should we?"

"Exactly," Tavia agreed. Her face held her usual quiet disapproval for these things, Lando noted. But at the same time, he could see some professional interest starting to peek through. This was a tactical challenge, and if there was one thing Tavia liked, it was a challenge. "Can you run us through his routine?"

"Sure," Rachele said. "He comes into the vault after being vetted by the Zeds outside—"

"Or by the human guards," Lando murmured.

"By whoever or whatever's inside the armor," Rachele agreed. "The vault's magnetic seal goes off when he opens the door, of course. He crosses the floor to the hover platform, and—"

Chewbacca gave a sharp rumble.

"Oh—right," Rachele said. "Sorry, I forgot to mention that part. The safe is set onto this ten-meter-diameter platform that hovers about a meter and a half off the floor on repulsorlifts and slowly moves around the room. I don't know whether it follows a constant circuit or runs a random path."

"Okay, *now* it's just getting ridiculous," Dozer said.

"Not really," Tavia said. "Back when we first started this thing someone mentioned the possibility of tunneling in from underneath. The other obvious approach is to cut through the ceiling and try to drop onto the safe from above without the guards spotting you. With the safe constantly moving around the room, both of those tactics are now useless."

"Those must be really impressive repulsorlifts," Bink commented. "A sphere of duracrete that size probably weighs upward of a hundred fifty tonnes."

"Easily," Rachele said. "And yes, the repulsorlifts are extremely powerful, so much so that they have their own fusion generator built in, probably in and below that thirty-centimeter pillar attaching the sphere to the plate."

"The guy's smart, all right," Bink agreed. "So he walks to the hover platform?"

"As he approaches the platform, the nearest set of stairs unfolds from beneath it," Rachele said. "By my count, there are fifty of those. Because while the platform is moving around the room it's also slowly rotating."

"Randomly, I assume?" Winter asked.

Rachele nodded. "I caught two small shifts in rotational speed while he was moving across the room. It's a slow rotation, but the speed isn't really important. The bottom line is that because of the rotation, the average intruder won't have any way of knowing where the safe's actual entrance is."

"But we do, right?" Bink asked.

"I think so," Rachele said. "There are multiple sets of paired finger-sized holes, spaced about four centimeters apart, all the way around the sphere at about chest height. Villachor goes to the proper set and inserts the first two fingers of his right hand, and the lower part of one of the sphere segments unfolds down onto the platform, leaving a gap about a meter and a half wide and two meters high through the duracrete that extends all the way in to the Hijarna stone center."

"Is the cabinet exactly in the middle of the sphere?" Zerba asked.

"No, it's about half a meter farther back," Rachele said, looking puzzled. "Why do you ask?"

Zerba shrugged. "Just curious."

"Do we know if the holes are fingerprint keyed?" Tavia asked.

"I don't think so," Rachele said. "The finger positioning seemed casual, and he never held them steady enough for a good print reading. Best guess is that it's a body-heat trigger, and you just have to know which ones to use."

"Or you do all of them," Zerba said.

"No need," Winter said, pointing. "There are two small scuff marks over the pair just to the left of the ones he's using."

"I see them," Bink said. "What's next?"

Rachele again keyed her datapad, and the holoprojector image zoomed in on the sphere, where a segment unfolded the way she'd just described. "We now have a short tunnel," she continued, "at the end of which is the door to the inner closet, another slab of Hijarna stone with a standard alphanumeric keypad set into it." The image zoomed in yet again, giving a close-up of the keypad.

"Done up in High Galactic letters, I see," Zerba commented.

"Aurebesh is for the common folk," Lando said dryly. "Snobs like Villachor are way too upper-level for that."

"We *did* get the code, right?" Tavia said.

"We've got this afternoon's code, anyway," Rachele said. "But given the rest of his security, I imagine the code changes regularly."

"Probably twice a day," Bink said, standing up and moving forward for a closer look at the image. "That particular model allows for a preset pattern with twice-daily changes."

"What do you mean by preset?" Kell asked.

"I mean that instead of some computer elsewhere in the house spitting out a random set of numbers every day that has to be transmitted to the safe—"

"And memorized by Villachor," Tavia added.

"And memorized by Villachor," Bink agreed, "he can precode the safe for weeks' or even months' worth of changes."

"How does he keep track of all of them?" Dozer asked.

"Two likely possibilities," Rachele said. "First, one of the Zeds inside could also have the sequence, and it feeds him the code on his way in. I didn't see that happen, but my angle might not have been right."

"Sounds risky," Kell said. "Especially since the droids probably get swapped out regularly for recharging and repair."

"And transmitting the sequence to a droid is no better than transmitting it directly to the keypad," Tavia added.

"Agreed," Rachele said. "The more likely possibility is that the sequence relates to some pattern Villachor already knows. Dates from family history, names of old girlfriends, vintage years of the wine in his cellar. Something like that."

"So now we have to read his mind, too," Dozer said heavily. "Great."

"Not his mind," Winter corrected calmly. "Just his history. *And* we have a known code to start from."

Dozer shook his head. "Still sounds like a candle in a canyon to me."

"True, but it's only one canyon," Winter said.

"And once we get through *that*," Rachele continued, "it looks like everything in the safe is exit-tagged."

"What does that mean?" Eanjer asked.

"It means that taking anything past the mansion's walls will trigger alarms all across Marblewood," Zerba explained.

"More than just alarms," Rachele said. "From the old purchase records, it looks like Villachor has also installed a spike-ring fence around the mansion. It's like a forest of close-spaced vertical poles a few centimeters apart that pop straight out of the ground when triggered," she added, looking at Eanjer. "The posts usually carry enough current to stun or kill."

"High-security places sometimes use them as a last-ditch defense against theft," Bink said. "You need an airspeeder to get over one, and even then you can't get too close or the current will arc up to you and fry your repulsorlifts."

"Depending on how high this one is, it may squeeze you close enough against the umbrella shield that you'd be effectively trapped inside," Tavia said.

"So we'll definitely want to shut the system down before we make our move," Eanjer concluded, nodding.

"Which we probably can't," Rachele said. "This kind of system usually includes a fine mesh throughout all the walls, which runs a low-level electrostatic field through all the doors and windows. It's self-contained and decentralized, and the only way to knock it out is to basically cut back the wall for about two meters around whatever door you plan to use." She considered. "Of course, once you do that, I suppose you really don't need the door anymore."

"So what we need to do is make sure that when the alarm goes off no one's in any shape to respond," Zerba said. "Maybe we could gas the place."

Bink shook her head. "You'll never get that much gas in without getting caught."

"And it wouldn't work on the droids, anyway," Kell added. "We'll also need enough detonite to blow up a section of the fence, and enough time to plant it."

"So we just make sure they're all too busy to respond?" Lando asked, looking at Han. "Is that the plan?"

"Mostly," Han said. "Is that everything, Rachele?"

"Yes," Rachele said. "Oh, except that the room directly above the vault is the guard ready room, where Villachor's security people hang out when they're not on duty."

"Luckily, most of them *will* be on duty during the Honorings," Han pointed out. "Thanks, Rachele. At least now we know what we're up against."

"Yeah, *I'm* sure going to sleep better tonight," Dozer growled.

"Glad to hear it," Han said in that innocent, not-quite-sarcastic tone he did so well. "That's it for tonight. Better get some sleep—tomorrow's going to be busy."

Standing up, he walked over and sat down beside Rachele, murmuring to her and gesturing at the holo. The others, taking the cue, got up and filed out.

Lando waited until everyone else was gone. "A word?" he asked.

"Sure," Han said, turning away from his quiet conversation.

"You want me to leave?" Rachele asked.

"No, I'd appreciate your input," Lando said. "Bink

said earlier that you or Dozer was going to have to take my place."

"Yeah, she did," Han agreed. "You want to put in your vote?"

Lando nodded. "I vote for me."

Rachele blinked. Han's face went into unreadable sabacc mode. "You just got grabbed," he reminded Lando.

"*And* got sprung," Lando countered. "I'm with an organization who doesn't think twice about luring senior Black Sun officials away, remember? A failed kidnapping shouldn't even throw me off my stride."

Han turned to Rachele. "What do you think?"

"He has a point," she said reluctantly. "Especially if Bink's right about Villachor himself not being involved. Whoever was behind the grab will still have to work around Marblewood security, *and* they'll now have to work around Lando's group as well. And since they don't know the size or extent of his team, they'll need to tread carefully."

"But you'll certainly need more security." Eanjer's voice came from the hall.

Lando turned, feeling a flicker of annoyance. Hadn't it been clear that he'd stayed behind because he wanted to talk to Han alone?

Apparently it hadn't. At least not to Eanjer.

"Something we can do for you?" Han asked, way more politely than Lando would have.

"I was thinking about security for whoever goes back into Marblewood," Eanjer said, coming the rest of the way into the room. He looked like he was planning to sit down, but he glanced at Lando's expression and apparently thought better of it. "It occurred to me that the weapons cache Winter found for you might also have some smaller blasters we could borrow."

"We don't need any more blasters," Han assured him. "Whoever goes in will just take Chewie with him."

Eanjer's single eye widened. "*Chewie?*"

"Sure, why not?" Han said. "There were plenty of Wookiees there the other two days."

"Wookiees *are* in high demand as bodyguards for the Iltarr City elite," Rachele confirmed.

"Yes, but—" Eanjer clamped his lips tightly shut. "Look. I know you have to play confident in front of"—his eye flicked to Lando—"everyone else. But this is insane. You can't possibly believe that we can quietly break into something like *that.*" He nodded at the holo floating overhead.

"You got a better idea?" Han asked.

"A direct, frontal assault," Eanjer said bluntly. "We bring in more of your friends, hit the place while security's busy with the Honorings—"

"Whoa, whoa," Lando interrupted. He'd never really liked Eanjer, but he hadn't been able to put his finger on exactly why. Now he knew. The man was an idiot. "Who do you think we are, the Five-oh-first? An attack on Marblewood would be instant suicide."

"Of course it would be risky," Eanjer countered. "But remember the payoff at the end. You can hire a lot of mercenaries for a hundred sixty-three million credits."

"Credits on hand, yes," Lando countered. "Credits promised isn't so good a draw."

"I know," Eanjer said. He huffed out his breath. "But I don't see any other way to get in."

"Me neither," Han said. "Lucky for us, we don't have to."

"What do you mean?" Rachele asked.

"I mean we don't have to get in," Han repeated patiently. "All we need is for Villachor to bring everything *out.*"

"*What?*" Eanjer demanded, his eye narrowing. "Oh, come *on.* Villachor's not going to just bring the credits and files out and hand them to you."

"I didn't say he was," Han said. "But if he thinks the vault's under threat, he'd have a good reason to move everything to a safer location. That's when we take it away from him."

"No," Eanjer insisted. "We can't do it that way."

"Why not?"

Eanjer's eye flicked to Lando. "Because it won't work," he said, speaking as if trying to explain something to a five-year-old. "He might—*might*—move the blackmail files if you worry him enough. But he's not likely to bother moving the credits."

"Well, then we just get the files," Han said. "I thought we decided they're more valuable on the open market than a few credit tabs anyway."

"Not without a cryodex they aren't," Eanjer insisted. "No, if we're going to pull this off, we have to actually get in there. We *have* to."

"Fine. Opinion noted." Han looked at Rachele and Lando. "Anyone else have thoughts they want to add to the pot?"

Something in his tone warned Lando that the proper answer was *no*. "Maybe later," he said. "I'm thinking I'll grab a quick snack—assuming Dozer's left anything for the rest of us—and get to bed."

"Me too," Rachele said, tapping her datapad and shutting off the holoprojector. "Except for the snack part. Good night, all."

Lando half expected Eanjer to follow him into the kitchen and try to argue some more against Han's new plan. Luckily for Eanjer, he didn't.

Lando and Eanjer disappeared down the hallway. Han waited a couple more seconds, just to be sure, then turned back to Rachele. "Can we be ready in two days?"

"Not a chance," she said. "Zerba's still working on

the silk tear-away outfits, and Tavia and the others only have about half the scramblers they'll need."

"And there's still no way to test them?"

"Not unless you want to try one out during the Honoring of Moving Water the day after tomorrow."

Han shook his head. "Too risky. What we get to see, they get to see."

"Yes." Rachele studied his face. "It's starting to come apart, isn't it?"

"I don't know," Han admitted. "Maybe a little. I never bought into this whole Qazadi story that Eanjer's buddy pitched, at least not the part about him being one of Xizor's top people. But if he's really the guy in charge now, he might bring down the hammer faster than we thought."

"But it might also force Villachor's hand," Rachele pointed out. "I realize that this whole side-switching offer was just so we could get Tavia's data card into the vault, but if we can genuinely talk him into defecting, we might get the credits and files with a whole lot less work."

"Not a chance," Han said firmly. "Not now that one of the Falleen has stepped in. Whoever it is, he's pretty well showed that he can commandeer Black Sun's assets on Wukkar. If he even suspects that Villachor's thinking about jumping ship, that's it for Villachor. He has to know that."

"I suppose," Rachele said, still eyeing him closely. "Which also means there's no way you can talk him into transferring the files elsewhere, because that move would look exactly the same as him absconding with them."

"Nope, no chance of that, either," Han agreed.

"So why did you tell Eanjer that was the new plan?"

"Mostly to see his reaction," Han said, standing up. "I'm heading to bed. Don't let Tavia sleep in—we've only got four days until the fire honoring, and we're going to need all the scramblers we can get."

"I'll make sure she and the others are up with the sun," Rachele promised. "What are you going to do about Villachor? He's expecting to meet Lando's boss at the Honoring of Moving Water the day after tomorrow."

"I guess I'll have to stall him," Han said. "We can work that out tomorrow." He headed toward the hallway and his room.

"So did you?" Rachele asked.

"Did I what?"

"Did you find out whatever it is you were looking for with Eanjer?"

Han grimaced. "Yeah, I think so," he said. "Turn out the lights on your way to bed, okay?"

CHAPTER FOURTEEN

The work of gearing up for the Honoring of Moving Water had been going on all day, and from the occasional glimpses Dozer had caught through the suite windows it looked like it was going to be as spectacular as the previous two Honorings had been.

But that was for tomorrow. Right now, for the next few minutes, the only thing on Dozer's mind was the Marblewood security guard getting tiredly out of his landspeeder in front of his home in a middle-class part of the city.

Han had assured him the man wouldn't simply shoot him down on the spot. That wasn't the way even Black Sun dealt with people doing odd but nonthreatening things. Han had promised that the man would simply listen, take the package, and let Dozer walk away.

Han was always persuasive. But he wasn't always right.

Especially given that they knew nothing about the guard except that he worked the early morning shift at Marblewood. They didn't know his name, his history, or anything else. They hadn't even known his address until Dozer followed him home.

Fortunately, with Rachele and her computer available to backtrack the address, they now also knew his name was Frewin Bromly.

He was working on getting a satchel out of the backseat, his bright blond hair shaded by the airspeeder's roof. Dozer walked up behind him and cleared his throat. "Excuse me?"

Bromly was every bit as good as one would expect from a man who worked for Villachor. He dropped the satchel back onto the seat and spun around in a smooth, fluid turn that left him facing Dozer with his hand in easy grabbing distance of his holstered blaster. A single, equally fluid glance took in Dozer and the entire area around him. "Yes?" he asked, his tone perfectly neutral.

"Quickline Courier Service," Dozer said, tapping his nameplate. "Got a package for Frewin Bromly. That you?"

"Yes," Bromly said, his eyes narrowing. "I haven't ordered anything."

"All I know is that I was hired to bring this to you," Dozer said, lifting his security case and popping the lid. "Here we go." He pulled out a small wrapped package and held it out.

Bromly made no move to take it. "What is it?"

"How should I know?" Dozer countered. He held out the package another second, then squatted down and set it on the driveway. "Fine. You don't want it, just leave it there. I've got a schedule to keep. Have a peaceful evening."

He straightened up, gave Bromly a polite nod, then turned and started back down the driveway toward his landspeeder.

"Hey!"

Dozer stopped, his throat tight. "Yes?"

"I don't want it," Bromly called. "Come back and get it."

"Can't do that," Dozer said. "You don't want it, give it away or feed it to the fish. Whatever you want."

He started walking again, his entire back a mass of

tense muscles. Sooner or later, probably before Dozer was out of sight, Bromly's curiosity would get the better of him and he would open the package.

And while five hundred credits didn't qualify as a windfall, it should be more than enough to grab some serious attention. Both from Bromly and, eventually, from Sheqoa and Villachor.

He half expected Bromly to chase him back to his landspeeder. But again, the man had been well trained. Either Dozer was an innocent courier, in which case confronting him wouldn't gain him anything, or else he was part of a serious bribery team, and anyone who so blatantly tried such a thing on a Black Sun guard surely would be smart enough to have arrived with backup.

No, Bromly's best move right now would be to take the package inside and immediately call in the incident to his superiors at Marblewood.

Or he could just pocket the credits. But that really would be too much to hope for.

Still, Dozer had two other guards on his list to follow home as their shifts ended. Maybe one of them would be gracious enough to accept the bribe.

Hopefully, none of them would be discourteous enough to shoot him in the back.

Sheqoa had never liked the Festival of Four Honorings. Even as a kid he'd found the spectacle too long, the venues too crowded, the food too weird, and the shows alternating between bombastic and boring. As an adult, he'd learned to enjoy some of the food and, even more, some of the drinks. Still, he'd continued to find the shows long and predictable.

As head of Marblewood security, he'd learned to utterly hate the event.

He understood why Villachor liked to host one of the

celebrations. It raised his status among Wukkar's upper echelons, which in turn brought more unsuspecting flies within range of Black Sun's webs. The Festival also provided perfect cover for clandestine meetings with those flies who were already trapped, as well as giving anonymity to potential new contacts with arms dealers, smugglers, and spice merchants. If the price for all those meetings had been merely the cost to feed and entertain a sizeable fraction of Iltarr City's population, he would have considered it credits well spent.

But the food and fireworks were only the snowy crest of the mountain. Having crowds of unwashed citizens wandering around the grounds strained Sheqoa's security forces to the limit. The oblivious or drunk pounded on locked doors, tripped over furniture, damaged serving droids, and sometimes started fights. At least once per festival his men had to roust a pickpocket or two and relieve various thieves of items both valuable and petty.

It was an extra strain and cost that Villachor never considered. And it was a cost that, if Sheqoa did his job properly, Villachor shouldn't even notice.

Except this year. This year was grimly, darkly different.

The mysterious glitterstim merchant. The cryodex man. The flash bomb incident outside Aziel's suite at the Lulina Crown Hotel. The still-unexplained firefight at the half-abandoned Golavere Industrial Complex, which might or might not have had something to do with one of the other three.

And now, just earlier this afternoon, the bizarre attempts to bribe three of his men.

It was Qazadi's fault, of course. Sheqoa had no doubts on that score. Whether the Falleen and his entourage had done something directly to cause all this chaos or whether their mere presence had sparked it was largely irrelevant. Either way, Qazadi was still the focal point.

And so, as he had most of the previous nights, Sheqoa had drifted off to sleep with unfriendly thoughts of Qazadi and his people floating through his mind.

Which, he dimly supposed, made it only fitting and proper that Qazadi's face was the first thing he saw when he was jolted violently out of that same deep sleep.

"You will be silent," Qazadi said, his voice soft and yet utterly vicious as Sheqoa's hand reflexively tried for the blaster under his pillow. A wasted effort; his arms were already pinned solidly to the bed. "I will ask questions. You will answer them. Or you will die. Do you understand?"

Sheqoa nodded, a barely perceptible movement of his head that was all he could accomplish with yet another hand entwined in his hair and a blade resting against his throat.

"Good," Qazadi said. "Tell me about the two men who came to see Master Villachor yesterday in his vault."

"He didn't—" Sheqoa broke off, fighting to work moisture into his mouth and fighting even harder to keep his voice from shaking with fear. A small part of him recognized that his terror wasn't real but was being driven by Falleen pheromones. But that knowledge did him little good. "He didn't take them into the vault," he managed. "Just to the anteroom."

"What did they do there?"

Sheqoa swallowed, his throat brushing unpleasantly against the knife blade, wondering fleetingly what he could say. Villachor was his superior, and Villachor had ordered him and the others not to say anything about that visit.

But he had no choice. A lie, or even a half-truth, and his own gushing blood would be the last thing he ever saw. "The visitors claimed they had a cryodex," he gasped.

Something in Qazadi's expression changed. "And did they?"

"Yes," Sheqoa said. "Master Villachor had them bring it to him so he could test it and see if it actually worked."

"Test it how?"

Again Sheqoa struggled with his conscience and his orders. But orders were one thing. Death was something else. "He brought a data card from the vault," he admitted reluctantly. "He wanted to see if their cryodex could decrypt it."

Qazadi's eyes flashed with anger, and Sheqoa braced himself for death. But the blade against his throat didn't move. "And could it?"

"Yes," Sheqoa said. "They decrypted the file of a Houk named Morg Nar on Bespin. He's supposedly trying to drive out Jabba's people but is secretly working with him."

"I presume you checked this out?"

Sheqoa started to nod, remembered the knife. "Yes."

Qazadi looked briefly at someone outside Sheqoa's field of view, then turned back. "Tell me about Dorston, Bromly, Uzior, and Tallboy."

Sheqoa frowned, trying frantically to figure out what those four particular guards had in common. But he couldn't think of anything. "Well, the first three had bribes delivered to them this afternoon," he said, stalling for time. "But Tallboy didn't—" He broke off as it suddenly hit him. "*He* was bribed, too?"

"Possibly," Qazadi said. "All I know is that the first bribe was sent to him."

"I don't understand," Sheqoa said. "He never reported it."

"Because he never knew about it," Qazadi said. "At least, not about this particular bribe. Unbeknownst to him, Lord Aziel had appropriated his name for use in various transactions at the Lulina Crown Hotel. The incident six days ago, when the small bomb was thrown at his suite, also involved a messenger delivering what appeared to be a bribe to that name."

Sheqoa felt his eyes narrow as some of the stranger aspects of that event suddenly became clear. "That's why you had the investigation halted," he said. "You didn't want the bribe part to come out in case Tallboy was actually involved in something."

"Correct," Qazadi said, an edge of unspoken threat in his voice. "And I *still* don't want it coming out."

"I understand," Sheqoa said.

Qazadi's eyes narrowed as he again glanced briefly away. "But Tallboy himself is of no especial importance," he said. "The larger question is not which of your guards received bribes and reported them, but which ones received bribes and *didn't* report them."

"My men are loyal, Your Excellency," Sheqoa said, again fighting the quaver in his voice. He already knew what happened to people in Black Sun who betrayed their loyalty.

"I'm certain they are," Qazadi agreed. "But are they loyal to Master Villachor, or are they loyal to Black Sun?"

Sheqoa swallowed again. "Surely those loyalties are the same," he said as firmly as he could.

"Perhaps," Qazadi said. "Perhaps not. Now that Master Villachor has confirmed that the strangers' cryodex is indeed genuine, what are his plans for it and for them?"

Finally, some relatively safe ground. "He's leading them on, hoping to learn who they work for," Sheqoa said. "If he can't draw them out for destruction, he should at least be able to obtain a spare cryodex for Prince Xizor."

"A noble goal," Qazadi said. "Yet yesterday he had the cryodex in a mansion full of armed men. Why didn't he take it then?"

Sheqoa swallowed again before he remembered not to do that. "The cryodex and case were booby-trapped," he said. "Detonite." He felt his eyes widen as another piece fell into the puzzle. "That firefight at the Golavere Complex. You were able to get the case open?"

"No," Qazadi said, and Sheqoa's already pounding heart picked up its pace a little as the other glared off into space. "I had ordered the services of two of the local police to take Master Villachor's visitors for questioning. When I learned of the detonite I also brought in Master Dempsey."

So that was where Villachor's explosives expert had disappeared to, and why he'd been so nervous and shaken when he returned to his lab in the north wing a few hours later. "Only their friends intervened?"

"For the first *and* last time," Qazadi said, his voice heavy with menace. "The only question remaining is whether they will die quickly or slowly." He cocked his head to the side. "Is there anything more you wish to tell me? Others, perhaps, who might be involved in this conspiracy against Black Sun?"

"There's a girl," Sheqoa said. "A human woman. Young, black hair, very—well, attractive to human eyes."

"And you think she wouldn't be attractive to my nonhuman ones?"

"I'm—I don't know," Sheqoa said, hurrying to get off the subject. "She's attached herself to me, probably hoping I can get her inside the mansion. She says her name's Katrin, but it's undoubtedly an alias."

"And you believe her to be with the cryodex merchant?"

"I don't know," Sheqoa said. "She might just be a regular thief hoping to rob the mansion. We get some of those at every Festival."

"You'll keep close watch on her." A faint smile briefly creased Qazadi's lips. "You'll see to that personally."

"Of course," Sheqoa confirmed. "Perhaps we should—"

He broke off as the knife suddenly pressed harder against his throat. "Silent unless asked a question," Qazadi reminded him coldly. He looked past Sheqoa again and twitched his head in an unspoken order. There was the sound of movement from that direction, a shuffling of multiple feet.

And out of the corner of his eye Sheqoa saw Villachor step into view, an armed Falleen on either side of him.

"Congratulations, Master Villachor," Qazadi said with ironic courtesy. "As you said, your people are indeed loyal."

"As am I," Villachor countered with the same hard-edged courtesy. He was standing stiff and defiant, but Sheqoa could see a sheen of sweat on his face. "And as you heard—*again*—my goal is and always has been to find out who this Kwerve and Bib are and whom they're working for. Nothing more."

"Perhaps," Qazadi said, his tone still courteous. "Still, the temptation to take the blackmail files for yourself must be nearly overwhelming. Especially with those files currently accessible only to you."

Sheqoa cleared his throat quietly.

"I believe Master Sheqoa was about to make a suggestion," Villachor said. "I'd like to hear it."

Qazadi considered, then looked down at Sheqoa. "Speak," he invited.

The knife eased back a fraction. "I was going to suggest that if Kwerve and Bib are trying to steal the files, perhaps we should simply move them," he said. "So far, all their activities have been under cover of the crowds at the Honorings. If we move the files tonight, when no one's watching, any future efforts they might make will be against an empty vault."

"Have you a suggestion as to where they should go?" Qazadi asked.

"Your ship was secure enough to protect them for the journey here," Sheqoa pointed out. "There's also Master Villachor's country estate in Baccha province. The safe there isn't as secure as the Marblewood vault, but the thieves would never think to look for the files there."

"How do you know?" Qazadi countered. "How do you know such a transfer isn't exactly what they're hoping for? How do you know they don't have people already in place at Baccha and Iltarr City Spaceport, waiting for us to deliver the files straight into their hands? How do you know they don't have people lying in wait outside the Marblewood wall even now for the airspeeders or landspeeders that would take the files away?"

"I . . ." Sheqoa looked helplessly at Villachor.

But Villachor wasn't looking at him. Villachor was looking at Qazadi. Thinking, measuring, perhaps scheming. Looking for a way to reinstate himself in the Falleen's good graces.

Trying to save himself.

"You make a good and valid point, Your Excellency," Villachor said. "Until we know the full extent of our enemies' reach, we can't afford to make any assumptions."

"On the contrary," Qazadi said. "There are two assumptions we can certainly make. First, they've offered you a functional cryodex. Therefore, they hope to lure you into treason against Black Sun."

"Which won't happen," Villachor said firmly.

"We shall hope not," Qazadi said darkly, and again Sheqoa felt his heart rate briefly increase. "Second, we know they're trying to subvert your security force." He looked down at Sheqoa. "And that they may have succeeded."

Never, Sheqoa wanted to say. But he remained silent. One warning about unsolicited comments was all he was likely to get.

"Since we can no longer trust your men," Qazadi continued, "you will immediately withdraw all human guards from the vault. From this point on, only the 501-Z droids will be stationed in that area."

Sheqoa felt his breath catch in his throat. That was a terrible idea. The whole point of mixing droids and humans was that potential intruders wouldn't know which they were facing at any given time.

SoroSuub claimed their Zeds were impossible to break or deprogram. But nothing in the universe was truly impossible. If Kwerve's people found out that the vault was guarded solely by droids, they might find a fatal weakness in their mechanism or programming and exploit it.

From the expression on Villachor's face, it was clear he was thinking the same thing. But it was also clear that he had no intention of arguing the point. "As you wish," he said. "I'll give the order immediately."

"Good," Qazadi said. "The guards can be reassigned to Festival duty. Perhaps a few extra eyes will provide a better view of those who seek to rob us. You *did* say immediately, did you not, Master Villachor?"

Villachor's lip twitched as he pulled out his comlink and gave the night duty officer the order for the guard change. "Will there be anything else, Your Excellency?" he asked as he returned the comlink to its holder.

"Not for now," Qazadi said. His eyes flicked down to Sheqoa, back to Villachor. "The Honoring of Moving Water begins in eight hours. You should both get some rest."

He turned and strode out of Sheqoa's view, followed by the Falleen flanking Villachor. A few seconds later, the knife at Sheqoa's throat and the hands gripping his arms and hair also disappeared. There was the sound of a door opening and then closing.

And Sheqoa and Villachor were alone.

Sheqoa looked up at his boss, trying to come up with

something to say. If Villachor took Sheqoa's admissions to Qazadi as a betrayal, he was dead.

But the words wouldn't come. And even with Qazadi and the Falleen's pheromone tricks gone, his pulse continued to pound in his neck.

Because, down deep, Sheqoa knew his statements to Qazadi *were* a betrayal.

Finally Villachor stirred. Sheqoa braced himself.

"He's right about the Honoring," Villachor said calmly. "Go back to sleep. I'll see you in the morning."

Without another word, he left.

Sheqoa took a deep breath, staring at the closed door. Something critical had just happened, he knew. Villachor had come to a decision.

Only Sheqoa had no idea what that decision was.

Slowly he rolled over onto his side. Like he was really going to get any sleep *now*.

CHAPTER FIFTEEN

It had been said that there were only three absolutes in life: death, taxes, and bad liquor. But as Lando strolled across the Marblewood grounds, he decided he could add a fourth to the list.

When you traveled with a Wookiee, people would move out of your way.

Of course, Chewbacca's two-meter-plus height also made the two of them easier for Villachor's security men to spot as they moved through the crowds. But then, that was the whole idea.

Chewie rumbled.

"Yeah, I see them," Lando said, making a face. He'd expected the entire Marblewood security force to be on their tail today. He hadn't expected to find himself also being watched by a pair of Falleen.

He especially hadn't expected one of those Falleen to be the would-be interrogator from the factory incident two nights earlier.

Chewie rumbled again.

"Don't worry, they aren't going to try anything," Lando assured him. "Not here."

Chewie warbled a not entirely confident comment.

"Sure, they're probably mad," Lando agreed. "But they want to question us, not kill us. At least not right away."

Or so he hoped. The logic certainly tracked, and most of the people Lando had faced across sabacc tables over the years would follow that same line of reasoning.

But there were species out there who would unhesitatingly pass up profit and vested self-interest in favor of immediate revenge. The Hutts tended that way. Maybe the Falleen did, too.

Still, they were on Villachor's grounds, and in the middle of one of his favorite bits of self-promotion. Surely he would keep them in line.

Which wasn't to say he and Chewie should press their luck. "Over there," he said, pointing away from the loitering Falleen. "That hanging waterfall looks interesting. Let's wander over and take a closer look."

Chewie growled.

"Right," Lando confirmed with a tight smile. "Looks like there's a spot right beside those other two Wookiees."

"I have to say," Bink commented as she peered up into Sheqoa's face, "that you *really* look tired."

"Thanks," he said dryly. "You look lovely, too."

"You're too kind," Bink said, smiling cheerfully. She let the smile fade into concern. "But I was being serious," she continued. "I guess people don't realize how hard something like this is on the folks who run the show. How long since you've had a real night's sleep?"

"It's been a while," he conceded. "Like you said, things get pretty busy during the Festival."

"Well, you need to make that time," she said firmly, reaching over and taking hold of his right upper arm. "If you don't get your rest—"

She broke off as he twisted his arm back out of her grip, simultaneously pushing her hand away with his left hand. "Gun hand," he said shortly. "Never do that."

"I'm so sorry," Bink apologized, screwing up her face into her best embarrassed wince. "Look, I can see you're not in the mood to just relax and have fun. Maybe I'd better go and let you concentrate on your work."

"No, that's all right," he said hastily as she started to back away. "I'm just a little twitchy this morning, that's all." He took her hand and gently pulled her around to his left side. "Come on, let's go see if they've got the ambrosia steamer up and running."

"All right," Bink said, wrapping her hand possessively around his left arm. This time, he didn't push her away. "But only if you promise to relax and have one of them with me."

"A small one only," he said.

They got two steps before he suddenly changed direction. "On second thought, let me show you something else first," he said, angling off through the crowd. "The hanging waterfall is one of the Honoring's highlights, and it's about to go into its quarter-hour show. We'll watch it and then go get the ambrosia."

"Sounds interesting," Bink said, a small red flag waving in the back of her brain. He was up to something.

New orders via his collar-clip comlink? Probably. Shifting her grip on his arm, Bink snuggled in a little closer. If the comlink's speaker hadn't been focused correctly, she might be able to get in close enough to hear what was going on.

Unfortunately, Villachor's tech people hadn't been that careless. But even as she eased casually away again, a hint of an odd scent touched her nostrils. Not enough for her to identify, but enough to tell her that she'd smelled it before. *And* that it was something significant.

It would be risky to move that close again so soon. But she had time. The scent was on Sheqoa, and Sheqoa had clearly been ordered to keep her close. There would be opportunities later to chase it down. More important right now was figuring out this sudden change in his schedule.

And then, just ahead, a pair of Kubaz moved aside, giving her a momentarily clear view of the hanging waterfall Sheqoa had mentioned.

The waterfall, and the big furry shape of Chewbacca towering over the crowd.

Apparently whoever had been watching Lando had decided it might be fun to throw Bink at him and see if the two of them knew each other.

Mentally, she shook her head. Of all of Han's group, she and Lando were probably the two *least* likely to show any of the reaction Sheqoa was hoping for.

Still, points for effort. Patting Sheqoa's arm, prattling on in the breezy, carefree way she knew he'd come to expect from her, she settled her mind for the immediate task ahead.

"—over by the hanging waterfall," Villachor was saying into his comlink as Han sauntered into eavesdropping range. "Take the girl over, spring her on him, and see if they recognize each other."

Han felt his throat tighten. He'd known ahead of time that Villachor would be taking it up a notch today. And if Villachor didn't, then Qazadi or Aziel certainly would. Trying to figure out how the various newcomers into their lives were connected was the obvious first step.

Still, throwing a ghost thief at a professional gambler would probably be a complete waste of time. Both Bink and Lando were more than capable of controlling their expressions and behavior.

Now it was Han's turn.

He squared his shoulders. He could do this. He'd faced down Jabba the Hutt, Imperial Commander Nyklas the sadist, and any number of other thugs and bandits. Villachor was just the latest in a long line. A couple more greeters and well-wishers wandered up to Villachor, babbling their thanks for the show under the watchful gaze of his two bodyguards. Han waited until they moved on, then walked over. "Nice show, Master Villachor," he said.

"Thank you," Villachor said, giving him a quick up-and-down look. "I'm glad you're enjoying it."

"I hear you have a really nice collection of airspeeders and landspeeders," Han continued, gesturing toward the garage at the north end of the mansion. "Any chance you'll be bringing them out to show us?"

"No, I don't think so," Villachor said with the same forced smile he was giving everyone else. "Not until an Honoring of Moving Vehicles is added to the Festival."

"I suppose not," Han said. He moved a step closer and lowered his voice. "What about the blackmail files? You going to bring *them* out?"

Villachor's smile vanished, and both bodyguards shifted their hands to their concealed blasters. "Excuse me?" Villachor said quietly.

"Easy," Han soothed. "I'm just here to talk."

"Then talk fast," Villachor snarled, hissing out the last word. "Did you bring the item?"

"No, and I'm not going to," Han said. "Not after what happened two nights ago."

"That wasn't my doing," Villachor insisted. He was starting to recover, and Han could see the little computer chips in his mind starting to spin again. "Are you the boss Kwerve promised to bring me?"

"No, and you're not going to see *him*, either," Han said. "If that wasn't you, who was it?"

"A misguided colleague," Villachor said. "Someone who felt we needed to know more about you before our discussions continued. If you didn't bring the item and we're not discussing terms, why *are* you here?"

"Mostly as a courtesy," Han said. "I wanted to warn you that another player has joined the game."

Villachor's face changed, just enough to show that the guards had indeed reported Dozer's off-duty visits. "What do you mean?"

"You know what I mean," Han said. "Someone's going around bribing your guards."

"*Trying* to bribe them," Villachor corrected. "All the men who were approached turned in the credits."

"You sure about that?" Han countered. "Because the numbers *I'm* hearing say that at least five of them took the packages and kept their mouths shut."

Abruptly a blaster muzzle jabbed into Han's ribs. "Who?" Villachor demanded. "Give me their names."

"I don't *have* their names," Han growled, glaring at the guard pressing the blaster into his side. "I told you, it's someone else who's doing that."

"A girl, perhaps?" Villachor suggested. "Black hair, medium height?"

"I . . . don't . . . know," Han said, biting out each word. "We don't know who they are."

"Or maybe *they* are *you*?" the guard growled.

"Use your head," Han growled back. "Our group is trying for a nice, quiet, civilized recruitment. Why would we risk that by throwing credits at employees who don't even matter?" He raised his eyebrows. "No offense."

"None taken," Villachor said. "Put it away, Tawb."

Reluctantly, the bodyguard returned the blaster to its hiding place.

"Enough small talk," Villachor continued. "Here's the bottom line. Before I make any decisions, I *will* meet with someone who has the authority to make me a deal. *And* I want to see the cryodex work one more time."

"You already got one sample," Han reminded him. "Didn't it pan out good enough for you?"

"Oh, it panned out quite nicely," Villachor assured

him. "The inquiries I sent to Bespin have confirmed this Morg Nar person your man identified is indeed working for the Hutt."

Han felt his stomach tighten. And if he knew anything about the way Black Sun did things, the inquiry alone was going to blow Nar's cover straight out the airlock. Jabba was *not* going to be happy about that.

And when Jabba wasn't happy, everyone connected to him paid the price. The faster they got Eanjer's credit tabs and Han could pay off his debt, the better.

"But any one-time winner could just be luck," Villachor continued. "A second sample will make things more definitive."

"That'll be up to the boss," Han said. "And before you ask, yes, he's already on Wukkar."

"Then what's the holdup?"

Han looked him straight in the eye. "He's waiting on confirmation that whoever grabbed Kwerve and Bib is under control."

"I can assure you there'll be no repeat of that incident."

"No offense, Master Villachor, but he's not looking for confirmation from *you*," Han said. "He's looking for confirmation from *us*. Don't worry, we're working on it."

"I see," Villachor said, his voice subtly shifting tone. "Any idea when you and he will deem the time right for such a conference?"

"Soon," Han promised. "I'm hoping I can bring him in two days from now during the Honoring of Moving Fire."

"And if you can't?"

"We will," Han assured him. "If that doesn't work—"

"Excuse me a moment," Villachor murmured, his eyes flicking somewhere over Han's shoulder as he pulled out his comlink. "Sheqoa? Anything? . . . Never mind. I've been informed that a man who may be yesterday's mystery courier is on the grounds. . . . Yes, that's the one. I think you should take your friend over there and see if they'd like to say hello to each other." He listened another moment, then closed down the comlink and turned back to Han. "I'm sorry. You were saying?"

"I was saying that if we can't secure the area by the end of the Festival, we should be able to set up a meeting for a day or two afterward," Han said, keeping his voice and expression calm and unconcerned. So security had spotted Dozer, or at least thought they had, and Villachor was sending Sheqoa and Bink over to confront him.

Problem was, while Han could trust Bink and Lando to handle the non-recognition game, he wasn't nearly so sure Dozer could pull it off without dropping any of the cues that Sheqoa would be watching for.

But there was nothing he could do. Villachor was watching, and if he made the slightest move to warn Dozer or to cut short the conversation, the other would be all over it.

In fact, that was probably the reason he'd made the call in Han's presence in the first place. Any reaction, and they would have the link between him and Dozer that Villachor obviously suspected.

Han could do nothing.

Luckily, he didn't *have* to do anything.

"But if you have a moment," he continued smoothly, "I have one other thought my boss wanted me to float past you."

"Certainly," Villachor said. "Come. Let's walk."

"Uh-oh," Winter said under her breath.

She thought she'd said it quietly enough not to be heard, but Rachele's ears were obviously better than average. Halfway across the room, standing on top of the low serving table, the other woman still caught the muttered word. "Trouble?" she asked.

"Nothing serious," Winter assured her, shifting the electrobinoculars a little as she pulled out her comlink. "Looks like Sheqoa's attempt to get Lando and Bink to react to each other has gone flat. So he's going to try it again with Bink and Dozer."

"With *Dozer*?" Rachele said, sounding worried. "That's not exactly *nothing*."

"Hold still," Zerba said testily. "You're going to pull out those arm seams again."

"I was just trying—"

"It's okay," Winter soothed, keying the comlink for Kell. Dozer was being watched, which meant she couldn't call and warn him without the timing looking suspicious. But Kell was under no such surveillance. "Kell, you need to get Dozer out of there," she said when he answered. "Can you do it without alerting his security playmates?"

"Sure," Kell said. "You want him all the way out, or just somewhere else on the grounds?"

"Better make it all the way," Winter said. Dozer had wanted another look at the Marblewood security setup, but with Sheqoa on the prowl it would be safer to just pull the plug.

"You sure?" Kell asked. "He could play hide-and-search for a long time without Sheqoa ever catching up with him."

"Out, and *now*," Winter said tartly, her memory flashing with the faces of all the Rebel operatives she'd seen push their luck too far.

"Okay, okay," Kell said defensively. "You don't have to shout. You want me out, too?"

"Only if you're spotted," Winter said, scowling to herself. She shouldn't have let the memories get the better of her. Especially not with Kell, who was going through the same agony of loss that she was. "Sorry."

"It's okay," he said. "Don't worry, I'll get him out."

"Don't be too hard on him," Rachele said as Winter put away the comlink. "He's young. The young always believe the dice are on their side."

"Enough reason right there to go hard on him," Winter countered, focusing the electrobinoculars back on Dozer. "I want him to live long enough to grow out of that phase."

"Or long enough to learn how to make the dice work for you," Zerba said. "How's it look?"

Winter's first impulse was to remind him that she had work to do, that she wasn't exactly loafing over here by the window. But Kell had been alerted in plenty of time, Bink had Sheqoa reasonably under control, and Lando, Chewbacca, and Han all seemed to be doing fine. She could probably spare a glance at Zerba's masterpiece.

It was well worth it. The last time Winter had seen the outfit, it had been mostly a stack of delicate pieces of red silk. Now, two hours later, Zerba had transformed the pieces into an elegant red formal-wear dress that could have held its own at one of Queen Breha's formal receptions.

In fact, except for the deeper waistline, higher collar, and slightly different shade, it was identical to one that the queen had worn at Princess Leia's twelfth-birthday celebration.

"Well?"

With a jolt, Winter realized she'd been staring as the memories flooded over her. "It's beautiful," she said. "The color suits you, Rachele."

"Thanks," Rachele said wryly. "I'd curtsy, except I'd probably pull out more of Zerba's seams." She shook her head. "I still can't believe I let you talk me into this."

"Tavia's busy, Bink's busy, and you're their size," Zerba reminded her.

"I know," Rachele said with a sigh. "But there's something fundamentally wrong about asking a woman to stand for a fitting when she's not going to get to wear the dress."

"Tell you what," Zerba offered. "When this is over, I'll make you one of your very own."

"You mean that?"

"Absolutely." Zerba ran his fingers gently across the silk. "And I'll even make it one like Tavia's that you can wear more than once."

Rachele chuckled. "That would be nice," she said dryly.

Winter turned back to the window and refocused her electrobinoculars. Dozer was on the move, drifting casually through the crowd and heading toward the double stream of people moving in and out of the grounds. Two of the security men were paralleling him, staying well back but keeping him in sight.

Mostly in sight, anyway. There was a spot, just before the gate, where the positioning of the trees and hedges would temporarily block him from their sight. Keying her comlink to Dozer's number, she got ready.

"So what exactly do you do for Mazzic?" Rachele asked.

"Procurement, mostly," Winter said. "I track through shipping manifests and warehouse throughputs and find him things he needs and people who are trying to hide their merchandise. The latter he can approach about smuggling work; the former he simply steals."

"Sounds like the kind of job where you sit at a computer and don't get shot at," Zerba commented wistfully. "Must be nice."

"It's not quite that easy," Winter told him. "I also handle security systems and alarms for him. That means being on-site for a lot of the work. But you're right—we mostly don't get shot at."

"I hope he pays you well," Zerba said. "You don't seem the type who lives for the thrill of the challenge."

Winter shrugged. Mazzic's pay scale was fairly tepid, actually. What kept her at the job was the fact that she could use his resources to find and break into supply and weapons storehouses, let the smugglers take what they wanted, and leave the way clear for her Rebel Alliance associates to slip in behind them and gather up the rest.

She was pretty sure Mazzic at least suspected her secret affiliation. But he'd never said anything. Apparently he was smart enough to see the mutual advantages of their relationship.

Though maybe that was why he paid her as little as he did.

"Not really," she told Zerba. "But it's worth it."

Dozer was nearly to the gate now, walking alongside a group of long-eared, buck-toothed Lepi, their arms gesticulating wildly as they strode along, chattering among themselves. Winter checked the positions of the security men, then double-checked the covering flora and prattling aliens.

As Dozer slipped momentarily out of sight, Winter tapped her comlink's call key. Without breaking stride, Dozer shrugged off his brown jacket, flipped it inside out to show the blue-and-silver jagged-slice pattern on the other side, and put it back on. As he settled it over his shoulders, he pulled a fold-up hat from the jacket's pocket and jammed it onto his head.

A moment later he had passed through the gate, past two security men who were starting to look puzzled as they scanned the crowds marching along in front of them.

Winter smiled in satisfaction. There were undoubtedly still cam droids floating around up there beneath Villachor's umbrella shield, and someone in the monitor room had probably caught the quick change. But the inevitable communication delay between monitor and gate had given Dozer just enough time to slip out.

Of course, now they knew he wasn't just an innocent

courier but a part of the mysterious gang throwing bribes at Villachor's people. But that was all right. That part of the plan was over. Hopefully, it had accomplished its goal of making Villachor doubt his guards' trustworthiness.

Her smile faded. Trust. That was indeed the duracrete foundation of every organization. Along with commitment, trust was what ultimately defined whether a group rose to victory or fell to destruction.

She trusted her friends and associates in the Rebel Alliance. Trusted them implicitly. Could she say the same about this assemblage of thieves and scoundrels that Han and Rachele had put together?

She smiled again, a very private smile this time. Yes, she could trust them.

Because Han was more than he seemed. Much more. And before this was over, she promised herself, she would make sure she got the whole story.

"What's happening?" Rachele asked.

"He's out," Winter said. "They're—looks like they're sending someone outside the gate to see if they can spot him."

Zerba snorted. "Fat chance of *that.*"

"Not with the zigzag he set up to get back," Rachele said, breathing out an audible sigh. "That was close."

"And we're all glad it's over," Zerba said, starting to sound testy again. "Now, will you please kindly hold *still*?"

"Think of it as an insurance policy," Han said. "Your own set of blackmail files, already decrypted and ready for your personal use."

"You mean for my personal execution," Villachor said darkly. "If I had such copies and Black Sun ever found out, I'd be dead within hours. Possibly within minutes."

"Probably," Han agreed. Villachor had mentioned Black Sun's quick retribution twice already in this conversation. From the rumors Han had heard over the years, he was pretty sure that was no exaggeration.

But Villachor was still listening.

"On the other hand, there's no reason they ever have to find out," Han went on. "I bring the cryodex in, we make copies, and you put the copies someplace secure. Maybe mix them in with all your other encrypted documents."

"Yes," Villachor murmured. "You realize, I presume, that your associate Kwerve has already made that suggestion."

"I know," Han said. "I thought it was worth making again."

"Worthwhile from *my* point of view, perhaps," Villachor said. "You offer what appears to be an attractive deal, yet ask nothing in return?"

Han shrugged. "It's a good-faith gesture," he said. "Sure, we're interested in the files, but we're much more interested in you personally. If that kind of deal gets you to join us, we'll figure it was a worthwhile long-term investment."

They walked a few more steps before Villachor spoke again. "Let me offer a compromise," he suggested. "When you bring your boss, you also bring the cryodex. I'll watch it work once more *and* allow you to make copies of five files, which you may take with you." He smiled thinly. "Consider that *my* good-faith gesture."

"That sounds reasonable," Han said, nodding slowly as if thinking it over. The cracks were starting to form in Villachor's resolve—he could hear that much in the man's voice.

But those cracks weren't very big. Unless something drastic happened in the next two days, there was no way

Villachor was going to be ready to desert Black Sun, or even move the blackmail files out of the vault.

Which meant they were going to have to go through with the original plan after all. Eanjer would be pleased by that.

"All right," he said. "Let me consult with my boss and see what he says."

Villachor snorted. "More delays."

"Can't be helped," Han said. "If it helps any, we're as anxious to wrap this up as you are."

"I'm sure you are." Villachor exhaled loudly as he came to a stop. "I trust you'll have some word for me by the Honoring of Moving Fire the day after tomorrow?"

"Absolutely," Han promised. "If I can't bring the boss to see you then, I'll at least bring an offer on when you two can meet."

"Very well," Villachor said. He looked into Han's eyes, and for a moment Han was startled by the intensity there. "We stand on the edge, my friend. Riches and power beyond compare, or a long and terrifying death. Be *very* certain you wish to continue."

With an effort, Han matched the other's gaze. No, he didn't want death, fast or slow. But he didn't want riches and power, either, at least not the kind Villachor was talking about. All he wanted was to be free of Jabba, and then to be free to do what he pleased.

But this was still the path to that goal. "I am," he said firmly.

"Good." The laser intensity of Villachor's gaze faded away. "Until the Honoring of Moving Fire, then."

Han nodded. "Good day, Master Villachor."

He forced himself to walk sedately the whole way back to the gate. The security guards there obviously had been alerted, and they watched Han closely as he passed. But none of them made any move to stop him.

Just the same, he was careful to follow the zigzag path that Dozer had created for travel back to the suite. Just in case.

Sheqoa tried to hide it, but from the changes in his expression over the past hour, Bink knew the afternoon had been a bust.

Not that she was really surprised. She and Lando had played their parts perfectly, walking the balance bar between guilty recognition and the opposite but equally suspicious complete ignoring of each other. She'd had some concerns about Sheqoa throwing her at Dozer, but from what she'd been able to glean from Sheqoa's side of his comlink communications it sounded like Dozer had made it out of Marblewood before anyone could pin him down.

Given Sheqoa's increasingly dark mood, Bink decided as she babbled away cheerfully, he would probably appreciate a good, warm hug.

"So anyway—oh, my *stars,* look at the time," she said, peering at her watch. "I'm sorry, Lapis, but I have to go. My boss has some Anomid clients in town and wants me to help take them to a high-class restaurant. You know how curious Anomids are about new cultures."

"If he wants to show them Wukkar culture, he should bring them here," Sheqoa said, his mind clearly on other things.

"That's what *I* said," Bink said, waggling a finger for emphasis. "But he's stubborn, and he's always looking for an excuse to eat fancy. You'll be around for the Honoring of Moving Fire, won't you?"

With a clear effort, Sheqoa brought his eyes and attention back to her. "Of course," he said, giving her a faint smile. "Will *you*?"

"Wouldn't miss it for the galaxy," Bink promised. "I'll

see you in a couple of days, then." Stepping close, she wrapped her arms around him—making sure not to pin his right arm—and pressed herself against his chest. "I had a wonderful day," she murmured into his neck. "Thanks for everything."

His first reflex was to go stiff with surprise. His next, a fraction of a second later, was to start to relax and enjoy her touch. His third, an even shorter fraction of a second after that, was to remember he was on duty and gently but firmly push her away.

And in and among all those reactions, she finally tracked down the scent she'd noticed earlier.

"I'll see you then," he said, his hands on her shoulders as he held her at arm's length. For a moment he gazed at her, then turned and disappeared into the crowd.

Bink turned, too, and headed for the gate. So along with not trusting her—which he certainly shouldn't—Sheqoa had decided to go all cute on her. The smell she'd picked up had been tracking dye, an invisible coating of stain that would leave indelible splotches on wandering fingers that would blaze into view under ultraviolet light.

Not surprisingly, Sheqoa suspected that her rapt attention was solely so that she could get hold of the key pendant on the choker chain around his neck, and he intended to have proof of her guilt if and when she made a grab for it. Simple, diabolical, and virtually foolproof.

Bink smiled to herself. In some ways, she almost felt sorry for him. Almost.

The grand finale was in full swing, the thundering corkscrews of water roiling and cascading over the cheering crowd filling the Marblewood grounds. The sparkles and glitters in the streams flashed and glowed and erupted, foreshadowing the huge fireworks display that would highlight the Honoring of Moving Fire at the conclusion of the Festival in two days. The fountains and tendrils leapt halfway to the sky, shot out to the sides and back in again, all of it carefully controlled and contained by the shifting repulsor fields that ensured that not a single drop fell on the audience below.

Standing on the presentation balcony, drinking in the noise and sights, Villachor permitted himself a moment of quiet gloating. So Kwerve and his secret organization were dragging their feet, were they? Hoping, no doubt, that the temptation of their cryodex, combined with the pressure from Qazadi, would force him into a swamp from which there was only a single means of escape. Theirs.

But they were wrong. So was Qazadi. Villachor didn't have to choose between the known power and ruthlessness of Black Sun and the ambiguous power and freedom of Kwerve and his group of unknowns.

Because there was, in fact, a third route. A path that neither of them would ever dream he might travel.

For that matter, he wasn't convinced himself that he wanted to travel it, let alone that he needed to. But options were life, and this was a path that basic caution insisted he at least explore.

He waited until the very climax of the water show, when virtually all eyes and thoughts across Iltarr City were focused on his presentation and the similar ones at the other Festival venues. Then he pulled out his comlink and punched in a number.

It took Donnal Cuciv nearly half a minute to answer. Probably busy watching a similar ceremony at one of the other venues across town. "Cuciv."

"Avrak Villachor," Villachor identified himself. "You may remember our conversation of a few days ago."

The silence was just long enough to confirm that Cuciv

did indeed remember that awkward, embarrassing, painful session. Villachor had seen blackmail victims respond with fury, embarrassment, and terror, but he'd never seen one who had left Marblewood so completely and hopelessly broken.

Qazadi had speculated at the time that Cuciv would simply go home and kill himself, though the Falleen hadn't sounded like he really cared one way or the other. Villachor had reminded him that suicide was a shameful act in Wukkar culture and that Cuciv would never add such additional debasement to his name. So far, Villachor was right.

"I remember," Cuciv said, his voice strained but steady. Apparently he'd made peace with his situation and had resigned himself to the fact that he'd be spending the rest of his life beneath Black Sun's hammer. "What do you want?"

"Something quite small, I assure you," Villachor said. "I've heard that a member of the Imperial court is in Iltarr City. I want everything you have on him: his name, his precise rank and position, his means of arrival, his current location, and the best way to contact him privately."

There was another pause. Across the grounds, a giant waterspout formed, then split into five branches, each with its own color of flashing sparkles. "What are you going to do to him?" Cuciv asked at last.

"That's not your concern," Villachor told him. "You just get me the information."

He heard Cuciv's sigh even over the crowd. "You want it tonight, I suppose?"

"Tomorrow will be soon enough," Villachor said. "Just make sure it's accurate."

"Everything I do is accurate," Cuciv said, professional pride momentarily eclipsing his shame and resentment.

"Good," Villachor said. "Tomorrow, then."

He closed down the comlink and put it away, permitting himself a small smile. Yes, Kwerve might think his cryodex was the ultimate lure. Qazadi might think Black Sun was the ultimate threat.

But there was another hand in this game. A hand that almost certainly would outlast them both.

Because if it came down to life or death, Villachor could do worse than abandon Black Sun, bring his knowledge of the organization to the Imperials, and see what kind of protection they could give him.

It was time to see what sort of bargain Lord Vader would be willing to offer.

CHAPTER SIXTEEN

The recording of the comlink conversation ended, and Dayja looked up from his datapad. "You must be joking," he said flatly. "*He* must be joking."

"It does sound like a joke, doesn't it?" d'Ashewl replied thoughtfully. "But if it's not, this could be the beginning of the end for Black Sun. A sector chief like Villachor will know all sorts of dirty secrets. And if he can bring Qazadi's blackmail files with him . . ." He raised his eyebrows.

"Maybe," Dayja said warily, staring down at the datapad. It couldn't be this easy. There was a hidden claw in this somewhere. "I notice that for all the words he spouted, there's a distinct lack of any solid statements or promises."

"Which isn't unreasonable for someone who's merely testing the waters," d'Ashewl said.

"Or someone angling for a one-sided deal," Dayja said. "This could also be a ploy to get us looking in the wrong direction."

"Possible," d'Ashewl agreed. "But whatever's going on, we have to treat it as if it's a genuine offer." He smiled tightly. "If only because the deeper we get into whatever scheme he's working, the more of it we'll see and the better our chances of turning it back on him."

"Unless the scheme is to draw out and kill a couple of Intelligence officers," Dayja warned.

"I never said I actually trusted the man," d'Ashewl said with a shrug. "I've already sent the recall order to Captain Worhven. He and the *Dominator* should be here by nightfall."

"And then?"

D'Ashewl pursed his lips. "Given that Villachor still doesn't know about the connection between us, I'm thinking it might be time for the two of you to have a face-to-face. Possibly as part of the glitterstim scam you've already set up."

Dayja thought it over. "Maybe," he said. "Though that might bump into whatever Eanjer and his team are up to."

D'Ashewl snorted. "If Villachor comes over, we'll have no need of Eanjer and his collection of scoundrels."

"If Villachor's just blowing soap bubbles, we might," Dayja countered.

D'Ashewl waved a hand. "You're the agent on the ground," he said. "Whatever you want to do about Eanjer, I won't second-guess you."

"Thank you," Dayja said. D'Ashewl was right, of course. This was Dayja's mission, with d'Ashewl only along for support and camouflage. All decisions were ultimately his.

So were the consequences of those decisions.

"Who are you calling?" d'Ashewl asked as Dayja pulled out his comlink.

"Eanjer," Dayja said, keying for echo to d'Ashewl's comlink and then punching in the number. "I can't believe Villachor just woke up this morning and decided he was tired of working for Black Sun. If he's being pushed, maybe Eanjer's team is doing the pushing. It might be a good idea to find out what exactly they've been up to."

The comlink made the connection. "Yes?" Eanjer said.

"It's Dayja," Dayja identified himself. "Can you talk?"

"Just a moment." The comlink went dead for a moment, then came back on. "All right, I'm clear," Eanjer said, his voice gone quiet.

"I'm calling for an update," Dayja said. "And to deliver a possible warning."

"What kind of warning?"

"You first," Dayja said.

"As far as I can tell, the plan's moving along properly," Eanjer said. "There's some talk about trying to push Villachor into moving the files elsewhere on Wukkar, but I can't see him panicking enough to go that route. Failing that, we'll have to go ahead and break into the vault."

"I see," Dayja said, smiling grimly to himself. So *that* was the angle Villachor was playing. "The Honoring should certainly provide enough distractions for a job like that."

"You don't know the half of it," Eanjer said. "Now, what's this about a warning?"

"Villachor may be trying to do an end sweep around you," Dayja said. "He's been making overtures to a member of the Imperial court who's currently in town. If he actually decides to defect, whatever lure or press you're prodding him with will suddenly become irrelevant. When that happens, you and your team may be in trouble."

"I see," Eanjer said slowly. "Thank you for the heads-up. When will you know whether or not that's going to happen?"

"So far they're in the *very* preliminary verbal dance," Dayja said. "If anything changes, I'll let you know."

"I'd appreciate that," Eanjer said. "Got to go. I'll talk to you later."

The connection broke.

"Interesting," d'Ashewl said, lowering his own comlink.

"Indeed," Dayja agreed. "And suddenly Villachor's offer has a whole second thread attached."

"He's thinking about moving the files, all right," d'Ashewl said. "But he knows better than to move them without adequate security."

Dayja nodded. "And what better security than a full Imperial escort?"

"What better security, indeed?" d'Ashewl agreed. "So he pretends to defect, has us escort some trivial equipment or personal items elsewhere, and then suddenly changes his mind."

"And since there's no way he can do that without Qazadi misinterpreting his move and taking his head off halfway along," Dayja added, "it follows that Qazadi is also in on the plan."

"So the files get moved and secured, and Eanjer's team is left empty-handed," d'Ashewl concluded. "And as a bonus for Black Sun, a couple of Intelligence agents are tagged."

"And possibly dealt with in their traditional pleasant manner," Dayja said sourly. "So much for Eanjer's approach."

"So it would seem," d'Ashewl agreed. "Question is, do you restart yours?"

Dayja tapped at his lip. "I suppose I have to," he said. "If Villachor is really planning to defect, it doesn't make much sense to muddy the water further. But if it's just a scam to get us to do the heavy lifting for him, then we'll still need a vector into Marblewood."

"*And* you'll need it before he moves the files," d'Ashewl warned. "Because wherever he gets us to take them, he'll be ready to spirit them away to some other location where we'll never find them."

"Unless we can take them en route, like Eanjer was obviously hoping to," Dayja pointed out. "But he'll have thought of that, too."

"Absolutely." D'Ashewl eyed him. "So?"

"So I guess I'll be attending the Honoring of Moving Fire at Marblewood tomorrow," Dayja said, heaving himself out of his chair. "Better go put together another sample package to wave under Villachor's nose."

"You've got a day to think about how you want to tailor your approach," d'Ashewl reminded him. "And don't forget, the *Dominator* will be here by then. If you need backup, it'll be available."

"Only if we want to blow the entire operation."

D'Ashewl shrugged. "If it comes to that point, the operation will already be blown," he said. "Better a dead operation and a live operative than the alternative."

"You have such a soothing way of putting things," Dayja said dryly. "You'll be wanting me to attend you during lunch, I assume?"

"If you have time," d'Ashewl said. "If not, I can explain your absence."

"No, we need to keep up appearances," Dayja said. "I'll see you for lunch."

"What was that all about?" Bink called across the conversation room.

Standing framed by the window and the cityscape beyond, Eanjer turned to face her. "Sorry?"

"That call," Bink said. She started to point at the comlink he was putting away, apparently remembered in time that she'd already pulled out stitches from two of the seams Winter was laboriously trying to finish, and nodded instead toward the comlink.

"It was my contact," Eanjer said. "He wanted to warn me that—"

"You're telling your *contact* about our plans?" Bink interrupted.

"He already knows," Eanjer said patiently. "He's the

one who told us about Qazadi and the blackmail files in the first place, remember? Anyway, he wanted to warn me that Villachor may be getting in some more Zed police droids."

Bink looked down at Winter, and Winter could see the uneasiness in her eyes. "How many?" Bink asked.

"And how soon?" Winter added.

"He didn't know," Eanjer said. "He's not even sure Villachor's actually getting them, or whether he's just *thinking* about getting them. He'll let me know if he hears anything more." He gestured down the hall. "I'm going to the kitchen. Either of you want anything?"

"No, thanks," Bink said.

"Me neither," Winter said.

"Okay." Eanjer hesitated. "Let me know if there's anything I can help with." He left the room.

"A few extra Zeds *aren't* going to hurt the plan, are they?" Winter asked.

"They shouldn't," Bink said. But she didn't sound 100 percent convinced. "One Zed or fifty, they all work off the same master control system."

Winter nodded. She'd assumed that was the case and was pretty sure Han had it covered. But he'd been keeping his cards pretty close to his vest, especially since the kidnapping, and she wasn't absolutely sure how or where he might be tweaking his plans. Eanjer, from what she'd been able to glean, was even more in the dark than she was.

On the other hand, if Eanjer was blabbing freely about their plans to this unknown contact, it was probably just as well Han wasn't telling him much.

"I haven't had a chance to talk to Tavia lately," Winter said as she studied the seam she was working on. She had no idea what kind of eye for detail Sheqoa had, but better to be safe than sorry. "Is she doing all right?"

"She's fine," Bink said.

"You sure?" Winter pressed, moving on to the next seam. This one, she knew, had to be a little crooked if it was going to match the one on the other dress. "She seemed pretty tired when I saw her at dinner last night."

"Tired, but happy," Bink assured her. "Sitting around putting electronics together is what she lives for. Even when it's the very same electronics, like now, being put together the same way over and over. Boring, if you ask me. But, hey—differences are what makes the galaxy spin, right?"

"So I've heard," Winter agreed. "It *does* sound like she prefers the quiet life, though."

Bink was silent long enough for Winter to finish with that seam and go on to the next one. "I gather she's been talking to you," she said at last. "Interesting. She must like you—she doesn't open up to just anyone. I suppose she's been telling you how much I enjoy the whole ghost-thief lifestyle and how I'm never content to stick to anything else for long?"

Winter hesitated. "She said you're very good at what you do," she said, deciding on the diplomatic approach. "We discussed a little about how people usually enjoy the things they're good at."

"And I suppose she told you how good she is at electronics?"

"None of us needs to be told *that,*" Winter said, hoping to deflect the conversation with a little humor. "We've all seen what she can do."

"Oh, she's good at her work, all right," Bink said. "What she's *not* so good at is realizing just how nasty the universe around her really is."

Winter frowned up at her. There was a deadly serious expression on the young woman's face, one that Winter hadn't seen there before. "I don't follow."

"Let me give you an example," Bink said, an edge of

bitterness in her voice. "I assume she told you about the Rivordak Electronics Company?"

"Not by name."

"It's the one she usually trots out as an example of me scuttling every decent thing that comes into her life," Bink said. "The pay was good, the boss was happy with her performance, and she really enjoyed the work. On the surface, it seemed perfect."

"So what was wrong with it?" Winter asked. "Did they drink their soup too loudly?"

"What was wrong was that the place didn't exist," Bink said heavily. "Or at least the place she *thought* she was working at didn't exist. The whole operation was nothing but a front for one of the Hutt syndicates. They were funneling spice, smuggled weapons, even slaves through the business, the whole thing prettified by innocents like Tavia."

Winter winced. She'd seen plenty of operations like that while scoping out likely places for the Alliance to hit. "You could have told her."

"I could have," Bink agreed with a sigh. "Maybe I should have. But she's so innocent that—look, I'm sure you've figured out by now that I have enough cynicism for both of us. Probably would have enough if we'd been triplets. I just don't want her to become like me."

"I understand," Winter said.

And, oddly enough, she realized that she genuinely did. She and Princess Leia had both had that same youthful innocence wrenched from their souls by the struggle against the Empire.

"I want her to be happy, Winter," Bink went on earnestly. "I really do. But I also want her to eat regularly, and I don't mean in a Kessel prison cafeteria. Until we have enough to set her up someplace safe—" She shrugged. "I have to keep doing this."

She seemed to suddenly come to herself. "Sorry. Did I pull out any of the seams just then?"

"No, you're fine," Winter assured her. "But don't do it again."

"Right," Bink said. The darker mood had vanished, and she was back to her old cheerful self. "Sorry."

The room once again fell silent. Winter settled back to work, pondering how the universe could look so different to two so similar sets of eyes.

Wondering, too, if this would be the score Bink and Tavia were both hoping for. The score that would finally give them freedom.

Or whether tomorrow would be the last day they would ever have together.

CHAPTER SEVENTEEN

The morning had dawned in full, cloudless sunshine, with all indications of a glorious day ahead. A few white clouds had made an appearance around noon, but they'd cleared out by early afternoon. Now, with the sun nearly to the horizon and the sky to the east already starting to darken, there was every indication that the fireworks that would bring the Festival of Four Honorings to an end would play out against a full starry background.

It was, Han thought, a good day to make 163 million credits.

It would not be such a good day to walk away empty-handed.

It would be a *really* bad day to get shot.

He scowled as he strode along with the cheerfully jabbering crowds, listening to them ooh and aah at the flame spurts and fire tornadoes whipping across the air above the Marblewood grounds. His mood had been all over the charts today, ranging from the insanely optimistic right down to the frozen fear that they were heading into catastrophic failure. Right now, as he walked toward the mansion framed by the taller city buildings beyond it, his mood was hovering near the really-bad-feeling end of the scale.

Which didn't make any sense. He'd done everything

he could. The equipment was ready, he'd been through every detail of the plan, and through skill or plain dumb luck he'd managed to assemble the perfect team to pull this off.

Maybe that was the problem. Maybe the team was *too* good. Aside from the overall planning, there wasn't really much for Han himself to do. Once he delivered the specially prepared data card to Villachor, in fact, his part was going to be over. He would go back to the suite, sit down in a comfy chair by the window, and watch it all unfold below him through electrobinoculars. He would have all the waiting, all the stress and worry, and none of the action.

He scowled a little harder. He'd been the one at the helm when he and Chewie did the Kessel run. He was the one in the gun turret when there were pirates or mercenaries that needed to be shot off the *Falcon*'s back.

And even though he'd spent most of that Yavin thing sitting quietly with the sun at his back, he'd known that if and when the time came, he would be the one who came blazing in to shoot those determined TIE fighters off Luke's tail.

Sitting around and waiting while someone else had all the fun wasn't what he was used to. But for once in his life, he would have to settle for that.

As usual, Villachor wasn't hard to find. All Han had to do was look for the spot with the most elaborate fire displays and figure out which way people were going when they weren't looking at the fire or heading toward the food and drink pavilions. Like most of the big shots Han had known, and pretty much all of the crime bosses, Villachor liked to be fawned over.

Sure enough, the man and his two bodyguards were hanging out at the edge of a crowd that was mostly staring in openmouthed fascination at a fire fountain that seemed to be matching precisely the flow and movements of the water fountain that had been there two days earlier. A nice trick, Han had to admit as he waited for the line of well-wishers surrounding Villachor to thin out.

Finally there was a lull. "Ah," Villachor said as Han walked up to him, his voice sounding a little odd. "I wondered if you'd show up."

"I said I would," Han reminded him. "I brought you—"

He broke off as one of the guards stepped around behind him and something hard pressed suddenly against his side. A second later, the other guard had joined his buddy, and both of Han's arms were being tightly held.

Han looked at the men, then at Villachor. "You're kidding."

Villachor's lip twitched. "Quietly, if you please," he said. Turning, he headed toward one of the service doors of the mansion, the bodyguards and Han following.

Han didn't spot any of the other security men along the way. Apparently Villachor wanted this kept quiet even from his own people.

The reason for that quickly became clear. Waiting a few meters inside the door were three Falleen. The one in the middle was dressed in an elaborate layered robe with a long, tooled sash. Probably the Qazadi character Eanjer had mentioned, especially since the two Falleen flanking him had the hard-edged looks of bodyguards. For the first half second Han thought about trying to get in the first word, but he decided calm silence would be the better way to play this one.

Probably just as well, since Qazadi clearly wanted that first word for himself. "There he is," he said before the door had even closed behind the little group. "The human who in arrogance and pride thinks he can subvert a Black Sun official from his sworn loyalties."

Han looked at Villachor. The other's expression was

steady enough, but there was sweat on his forehead. "I'm just an employee, Master Qazadi," Han said, turning back to the Falleen. "I'm not allowed to have arrogance and pride. I just deliver messages."

"Perhaps I should deliver a message of my own," Qazadi suggested calmly. "Your body, for example, shredded into small bits of flesh and bone. Would such a communication be a clear enough message of the cost of challenging us?"

Han swallowed. He could feel his heart racing as the fear flowing through him edged rapidly toward panic.

It was the Falleen's pheromones, he knew, that were driving that emotion. But knowing that didn't do a bit of good. "I'm sure there are better ways to get what you want," he said, keeping his voice as calm as he could.

"What I *want*?" Qazadi asked, raising his eyebrows in feigned surprise. "What makes you think I want anything except your death and the death of everyone in your organization?"

"The fact that you're talking and not shooting." Han lifted his hands, about all the gesturing he could do with Villachor's bodyguards still holding his arms. "So?"

Qazadi smiled thinly. "He is indeed a clever one, Master Villachor," he commented. "Very well. I want the cryodex."

Even knowing that would be Qazadi's demand, Han still felt a fresh ripple of fear run through him. "And in return?" he asked, knowing what the Falleen's answer would be to that one, too.

He was right. "A quick death," Qazadi said. "Or, depending on what you can tell me about your people and your assets, there is a *very* slim chance that you may in fact walk out of Marblewood with your life intact."

"Sounds like a reasonable deal," Han said. "I'll need to call my contact."

Qazadi made a small gesture, and the guards released

Han's arms. Pulling out his comlink, he punched in Lando's number.

Lando wasn't going to like this. Not one bit.

"But why take him inside?" Rachele asked worriedly, her electrobinoculars pressed to her face as she stood by the conversation room window. "All he had to do was deliver a data card. Why couldn't they do that outside?"

"Maybe Villachor wanted privacy," Lando said, wondering if it sounded as lame to the others as it did to him.

It did. "Since when?" Winter countered. Her voice was under better control than Rachele's, but Lando could hear the same concern. "Up to now he's always preferred keeping us outside whenever possible. Changing that pattern is a bad sign."

Chewbacca warbled ominously.

"Easy," Lando cautioned. "Han's a big boy. Whatever Villachor's got in mind, I'm sure he can talk his way out of it."

At his side, his comlink signaled. Lando pulled it out and clicked it on. "Yes?"

"Hey, Kwerve." Han's voice was just a little too casual. "Got a situation here."

"What kind of situation?" Lando asked, beckoning to the others as he keyed the comlink's speaker to wide focus.

"I'm at a meeting with Master Qazadi," Han said. "He'd like to see our cryodex."

Uh-oh. "You mean he wants to see it work?" Lando asked carefully.

"Yeah, something like that," Han said. "I think it would be in our best interests to show it to him."

Lando glanced at the others gathered around him. Rachele and Tavia looked stricken. Winter looked controlled and calculating. Dozer looked jumpy. Chewbacca looked ready to go on a rampage. And Eanjer—

Lando frowned. Eanjer looked oddly guilty.

What exactly could Eanjer have to look guilty about?

"I can ask the boss," Lando said into the comlink. "He'd have to be shown there would be a decent payoff for it."

"Let's just say there'll be some pretty nasty payoff if he doesn't," Han said grimly.

For an instant Lando flashed back to that awkward scene on Nar Shaddaa, back after the Ylesian fiasco, when he'd been so mad at Han that he'd threatened to put a blaster bolt in his friend's head. Han tended to spark that kind of reaction in people.

But Lando had spoken in the heat of rage and frustration and betrayal. Qazadi's threat was cold and calculated and very, very serious.

"I'll tell him," Lando promised. "I'll get back to you as soon as I have his answer."

"Make it quick," Han said. "Master Qazadi doesn't strike me as the patient type."

"Got it," Lando said. "I'll get back to you soon."

He clicked off. "Well, *that's* made the day more interesting," he commented. "Any thoughts?"

Chewbacca warbled threateningly.

"Of course we get him out," Rachele agreed tightly. "I think the question is *how.*"

"Actually, the first question is *why,* as in why the bottom is suddenly falling out of this thing," Lando said. "Eanjer? You got something to say?"

Eanjer started. "What do you mean?"

"You got a call from your contact yesterday," Winter said. "Did he say anything about this?"

Eanjer swallowed hard. "I—" He stopped. "I mean—"

Chewbacca took a step toward him. Eanjer twitched back, then seemed to shrink in on himself. "I'm sorry," he said, almost too low for Lando to hear. "I didn't think . . . he mentioned that Villachor had been making overtures to the Imperials."

"And you didn't think this was worth *telling* us about?" Tavia bit out. "Blast it, Eanjer—if he makes a deal with the Imps, we've got no hold over him. He can play us without ever having to put any chips in the pot, knowing he's got a pass if his hand doesn't pan out."

"I know, I know," Eanjer said, looking even more pained. "I just didn't think anything could happen this quickly, that's all."

"I guess it did," Dozer said heavily. "So now what?"

"You heard Chewie and Rachele," Lando said. "We get him out."

"How?" Dozer retorted.

"Somehow," Lando said with strained patience, his mind scrambling for a plan. "Winter, are there any other weapons caches lying around town we could raid?"

"There are two that I know of," Winter said. "But anything small enough to be smuggled in through the gates wouldn't be nearly powerful enough to get through the mansion's doors, walls, or windows."

"Not to mention all the security men," Dozer pointed out.

"The umbrella shield will have to be shut down for the grand fireworks display later," Rachele pointed out. "Maybe we could get something big enough to breach the wall from up here."

"We can't wait that long," Lando said. "I don't know how much patience Qazadi has, but I doubt it's going to last more than an hour or so."

Eanjer cleared his throat. "I have an idea," he said hesitantly. "Winter, how accurately did you duplicate the other cryodex?"

"Completely," Winter said.

"I mean, *really* accurately?"

"What part of *completely* don't you get?" Lando growled.

"No, no, I understand," Eanjer said. "I was just thinking . . . if we let Qazadi see the cryodex, and if he's seen Aziel's enough times up close . . ." He paused, looking around expectantly.

Rachele got it first. "He'll think it's Aziel's," she said. "And that Aziel . . . no. Would he?"

"What, think Aziel's behind Lando's bid to get the blackmail files?" Winter asked. "Sure, why not?"

"She's right," Tavia agreed. "If he suspects Villachor of possible treason, why not Aziel?"

"Playing the corners against each other," Lando agreed. Eanjer might be on to something here. "So if we can convince Qazadi that Aziel is a traitor . . ."

"He won't just let Han go," Tavia said slowly. "But he'll definitely figure he's worth more alive than dead."

"Especially if he thinks Han can fill in the details of Aziel's plan," Rachele added. "It should at least buy us some time."

Chewbacca rumbled a warning.

"Good point," Lando agreed grimly. "It only works until Aziel shows up at Marblewood with the real cryodex."

"Which means we have to get to Aziel—right now—and steal the real one," Rachele said.

"What about the guards and the window alarms?" Dozer objected.

"We'll just have to take the risk," Rachele said. "If Villachor sees the two cryodexes together, Han is dead. Tavia, do you think Bink can pull it off?"

"I don't know," Tavia said, her face screwed up in thought. "This fast, and before full dark . . . I don't think so. But if it's the only way, I know she'll be game to try."

"If we pull her out now, we may lose our chance at

Villachor's vault," Winter warned, picking up the electrobinoculars and going back to the window.

"Han's worth more than all the files in the galaxy," Rachele called after her. She sent a quick glare at Eanjer. "*And* all the credits, too."

"Let's not make it an either-or just yet," Lando said. "Winter? Can you see her?"

"Yes," Winter said, shaking her head. "Sorry—she's already hooked up with Sheqoa. If we pull her out now, especially with him probably already suspicious, it's over."

"Unless we can get her back in time," Dozer said.

"Not a chance," Tavia said.

"Which leaves only one other shot," Winter continued calmly. "Dozer and I don't have anything else to do right now. We'll go to the Lulina Crown and keep Aziel there."

"Whoa," Dozer said, his eyes going wide. "Us against—? No. Not a chance."

"Relax," Winter said. "I'm not suggesting we hammer him and his collection of bodyguards. We just have to keep him locked down in his suite at the hotel."

"Oh, yeah, *that'll* work," Dozer said sarcastically. "He wouldn't have a comlink or anything he could call Qazadi with. Not a chance."

"Hang on," Lando said, the first bit of hope stirring inside him. "Winter's right. Calling Qazadi doesn't do Aziel any good. Of *course* he'll say he still has the cryodex. But he'd say that whether he did or didn't."

"So how do you pin someone in his room?" Rachele asked.

"I don't know yet," Lando said. "Let's run a quick inventory of what we've got on hand and see if we can come up with a plan."

"Unless you're still too afraid of the Falleen to do

this," Rachele added to Dozer, an edge of challenge in her voice.

Dozer flashed a glance at Winter's back and squared his shoulders. "Let's find a workable plan first," he said. "As far as gear goes, I've got some vehicle remotes, some universal door decrypt openers—"

"Excuse me," Winter said, still standing at the window. "Any of you know if Han smokes?"

"Not that I know of," Lando said, frowning. "Chewie?"

Chewbacca rumbled a negative.

"Maybe a long time ago, but not lately," Lando said. "Why?"

"Because I think," Winter said thoughtfully, "he may just have sent us a message."

Han keyed off the comlink. As he started to put it away, one of the guards plucked it out of his hand.

"Okay, I sent the message," Han said to Qazadi. "I guess we wait."

"Yes," Qazadi said. "We shall hope your superior considers you more valuable than his cryodex." He smiled thinly. "Especially since underlings are so much more easily replaced than rare artifacts."

"Not the good ones," Han countered, looking back at Villachor. The man was about two paces away. It should work. "I suppose I'm going to be your guest for a while?"

"A short while only," Qazadi said. His eyes flicked to Villachor's bodyguards. "You two, escort him to the guards' quarters across from my suite. The closet there is lockable. Put him inside."

"Manning can take him," Villachor said firmly. "Tawb will stay with me."

"They'll *both* take him," Qazadi said.

For a second he and Villachor locked eyes.

And in that second, Han made his move.

The bodyguards were still gripping his upper arms, but both forearms were free. Giving his left shoulder a little hunch as a distraction, Han dipped his right hand into his side pocket and got a grip on the data card there. In a single smooth motion, he drew it out and flipped it toward Villachor.

He had just enough time to see Villachor reflexively reach up and catch it before the two bodyguards yanked him backward and slammed him down onto the floor.

"Take it easy," Han said hastily, wincing with the sudden pain in his shoulders as the whole room seemed to sprout blasters. "It's just a delivery from my boss. I was ordered to give the card to Master Villachor."

For a long moment no one moved. Out of the corner of his eye, Han could see Villachor turning the data card over in his hands.

"What is it?" Qazadi asked.

"The details of his offer," Han said. "Not that it matters now, I suppose."

"I never said I was going to join you," Villachor insisted, tossing the card back at Han as if he were getting rid of a baby gundark.

Han gave a little shrug. "Like I said, I was ordered to deliver it."

For a few more heartbeats no one moved or spoke. Han held his breath . . .

And then Qazadi stirred and gave Han a small smile. "I admire a man who spends his last breath carrying out his orders," he said. "Let him up."

The hands pinning Han's arms to the floor reversed direction, pulling him upright again.

"And I'll take that data card," the Falleen added, almost as if it was an afterthought. "Dygrig?"

One of Qazadi's guards retrieved the data card and handed it to his boss.

"You have your orders," Qazadi continued, eyeing the card thoughtfully.

"Sir?" one of Villachor's bodyguards asked.

"Yes, go ahead, Manning," Villachor said with a hint of a sigh. "Tawb, go with him."

"Move," Manning growled in Han's ear as the hands tightened around his arms again. His breath carried a hint of tabac; apparently the man was a cigarra smoker.

They led him down a long hallway and up three flights of steps to the fourth floor. Along the way, Han noted with some interest, they passed exactly one other person, an older man in a chef's outfit hurrying toward the kitchen area. Apparently all of Villachor's people were either outside or on duty in the mansion's various working areas.

"Where are we going?" Han asked, glancing up at the skylights above him as they headed down the corridor into the northeast wing.

"You heard His Excellency," Tawb growled.

"Yeah—a closet in his guards' room." Han looked sideways at Manning. "I don't suppose you could give me a cigarra to help pass the time."

Manning snorted. "Yeah. Sure."

"No, really," Han pressed. "I really need one, and I know you smoke—I can smell it on you. Come on, give me a break. I really need it."

"You really need a smoke?" Letting go of Han's arm, Manning took a long step forward and fell into step beside him, pulling a long, thin cigarra from his pocket. "Like this one?"

"Watch it," Tawb warned. "Qazadi's not going to like it if you get smoke in his rooms."

"I won't," Manning assured him. He lit the cigarra and puffed out some smoke. "Smoke like this?" he asked Han, puffing out another cloud.

"Yeah, like that," Han said, straining against Tawb's

grip as he tried to get closer to the twisting tendrils of smoke, hoping he could mask his actual disgust for the stuff. "Come on, let me at least *smell* it."

"Because I'd be in real trouble if I gave you anything," Manning continued, walking backward as he inhaled more smoke and puffed it back at Han, always keeping just far enough away that Han could only get a whiff from the edge of each cloud before it drifted up to the ceiling. "Especially a cigarra. Especially in Qazadi's suite."

"Come *on,*" Han pleaded. He could practically feel his nose hairs curling as he inhaled the smoke, and his lungs were hovering on the edge of a violent coughing fit. But he had to make this look real if he wanted Manning to keep up the game.

"Enough," Tawb snapped. "Come on—we're too close as it is."

"Relax," Manning soothed. He gave one final puff and then slipped a cap on the cigarra to extinguish it. "I'll save the rest for later," he said, dropping it back into his pocket. "Enjoy the memories." He stopped at an open door and gestured inside. "In here."

"Sure," Han said. Winter and Rachele would be up in their suite right now, keeping a close eye on the mansion and grounds, and an odd pattern of smoke puffs in one of the skylights should be just the sort of thing one of them might notice.

Or they might miss it completely. But if they *did* spot it, they might figure out that Han was pointing them to the part of the mansion where he was being taken.

It was a long shot. But sometimes long shots paid off.

The room they ushered him into was surprisingly large, equipped with a small table and four chairs, a couple of floor lights, and six beds spaced around the living area. Guards' quarters, all right, furnished for men or Falleen who would use the room for little except sleeping. Manning led the way across to a wide door on the side wall that had an oversized keypad beside it. He punched in a simple code—one, two, three—and the door slid open to reveal a large walk-in closet. Tawb walked Han over to it and gave him a shove inside.

"You've got to be kidding," Han protested as he regained his balance and looked around. No clothing, no storage boxes—the closet was completely bare except for a couple of long hanging rods along the side walls, some moveable shelves, and about a dozen hangers. "How about you at least give me one of those chairs?"

"How about we don't," Tawb said, giving the closet a quick once-over of his own and then backing out. "Enjoy your stay. We'll be back when Master Villachor calls for you."

"More likely when Master Qazadi calls," Han called as the door slid shut. "He seems to be the one running things now."

There was no comment from either of them. Han hadn't really expected one.

The closet was pitch-dark, but Han had spotted a switch by the door on his way in. He tapped it, and a set of soft lights went on along the closet's upper edges.

He spent the next couple of minutes looking around the room, hoping there might be something useful that he'd missed on his first sweep. But there was still nothing. The hangers were high-class types, polished hardwood with chrome hooks—marginally useful as clubs, but nothing that would do any good against a heavy wooden door. The shelves and clothing rods were the same polished hardwood, again not offering much in the way of escape material. The walls and floor were also hardwood, a different kind from that of the shelving but just as solid. The ceiling—

The ceiling.

Han looked up. The ceiling looked to be made of some kind of ceramic. But back when Rachele had been talking about the vault, she'd mentioned a gap between the ceiling and the floor above it. If the same design was in play up here, that ceiling shouldn't be supporting any weight, and might not be all that thick.

And if the between-floors gap was big enough for him to fit into . . .

It took a couple of minutes to take down the shelves and set them up against the side walls, angled from floor to ceiling in opposite directions to create a sort of make-shift scaffold. Picking the sturdiest-looking of the wooden hangers, he climbed up onto the shelves and gave the ceiling an experimental tap.

Nothing happened. He tapped a little harder, then a little harder, wondering if the noise was going to draw unwelcome attention. But no one rushed in. He kept at it until finally, with a medium-hard tap, the hanger broke through the ceramic.

He'd been right—the material wasn't very thick. Working along the spiderweb of cracks radiating outward from the impact point, he broke off enough to make a twenty-centimeter opening. He climbed the rest of the way up his scaffolding and eased his head through.

There was a between-floors gap, all right. Unfortunately, it was no more than twenty or thirty centimeters deep, with a narrower framing above the closet door. Bink might have been able to get through, especially with proper climbing gear, but there was no way Han was going to.

But if he could tear away enough of the ceiling outside the closet, he might be able to use one of the clothing poles to work the keypad and open the door. The one-two-three code Manning had punched in was probably a default setting and would be easy enough to duplicate.

Climbing back down, he moved his scaffolding to a spot right in front of the door and got to work.

From everything Dayja had read in the visitor brochures, the Honoring of Moving Fire was the climax of the Festival, the day when the various venues around the planet worked the hardest to outdo each other. Someday, Dayja decided, he would have to take the time to come here and actually watch it.

But today wasn't that day. Today he had eyes only for the crowd wandering the Marblewood grounds.

There were eleven people on Eanjer's team, he knew. Peeking in from their balcony nine days earlier, he'd seen them all in their suite's conversation room. And though he'd seen one of the women only from behind, he'd had clear views of all the others' faces. Today, right now, was their last and best chance to breach Villachor's mansion and get into his vault. They should be here, ready to play their parts in whatever scheme Eanjer had come up with.

He'd already spotted three of them. Two of them, the team's youngest human male and the shifty-eyed Balosar, seemed to have the same job: to stroll around and surreptitiously attach something beneath the flame-patterned gowns of the various serving and maintenance droids. Restraining bolts, Dayja guessed, or possibly small detonite charges. The third team member, a black-haired young woman dressed in a long and vibrant red gown, had attached herself to Sheqoa, the Marblewood security chief. She, obviously, was setting up to be the diversion.

So where in blazes were the other eight?

Off to his left, a sudden geyser of blue-yellow flame burst up toward the sky, sending a wave of warmth across the assembled crowd. Dayja gave the fountain an absent-minded look, then changed direction and headed toward the drink pavilions. The sun was just about down, with full darkness and the climactic fireworks display maybe an hour and a half away. He would give Eanjer that first hour to make his move, he decided. After that, if there was still nothing happening, he would go find Villachor and try to pick up the threads of his original penetration plan.

In the meantime, the Marblewood food and drink pavilions were still impressively stocked. He might as well take advantage of that.

The room ceiling just outside the door was as easy to break through as the closet ceiling had been, though Han winced at each snap and crack that the ceramic made as the pieces came loose. He could see that the room door was partially open, and he was mildly surprised that no one out there had noticed the noise he was making.

Still, as he'd already noted, most of Villachor's people were busy elsewhere. That, plus the noise of the crowd and the show outside, was apparently enough to cover his activities.

The first snag came when he realized that the clothing poles were too long to maneuver through the holes, into the between-floors gap, and down through the hole outside the door. They also stubbornly refused to break, even when he angled one of them against the wall and jumped on it.

But there were still the fancy hangers. By hooking them together, he was able to make a flexible chain long enough to dangle through the opening and tap against the keypad.

Not that it was easy. It took a multitude of attempts and more patience than Han thought he had. But in the end, he got the door open.

Luckily the main room was still empty. Holding one of the hangers ready like a club, a small part of his mind recognizing how ridiculous such a weapon would be against knives, neuronic whips, and blasters, he crossed the room and eased a look outside.

And found himself well and truly blocked. Fifteen meters down the hallway, standing on opposite sides of one of the doors, were the two Falleen bodyguards he'd seen earlier.

Evidently Qazadi was the one person in Iltarr City who wasn't outside watching Villachor's fire show.

Mouthing a curse, he eased back from the door. Okay, so he was trapped in here. But that wouldn't last forever. As soon as Lando showed up with their fake cryodex, Qazadi would surely go downstairs to take a look. Where Qazadi went, the bodyguards would also go.

And with the rest of Villachor's people out and about, once the Falleen were gone Han basically should have free run of the mansion.

Assuming Lando did indeed bring the cryodex.

Get this through your head, Solo, Lando's angry words whispered through his memory. *We've been friends in the past, so I'm not going to do what you so richly deserve and blow your head off. But don't ever come near me again.*

Lando had told him earlier that he'd cooled down since that rant, that he'd grudgingly realized Han hadn't stiffed him on purpose. Given their long history together, Han had accepted the cease-fire as genuine.

But what if it wasn't? What if the not-quite-apology had simply been the words Lando figured he had to say in order to get a shot at Eanjer's 163 million credits?

In that case, all Lando had to do was stick with the original plan, help the others raid the Marblewood safe, and leave Han to whatever Qazadi decided to do with him. Neat and clean, with no need for Lando to dirty his own hands.

And it would pretty much guarantee that he'd never have to worry about Han coming near him again.

Han took a deep breath. No, Lando wouldn't do that to him. Not that way. Definitely not with Chewie breathing down his neck.

He just had to wait. That was all. Just wait.

Backing across the room to one of the beds, he settled down onto the floor behind it, slouching enough to put his eyes just above mattress level, where he could see the hallway but wouldn't be immediately visible himself unless whoever was passing took a careful look.

Lando and the others would come up with something. He just needed to be ready when they did.

Carefully, Lando settled their fake cryodex into its case and sealed it. "Everyone ready?" he asked, looking around the room.

A chorus of affirmatives ran through the group. They certainly *looked* ready, Lando decided. Even with a brown floppy hat obscuring half her face and the tension of anticipation lying before her, Tavia was stunning in her demure brown dress. Rachele had moved her computer over to the window, ready to provide whatever support anyone needed, whether it involved data fishing or high-sky visual work. Winter and Dozer were dressed in outfits that wouldn't draw a second glance on the street but which were tailored to allow ease of running, dodging, or shooting. Chewbacca, typically, just looked impatient to get going.

"Okay," Lando said, carefully adjusting the edge of the nondescript silk tear-away jacket Zerba had made for him. "Let's do this."

"Hang on!" Eanjer called from down the hall.

Lando turned, wondering irritably what the other man wanted now.

He felt his mouth drop open. Eanjer had put on a long dark blue coat, its upturned collar hiding much of the medseal that covered the right half of his face. Draped jauntily across his head was a wide burgundy beret with a side spray of drooping feathers at the lower edge that hid most of the rest.

"What are you all dressed up for?" Lando demanded.

"I'm going with you," Eanjer said, his voice firm. "It's my fault Han's in this mess. I'm not going to just sit here and do nothing."

"What if Villachor's people recognize you?" Tavia asked.

"They won't," Eanjer assured her.

"And if they do?" Tavia persisted.

Eanjer's single eye looked like something cut from flint as he slowly turned to face her. "Then you and Bink will have an extra bit of diversion to do, won't you?"

Chewbacca growled and gestured impatiently toward the door.

"Yes, and we don't have any to waste," Lando agreed reluctantly. He didn't want Eanjer in there with him. But unless they threw binders on the man's wrists or ordered Rachele to sit on him, there wasn't any practical way to keep him in the suite. "Fine. *But.*" He leveled a finger. "You'll stay in the background, do *only* what one of us tells you to do, and will *not* make yourself a diversion of any kind. Understood?"

"Understood." Eanjer smiled cynically. "After all, if Villachor gets me, your hundred sixty-three million suddenly shrinks to eight hundred thousand. Can't have that, can we?"

"Never mind the shrinkage," Lando growled. "We know what we're doing. You don't. So stay out of the way."

"Trust me," Eanjer said softly. "I have no intention of dying today."

"Good," Lando said. "Because neither do the rest of us." He took a deep breath. "All right. Let's go."

There was another round of muted agreement as they all headed for the door.

As he joined them, Lando felt a frown crease his forehead. It had been hard to tell through all the rest of their murmurings. But he could have sworn Winter had just said—

"Winter?" he asked.

"Yes?" she said, looking at him.

Lando felt his lip twitch. "Nothing," he said, and kept walking.

Because, really, no one said *May the Force be with us* anymore. No one but Rebels and religious nuts.

And if Winter was one of either group, he really didn't want to know about it.

CHAPTER EIGHTEEN

Dozer settled the airspeeder down onto the rooftop landing area half a block from the Lulina Crown Hotel and cut the engine and lights.

"In position," Winter reported into her comlink. She listened a moment, then nodded. "Okay. Let us know when."

She clicked off and put it away. "The others are heading in," she told Dozer. "Lando will call when he wants us to make our move."

Dozer nodded, staring through the gathering darkness at the entrance to the Lulina Crown's airspeeder garage floor. "Great," he muttered.

"You ready for this?"

Dozer clenched his teeth. No, he kriffing well *wasn't* ready for this. And if Winter had any brains, she wouldn't be ready, either.

Because that was a Falleen in there. A *Falleen.* More than that, a Falleen who'd already once brought Dozer to the edge of saying things he didn't want to say.

And he'd done it just by smiling, asking nicely, and filling Dozer's lungs with biochemical poison.

Dozer had always prided himself on being in control. Always. Even when he was working for someone else, there were still important bits of freedom that he possessed and would never give up. *He* was the one who chose whether to obey questionable or dangerous orders. *He* was the one who decided when and how to close the deal he needed to close. *He* was the one who knew when he needed to stick with it and when he needed to bail.

With the Falleen, he no longer had those freedoms. The Falleen could take all of them away from him.

He looked sideways at Winter. She was gazing straight ahead at the garage entrance, but he knew she could feel his eyes on her.

And there was no fear in her face. Nothing but calmness and determination.

Dozer felt his lip twist. She was barely half his age. Certainly no more than half his size. But even she should be smart enough to be concerned about the odds of going up against a Black Sun official and his bodyguards.

Maybe she *was* nervous. Maybe she just wasn't showing it.

Or maybe she just didn't care. Maybe all she cared about was getting the job done.

And Dozer would be damned if he let a half-baked girl show him up.

In fact, come to think of it, the whole bunch of them had been pretty much ignoring him from the day this whole thing started. He'd been scheduled as front man, and then Calrissian had showed up and been handed the job. He'd expected to have to boost airspeeders, but Eanjer had just gone out and rented the things. Aside from the Z-95 and that other job Han had asked him to do, he'd basically done nothing to earn his slice of the pie except pass out bribes that everyone knew Villachor's people wouldn't even take.

Well, that was going to change. He, Dozer Creed, was going to make Eanjer's 163 million look like pocket change. And when he did, the others would treat him with more respect. A *lot* more respect.

"Yeah," he growled to Winter. "I'm ready."

And to his mild surprise, he found that he actually meant it.

A hissing curl of flame rolled past directly above them like a flaming snake. Lando ducked reflexively, even though the fire was contained by a repulsor field and a good two meters above his head. Chewbacca, who was even closer to the flame, didn't even flinch.

But then, Chewbacca was seriously focused right now. Having seen him in that mood before, Lando was just as glad the Wookiee's focus wasn't on him.

The fire blew past, and Chewbacca rumbled.

"He's here," Lando said.

"Where?" Eanjer asked.

"Over by the security station at the south end of the children's play pavilion," Lando told him.

Eanjer grunted. "I'm a little surprised he was willing to meet out in the open like this."

"I wasn't offering him any choice," Lando said grimly. "I doubt he's very happy about it."

"We don't always get what we want," Eanjer said philosophically. "Is Qazadi with him?"

Chewbacca rumbled again.

"No sign of any Falleen," Lando reported. "Okay. Ten more steps, and it'll be time for you and Chewie to break off and go find Bink."

"Wait a minute," Eanjer objected, frowning at Lando with his good eye. "I thought I was going with *you*."

"I don't know where you got that idea," Lando said. "You're going with Chewie."

"But—"

"And if you give either of us any static about it, he's going to toss you over his shoulder and carry you out of here like a child throwing a tantrum," Lando told him. "Clear?"

Eanjer threw a look upward at Chewbacca. "Clear," he said reluctantly.

"You came here to get Han out," Lando reminded him. "That's Chewie's job, and I know he can use your help."

Chewbacca warbled his opinion of *that*.

For once, Lando decided it would be best not to translate. "Me, I'm just delivering a package and then getting out," he said instead.

Which wasn't quite true, either. Again, Eanjer didn't need to concern himself with the details.

Chewbacca growled a warning.

"Time to go," Lando said, underlining his order with a firm push against Eanjer's shoulder. "Good luck."

With a curt nod, Eanjer veered off into the crowd, Chewbacca striding along behind him. Lando waited until the Wookiee was just a head bobbing along above the crowd, then pulled out his comlink. "Rachele?"

"Looks like a total of eight bodyguards in the clump," she reported. "But there are at least four more security types loitering in a ring twenty meters out from the main group. There might be more that I haven't tagged."

Lando nodded. He'd expected Villachor to come heavily prepared, and he'd been right. "Qazadi?"

"No sign of him. Villachor may be planning to take you inside for that part of the meeting."

"I'm sure he is," Lando said sourly. Going inside the mansion was what had gotten Han locked up, and Lando had no intention of offering Villachor a two-for-one special. Especially given what he was wearing beneath his tear-away outfit. "Did Tavia make it in okay?"

"She's in, and hanging around the main flame geyser setup," Rachele said. "Hold it . . . Yes—she's seen Chewbacca. Starting to move southeast . . . okay, I see Bink now, coming out of the drinks pavilion with Sheqoa. Chewie and Tavia are drifting to intercept."

"Good," Lando said. He thought briefly about having Rachele give Tavia a quick call to remind her about the newly tweaked timing, then decided against it. She and Chewbacca knew what they were doing, and Bink already knew to wait for their lead. As long as they didn't push it, the timing ought to be all right. "Okay, I'm going in," he said. "How's the north end of the children's pavilion look?"

"Clear, as far as I can tell," Rachele said. "But I can't tag all of Villachor's people from here. Watch yourself."

"I will," Lando said. "Don't forget, odds are Villachor hasn't spread my face around too widely, not even to his whole security force."

"That may be what *your* calculations tell you," Rachele said darkly. "Me, I'm not so sure."

"I'll be fine," Lando said. "I've got those squeaker charges from Kell's pack. If worse comes to worst, I can start tossing them around and try to get away in the confusion."

"Just don't make it *too* confusing," Rachele reminded him. "The last thing we want right now is a full-blown panic."

"I know," Lando said. "I'll check in again after I make the drop."

The children's pavilion was easy to identify, full of colorful play equipment and bursting with excited shouts and laughter. Lando approached the north end cautiously but didn't see any hard-eyed men hanging around. Through the maze of colorful climbing and play structures he caught occasional glimpses of Villachor and his clump of guards, waiting for Lando at the south end, where Lando had told them to wait.

Villachor wasn't going to be happy about being stood up this way. But people didn't always get what they wanted.

As he walked past the pavilion he dropped the case casually inside the northwest corner's vertical support pillar.

He walked for another minute, weaving in and out of traveling clumps of people, at one point slipping through a double line as they moved back and forth between one of the flame fountains and the drink pavilion. Only then did he pull out his comlink and punch in Villachor's number.

The other man answered promptly. "Villachor."

"Kwerve," Lando identified himself. "The package is waiting for you at the northwest corner of the children's pavilion."

There was a brief pause. "I thought we were going to have a face-to-face discussion like civilized gentlemen."

"I know," Lando agreed. "My boss decided there wasn't really anything more we needed to say to each other right now. He also wants to know when we can expect his other employee to be released."

"After we've checked out the device," Villachor said. "And if it isn't where you say—or if there happens to be an explosion when we open it—I promise you his only release will come from a *very* slow death."

"There won't be any explosions," Lando promised, wincing. Chewie's plan for getting Han out had better work. "My boss told me to tell you in turn that if any of his people are harmed, *you'll* be the one who'll die very slowly."

"I'm sure he did," Villachor said with deceptive calmness. "Tell him I'm looking forward to meeting him someday."

"Someday," Lando promised, trying to match the other's tone. "Enjoy the package. We'll look forward to seeing our friend soon."

When it happened, it happened all at once.

One minute the hall outside Han's room was as dead as a Hutt's list of friends. The next it was suddenly hosting a parade. Keeping as low as he could, he watched as six humans and three Falleen went marching past, one of the Falleen dressed like he was getting an Imperial citation, the other Falleen and the humans armed right up to their collarbones.

Somewhere out there, Lando had apparently delivered the cryodex.

He waited until the procession had passed, and gave them another minute after that just to make sure. Then, easing up out of his slouch, he headed silently to the door. A quick check in both directions showed that the hallway was again deserted. Trying to watch both directions at once, he headed back toward the central section of the mansion.

There wasn't much he could do yet, he knew. Not until the plan kicked off in earnest. With no weapons, allies, or comlink, all he could do was find a place to go to ground for a while.

Fortunately, having had some time to think about it, he'd come up with the ideal spot.

Only the major rooms on Rachele's schematics had been labeled, but her analysis of this particular second-floor cluster of small rooms had suggested they were probably a security station. At the moment, with the Marblewood guard contingent stretched thin, it stood to reason that the smaller substations were likely to be deserted.

The main security room part of the cluster, where the

equipment and weapons were probably stored, was solidly locked. But the lounge area to the side was open and empty.

Best of all, it was conveniently located right down the hall from the main guards' quarters and ready room, the room right over the junior ballroom.

The room where, if all went according to plan, the team would be assembling to breach the vault.

There was a good chance, Han knew, that no one would disturb him until the unexpected entertainment Kell and Zerba had arranged started up outside. But just in case someone did . . .

The lounge turned out to be stocked with plenty of snack foods and bottles of water, fruit juices, and caf drinks. Finding a tray, Han took it to the sideboard and loaded half the drink bottles and half the bowl of fruit onto it. Then, positioning himself with his back to the door, he slid the hanger he'd taken from his closet holding cell into his belt where it would be handy.

A roving guard would probably be instantly suspicious of a stranger wandering the mansion's hallways. He shouldn't be nearly so suspicious of a simple worker who had come to restock the snack selection.

With luck he'd remain unsuspicious long enough for Han to get in the first shot.

Eyeing the snacks, wondering if it would look suspicious if a guard caught one of the food-service workers eating on the job, Han settled in to wait.

Dayja was still circling the grounds, looking in vain for the rest of Eanjer's team, when he finally spotted one of them.

Not that the discovery was anything to be especially proud of. The Wookiee towered over all the humans and most of the other aliens mixed into the crowd—tall enough, in fact, that he and the others of his species were probably in danger of being singed by some of the lower flowing-fire exhibits. He was heading northwest, Dayja saw, striding through the crowd with a determination that confirmed he wasn't just aimlessly enjoying the show.

Smiling tightly, Dayja plotted himself an intercept/tracking course and headed off to see what the Wookiee was up to.

He'd gotten four steps when a hard object abruptly jabbed into his ribs, bringing him to an equally sudden stop. "Well, well," a voice murmured in his ear. "About time you showed your face."

Dayja swallowed a curse. In all that had happened over the past few days, he'd nearly forgotten that voice. "Hello, Crovendif," he said casually. "Enjoying the show?"

"Enjoying it a lot more now," Crovendif growled. "Master Villachor's been all up on my back, wanting more of that glitterstim you foisted off on me. Only you never showed. Anywhere."

"I've been busy," Dayja said, looking casually over his shoulder. If he could twist himself out of Crovendif's line of fire, he should to be able to take him down quietly enough that the crowd flowing around them wouldn't even notice.

Unfortunately, that lack of awareness probably wouldn't extend to the two Marblewood security men watching him from a few meters away.

He'd tagged Crovendif as too stupid or too careless to secure backup before confronting a potentially dangerous suspect. Clearly he'd underestimated the man. "I trust Master Villachor found the sample intriguing?"

"I don't know," Crovendif said. "What say we go ask

him?" He pressed the blaster harder into Dayja's side. "Right now."

Villachor had been glowering across the children's pavilion for nearly two minutes, planning in exquisite detail exactly what he would do to his prisoner if Kwerve was lying, when confirmation finally came. "They've got it," Manning announced quietly, leaning a little closer to his comlink clip. "Same case he brought in before."

The same case. Did that also mean the same booby trap? "Did they open it?"

"No, sir," Manning said. "They're taking it to the guardroom."

Where Dempsey and his bomb-scanning equipment were already set up. "Good." Villachor glanced around, half expecting to see Kwerve watching him from the fringe of the crowd. But the man was nowhere to be seen. "Back inside," he ordered. "Alert His Excellency that we should have the cryodex in the southwest foyer within a few minutes."

"He's already there," Manning said uncomfortably. "Bromley says he looks impatient."

Villachor swallowed a curse. Of course Qazadi was impatient. He wanted someone dead.

But at least that someone wouldn't be Villachor. Not once he proved that Kwerve really had shown him a cryodex.

Though why Kwerve had given it up so easily still bothered him. Was their prisoner worth that much to his boss? Or was there something else still going on beneath the surface?

"Do you want us to go after him, sir?" Tawb asked. "Or shall we send out a full alert? We have Kwerve's description."

"But not his face," Villachor growled.

Tawb winced. "No, sir."

Villachor shifted his glare to the sky above him. Cursed useless cam droids, and the techs *still* hadn't figured out why they couldn't take decent pictures. "Forget it," he decided. His two bodyguards and Sheqoa were the only ones who'd actually seen the man, and right now he needed all three of them to stay exactly where they were. "There's no serious damage he can do out here. Not now."

He gestured to the other security men. "The rest of you, return to your patrol areas," he said, raising his voice over the noise of the crowd. "And keep your eyes open."

Someone else, even another crime lord, might have expressed his impatience by pacing back and forth across the foyer. But vigos didn't pace. At least this one didn't. Qazadi was standing perfectly still as Villachor and his two bodyguards walked in through the doorway, his eyes cold as he stared at and through Villachor.

"The cryodex is in our hands, Your Excellency," Villachor announced. "It's being checked for traps as we speak."

"And this Master Kwerve?" Qazadi asked.

"He skipped the meeting and left the case in a different spot," Villachor said. "He's probably already left the grounds."

"Without his companion?" A hint of an icy smile touched Qazadi's lips. "I think not. Alert your guards to watch the doors carefully. Sooner or later he'll attempt to enter the mansion."

"The guards are already on alert," Villachor said, trying not to scowl. He didn't need a vigo to tell him how to run his own territory. "The doors are quite secure."

"Good," Qazadi said. "I wish to see this alleged cryodex. How soon until the check is complete?"

Across the foyer, the guardroom door opened and Dempsey emerged, his gait an ominous mixture of urgency and reluctance. He was holding the cryodex in front of him in both hands as if it were a priceless work of art.

"I would say it's complete right now," Villachor said, beckoning to Dempsey. "Bring it here," he called. "I gather there were no explosives?"

Dempsey's eyes flicked to Qazadi. But instead of answering, he merely picked up his pace.

Villachor felt a stirring of fresh anger. He wasn't accustomed to having his questions ignored. "I asked if there were any explosives," he repeated harshly.

"No explosives, Master Villachor," Dempsey said as he came to a jerky halt a few meters away from the group. He seemed now to be trying very hard *not* to look at Qazadi. "But there *was* a trap: a pressurized gas canister set to explode in a cloud-spray pattern when the case was opened."

So Kwerve *had* had one last lethal trick up his sleeve. He and his people would pay dearly for that. "What kind of gas?"

"I'll need to take the canister back to my lab to run a proper chemical analysis," Dempsey said. "But the label—" His tongue swiped across his upper lip. "The label identified it as white fieljine."

A violent hiss exploded from somewhere in Qazadi's group, a sound unlike anything Villachor had ever heard before. He jerked in reaction, twisting around to look.

He'd thought he'd seen Qazadi angry before. He'd been wrong. *This* was what an angry Falleen looked like. "Your Excellency?" he asked cautiously.

"You will find this human Kwerve and bring him to me," Qazadi said in a voice that sent a shiver through Villachor's body. "Then you will find everyone in his organization and bring *them* to me, as well."

"I understand, Your Excellency," Villachor said, wishing like hell that he did. He spun back to Dempsey. "What in the galaxy is white fieljine?"

"It's a poison," Dempsey said, visibly shaking now. "That only kills Falleen."

Villachor stared at him, feeling the blood draining from his face. In a single heartbeat this had gone from business rivalry to something bitterly personal.

Kwerve was dead, all right. So was everyone in his organization, and probably everyone his organization had ever dealt with.

And unless Villachor nailed the son of a Sith, and fast, he very likely would join them. "I see," he managed. "Well—"

He broke off again as the door behind him suddenly opened. He spun around, half expecting to see Kwerve and a heavily armed assault team charging in to rescue their comrade.

But it was only two of his security team, Becker and Tarrish, standing in the doorway, an unknown man wearing field binders pressed between them. "What?" he snarled.

"Someone outside named Crovendif told us to bring him to you, sir," Becker said, his professional demeanor cracking as he picked up on the tension shimmering across the foyer. "He said it's the man who gave him the glitterstim sample a few days ago."

Villachor felt a trickle of relief. Finally, some good news, and the timing couldn't have been better. "You asked for Kwerve's organization, Your Excellency," he said, motioning them in. "Here's the first of them."

"Really," Qazadi said, eyeing the newcomer. His brief burst of rage had apparently ended, Villachor noted uneasily. With Falleen, he knew, that could be a bad sign, or a *very* bad sign. "Bring him to me." Qazadi beckoned to Dempsey. "*And* the cryodex."

Villachor nodded confirmation of the order. Becker and Tarrish walked their prisoner over to Qazadi, stopping a few meters away as two of the Falleen's bodyguards intercepted them and silently but firmly took the man into their own custody. At the same time, Dempsey walked gingerly over to the group and likewise handed the cryodex to one of Qazadi's Falleen, who in turn handed it to Qazadi.

"As you can see, Your Excellency, it's indeed a cryodex," Villachor said, watching as Qazadi studied the instrument. "And as I also told you, my sole intent was to draw out him and his organization—"

"What is this?" Qazadi snarled, his rage suddenly back again. "Where did you get this?" He sent the prisoner a laser-edged glare. "Where did you get this?" he demanded.

"I don't know," the prisoner protested, wincing back from the Falleen's fury. "Whoever these people are, I'm not with them—"

Abruptly, Qazadi took a long step forward and slapped the man hard across his face. He staggered back, only the guards' grips preventing him from toppling onto the stone floor.

"Your Excellency, what is it?" Villachor asked carefully.

Qazadi turned vicious eyes on him. "This is not some random cryodex," he bit out. "This is Aziel's. *Aziel's!*"

"Aziel's?" Villachor echoed, thoroughly confused now. "He has his own—?"

And in a sudden, horrible rush he understood. Aziel didn't have the key codes to a cryodex that Qazadi kept in his suite, the way Qazadi had told him. He never had. Instead, Aziel was the keeper of the cryodex itself.

But if this was Aziel's cryodex, then Kwerve's offer to copy the blackmail files . . .

He caught his breath. It was impossible. For an aide to

a Black Sun vigo to even *think* about betrayal was utterly impossible.

And yet there it was, handed to them by Kwerve himself. Aziel's cryodex.

Or something that *looked* like Aziel's cryodex. "It has to be a copy," he said into the taut silence. "A forgery."

"How?" Qazadi demanded. "There are marks on the back that only his cryodex has. Marks that no one else would ever see. Certainly that no one else would ever notice. Why would they have been included?"

"I don't know," Villachor said. "But it has to be a trick. Because if it's really Lord Aziel's cryodex—" He broke off, realizing he didn't dare say it.

Qazadi had no such compunctions. "Then Aziel is a traitor," he said quietly. "And so, perhaps, are you."

"No," Villachor said quickly. Possibly too quickly. "If I were planning something with Lord Aziel, he and I would hardly need to go through all this complication. I could have given him the files long ago."

"Perhaps you did," Qazadi said. "Perhaps this was merely your preferred method of drawing my interest to this matter and then arranging my death." He lifted the cryodex slightly. "Certainly once I was dead it would be unlikely that the true ownership of this device could ever be proven."

Villachor felt his stomach tighten. The whole thing was utterly insane.

But a Black Sun vigo didn't need courtroom-level proof to make decisions and pass judgments. He could do it purely on his own suspicions.

"But I don't think poison suits your style," Qazadi continued. "If not you, perhaps one of your men has been acting in collusion with the traitor."

Villachor's first impulse was to deny it. His men were loyal, hand-screened by Sheqoa himself.

His second impulse was to keep his mouth firmly shut.

If Qazadi's threat of death was pointed at someone else, it wouldn't be pointed at him.

Qazadi knew that, too. "I see you don't deny the possibility," he commented.

"Unfortunately, anything is possible, Your Excellency," Villachor said, choosing his words carefully. "Before today, I would have said all of my men were unquestionably loyal to Black Sun. Now—" He shook his head.

"Yes," Qazadi said, the word coming out as a snake's hiss. "You've removed all human guards from the vault, as I ordered?"

"Yes, Your Excellency," Villachor confirmed. At the time, he'd thought the order dangerously stupid. Now he was very glad he'd obeyed it. "And I checked the vault after they left. The data cards were still in place." He nodded at the prisoner, who'd pulled himself mostly back to his feet and was sagging between his guards. "What do you want me to do with him?"

"*I* will deal with him," Qazadi said, eyeing the man coolly. "You say you aren't with these people, human?"

"I've never even heard of this Kwerve person," the man said, his voice strained, his breathing shallow and rapid. "Or this Aziel, or a cryodex, or any of the rest of it. I just have a good source of glitterstim, and I'm looking for someone to distribute it for me. I even brought another sample—he's got it right there." He started to lift one hand to point to Becker.

And gave a strangled gasp as Qazadi's guard bent his arm against the elbow joint. "I'm not with them," the prisoner moaned. "I swear."

For another moment Qazadi stared at him. The man squirmed under the Falleen's gaze, avoiding his eyes, looking like he was on the verge of tears. A far cry from the arrogant, overconfident drug dealer Crovendif had described, Villachor thought contemptuously.

"Take him to my quarters," Qazadi said at last. "What was he carrying?"

"A comlink, a holocamera, and a small vial," Becker said. "Maybe the glitterstim. No weapons."

"Bring them here."

Again Becker glanced at Villachor for confirmation, then stepped forward and handed the items to one of the men holding the prisoner. "Take those to my quarters as well," Qazadi ordered. "Wait for me there."

"We obey, Your Excellency," one of the guards said. He nudged the prisoner, and the three of them headed toward the service turbolift at the rear of the foyer.

Qazadi watched them go, then turned to one of his four remaining human guards. "Take two others and my airspeeders and position yourselves in observation sites around the Lulina Crown Hotel," he ordered. "I'll order Lord Aziel to bring his cryodex here. If Master Villachor is right and this is merely some clever copy, he'll answer the summons without hesitation or fear."

He looked at Villachor. "If Master Villachor is wrong and this is indeed Aziel's cryodex, he will attempt to run. By his own actions he will be condemned."

The guard bowed. "I obey, Your Excellency," he said. Pulling out his comlink, he strode briskly from the foyer, heading in the direction of the garage.

"May I offer the assistance of my own security forces?" Villachor asked hesitantly.

"Are there any you can trust with your life?" Qazadi countered.

Under the circumstances, Villachor knew what the correct answer had to be. "No," he conceded.

"Then your men may not help," Qazadi said. "I'll let you know the results of my interrogations in due time."

He turned and headed toward the stairs, the two Falleen and three humans forming a moving box around him.

Villachor watched him go, a hollow sensation in the pit of his stomach. In the nearly three weeks since Qazadi and his entourage had arrived, he'd seen the Falleen's guards take up such an obviously defensive formation only on the rare occasions when they moved from the safety of the mansion out onto the grounds. Clearly, Qazadi no longer felt safe inside Villachor's home.

Villachor could hardly blame him. If the cryodex was a fake, how had it been done? If it was real, what could possibly have possessed Aziel to make this insane bid for power?

Unless Kwerve's people hadn't been targeting only Villachor. Maybe they'd been working both sides: Aziel for his cryodex, Villachor for the files themselves.

Or perhaps there was no treason at all. After all, he had only Qazadi's word that Kwerve's cryodex was identical to Aziel's. Could this be Qazadi's way of painting Villachor with the suspicion of treason?

If so, there was likely nothing he could do about it. He was a sector chief; Qazadi was a vigo. Whether Aziel was genuinely a traitor or whether Qazadi was manipulating nonexistent evidence to implicate Villachor, it was one side's word against the other's.

And there was no doubt at all which of them Prince Xizor would believe.

Suddenly, a deal with the Imperials was looking better and better.

"Sir?" Tawb said.

Villachor snapped out of his dark thoughts, fresh determination flooding through him. He wasn't going to go running off to Lord d'Ashewl, Darth Vader, or even the Emperor himself. He was going to stand his ground and fight for the power and territory that he'd worked so hard to build. The power and territory that were rightfully his. How could he even have thought about giving in?

And then he realized how he could have thought about it, and he bared his teeth in a vicious snarl.

Curse Qazadi and his Falleen pheromones, anyway.

"Sir?" Tawb repeated, more urgently.

"What?" Villachor snapped.

"I'm getting reports of a commotion outside," the bodyguard said urgently.

"What kind of commotion?" Qazadi's voice wafted across the room.

Villachor turned around. The Falleen and his guard had paused near the foot of the stairway and were looking back at Villachor and the others.

Villachor turned back to Tawb. And curse Tawb and his big mouth, too. "You heard him," he growled. "What kind of commotion?"

"It appears—" Tawb frowned and leaned closer to his comlink clip. "It appears that some of the droids are . . . going crazy."

The sky was darkening, and Bink was wondering if something had gone wrong, when she finally spotted Chewbacca drifting casually toward them.

She breathed a quiet sigh of relief. Sheqoa's comlink clip had been spitting out new orders or updates every few minutes for the past hour, and though she couldn't hear any of them distinctly as she nestled against his side, she could tell by his facial muscles and body tension that something wasn't going well in Villachor's little corner of paradise. The fact that Sheqoa apparently was ignoring the updates in favor of continuing to wander the crowds and pretending to enjoy Bink's prattle confirmed that Bink was still his current assignment.

Which was, of course, exactly how she wanted it.

Chewie was moving closer, his attention apparently on something off to the side. Bink hadn't seen Tavia yet, but she had no doubt her sister was moving up behind her, exactly as she was supposed to.

Casually, she extricated her right hand from Sheqoa's left arm, reaching up to brush a lock of hair out of her eyes and taking the opportunity for one last visual check of the fingersnips fastened all but invisibly beneath her nails. They were set and ready to go. Out of the corner of her eye she spotted Chewbacca moving in from her left . . .

And suddenly there he was, angling sideways straight into her as he looked at something off to his own left. Bink jerked away from the big furry wall bearing down on her and ducked sideways in front of Sheqoa. She pivoted around to face him as she continued her evasive motion, her left hand clutching at Sheqoa's shoulder, her right pressed briefly against his upper chest as she breathed a startled and panicky gasp into his face.

As she continued around to his other side, the fingersnips on her right hand deftly cut through the small chain connecting the key pendant to the choker around his neck. The fingertip-sized glazed stone dropped into her hand, and as she palmed it, she continued on to Sheqoa's right side, grabbing his right arm with both hands.

Which was his gun hand, which he'd already warned her not to grab. Sure enough, before she could even get her feet planted, his forearm lurched reflexively up and back, throwing off her hands and sending her falling backward into the flowing mass of people behind her. She half turned as someone grabbed her, caught a glimpse of a brown dress and floppy hat and Tavia's face. As the two of them spun around, fighting for balance against Bink's momentum, Bink's flailing right hand came up beneath the brim of Tavia's hat, flipping it back and off her sister's head. As the hat sailed up into the air, Bink's left hand slipped into a fold of her skirt and caught hold of Zerba's magic egg. She squeezed the activator—

And in the blink of an eye, as the two of them toppled to the ground, Bink's red silk dress was ripped instantly away into the egg, leaving her dressed in a duplicate of Tavia's brown dress, as Tavia's brown dress similarly vanished to reveal the copy of Bink's red one.

Their twirling movement as they fell had landed Bink on the bottom of the two-woman heap. Tavia was off her in an instant, rolling away so as to give Bink the necessary freedom of movement to flip over onto her stomach and get her face turned away from Sheqoa. She finished the roll, then got her hands under her and pushed herself shakily up onto her knees. A second later, half a dozen hands closed around her arms, another half dozen grabbed Tavia's, and a moment later both women were back on their feet. Standing behind her sister, listening tensely for the cues that would mean Sheqoa hadn't been fooled by the trick, Bink brushed herself off and drifted farther into the crowd, murmuring her assurances to the anxious people around her that she was fine. Someone handed her Tavia's floppy hat as she passed; she smiled her thanks and set it carefully onto her head.

"You okay?" Sheqoa said gruffly from behind her. Bink tensed—

"I'm fine," Tavia said, sounding breathless. "I'm so sorry. I didn't mean to grab you like that."

"It's okay," Sheqoa said. His voice was still gruff, but Bink could hear that the growl was coming from embarrassment, not suspicion. "Stupid clumsy oaf of a Wookiee. Did he hurt you?"

"No, no, I'm fine," Tavia said again. "I thought for sure he was going to run me straight down."

"It's okay now," Sheqoa said, and Bink could visualize him taking her arm and pulling her gently but firmly back to his side.

Somewhere in the near distance, audible over the roar of the crowd and the hissing of the various flame jets, came the sound of crashing tableware. "Uh-oh—sounds like someone's going to have some cleanup to do," Tavia commented. "I guess Wookiees aren't the only clumsy oafs here today."

The words were barely out of her mouth when two more crashes sounded across the grounds, each of them coming from a different direction. A half second later, an even louder crash echoed off the mansion wall, this one accompanied by a woman's or child's scream.

"That's not someone being clumsy," Sheqoa bit out. "Come on."

Out of the corner of her eye, Bink saw them head off quickly in the direction of the latest crash, disappearing within seconds into the crowd.

She smiled tightly to herself as she made a more leisurely departure from the area. So much for her worries that something had gone wrong.

The plan was back on schedule. Chewbacca and Tavia had done their jobs, and from the ever-growing cacophony of crashes, screams, and shouts it was clear that Kell and Zerba had done theirs.

Time for Bink to do hers.

The others would be waiting for her at the garage door. Picking up her pace, wondering just how big a mess the droids were making, she headed north.

Dayja had never been hit by a Falleen before, and if Qazadi's slap was a representative sample of their work, he was pretty sure he never wanted to be hit by one again. That single blow was still throbbing through his cheek, his head, and most of the upper half of his body.

But the residual effects from the slap paled in comparison to the mental dizziness that had been created by the revelations ricocheting across his brain.

A cryodex. So *that* was how Xizor had encrypted his blackmail files. Imperial Intelligence had managed to collect alleged bits of those files over the years but had never been able to crack the encryption or even to figure out how it was done. There were many analysts, in fact, who flatly rejected the idea that those bits were genuine Black Sun files and assumed they were simple disinformation designed to keep Intelligence running in loops.

A cryodex explained everything. And if the blackmail files, why not other sensitive information? In fact, why not the whole Black Sun information network?

Dayja wrinkled his nose. Intriguing, but highly unlikely. There might yet be other cryodexes still floating around, any one of which could instantly slice the unsliceable code. Xizor was far too smart to put too many hatchlings in the same basket.

But even if it was just the blackmail files, getting hold of that cryodex would be a major accomplishment. Especially now that most of the remaining models were part of the expanding dust cloud that had once been Alderaan. Dayja had no idea how Eanjer's team had gotten hold of Aziel's device, but he had no intention of letting Qazadi or anyone else kick it back into the shadows.

Assuming, of course, that the device he'd left Qazadi holding was indeed the real cryodex.

Mentally, he shook his head. He was with Villachor on this one. Stealing Aziel's cryodex or duplicating it both seemed to be at roughly the same level of impossibility. The whole thing was smelling suspiciously like a con man's shell game, and until he knew which shell the real cryodex was under, there was no point making any moves.

Except, of course, for the first move in any and all future plans, which was to get free of Qazadi's thugs.

"Get in," one of the thugs growled as the turbolift door slid open. Hunching his shoulders in the very image of demoralization, Dayja obeyed. The guards joined him, and they headed up.

Holodrama writers, Dayja had noticed over the years, had a strange fascination with turbolifts. They especially liked casting such places as the perfect spot for a captured hero or heroine to burst into action against evil captors, using hands or feet or concealed weapons to render their opponents dead or unconscious, usually before they even reached their designated floor. Maybe it was the drama of the close quarters that the producers liked, or maybe it was simply that turbolift fights required no set dressing and left minimal damage to clean up afterward.

It was, of course, ridiculous. The close quarters meant there was nowhere a would-be escapee could run to, along with the added disadvantage of having to fight an entire circle of enemies at the same time. The lack of furniture or decoration meant no impromptu weapons close at hand. There was also no telling what kind of setting or situation the turbolift door would open up on. Even if the hero made it through all that, a turbolift car had no place in which to hide the bodies.

Finally, the fact that the bad guys watched those same holodramas meant that they fully expected trouble to break out in turbolift cars. As a result, guards had a tendency to press even more closely around a prisoner in such a setting, their senses alert to any sign of trouble.

Unfortunately for them, the fact that they were watching for signs of impending violence tended to make them oblivious to everything else. Which made turbolifts the ideal place for a prisoner to pick his binders.

Dayja had his unfastened by the time the door slid open on the fourth floor. "Where are we going?" he asked, peering nervously out through the opening. The hallway was exquisitely decorated, with potted plants and expensive artwork along the walls, a thick carpet on the floor, and a molded glitter-coated ceiling above them. A guest floor, undoubtedly, with Qazadi and his guard contingent probably the only current residents. Several of the doors lining the hallway stood open, but there was no one in sight.

"To your own personal hell," one of the guards answered, giving him a shove out of the car. "Move."

Turbolift cars were rotten places to pick a fight. Turbolift car *doorways,* on the other hand, were ideal.

The nearest open door led into a sleeping room that was even more nicely furnished than the hallway. The walk-in closet had a lock, but there was enough room on the far side of the massive bed for both of the bodies. Dayja paused long enough to relieve the late guards of his appropriated comlink and holocamera, then headed back to the turbolift. It would have been nice to take one of their blasters, too, but he wouldn't put it past Qazadi to have all his guards' weapons track-chipped. Once the alarm went up and the hunt began, there was no point in making it too easy for them to find him.

The original plans for the governor's mansion had included a roof stairway beside the dumbwaiter shaft that led up from the kitchen in the building's central section. There was a chance Villachor had sealed it up as unnecessary and a possible security risk, but it was worth a try.

To his mild surprise the stairway was still there, its entrance concealed behind an impressive four-panel wall painting. He got the door open and slipped inside, closing the painting behind him as best he could.

Rooftops were traditionally a bad place for a fugitive

to be trapped, especially rooftops high enough that jumping would almost certainly lead to death or serious injury. But his escape probably would be discovered within a very few minutes, and the same logic that argued against rooftops as a hiding place should send Villachor's searchers running off to check all the other likely places first. At the very least, it should buy Dayja a little more time.

And right now, time was what he needed most.

Taking the stairs as quietly as he could, he pulled out his comlink. He only hoped his call wouldn't be too late.

CHAPTER NINETEEN

Across the darkening grounds came the sound of crunching wood. "There," Tawb said, pointing in that direction. "There goes another one."

"Sounds like a maintenance droid kicking over a bench," Manning added. "Yes—make that an affirmative. Tallboy's heading over to try to tackle it."

With an effort, Villachor held on to what was left of his patience. A few malfunctioning droids, and his so-called professional security men were panicking? "We have tech people for this," he growled, spinning around and heading back toward the open doorway behind him. "Call *them*."

"No," Qazadi's voice came from inside the doorway.

Villachor stopped, swallowing a curse. "They're malfunctioning droids, Your Excellency," he bit out. "It happens all the time. Probably a frequency bleed-through between motivators—"

"Or a deliberate attack," Qazadi cut him off. "Your security chief himself seems to think so."

Villachor frowned. "What?"

"He comes to you now," Qazadi said.

Villachor turned back around. Sure enough, Sheqoa had appeared from the edge of the crowd and was hurrying toward him, his hand locked around the wrist of a young woman in a red dress as he half pulled, half dragged her behind him.

And there was definitely a hard set to his face.

Villachor bared his teeth. Treason and betrayal all around him, prisoners who might hold the key waiting to be interrogated, and all these fools could worry about were a few rampaging *droids*?

But Qazadi was concerned, and Qazadi was the one calling the shots. All Villachor could do was get the mess fixed as quickly as possible and get back to the real issues.

"It's the droids, sir," Sheqoa said as he came up to them. "Serving and maintenance both."

"Yes, I can hear them," Villachor snarled as another crash and startled scream came from somewhere to the northwest. "I've already called Purvis. If there's a programming glitch, he'll fix it."

"I don't think it's a glitch," Sheqoa insisted. "I think this is a deliberate diversion. My men are already stretched thin, and this is distracting them even more—"

"Sheqoa!" Villachor snapped, feeling a surge of horror and fury. The man's neck— "Your key pendant!"

Sheqoa's free hand went to his throat, his eyes widening in the same horror as he touched the spot where the pendant should have been. Then, with a curse, he hauled the woman around in front of him. "Where is it?" he bit out as she stumbled to a halt between him and Villachor. "Curse you, where *is* it?"

"Where is what?" she protested, shrinking back from his glare. "I don't know what you're talking about."

Sheqoa swore again and shoved her toward Tawb. "Hold her," he ordered as he dug into his pocket and pulled out his glow rod. Spinning the selector to ultraviolet, he grabbed the woman's right hand, pulled it close, and turned the light on it. Villachor took a step closer and peered down at the hand.

Nothing. Just plain skin, the calcium in her fingernails

glowing the usual white, with no signs anywhere of the tracking dye that coated all the key pendants.

Sheqoa flashed Villachor an unreadable look, dropped the girl's right hand, and tried the UV light on her left. Still nothing.

"And?" Qazadi prompted from inside the doorway.

"She took it," Sheqoa said blackly. "I don't know why there's no dye, but I know she took it." He dropped her hand, all but throwing the arm back to her side. "Maybe with—" He grabbed her left hand again, this time turning it so that he could look closely at the undersides of the fingernails. He swore under his breath and swapped it out for her right hand, giving that set of nails the same scrutiny.

"Fingersnips?" Villachor asked.

Again Sheqoa flung the woman's hand back at her. "She must have gotten rid of them somehow," he growled.

"What are you talking about?" the woman demanded. "Look, I don't want to bring any trouble on you people, but enough is enough. I have rights, and I don't have to—"

"Shut up," Sheqoa cut her off. He turned and looked out over the crowd, reaching for his comlink clip. "Kastoni should be closest. I'll have him take her inside and do a complete search."

"No," Qazadi said calmly. "*I* will take her."

Villachor turned, frustration surging through him. "With all due respect, Your Excellency, you have other prisoners to interrogate," he said as civilly as he could. "Prisoners we *know* are involved."

"She's involved, too," Sheqoa insisted.

"The others will keep, Master Villachor," Qazadi said. "But this one's a female. We Falleen have a certain way with females."

Villachor looked at the woman. Her face had gone rigid. "Anything you want to tell us?" he invited.

She swallowed. "I have nothing to do with whatever it is you're all talking about," she said firmly. "I came here today to honor moving fire, and—"

"Take her inside, Sheqoa," Villachor said, jerking his head toward the door. "If His Excellency wants her, His Excellency can have her."

"Yes, sir." Sheqoa took her wrist and once again half pulled, half dragged her to the door and the waiting Falleen.

"And then pull some men from the grounds and do a sweep of the mansion," Villachor called after him. "Starting with the prisoners."

"Yes, sir."

Villachor turned back to the grounds, snarling under his breath at each distant crash or thud or scream. Apparently, Kwerve's boss wanted his people back.

Time to see just how big a price he was willing to pay for them.

"They've taken her inside." Rachele's tense voice came from Lando's comlink. "Someone in there took her—I couldn't see who it was."

Lando gazed across the darkening grounds, ducking reflexively as a spiraling fireball overhead briefly lit up the area. "I'll lay you odds it was Qazadi," he said. "At least I hope so."

"You *hope* so? Lando, do you have any idea what Falleen do to women?"

"Yeah, I've heard the stories," Lando said grimly. "I'm hoping he's got her because I figure he's got Han, too. And we know where Han is."

"Maybe," Rachele said. "*If* Winter was right about the smoke."

"I haven't seen her wrong yet," Lando reminded her. "And begging a cigarra from someone just so he could send a few puffs into a skylight is exactly the sort of thing Han would do."

"Fine," Rachele said. "You just better get in there and get them both out. And fast."

"As fast as we can," Lando promised. "Give me the signal."

"Right," she said reluctantly. "Just watch yourselves, and don't forget Dozer's run-in with Aziel. They're almost as bad with men as they are with women."

"We'll be careful."

He keyed off and looked at the sky. Night was rapidly falling, with the main fireworks display no more than half an hour away. They had to get this thing done before then.

Only he and Chewbacca couldn't move. Not yet. Not until Bink had the others safely inside the vault.

For her sister's sake, Bink had better be on schedule.

Kell and Zerba were waiting near the garage door when Bink arrived. "You get it?" Kell asked.

Bink nodded, reaching into her mouth and retrieving the key pendant from where she'd concealed it under her tongue. The tracking dye tasted exactly the way it smelled, only stronger. "Nice work with the droids, by the way," she said as they hurried to the door and went through. Beyond was a plain tan-colored service corridor. "Where to?"

"Droid repair room is this way," Kell murmured, heading off down the service corridor. "Droid control and operations are typically bundled into the same area."

"Go ahead," Bink said to Zerba, pulling at the sealing strips of her brown dress. "I'll catch up."

"Right," Zerba said, pulling a hold-out blaster from his belt. "Lightsaber?"

Bink pulled up the hem of her skirt and unstrapped

the lightsaber from her inside calf. She handed it to Zerba, accepted the blaster in exchange, and as he trotted down the corridor after Kell, she returned to the task of getting rid of her dress.

It wasn't the same easy tear-away material as the red dress that she'd worn on top of it. But Zerba had at least made sure there were no complicated hooks, laces, ties, or any of the other annoyances often associated with this class of dress. Within a minute she had the dress off and the tools and other bits of equipment fastened to her lower legs back to more convenient spots on belt and hip.

Her last task was to embed the key pendant in a glob of rock putty, open the door a crack, and toss the putty to the ground beside the door. Now, whenever Lando was ready to make his move, he could get inside without having to bully some security man into unlocking the door for him.

She was less than two minutes behind the others. But those two minutes had made all the difference in the universe. Just beyond the droid repair room, she spotted a door with a long, black-edged slice cut into it. Wincing, she hurried over and looked through the crack.

It was the droid control room, all right, its walls lined with controls, computer consoles, and status displays. Kell and Zerba were inside, moving around and between three unmoving bodies sprawled on the floor near various chairs. Grimacing, she eased the door open and went in.

Zerba spun around as the door opened, his hold-out blaster tracking toward her. He lowered the weapon again as he saw who it was. "What kept you?" he asked.

"*You* try getting out of one of those dresses," she countered, nodding back toward the door. "I never realized lightsabers made that much of a mess."

"Mine does," Zerba said, still sounding a little annoyed. "Why did you think I didn't want to use it on the outside door? Come here and tell me what I need to do."

"Probably nothing," Bink said, gingerly stepping over one of the bodies. "I hope you remembered Han's order not to kill anyone if we could avoid it."

"Don't worry—they're just stunned," Kell assured her. "I think this is the Zed console over here. But it looks pretty solid."

"Not a problem," Bink said, glancing over the console Zerba was standing beside. "Zerba, that keypad there. Enter eight or nine numbers—any eight or nine will do—then repeat three or four times."

"Right," he said, and got to work.

She crossed to Kell's console, a more heavily armored version of Zerba's. "Same thing," she told him, pointing to one of the keypads. "Zerba, toss me that lightsaber, will you?"

"I'll do it," Zerba said. He keyed in one final number and then walked over to them, pulling his lightsaber from his belt. "Sorry, but it's temperamental enough as it is. What do you need?"

"A small cut right here," she said, running her finger along one of the rear connections. "About three centimeters long, and *don't* cut any of the wires behind it."

"Got it." He ignited the lightsaber, which gave a gurgly sort of hissing that didn't sound a thing like the ones in old holodramas. The blade didn't look like anything she'd ever seen, either, a sort of sickly yellow that was no more than fourteen or fifteen centimeters long.

"I know," Zerba growled as he positioned it carefully at the spot Bink had indicated. He probably found himself apologizing for the weapon a lot.

Still, useless as it would be in a fight, it was perfectly adequate for what she needed. The tip of the blade cut easily, if noisily, through the metal, leaving another blackened scar like the one on the door. "Good," she said. "Close it down, and let's get out of here."

"You figured out a spot where we can go to ground?" Kell asked as they crossed back to the door.

"I think so," Bink said, easing the door open and looking out. The corridor was still deserted. "Service stairs twenty meters that way, and up to the second floor."

"Wait a second," Kell said, pulling a flat disk from his pocket and gazing up at the ceiling. "Any idea where the intercom and alarm wires would be?"

"What in space do you need those for?" Bink asked.

"That's right—you don't know," Kell said. "Lando called while you were chatting up Sheqoa. Villachor grabbed Han when he came in earlier."

Bink felt her breath catch in her throat. "What? Oh, bloody—"

"It's okay—we've got a plan," Zerba hastened to assure her. "We'll clue you in later."

"Right now we need an excuse for Lando to come in and make some noise," Kell said. "That's this." He wiggled the disk.

Bink clenched her teeth, running a practiced eye over the top of the door. If the system was laid out like they usually were . . . "Probably there," she said, pointing at the right-hand upper corner of the door. "That should be one of the nexus points, anyway."

"Good enough." Straining to his full height, Kell pressed the disk into place against the wall. "Okay, let's go."

Bink nodded, frowning back over her shoulder at the disk as she again started down the corridor. "What does it do?"

"Absolutely nothing," Kell said. "But they won't know that."

"We should be quiet now, right?" Zerba suggested.

Bink nodded. She had a lot more questions, but they would have to wait.

The service stairs opened up into a gorgeous hallway, and as Bink led the way across the thick carpet she decided that this was, without a doubt, the nicest target she'd ever hit.

"Where are we going?" Kell murmured.

Bink smiled. They had secrets? Fine. So did she. "You'll see."

"What do you mean, they're gone?" Villachor demanded. "*Both* of them?"

"Yes, sir," Kastoni said, his tone one of barely controlled fury. "*And* two of Master Qazadi's guards are dead. Looks like our glitterstim peddler is more than a typical drug dealer."

Villachor squeezed his comlink hard enough to hurt. That, or they'd had help from whoever had stolen Sheqoa's key pendant. "Find them," he ordered, his own anger and frustration dropping to a quiet simmer. Overt fury would only keep him from thinking clearly, and that was the last thing he could afford. "Pull as many men off ground patrol as you have to, but *find them.*"

"Sir, they're probably already off the grounds—"

"If they are, we'll deal with them later," Villachor cut him off. "You concentrate on making sure they aren't hiding somewhere in my house. Is that clear?"

"Yes, sir."

Villachor keyed off, snarling a curse under his breath, and keyed for Sheqoa. "The prisoners are loose," he said when the other answered.

"Yes, I just heard," Sheqoa said grimly. "I've sent Kastoni five more men, and I'm trying to pull enough guards from the grounds to put one on every door."

"Good," Villachor said. "Make it clear that no one goes in *or* out without my express order."

"Yes, sir," Sheqoa said. "Do you want me to assign a couple more men to you?"

"You mean in case they catch Manning and Tawb napping like they did Master Qazadi's late guards?" Villachor said acidly. "I think that very unlikely."

"Yes, sir," Sheqoa said. "If they're still here, we'll find them."

Han had rearranged the snacks and drink bottles on the tray for probably the seventh time, and was wondering how much farther he should try to press his luck, when he heard the soft sound of multiple footsteps coming his way down the hallway.

He froze, one of the apples still in his hand. Then, deliberately, he set it back on the tray and began once again moving the items back onto the sideboard. If whoever it was decided to take a closer look, he decided, the tray itself would be his best bet. He would swing it at whoever was first in line, flinging its current contents into the guard's face, then try to get to the second guard fast enough to hit him with the tray itself. The footsteps got closer . . .

And passed the door without slowing.

Han took a deep breath, some of the tension fading. That had been close.

He frowned, taking another deep breath. Wafting in from the hallway was a faint but highly distinctive scent.

The perfume Bink and Tavia had both been wearing this morning.

He was at the door in three quick strides. Sure enough, hurrying quietly down the hallway were Bink, Kell, and Zerba. At least he assumed it was Bink. "Bink!" he stage-whispered, slipping out into the hall and heading after them.

All three spun around, their blasters spinning toward him as well. All three sets of eyes widened as they saw who it was. Bink beckoned him urgently forward, her gesturing hand shifting to a warning finger across her lips.

Han nodded. He'd already figured out that part.

The three of them had stopped in front of a plain metal door by the time Han caught up to them. "We thought you were a prisoner," Kell whispered as Bink crouched down by the door with her lockpick.

"I was," Han whispered back, eyeing the ELECTRICAL CLOSET sign on the door. "There going to be enough room in there for all of us?"

"Easily," Bink assured him. There was a soft click, and the door popped open. "Inside. *Quietly.*"

Han had seen electrical closets before. In fact, he'd spent a fair amount of time hiding in such places off and on over the years. But he'd never seen one nearly this big. It was a good two meters square, with a ceiling that was pushing three meters, and there were a dozen twenty-centimeter-diameter cables running vertically along the back wall. "What are they powering, a Star Destroyer?" he muttered, looking at the massive cables.

"Close," Bink murmured. She had her syntherope dispenser out and was fastening the end of the cable to a small glob of rock putty. "These are the cables from the generator in the north subbasement to the south-section umbrella shield projectors on the roof." Unfolding a small slingshot, she fired the rock putty at one edge of the ceiling, the dispenser feeding a thin line of syntherope behind it. "Kell, that one's yours," she said, cutting the line with her fingersnips and refitting the dispenser with more rock putty. "Give it a ten-count, then hook in your belt link and go all the way to the ceiling."

By the time the putty was solid enough for Kell to start pulling himself up, she had two more lines in place. "I guess you and I are going to have to share one," Bink said, slipping out of her climbing belt and handing it to Han. "Ever had someone sit in your lap two meters off the ground?"

"Not lately," Han said as he fastened the belt around his waist. By the time he was ready, Kell and Zerba were all the way up at the ceiling, their bodies pressed flat against the ceramic. "What do we do if they look up?"

"Got it covered," Bink assured him. She stepped over to him, threaded the syntherope through the belt link, then turned around and backed way too cozily against him. "You want to operate it?" she asked. "Or shall I?"

"I'll do it," Han growled, feeling an unexpected flush of annoyed embarrassment. Whether she'd meant it that way or not, there was a time and a place for flirting, and this was neither. Finding the control, he sent them swinging up off the floor as the belt reeled in the line. A few seconds later, the two of them were pressed against the ceiling between Kell and Zerba. "Now what?" Han asked.

"Take this," Bink said, handing him a thick, hand-sized piece of something that felt like the silk Zerba had used to make the women's tear-away outfits. In the center of one side was a flexible finger-sized ring. "Get a grip on the ring, hold it beneath you, and slip off the loop that's around the edge. And *don't* drop it."

Lowering his hand, Han did as instructed—

And jerked in surprise as the material unfolded outward in all directions, each edge expanding until it ran into the wall on that side.

"Chameleon cloth," Bink explained. "Instant wall or ceiling, in a handy carry size."

"Won't they notice the ceiling's lower than it's supposed to be?" Kell asked.

"People never know how high ceilings are supposed to be," Bink said with a shrug. "You two, get a grip on the edges and stabilize it. Great. Now all we have to do is wait for the searchers to pass this part of the—"

She broke off as a soft click came from below them. A second later, the door was flung open and a glow rod flashed, its light flickering faintly across the edges of the chameleon cloth as whoever was below waved it around the room. Han tensed, waiting for the inevitable shout of discovery . . .

And then, without any such shout, the door was slammed shut.

Bink gave it a full twenty-count before she spoke again. "And then we'll be almost ready to go," she finished.

"Not quite," Zerba said, pulling out his comlink. "I have to call Rachele and give her the go-ahead."

"The go-ahead for what?" Han asked.

"After you were grabbed, we decided we couldn't afford to let Villachor figure out the droid thing by himself," Zerba explained. "So Lando's going to help."

"Lando?"

"Yep," Zerba said. "Too bad we'll miss his performance. It should be the crowning point of his career."

"Really?" Han asked, frowning. "What's he going in as?"

"The last thing you'd expect," Zerba said, and Han could visualize him smiling in the darkness. "He's going as someone *respectable.*"

CHAPTER TWENTY

Lando had never liked Bink's idea of hiding in an electrical closet. He'd liked it even less as the afternoon wore on into evening, and first Han and then Tavia were grabbed. Marblewood security would be on even higher alert after all that, and having had the chameleon cloth demonstrated for him hadn't helped his doubts.

So when he finally got Rachele's call, it was with both relief and a fair bit of surprise.

And there was even a bonus on the relief part.

"And Han *is* with them?" he asked, just to make sure.

"Unless Zerba messed up with the tap code," Rachele said. "He didn't send any details, but if Han had been hurt, I think he would have said something."

"Probably," Lando said. So Han had gotten loose on his own. He should have guessed they couldn't hold him for long. "What about Tavia?"

"No word," Rachele said grimly. "But if Qazadi has taken over—and we've certainly given him enough reasons to do so—it's likely that both she and Han would have been taken to wherever he's set up shop. Zerba has confirmed that those puffs of smoke we saw were a signal from Han, so Tavia's probably in that same area."

"It's the place to start, anyway," Lando agreed, peering around the corner of the portable refresher station at the garage door fifty meters away. One of Villachor's men had taken up position there, his spine straight and stiff, his head moving back and forth as he continually scanned the area around him. Villachor and Qazadi were jumpy, all right. Time to push them over the edge. "Okay, I'm going in," he said. "Tell Chewie and Eanjer the door should be clear in a couple of minutes."

"Got it. Good luck."

Lando keyed off the comlink and put it away, moving back around the side of the refresher and glancing casually around. Villachor's techs and security men had chased down most of the scrambler-rigged droids that Kell and Zerba had turned loose, but there were still enough of them running around to give an edge of distracted concern to the otherwise festive crowd. Between that and the fire jets and fountains still going off all over the grounds, there wasn't a lot of attention left to spare for someone like Lando just standing quietly off to the side.

Bracing himself, he pulled out Zerba's egg and squeezed the activator.

He'd expected to feel a shock or a jolt as the silk outer clothing was ripped away into the egg. But there was barely a whisper of sensation. A neat trick, Lando decided, and one he'd have to look into for future use.

He took a moment to examine the Iltarr City police uniform he was now wearing, brushed off a piece of silk debris that somehow had come loose during the ripping process, and pulled out the flattened cap tucked into the tunic. He settled the cap on his head, making sure the bill was pulled down low over his eyes, and sent one final hope skyward that the gadget Bink and Tavia had planted to mess up the cam droids had done its job. It wouldn't do to have the guard over there recognize him as the same man who'd brought in a contraband cryodex for his boss to look at.

Taking a deep breath, stiffening into the arrogant official posture he'd seen way too many times on police and security officers, he rounded the corner of the refresher station and strode toward the garage door.

The guard's first reaction as he spotted the approaching figure was to slip his hand beneath the edge of his tunic toward his concealed blaster. His second reaction, as a flame jet across the grounds briefly lit up the scene and Lando's uniform, was to not budge a single centimeter from that pose. "What do you want?" he called.

"Sergeant Emil Talbot, Iltarr City police," Lando said curtly. "I need to check out an emergency call we've received from someone inside."

Another flame jet went off somewhere behind him, this one a whistling spiral, and in the light Lando saw the guard's eyes narrow. "I'm sorry, Officer, but I have orders not to admit anyone without authorization from—"

"It's *sergeant,* not *officer,*" Lando snapped. "And I don't need your permission to investigate an emergency situation. Someone in your droid control room called in that he was under attack. I was already on the scene, so—"

"The *droid* room?" the guard asked, stiffening.

"Yes, the *droid* room." Lando jabbed a finger at the door behind him. "Now, you get that door open right now, or I swear to you—"

"Yes, of course," the guard said, taking a step back and reaching up to his shoulder comlink clip. "I just need to call it in . . . Sir, this is Pickwin. I've got an Iltarr City police sergeant here who says they've had an emergency call from the droid control room . . . Yes, sir, right away."

He reached behind and opened the door. "Master Villachor's sending some of our men to check it out," he said.

"I still need to take a look for myself," Lando insisted.

"Understood, sir," Pickwin said. "As always, Master Villachor is more than happy to cooperate with the police. If you'll come this way, I've been ordered to escort you to the scene."

"Thank you," Lando said. He brushed past the guard and strode through the doorway, pausing just inside to wait for Pickwin. The other man followed, closing the door behind him.

And just before it shut, Lando caught a glimpse of a pair of figures moving across the grounds toward the door: one of them the size of a normal human, the other the towering bulk of a Wookiee.

"This way, sir," Pickwin said, heading down the hallway.

Lando followed, resisting the urge to throw a furtive look behind him. If Bink had followed the plan and left her stolen key pendant where Chewbacca could find it, he and Eanjer should be right behind him.

If she hadn't, Lando was on his own.

"Confirmed, sir," Kastoni said grimly. "The droid control room was definitely broken into. Probably a plasma torch, though the cut looks a little strange. Three techs are down, including Purvis. The good news is that they were just stunned."

"Yes, that's wonderful," Villachor snarled as he glared out across the darkened grounds at the pockets of chaos still rippling through the crowds. Purvis was the droid chief, with more working knowledge of the cursed machines than any five of Villachor's other men. With him out of commission, the servers and maintenance droids running amok outside would probably have to be taken down one by one. "Why in hell didn't they call for help? Even a plasma jet would take time to get through that door."

"They probably tried," Kastoni said. "There's something on the wall on top of the intercom and alarm lines. Signal damper of some sort, probably."

"And they didn't think to use their comlinks instead?"

"Sure—that's how the cops got wind of it," Kastoni said sourly. "I'm guessing they couldn't get through to anyone here until it was too late."

Because all the security men had also been on their comlinks, chasing malfunctioning droids and searching for missing prisoners. Villachor glared at a set of flame fountains in the distance, twisting to the rhythms of a song too distant for him to hear. "What about this cop? You check him out?"

"Yes, sir," Kastoni said. "Sergeant Emil Talbot. Don't know him personally, but his ID looks good and he's in the system. Seems to know how to handle a crime scene, too."

"Keep an eye on him anyway," Villachor ordered, his mind flicking back to the incident at the Lulina Crown Hotel and how Qazadi had manipulated Villachor's contacts in the police department to bury that investigation. "Is Pickwin back on the door?"

"Yes, sir," Kastoni confirmed. "I sent him back out as soon as he'd passed Talbot over to us."

"Good," Villachor said, though there wasn't a single thing that was good about this situation. "I'm sending Sheqoa to take over. As soon as he arrives, you and Bromley rejoin your search team."

"Yes, sir."

Villachor keyed off, scowling again at the fire-filled darkness, and keyed for Sheqoa. "Have you heard anything from Qazadi about Aziel and his cryodex?" he asked when the other answered.

"Not from him, sir, no," Sheqoa said. "But our men at the hotel just reported that Lord Aziel and his guards have left the suite and are heading to the airspeeder garage. I was just about to call you."

"Have them follow him," Villachor ordered. If this was some game Qazadi and Aziel had cooked up between themselves, he wanted to at least have eyes on the situation. "Then get over to the droid control room. We've had a break-in, and I want you to supervise the cop who's come to investigate."

"Yes, sir."

Villachor keyed off and sent another glare at the grounds. It would be time soon for the fireworks to begin. Normally that was the most festive and eagerly anticipated part of the Festival.

But Villachor wasn't looking forward to it. Not at all.

Because a proper fireworks display required him to shut down his umbrella shield.

He peered up at the sky. Cancelling the display would be a tremendous loss of face in the community.

But if Qazadi or Aziel had some kind of aerial attack planned . . .

Fortunately, there was no need to make that decision. Not yet. He could wait until they'd either caught the prisoners or confirmed they'd left Marblewood, and until Sheqoa's men found out what Aziel was up to at the Lulina Crown.

And he would definitely not make any decisions until Sheqoa and Sergeant Talbot found out what the intruders had been doing in the droid control room.

"We about set?" Dozer asked.

"I think so," Winter said, lowering her electrobinoculars and giving her eyes a quick rub with her fingertips. Four airspeeders had gone into the Lulina Crown Hotel parking garage, three others had come out, and between them she had the procedure and the timing down cold.

"We'll want to start moving as soon as an airspeeder passes the fourth opening from the entryway," she continued, pointing toward one of the wide vents that lined the garage wall. "That should let us ram into him without giving him enough time to get out of the way, while still making it look like an accident."

"And our angle's okay?"

Winter frowned at him. He'd been staring intently at the garage ever since they arrived, intently enough that she could practically hear the gears turning in his brain. "The angle's fine," she said. "We'll hit them from their blind spot, and with the attendant facing the other way for the checkout procedure, he won't see us coming, either. You okay?"

"I'm fine," he assured her. "I'm thinking that after we ram them and block this entrance, maybe you should stick around and keep the attendant busy while I go across and block the one on the other side."

"I thought you wanted me to come help you."

"I don't think I'll need you," he said. "You might as well stay at this end, where you're out of the way."

"Where I'm out of the *way*?" Winter echoed. "What's that supposed to—"

"Here's one," Dozer cut her off, resettling his grip on the wheel and turning on his lights. "Hang on." The airspeeder passed the vent Winter had pointed out—

She grabbed for her restraints as their vehicle leapt forward, accelerating toward the garage entrance. She tensed reflexively, then forced her muscles to relax. Better chance of escaping injury that way. The target vehicle moved into view past the attendant station and started its leisurely turn into the opening. Dozer accelerated a half second longer, then hit the brakes as if he'd suddenly noticed the obstacle.

With a stomach-churning crash, Winter's whole world seemed to ram itself into her chest, flip itself up over her head, and drop like a sack of vegetables onto her shoulders. There was a horrendous screeching of metal and plastic and ceramic that ground across her ears like a rasp file.

And then, abruptly, all was silence.

Winter blinked twice, and with the second blink her confused world abruptly resolved itself. The airspeeder was canted to the right at a thirty-degree angle and pointed upward with its nose nearly touching the garage ceiling. Something nearby was hissing; beneath the hiss, she could hear the faint sounds of people shouting. There were plumes of white smoke everywhere, probably a mixture of coolant from a ruptured turbojet and spray from the airspeeders' fire suppression systems.

And Dozer was gone.

Winter shook her head, the movement helping clear it, and popped her restraints. If he thought she was going to just sit here looking helpless, he had some serious rethinking to do.

The commotion was even louder and more frantic-sounding with the door open, and the air reeked of coolant and fire mist. Winter listened carefully as she rolled out through the opening and eased herself to the floor, but the shouts were more along the line of dismay and fury than of actual pain or injury. At least Dozer had followed *that* part of the plan correctly. She took a second to confirm that the two airspeeders were indeed completely blocking this entrance, then slipped away through the smoke. Staying low behind the neat rows of parked vehicles, she headed for the entrance at the hotel's opposite side.

The attendant at the booth there was gazing anxiously across the floor at the smoking wreck but was making no move to head over to help. He probably had strict instructions to stay at his post no matter what, Winter guessed.

Though that would probably change when the biggest vehicle in the garage came roaring at him, did a half flip, and wedged itself solidly across his entrance. There were, Winter saw, three perfect candidates for the job, all of them within four rows of the entrance.

Dozer wasn't at any of them.

For a moment she leaned back against the last of the big airspeeders, breathing in the faint fumes drifting across the garage from the fire mist, her pulse thudding loudly in her ears. What the hell was he up to? All Lando had asked them to do was keep Aziel from bringing the real cryodex to Qazadi.

Unless Dozer had decided to get creative.

Sure enough, she found him at the rear of the garage, lying on his back beneath one of Aziel's four black landspeeders. "What are you *doing*?" she demanded as she knelt down beside him.

"About time you showed up," he said with a grunt. "You're the one with the insane eye for detail. Is there a particular one of these that Aziel usually rides in?"

"Dozer—"

"I know, I know," he cut her off. "Yell at me later. Right now, just tell me which one is his."

Swallowing a word that had once gotten both her and Leia in trouble, Winter looked at the landspeeders. The small, minor marks . . . "That one," she said, pointing to the one to Dozer's right. "They line them up in random order when they travel, but he always rides in that one."

"I knew it," Dozer said, grunting again as he pulled himself out from under the landspeeder and slid under the one Winter had identified. "These guys are always so predictable."

"Sure," Winter said. "Speaking of insane eyes, are you completely out of your insane *mind*? Aziel could be here any minute, and you're trying to hotwire his landspeeder?"

"Not *trying*," Dozer corrected, his voice punctuated by the clink of tools. "Anyway, we all agreed the blackmail files are worth a whole lot more if we have a cryodex to go with them, right?"

Winter felt her mouth drop open. "Are you *insane*?"

"You already asked me that," Dozer reminded her. "Here—peel the insulation off the ends, will you?"

A small finger-sized cylinder rolled out from under the airspeeder.

"Dozer, you're not thinking this through," Winter persisted, crouching down and starting to pull the insulation off the ends of the wires sticking out from one end of the cylinder. "Do you even have a blaster? Because I don't."

"Don't need a blaster," Dozer said. There was a double clink as he tapped one of his tools against the edge of the vehicle's frame. "I've got this. You finish that yet? Great—thanks."

Winter rose into a low crouch and peered across the landspeeder's hood at the bank of turbolift doors along the wall. "How long is this going to take?"

"Not long," Dozer said, the last word coming out as a grunt. "I just have to bypass the security system—which is absurdly easy; Black Sun really needs to invest some credits in a *real* system—and then hook up the remote. I'll be finished in no time."

Across the garage, one of the turbolift doors slid open.

"I hope you're right," Winter murmured urgently. "Because here they come."

"I don't know," Kastoni said, looking back and forth across the monitors and keypads. "I'm sure they changed some settings *somewhere.* Why else would they come in here? But I haven't got a clue which ones."

"We're going to need a tech," Lando agreed, pretending to look around. He'd spotted Zerba's sliced console almost as soon as he'd walked into the room. But, of course, he'd known what to look for. He also knew better than to point it out too quickly. "I've put in a call, but all our techs are scattered across town at the various Festival venues. It'll take a while to get anyone back in."

"That's okay," the other guard, Bromley, said from across the room. "I don't think Master Villachor would want your people poking around here anyway. Our droid master can fix it when he wakes up."

"I hope so," Lando said, glancing casually out the door.

And froze. At the far end of the hallway, talking intently toward his comlink clip as he strode toward the control room, was Sheqoa.

One of the handful of people in Marblewood who knew Lando by sight.

And Lando had suddenly run out of time. "Wait a second," he said, jabbing a finger at the damaged console. "That console—see the cut?"

"Yeah," Kastoni said as he crossed toward it. "Looks like the same whatever they used to slice open the door."

"Sure does," Lando said, joining him and looking over the console itself. There was nothing identifying it as a 501-Z control panel, at least nothing he could see. But obviously Bink had figured it out, and if she could, Police Sergeant Talbot certainly could. "Looks like a 501-Z control console," he commented. "You have Zeds patrolling the grounds somewhere?"

Out of the corner of his eye he saw Kastoni's head jerk toward him. "This controls the *Zeds*?" he breathed. "Oh, *hell.*" He tapped his comlink clip. Lando held his breath . . . "Kastoni, sir," Kastoni said quickly. "It looks like they hit the Zed control panel . . . Yes, sir."

He took a step back and craned his neck to look out into the hallway. "Yes, I see him . . . Master Sheqoa?" he called. "Master Villachor wants you."

Kastoni stepped into the doorway. Lando turned his back, leaning over the Zed console, pretending to examine the jagged cut Zerba's lightsaber had made. Behind him, the two men conversed in low tones, and though Lando couldn't make out the words, he could hear the shift in Sheqoa's tone as he stopped talking to Kastoni and started talking to Villachor. The conversation ended, and Lando heard footsteps heading rapidly away.

"Gone to check on your Zeds?" Lando asked over his shoulder.

"Yeah, if they're still there," Kastoni growled, coming up beside him.

"You cops know any fast ways to bring someone out of a stun blast?" Bromley asked. "Some drug or something we can use?"

"Nothing that would be legal," Lando said. "Sorry. Here, help me move this other console out of the way, will you? We need to see if they got into the wall conduits, too."

The echo of the hard service corridor gave way to the silence and softer cushioning of the main mansion hallways.

Sheqoa hardly noticed.

So it was the Zeds they'd been after. Kriffing obvious in retrospect, especially after Villachor replaced all the armored human guards in the vault with more of the kriffing droids.

All of which had been Qazadi's idea. Curse the stupid green-scaled Falleen idiot, anyway.

Unless it *hadn't* been stupidity. Unless it was part of whatever insane plan Qazadi and Aziel and Kwerve and maybe Prince kriffing Xizor himself had worked up to bring down Villachor and put someone else in his place.

Well, they could just dream on. Whatever success the mysterious intruder had managed with the serving and maintenance droids outside, he'd find the Zeds a much harder nut to crack. They were horribly difficult to reprogram or disable, especially without the general access codes that only Villachor and Purvis, the droid chief, had. Once Purvis recovered from the stun blast, he could check on the Zeds and fix any damage the intruder had managed to inflict. In the meantime, Sheqoa and Villachor would go into the vault—alone if necessary—and guard the safe and Xizor's precious blackmail files.

Unless Purvis was part of the plot.

Sheqoa glared at the fancy hallway. A nice, complicated Festival of Four Honorings had suddenly become a maze of spinners within spinners within spinners. With Qazadi and his hidden agenda on one end and someone throwing bribe credits at the Marblewood staff on the other, he no longer had a clue as to whom he could trust.

"Master Sheqoa?"

Sheqoa pulled his lips back in a snarl. He *absolutely* didn't trust this one. "What do you want, Barbas?" he growled, not bothering to turn around or even slow down.

"We have a message from His Excellency," Barbas said. There was the soft sound of hurrying footsteps, and Barbas and one of Qazadi's other guards—Narkan, Sheqoa tentatively identified him—came up on Sheqoa's sides. "His Excellency requests the pleasure of your presence."

"His Excellency will have to wait," Sheqoa told him shortly. "Right now we've got a possible crisis on our hands."

"A crisis for Master Villachor and Marblewood?" Barbas asked pointedly. "Or a crisis for Master Lapis Sheqoa?"

Sheqoa shook his head. "I have no idea what you're talking about."

"Then let me make it clearer," Barbas said. "The woman you sent to us has been making some fascinating statements to His Excellency. One of those statements is that she can't remember seeing your key pendant for at least an hour before Master Villachor finally noticed it was missing."

Sheqoa felt a surge of contempt over his anger. "And you believed her? A kriffing thief, and you actually *believed* her?"

"Yes, about that," Barbas said. "We've examined her thoroughly and have found nothing. No hint of tracking dye; no fingersnips, or even marks where fingersnips might have been attached; no weapons, tools, or contraband of any sort. As far as we can tell, she's nothing more than the brainless social floater that she appears."

"Then dig deeper," Sheqoa growled. "She's the thief. I know it."

"And His Excellency would be delighted to have you prove that to him," Barbas said. "This should take only a few minutes of your time."

"I don't think so," Sheqoa said, and stopped dead in his tracks.

Barbas and Narkan were caught completely by surprise, each of them taking another step before they could react. They stopped, turned to face Sheqoa—

And froze at the sight of his drawn blaster.

"Let me tell you what's going to happen," Sheqoa said into the taut silence. "I'm going to the vault, and I'm going to confirm that the safe and its contents are secure. After that, if Master Villachor feels he can dispense with my services for the few minutes you mentioned, I'll be happy to answer any questions His Excellency has for me." He lifted the barrel of his blaster a couple of centimeters. "You can come with me, you can return to His Excellency and wait, or you can die. Your choice."

"You wouldn't dare," Barbas said darkly.

"We have two escaped prisoners and possibly another intruder inside these walls," Sheqoa reminded him. "One of them could easily have picked up a blaster."

Barbas's lips twitched in a small smile. "Very well," he said. "We accept your gracious invitation. After all, the most valuable item in the safe is His Excellency's, so it only makes sense for us to help you secure it." He gestured down the hall. "Lead the way."

Sheqoa brushed past them, jamming his blaster back into its holster as he did so. Barbas could smile all he wanted, but Sheqoa knew the other wouldn't forget this.

That was okay. Neither would Sheqoa.

Aziel's landspeeder hadn't been nearly as easy to slice as Dozer had made it sound. Far from it. But he was the best, he was determined, and Black Sun really *did* need to spend their credits on better security.

Still, he could hear the approaching footsteps on the duracrete by the time he finally finished and rolled across the floor to safety.

Winter was waiting for him five rows over, crouched behind a classic and lovingly restored Incom T-24. "Nothing like cutting it straight to the wire," she murmured.

"Keeps the heart pumping," he murmured back, peering around the T-24's ventral fin and wondering briefly whether *its* owner had opted for a decent security system. There were twelve of them striding across the floor, including Aziel. The whole contingent, if Rachele's earlier estimate of their numbers was correct. Wrapped around Aziel's waist was a hip pouch that presumably held the cryodex.

"What's the plan?" Winter asked.

"First part of every plan is always the same," Dozer told her, unfolding the control pad for the remote he'd hooked into the landspeeder's system. The timing here was going to be critical. "You separate the goodies from the people hired to guard them."

"If you mean you're hoping he gets into that airspeeder all by himself, that's not going to happen," she warned. "Back at Marblewood, the driver and two guards always got in the same time he did."

"I know," Dozer said. "We'll just have to do what we can with what we've got."

The first human in line stopped at Aziel's landspeeder and climbed in the driver's door. As he did so, the next man in line passed him and opened the rear passenger door. He climbed in and was followed by Aziel, who was followed in turn by the next man in line. The rest of the guards waited until both doors were closed, then headed toward the other three landspeeders. Straining his ears, Dozer heard the first landspeeder's engine activate.

And in the half second between the activation and the driver keying in his power train access, Dozer hit the reroute switch on his pad.

With a roar, the engines kicked to full power. Keying in the boost and twisting the level control all the way over, Dozer sent the vehicle leaping straight up to slam hard into the duracrete ceiling.

The guards were good, all right. Not a single one of them wasted time gaping at the landspeeder's sudden and inexplicable movement. Instead, all eight snatched out their blasters and spread out, looking for whoever was responsible for the jacking.

A second later, they were scrambling frantically for

cover as Dozer dropped the landspeeder squarely into their midst.

"You got one," Winter called softly from her new position at the T-24's nose. "The rest are taking cover between other vehicles."

Where Dozer couldn't get at them. But it was an obvious defensive move, and he'd expected it. All he'd really wanted to do was slow them down and get them reacting instead of thinking.

Because it was time now to get them away from him. Lifting the landspeeder back up above the general vehicle level, waggling it violently back and forth to keep the passengers flopping around inside, he sent it careening across the garage toward the two-vehicle wreck he and Winter had assembled earlier.

With the perfect mix of frustrated anger and unthinking reaction he'd hoped for, the whole batch of guards rose from their hiding spots and tore off after it.

Dozer smiled tightly. Perfect. Now all he had to do was keep the vehicle bouncing around enough that the driver couldn't get to the engine kill switch, let the guards go hunt for the jacker who they naturally assumed was somewhere near the vehicle's end point, and then fly it back here. Before the guards could return he should be able to flip the thing over on its head, pop the door, grab the cryodex from Aziel's pouch while the Falleen and his guards were still too dazed to do anything, and get the hell out of here.

"Watch it—three of them are getting into one of the other landspeeders," Winter warned.

Dozer felt his smirk turn into a wince. Okay, so Aziel's guards weren't as dumb as he'd thought. They were hedging their bets, one group handling the ground-level search while another went airborne.

Which meant he had less time than he'd thought to

finish this up. "Can you hotwire an airspeeder?" he asked Winter.

"Probably," she said, and out of the corner of his eye he saw her looking around. "Any one in particular?"

"Never mind," Dozer said, backing up to her and thrusting the control pad into her hands. "Forward—backward—sideways—wiggle—boost," he said briefly, touching each control to identify it. "Keep it over there, and keep it moving."

"Dozer—"

"And if it drops out of the sky, that means the driver's killed the engine, and we give it up and run," he added, glancing over the nearest parked vehicles. The OS-20 two vehicles over, he decided.

"Dozer—incoming!"

He spun back around. A black airspeeder was roaring through the unblocked entrance, with two more hovering in guard positions behind it. The first vehicle stopped just inside the garage as the driver apparently paused to assess the situation.

"They're Villachor's," Winter said tensely. "The license tags—"

"Yeah, yeah," Dozer cut her off, snatching back the control pad. "Get us a vehicle—I'll hold them off." The new arrival finished his assessment, turned toward Aziel's hovering landspeeder—

And twisted hard to the side, trying to get out of the way, as Dozer sent the jacked vehicle shooting straight at him.

The other pilot almost made it. Aziel's vehicle caught his fender a glancing blow, bouncing the vehicle into the side wall with a grinding crash. A flicker of motion caught Dozer's eye: Aziel's other landspeeder was off the floor now, boosts at full power, heading toward the jacked one.

And with that, Dozer's numbers had suddenly gone

straight to zero. With two other vehicles in the game and two more hovering outside waiting for their chance to join in, it was only a matter of time before they'd be able to box Aziel's jacked vehicle in long enough for the driver to untangle himself from the seats and get to the kill switch.

It was now or never.

"Cover," he snapped, and turned the control over hard. The jacked airspeeder reversed direction, slamming again into the newcomer. Dozer switched back to forward motion and ran it straight toward where he and Winter were crouching. Peripherally, he noted that the two vehicles outside had disappeared somewhere. He brought the jacked vehicle almost to them, rammed it one final time into the ceiling, and then flipped it over and sent it crashing to the floor in front of them.

He had no idea how long it would take the men and Falleen inside to recover from that double punch. He also had no intention of hanging around long enough to find out. Jumping up from his crouch, he ran to the turtled vehicle, keyed the lock control, and pulled open the door.

The landspeeder's interior was nearly as much of a mess as its exterior. Apparently Aziel had had a miniature refreshment bar set up for his convenience, the contents of which were now scattered or dripping across the fancy seats.

But none of that mattered. All that mattered was that the cryodex was fastened around a dazed Falleen's waist, and there were no blasters pointed at him. Unfastening the hip pouch, Dozer ducked back out and sprinted toward the turbolifts. No time to get an airspeeder now, he knew, even if there'd been anywhere to go with it. Their only chance was to try to beat the pursuit out of the garage and take their chances on the ground.

Winter was crouched beside one of the airspeeders,

working on the lock. Dozer grabbed her wrist as he passed, yanking her to her feet and dragging her after him. Behind them, the garage exploded with the flash and fury of multiple blaster shots, and Dozer winced as several of the bolts blazed past overhead. He thought about looking back to see how close the pursuit was, decided he needed to focus all his attention on running. The turbolifts were no more than thirty meters ahead. The doors slid open, all of them at once—

And with a horrified curse, Dozer stumbled to a halt. In the sudden blink of an eye, the situation had suddenly ended.

The game was over . . . and he and Winter had lost.

CHAPTER TWENTY-ONE

Villachor had been waiting impatiently in the vault anteroom for nearly two minutes before Sheqoa finally showed up.

Only he wasn't alone. He'd thoughtfully brought guests.

"What are *they* doing here?" Villachor demanded. "I didn't call for anyone except you."

"I didn't call for anyone, either, sir," Sheqoa growled. "They invited themselves. And I didn't think I had time to kill them."

Villachor glared at the two thugs, sorely tempted to order them away and to back up the command with the Zeds currently standing motionless in front of the vault doorway.

But Sheqoa was right. There would be time to deal with Qazadi's thugs later.

With a derisive snort, he turned his back on them. They wanted to watch? Fine—let them watch. He was still the master of Marblewood, the Marblewood vault, and everything inside it. And for the moment, at least, there was nothing Qazadi's men or even Qazadi himself could do about it. Striding to the key Zed, he held his hand up to the droid's face for the usual scent confirmation. He and Sheqoa would go inside, he decided, double-check that the safe was still secure, and then reconfigure the Zeds inside the vault for possible intrusion. At that point, he could either leave or wait inside with them—

He frowned. His hand was still in the Zed's face, but the Zed was just standing there. "Smell," he ordered, moving the hand a little closer. The passcode cologne couldn't have worn off. It *never* wore off. "I said *smell,*" he repeated, this time pressing his hand right up to the metal.

He barely snatched it back in time as the Zed suddenly came to life, one massive hand reaching for Villachor's arm, the other going for the neuronic whip coiled at its side.

"Sir!" Sheqoa said, leaping forward.

"I know, I know," Villachor snarled as he hastily backed up out of the whip's range. The Zeds were programmed to react strongly if they were touched.

And then the full implications of that reaction turned his blood cold.

The intruder had gotten into the Zed programming, all right, just like the cop in the droid control room had warned. But he hadn't simply shut all of them down, the way an unimaginative thief would have. Instead he'd reprogrammed their loyalties, flipping them to his side, so that instead of keeping out intruders, they were keeping out *Villachor.*

There was only one reason to do something that complicated and time-consuming: to buy more time at the other end of the road.

The intruder wasn't hoping to break into the vault. *He was already inside.*

With a curse, Villachor yanked out his comlink and punched for Kastoni. "Is Purvis awake yet?" he snapped.

"I don't know, sir," Kastoni said. "Bromley and two of the techs took him and the others to the infirmary—"

"Never mind," Villachor cut him off. So the intruder thought he could turn the Zeds against their master? Fine. Two could play that game. "Go to the Zed control board and pull up the main status page."

"Yes, sir."

Villachor motioned Sheqoa closer. "You still have men on standby in the ready room?" he asked, keeping his voice low.

"Yes, sir, five of them," Sheqoa confirmed. "Uzior's in command."

"Have them suit up," Villachor ordered. "Full gear, and get them down here as quickly as possible."

"Yes, sir." Sheqoa touched his comlink clip, his eyes flicking to Qazadi's men, standing off to the side. "Sir?"

"I know, and I don't care," Villachor growled. "The intruder's in there, or will be soon, and he's got the Zeds running interference for him. So we take them out of the equation."

Sheqoa looked at the double line of Zeds. "Yes, sir," he said, not sounding at all happy at the idea. "Sir, do you think—"

"I have the status page, sir," Kastoni cut in.

"Go to the code input box at the upper left," Villachor directed, closing his eyes and visualizing the sequence. "Input the following numbers: eight, four, five, five, two . . ."

He ran through the full string, then had Kastoni read it back to him. "Good," Villachor said. "Now hit activate."

"May I ask what you're doing, Master Villachor?" one of Qazadi's men called.

"I'm solving a problem," Villachor said, glowering at him. "I trust you're not planning to become another one."

"No, sir, not at all," the man assured him, smiling

faintly. But Villachor noticed that the smile didn't go all the way to his eyes.

And his hand was resting very close to his blaster.

It wasn't until the heavy footsteps began thudding along the hallway outside the electrical closet that Han really began to believe that this whole thing might actually work.

It was an astonishing thought. Most of the time he figured his plans for about a 50 percent chance of success, and even then only if he scrambled like crazy when the original idea started coming apart at the edges. But this one, for some reason, seemed to be working exactly like it was supposed to.

Minus the couple of small side glitches they'd had along the way, of course.

"Sounds like five of them," Bink murmured, her ear pressed to the door. "In a hurry, too."

"I guess Han and his magic data card came through," Zerba said. He seemed even more astonished than Han that the plan was working. "What was on it, anyway?"

"Just plain simple flux perfume base," Bink said, sliding a slender optic line under the door and adjusting the eyepiece over her eye. "The kind that adapts to your body chemistry through the day. One touch was enough to get the solvent reagents into the cologne on Villachor's hand and alter it just enough to be unrecognizable to the Zeds. Okay, looks clear."

Han nodded. "I'll go first," he said.

The hallway was indeed deserted. The guards who'd just thundered past had remembered to lock the ready room on their way out, but it was an ordinary lock and Bink was through it in seconds. The four of them slipped inside, closing and relocking the door behind them.

It was about as close a copy of a standard military

ready room as Han had ever seen. Two of the walls were lined with suits of the Zed-droid-mimicking armor Kell had warned them about, set into the same type of multi-armed self-suit frameworks that Imperial spacetroopers used to help them get into their armor. The other two walls were given over to clothing lockers, equipment cabinets, and a refreshment sideboard like the one back in the lounge where he'd been hiding out earlier. In the center of the room were a couple of game tables and chairs, with a group of three-tier bunks visible through an open door in a back room. "Where do we start?" he asked Bink.

She was crouched between the two tables, holding a small sensor just above the floor. "Right here should do nicely," she said, drawing a small circle on the thin carpet with her finger. "Zerba?"

"How deep?" he asked, crouching beside her and igniting his lightsaber.

"About ten centimeters," she said, attaching a hook to the carpet at that spot. "Doesn't have to be precise—there aren't any sensor wires under it."

He nodded and carefully sliced a circle around the hook. He closed down the lightsaber, and she pulled out the plug. "Now, if they've done this properly," she commented as she inserted the end of her optic line into the hole and moved it around, "they should have a criss-cross grid of sensor wires . . . yep, there they are. Okay, Zerba: a meter-diameter circle from *here* to *here.* This deep." She held up the plug to demonstrate. "This time, neatness counts."

"Right." Igniting his lightsaber again, Zerba got to work.

Han looked around the room, suddenly struck by an odd thought. His part of the field work was supposed to have ended with the delivery of the gimmicked data card to Villachor. In fact, according to the original plan, he should be in the suite right now, watching the Marblewood grounds with electrobinoculars and helping Rachele and Winter coordinate the rest of the operation. Right here, right now, he basically had nothing to do.

His eyes fell on the line of armored suits. Or maybe he did.

"Kell?" he invited quietly, walking over to the nearest suit. It didn't look that complicated to get into.

"What?" Kell asked, coming up beside him.

"You know anything about these?"

"Nothing specific," Kell said, running his fingers thoughtfully along the metal of the helmet. "Full life support, probably. Certainly has motion-echo power enhancement, half-face heads-up display, comm capability, and a partial sensor suite. Possibly targeting optics, too."

"Thanks," Han said dryly. A shame the kid didn't know anything specific. "Give me a hand, will you?"

"Going someplace?" Bink asked, looking up from Zerba's work.

"Thought I'd wander downstairs and see what Villachor's up to," Han told her, pulling experimentally on the armor's torso. It lifted easily on its counterbalanced self-suit arm. "You three look like you've got this end pretty well covered. Don't you?"

"Pretty much," Bink said as she and Zerba lifted out the circle of flooring and set it to the side.

Han craned his neck to look into the hole as he worked his left leg and hip into the lower section of armor. Beneath the main floor was a multiple zigzag grid of wires a couple of centimeters apart set into a subfloor. "Is that the alarm?"

"That's it," Bink confirmed. "A randomized, variable-pulse flicker field, to be specific. You can put jumpers across the lines all day and still not hit all the combinations."

"So what do we do?" Kell asked.

"We first make sure there aren't any unwelcome surprises waiting for us below," she said, tapping a part of the subfloor between two of the wires. "Zerba? A hole straight through here, if you please. As small as you can manage."

Zerba nodded and again ignited his lightsaber. This time, instead of cutting with the edge, he carefully pushed the blade straight down into the floor. There was a small jolt as he broke through the other side, and he quickly closed it down. "I guess a lightsaber cuts through magsealed armor plate just fine," he commented.

"Never thought it wouldn't," Bink assured him. She slipped her optic line into the hole, turned it around a couple of times.

"Well?" Han asked.

With a puff of exhaled air, Bink pulled out the line and leaned back. "He did it," she announced. "Villachor shut down the Zeds for us."

"Awfully nice of him," Kell said. "What about the alarm?"

"Patience, child, patience," Bink said. She took another deep breath, puffed this one out as well, and leaned forward again. "First job is to slow everything down to a manageable rate," she continued, putting her optic line back into the hole and turning it slowly around. "See, the regulator and randomizer cascade switch for the whole thing are . . . right over there." She pointed toward the wall beneath the sideboard. "Hitting them in just the right spots will slow the flicker pattern without shutting it down completely, and therefore not trigger any alarms."

"You need me to cut you a hole over there?" Zerba asked, starting to get to his feet.

"Don't bother," Bink said. Pulling her hold-out blaster from its belly holster, she lowered it into the hole, lined it up carefully with the optic line, and carefully squeezed the trigger. The hole lit up briefly with the shot; shifting aim slightly, she fired again. Setting the blaster on the floor beside her, she ran her sensor over the zigzag wires again. "Perfect," she said.

"Now what?" Zerba asked.

"There are a couple of ways of bypassing a grid like this," she said. "But they take time, and we're in a hurry. So we're going to be clever." She nodded back toward the equipment cabinets behind her. "Zerba, go find me one of those neuronic whips, will you?"

"A neuronic *whip*?" Zerba echoed, frowning, as he stood up.

Han glanced at the collection of weapons racked beside his armor. Along with a half dozen blasters were two of the whips. "Here," he said, detaching one from its peg and tossing it across to Bink. "I can't *wait* to hear this one."

"It's really very simple," she said as she uncoiled it. "Neuronic whips adapt to the neural characteristics of whatever skin they happen to be touching, right?"

Kell's mouth dropped open. "You're joking."

"Not at all," she assured him as she carefully laid out the whip in a circle on top of the wire grid. "It's not fast enough to adapt to a normal flicker-field, which is why no one bothers to worry about them. But with the randomizer slowed down, the whip should pick up the incoming pulses and echo them just fine." Giving the whip's positioning a final adjustment, she reached in to the handle and activated the switch.

There was a crackle of energy from the whip, accompanied by a flash of blue-white light. The whip flashed again, then settled down into a flickering blue glow.

"And that should be that," Bink concluded.

"Do we need to be worried about the *should* in that sentence?" Zerba asked.

"Let's find out." Bink gestured into the hole. "Make a hole, Zerba. Be sure to stay inside the circle of the whip."

Zerba took it slow and careful, clearly expecting a blare of alarms to go off somewhere midway through the procedure and just as clearly surprised when they didn't. As he worked, Bink unfolded a small but sturdy tripod lifter and set it up over the hole, and Han could see its legs strain as it slowly took the weight of the section of subflooring and the armor plate beneath it. By the time Kell eased the helmet shut over Han's head, they had the hole cut and the plug ratcheted up, and they were maneuvering the circle of material out of their way.

"How's it look?" Han asked.

"See for yourself," Bink's muffled voice came faintly through the helmet.

"How?" Han growled, glaring at the darkness in front of him.

And then, suddenly, the inside faceplate lit up with a view of the room, overlaid with range markings. There was a tiny inset infrared version in the upper right corner and an equally tiny rear view in the upper left. "That better?" Kell's voice came normally in his ears.

"Yeah," Han said, looking over the display. There was a status bar running along the bottom of the image, marking comm setting, power levels, auditory levels, and advanced sensor options.

"Controls should be right here," Kell said, turning Han's left arm over and indicating the inner wrist area. "You see anything?"

"I do now," Han said, smiling tightly. Where he'd seen only bare metal from outside the suit, the heads-up display now indicated a half dozen buttons and touch sliders. Experimentally he reached over with his right hand and tapped the telescopic button, then ran the finger along the slider. The image in front of him jumped, zooming in on the controls, the arm, and the section of floor beyond them. "Yeah, got it," he said, moving the slider back and keying off the telescopics. "Any place in here to put an extra comlink? I'm guessing this one is locked into the security circuit."

"Yeah, there should be room right here," Kell said, touching the helmet behind the right-hand cheek flange. "There's a disguised air intake behind the flange. Let me see if I can wedge mine in there for you . . . Okay, that should do it. Zerba?"

Zerba pulled out his comlink. "Testing?"

"Got it," Han said. The sound from the comlink was faint, but as long as it didn't get too noisy outside he should be able to hear well enough. "Okay, I'm heading down. Good luck with the safe."

"Wait a second." Bink pulled a small comm signaler from her pocket and tossed it to Kell. "As long as you're in an accessorizing mood, Kell, see if you can find a spot for this."

"No problem—it should fit right below the comlink," Kell said. "Let me see . . . there. Right below the comlink, Han. Push it straight forward to trigger."

"Wait a second," Zerba said, frowning at Bink. "I thought *you* were going to handle that part."

"Han's going to be down there watching the show anyway," Bink pointed out. "He might as well have the honor. Besides, he'll have a better view and angle than I will."

"She's right," Han agreed, looking at the weapons rack. All he needed to complete his new outfit was something that packed the maximum punch at close range.

His eyes fell on a Caliban Model X heavy blaster pistol: fifty shots fully charged, a sixty-meter range, and nearly as powerful as a full blaster rifle. It would do nicely.

He slipped the Caliban into his armor's right-hand side holster. Then, almost as an afterthought, he unhooked the other neuronic whip and secured it to his left hip. "Watch yourselves," he said as he headed out.

"You too," Kell said.

A moment later Han was on his way, clumping along the hallway, a bad feeling tugging at him. This was Bink's part of the operation, and if she pulled it off, it would be the crowning point of her entire career. There was no way in the galaxy she would hand off the grand moment to him. Not unless she had a very good reason to do so.

Unfortunately, that reason wasn't hard to guess. The minute she had the safe open, she was going to head across the mansion and find her sister.

He muttered a curse, feeling the breath bounce off his heads-up display back into his lips. Problem was, she'd never make it. Not alone. Absolutely not alone and with Marblewood's whole security force stirred up the way they were. The division of tasks in this whole thing had been very clear: Lando and Chewbacca at the mansion's north end would go after Tavia; Bink, Zerba, and Kell at the south end would deal with the safe. That had been the arrangement from the start, and none of Lando's last-minute tweaks had changed it.

Bink, apparently, was going to do so anyway.

And there was nothing Han could do about it. Not unless they wanted to scratch the job and have all of them troop off after Tavia together, and they'd come way too far for that.

All he could do was hope that Bink would calm down and think it through. As long as Qazadi didn't know who was on whose side—or even what the sides were—he would be a fool to push Tavia too hard. Especially with the question of the cryodex still up in the air. If Bink would just relax a little, maybe she'd see that she could back off and let Lando and Chewbacca get her sister out.

Because if she didn't, they might well wind up with two prisoners to be rescued instead of one.

And there was a very good chance that Qazadi would decide he didn't need to keep *both* of them alive.

With a sizzle of old-fashioned chemical propellant, the first of the fireworks shot upward from the Marblewood grounds. The propellant burned out, and there was a moment of anticipation as nothing seemed to happen. Then, with a burst of vibrant color, the rocket exploded, shooting tiny stars into the air to soar, swoop, and then fade into oblivion.

Sitting against one of the chimney spires where the shadows were the deepest, Dayja frowned. Fireworks, he knew, were the traditional finale to the Festival of Four Honorings. But that finale was supposed to wait until full dark, and they still had fifteen or twenty minutes until then. Had something else gone wrong?

Maybe. On the other hand, maybe someone had noticed that the spate of rampaging droids had threatened to spark a mass exodus of the visitors and was hoping to stem that flow by starting the fireworks a little early.

If that was the plan, it definitely seemed to be working. As a second rocket sizzled upward and then burst, Dayja could see that the flow of people toward the exits had slowed as the visitors turned back to watch the show.

Only . . .

Frowning, Dayja broke open his fake holocamera and extracted the knife and the small but powerful electrobinoculars tucked away inside. Slipping the weapon into his sleeve, where it would be handy if he needed it, he activated the electrobinoculars and focused on the low wall surrounding the grounds.

According to the faintly glowing indicator lights, Marblewood's umbrella shield was still active.

A third rocket exploded overhead, this one spitting its stars into a serise-flower pattern. Leaving the shield up for these smaller ones was all well and good. But the larger, more elaborate fireworks later in the show were designed to travel considerably higher before exploding. If the shield was still up when those were fired, they were either going to spatter early or possibly even ricochet down into the crowd.

Maybe Villachor already had that covered and would be dropping the shield before the show got to the point of endangering the visitors.

Or maybe endangering the visitors was exactly what someone else had in mind.

Either way, it would be very interesting to watch.

The big round safe was halfway across the room, moving ponderously on its floating platform, as Bink slid down through the hole in the ceiling.

To her relief, the Zeds spaced around the room remained silent and motionless. There'd always been the chance, however slim, that Villachor would reconsider his strategy and reactivate them. Watching through the hole above her, Zerba and Kell were almost as silent as the droids.

Which was just as well, since Bink didn't feel like talking to anyone right now.

Had Han figured it out? Probably. He could be a pretty fair judge of people when he put his mind to it, and he knew her well enough to be able to read her reactions. Of course, just giving him the spare trigger should have been all the hint he'd have needed.

But he hadn't done anything to stop her. He hadn't even said anything. Probably had known it would be a waste of time.

Because Tavia was in danger, and Bink was the one who'd put her there. And as much as she liked and trusted Chewbacca, she had no intention of letting him carry the football on this one alone.

But first she had a job to do, if for no other reason than that it would ensure that this was the last time her sister would ever have to be in this kind of danger.

She landed with a quiet thump on the floor, glancing once at the doorway and then moving toward the floating safe, studying it as she walked. As Rachele had described earlier, the platform was slowly rotating as it traced its path around the ballroom. Not very quickly, probably only about once every three minutes.

Unfortunately, at this point any rotation was a problem. Their first task, therefore, was to get it stopped.

There was a soft thump from behind her, and she looked back to see Kell disengaging from the synth-erope. "Anywhere in particular you want me to start?" he stage-whispered.

"You don't need to whisper," Bink told him. "The place is completely soundproof."

Kell glanced up, as if he was going to point out that the open hole above them was most definitely *not* soundproof. Fortunately, he seemed to think better of it. "I was thinking we should kill the platform's movement," he continued in an only slightly louder voice as he hurried toward her. "Otherwise, the timing—"

"Exactly," Bink cut him off. "Think you can do that without dropping everything?"

Kell nodded. "No problem."

"Then do it."

He nodded again and strode past her, pulling out his compact tool kit and one of his small detonite charges.

Bink watched as Zerba rappelled down, landing with considerably more bounce than either she or Kell had managed. "You ready?" she asked.

"Sure," he said, hurrying toward her. "You going to be able to find the door? I'm not crazy about the idea of poking randomly into that thing."

"I wouldn't be crazy about it, either," Bink said. "Don't worry, I'll find it."

The stairs unfolded as they approached, just as Rachele had said they would. Bink climbed up onto the platform and began slowly circling, running her fingers over the surface of the duracrete, looking for the telltale scuff marks Winter had identified. Midway through the operation she felt the platform come to a smooth halt. "Got it," Kell called up to them. "I'll start setting the charges."

"Good," Bink called back, scowling at the safe. It would be just her luck if she'd started right past the proper finger holes and was going to have to go all nine and a half meters around the edge of the sphere before she found them.

But the universe had decided to play nice today. Two steps later, she spotted the marks.

The finger holes just to the right, Winter had said. Bracing herself, Bink slipped her fingers into the holes.

And with a gratifying lack of fuss or bother, the bottom segment folded down, exactly as Rachele's simulation had showed. Bink stepped to the side out of the way as it settled onto the platform, and peered inside.

The tunnel had its own lighting system: a set of tiny glowbugs set into the ceiling, with a larger glowpanel over the black stone door and the keypad at the far end.

"I hope you're not going to ask me to cut through that," Zerba warned from behind her. "I read up a little on Hijarna stone. I doubt my lightsaber can even begin to handle it."

"Wouldn't dream of putting your lightsaber through that," Bink assured him, pulling out her sensor and stepping into the tunnel. The spit-mitter inside the fake data card had been silent since Villachor shut it up in the safe, its lower-powered transmitter incapable of punching a signal through both Hijarna stone *and* magsealed vault walls. But Tavia had calculated that it should be able to get a signal through the stone if the receiver was close enough to the safe.

As usual, she'd been right. The signal was faint but readable. "What have we got?" Zerba asked.

"Villachor opened the safe three more times in the past four days," Bink said with satisfaction.

"So four total, counting the one when he put it in there," Zerba said doubtfully. "I don't know. Going to be tricky to pull a pattern with only four points."

"Rachele and Winter can do it," Bink said firmly, backing out onto the platform again. "Don't you have some work of your own to do?"

"Just waiting until I was sure it wasn't going anywhere," Zerba said. He leaned over the edge of the platform. "Kell?"

"It's not going anywhere," Kell confirmed. "And if we don't get this done before Villachor's men get in, none of us will be going anywhere, either."

"Point taken," Zerba said. He peered at the door, then turned his back on it and crouched down beside the short pillar that connected the duracrete ball to the platform. Igniting his lightsaber, he set to work.

Bink took a couple of steps away from him and the hiss of his lightsaber and keyed her comlink.

Rachele picked up almost before the call signal sounded. "Bink?"

"Yes," Bink confirmed. "We're ready here. Can you get Winter hooked in?"

"I'm trying," Rachele said tautly. "I haven't heard from either her or Dozer since they went in."

Bink squeezed her comlink. "You think something's happened to them?"

"I don't know," Rachele said. "I'm starting to wonder if we're going to have another rescue mission on our hands."

Bink hissed between her teeth. "I hope to hell not."

"Me too," Rachele said. "But either way, I think you and I are on our own."

The five armored guards came clumping through the door into the anteroom, to Villachor's simultaneous relief and annoyance. About kriffing time. "I want to get into my vault," he growled. "Those Zeds are in my way. Move them."

"Yes, sir," Uzior's filtered voice came from the lead guard. "We'll have them clear in no time."

Villachor threw a sideways look at Barbas and Narkan, still standing silently against the wall, their expressions unreadable. Probably already working out how they were going to report this to their boss.

Let them. Let them say anything they wanted. One way or another, Villachor was going to get through this. "Make it fast," he told Uzior. "Very fast."

CHAPTER TWENTY-TWO

The game was over, Winter thought distantly. She'd played it well and survived far longer than she'd ever expected. Certainly longer than many of her comrades. But now it was over.

And she'd lost.

There were at least thirty of them, she estimated numbly as she watched them pour out of the turbolifts. Thirty Imperial stormtroopers, their white armor gleaming brighter than it should have in the garage's muted light, their blaster rifles held ready as they spread with silent efficiency across the garage.

"So much for making a run for it," Dozer murmured beside her. "At least we know why those other two airspeeders suddenly found somewhere else to be."

Winter looked over her shoulder. Hovering outside the garage entrance, gleaming like the stormtrooper armor in the diffuse city lights, was an Imperial landing craft, *Sentinel* class, its laser cannons and rotating blasters covering the garage.

"You," a filtered voice said brusquely.

Winter turned back. Two of the stormtroopers had come up to her and Dozer, their blaster rifles not *quite* aimed at them. "Come with us."

And now the game really *was* over.

Another man had emerged from the open turbolifts by

the time Winter and Dozer arrived. He was something of a surprise: an older man, his face ruddy, his body far more overweight than even a senior Fleet officer should be allowed to get away with, his clothing casual but expensive. Someone important, judging from the way their stormtrooper escort stiffened to attention as they stopped in front of him.

"Ah," the man said, his lips smiling genially, his eyes sharp and clear and knowing. "Is that it?"

"Is that what?" Dozer asked, genuine-sounding puzzlement in his voice. "I don't know what's going on here, Master, but I'm very glad you and your troops showed up. Those people"—he jerked a thumb over his shoulder—"were going crazy in here. Just *crazy.*"

"Really," the man said calmly. "Flying about like maniacs, were they?"

"And crashing into the ceiling and parked vehicles and just ripping up the whole place," Dozer said, warming to his story. "I thought we were going to be killed for sure."

"A frightening experience, indeed," the other commiserated, almost as if he genuinely believed it. "But don't worry. It's all over now. We'll take everyone in and get it sorted out." He nodded toward Dozer's side. "And thank you so much for retrieving my hip pouch for me. I'm not sure how you managed it, but I'm pleased you were able to rescue it before their antics could damage it further."

Winter felt her heart seize up. So the Imperials even knew about the cryodex.

"Your hip pouch?" Dozer asked, frowning as he looked down at the one in his hand. "No, no, this is—"

"This is *my* pouch, which was stolen from me," the man cut him off firmly. "Which is why, when I received a tip as to its whereabouts, I immediately called Captain Worhven of the Imperial Star Destroyer *Dominator* and asked him to help retrieve it." He smiled again, and this time the smile had a brittle edge. "I'm sure you understand how difficult it can be sometimes to work with locals."

Winter swallowed. Especially when the locals were essentially owned and operated by Villachor and Black Sun. This man knew, all right. He knew everything.

"We're glad we could help," Winter said, giving Dozer a nudge. Under the circumstances, there was really no point in dragging this out any further.

With a resigned sigh, Dozer handed him the pouch. "Immensely glad," he said.

"Thank you," the man said. He opened the pouch and peered inside. "Yes, this is it, Commander," he confirmed, closing it and turning to the stormtrooper beside him. "Have your men gather everyone and take them to the Tweenriver garrison for questioning. What became of those other two airspeeders, by the way? I trust you didn't let them get away."

"No, my lord, we have them," the stormtrooper said.

"Excellent," the man said. "No communications are to be allowed from any of the prisoners, of course."

"Yes, my lord." The stormtrooper nodded at Dozer and Winter. "What about these two?"

The man looked back at Winter and Dozer, and it seemed to Winter that his smile this time had an edge of ironic enjoyment to it. "Master and Mistress Smith can go," he said. "Will you need assistance with your vehicle?"

There was a brief pause as Dozer apparently tried to find his voice. "No," he said. "Thank you. We can manage."

"Very good," the man said briskly. "Farewell." Turning, he strode back to the turbolift, one of the stormtroopers following respectfully behind him.

The other stormtrooper gestured with his blaster. "You

heard him," he said gruffly. "Move along." Without waiting for a response, he brushed past and headed across to where the other Imperials were collecting Aziel's furious men into small knots for disarming and binding.

"Come on," Dozer muttered, taking Winter's arm and heading back toward the airspeeder she'd been working on. "Is it open?"

"Yes," Winter said, her head spinning. This had to be some kind of trick. Some game the predator was playing with his prey.

She was still waiting for the hammer to fall as Dozer hotwired the airspeeder, got them into the air, and edged gingerly through the exit under the watchful eye but silent lasers of the *Sentinel* standing guard.

"So much for secrecy," Dozer said sourly as he lifted them toward the traffic pattern flowing across the lights of the city.

"What do you mean?" Winter asked.

"Isn't it obvious?" he growled. "The Imperials are on to the whole thing. They let us get the cryodex for them, and now they're letting us run loose in hopes we can get them the blackmail files, too."

Winter felt her stomach tighten. Of course. She'd been so focused on her life with the Alliance that she'd momentarily forgotten that she was on an entirely different side this time. "Eanjer's contact," she murmured.

"Who else?" Dozer said darkly. "No wonder the man knew so much about Black Sun and Qazadi."

"I wonder what kind of deal Eanjer's made with him."

"Whatever it is, he's not delivering on it," Dozer said firmly. "We got here first. Still, this should make a pretty puzzle for Villachor and Qazadi to chew on."

"You mean Aziel and the cryodex disappearing without a trace?" Winter asked, pulling out her comlink and trying the signaler. No good—they must still be inside the Imperials' jamming field. "It won't be for long, you know. They'll have to let him go."

"Sure, but hopefully not until we're long gone—"

"Hold it," Winter said as her comlink signaled. She keyed it on. "Rachele?"

"Yes," Rachele said, sounding relieved. "Are you all right? I've been calling and calling."

"We're fine," Winter assured her. "The Imperials had a jamming field set up over the hotel."

"The *Imperials*?"

"Long story; no time," Winter said. "What's happening with Bink?"

"Wait a second," Bink cut in. "You can't just leave it at that. What's going on with Aziel?"

"The Imperials came in and snatched him," Winter said. "Him and the cryodex both."

"Which should actually work to our advantage," Dozer put in. "Depending on how fast Villachor's spy network picks up on this, he'll either assume Aziel has gone over to the Empire or else figure that he's made a run for it."

"I don't see how that helps us," Rachele said. "If they think Aziel's on the run, they could decide to squeeze Tavia to find out what he's up to."

"Except that they only have Sheqoa's word that she's even involved," Dozer pointed out. "Sheqoa means Villachor, and Qazadi doesn't trust Villachor farther than he can throw Villachor's safe. He's not going to interrogate someone purely on Sheqoa's say-so."

"Look, we can talk about this after Bink cracks the safe," Winter said. "What have we got?"

"Three more code sequences," Bink said. She read them off. "You'll note they're different lengths, which means they're not just variants of some standard multidigit code or something."

"So far the computer hasn't come up with any patterns," Rachele said. "Any thoughts?"

Winter stared off at the city stretched beneath them, visualizing the standard High Galactic keypad layout Villachor was using and superimposing their four known sequences over it. "The series seems to be in alphabetic order," she offered.

"Yeah, we already got that part," Bink said tersely. "You're the one who's read everything there is on Villachor. Could it be a list of famous battles, or his old pets or schools—"

"Got it," Winter said as it suddenly fell into place. Of course. "Try this: seven two nine two three four."

There was a short silence. "No good," Bink said.

Winter frowned. No good?

She smiled tightly. Of course no good. Served her right for not following the other sequences all the way to the end. "Try the same sequence, followed by three two five five three three six."

Another short silence. Dozer lifted them into the next airlane and picked up speed.

"That's it," Bink said, all but crowing. "We're open . . . here we go. A box of Black Sun blackmail cards—a *really* pretty box—plus a stack of other data cards Villachor no doubt would also hate to lose. *And* a whole fistful of the prettiest credit tabs you've ever seen."

"I give up," Rachele said, sounding excited and bewildered at the same time. "The computer can't find a thing with that sequence."

"That's because the computer looks for standard words but can't cover the whole spectrum of proper names," Winter said. "Today's code is *Qazadi Falleen.* Villachor's rotating through an alphabetical list of Black Sun's nine vigos, with their respective species attached."

"Beautiful," Dozer said. "Boot-licking subservient, and it's a list he has to have memorized anyway."

"Exactly," Winter said. "How's the rest of it going?"

"We're on track," Bink said. "Kell's got my sensor and is setting his final charges, Zerba's clearing out the safe, and I'm heading back up to the ready room."

"Just be sure you're right behind them when the charges go," Rachele warned. "That part of the universe is going to be a *very* unhealthy place to be for a long time afterward."

"Don't worry, I'll be fine," Bink said softly. "See you."

"Wait a second—I'm not done talking about Tavia yet," Rachele said. "Maybe we should send Lando and Chewie in earlier than planned."

"If you do, we'll risk losing both teams," Dozer warned. "The whole idea was to have everything happen at once so that Villachor doesn't know which way to jump. Remember?"

"Han?" Rachele called. "This is your plan, really. What do you think?"

"Let's hold off for now," Han's voice came, soft and with an odd echo to it. "I don't think Qazadi would do anything without telling Villachor about it first. If that word comes through, we'll know fast enough to get Chewie and Lando moving."

Winter frowned at Dozer. "How does he expect to know what Villachor is or isn't doing?" she murmured.

Dozer shrugged. "It's Han," he said, as if that was all the explanation she needed. Or, more likely, all the explanation she was going to get.

"So we sit on it," Rachele said. She still didn't sound happy but was apparently willing to accept Han's decision. "But stay on him, okay?"

"Sure," Han said. "Conference over. Everyone back to your jobs."

Winter looked at Dozer questioningly. He shrugged and gestured, and she keyed off. "What now?" she asked.

"I don't know," he said slowly. "Eanjer's contact probably knows where the suite is. Then again, he might not. I'm *really* hoping he doesn't know where the rendezvous is."

"So we don't go to either the suite or the rendezvous?"

He shrugged again. "I was just thinking it's a nice night for a drive. Care to join me?"

Winter looked out across the city. In the distance, one of the climactic fireworks displays was starting. "Sure. Why not?"

With a quiet sigh of relief, Kell settled the last of his detonite charges in position and gently switched on its arming switch. Working around explosives was one thing. Working around someone else's booby trap explosives was something else entirely. "Zerba?"

"All set," Zerba announced, stepping around the curve of the safe and fastening his now-bulging hip pouch around his waist. "You?"

"Ready," Kell said, looking up at the hole in the ceiling. Bink should be up there, looking down to make sure they were still on schedule.

Only she wasn't. She was nowhere in sight. "Bink?" he called softly.

"Don't bother," Zerba said with a grunt. "She's long gone."

Kell felt his jaw drop. "She's *gone*?"

"Of course," Zerba said. "Why do you think she gave Han the trigger? She was never planning to stick around once she got the safe open."

"But—" Kell looked up again. "Where did she go?"

"Where do you think?" Zerba said sourly. "She's charged off to rescue her sister."

A lone woman, wearing a burglar outfit loaded with

burglar tools, with no weapon except a small hold-out blaster. "She'll never make it," Kell murmured.

"Nope," Zerba agreed grimly. "I just hope she doesn't get caught in time to foul it up for the rest of us."

Kell stared at him. "How can you—"

"Because that's the kind of business this is, kid," Zerba said quietly. "You can join up with someone for a job like this, but you learn not to make any long-term commitments. Not even in your own mind."

He gestured. "Come on. Time to get ready."

Han hadn't tried to stop her, Bink mused as she headed across the mansion. Zerba hadn't, either. Kell might have, except he'd probably completely missed the fact that she was running out on them.

That part of it bothered her. She'd worked with a fair number of people over the years, and she'd never failed any of them before.

She wasn't failing Zerba and the others here, either, of course. Not really. Han had the trigger, and Han knew what he was doing. Usually.

But sometimes the perception of guilt was more important even than the guilt itself.

She set her jaw. It was her sister. If they couldn't see that or didn't care, then to chaos with all of them.

And especially to chaos with anyone who objected on the grounds that she'd just walk up to the door of Qazadi's suite and get herself killed. That one was not only a misunderstanding but also a professional insult.

Directly ahead, the between-floors gap narrowed into another of the tightly framed doorways she'd already passed twice. Releasing the climbing grip clamps from the ceiling above her, she worked her head and shoulders through the gap, reconnected the clamps on the other side, and kept moving. Han at least shouldn't have been worried on that score—from what she'd heard of his story while they were waiting in the electrical closet, it was clear he'd already looked up here and seen that there was plenty of room for her to make her way invisibly across the mansion.

Though in all fairness, maybe what he'd been worried about was how she was going to handle the vertical distance between the second and fourth floors. The elevator shafts were the obvious routes, which of course meant that Villachor's people would have them covered.

Luckily for her, there was a route that would probably never occur to any of them.

It always amazed her how many buildings more than a hundred years old included hidden rooms or corridors somewhere. Maybe the rich and powerful in those eras had been more paranoid than their modern-day descendants, or maybe they'd just liked the old-fashioned romance and glamour of it all. Given that Villachor's mansion had once housed a sector governor, she would bet heavily that there was a whole set of emergency passages tucked away coyly somewhere between the walls.

Unfortunately, Rachele's schematics hadn't included any hidden boltholes, and she didn't have time to search them out.

Fortunately, those same schematics *had* showed the dumbwaiter.

She broke her way through the wall with little effort and even less noise. The shaft was just as narrow as she'd expected. It was also as easily passable for someone her size who knew what she was doing.

Climbing into the narrow space, she headed up.

The Zeds were heavy, bulky things, and even with the armored suits' power assistance it took Uzior and his men nearly ten minutes to move the first row of five out of the way. Villachor watched in silence from beside Sheqoa, listening to the seconds tick away, furiously anxious to know what was happening behind that door but equally determined to keep his fears and frustration invisible to Qazadi's men.

Uzior had started on the second row when Villachor suddenly noticed that a sixth armored guard had slipped unseen into the anteroom and was watching silently from the wall across from the vault door. "Who are you?" he demanded. "Who is he?" he repeated, glaring at Sheqoa.

"I assumed that you called him in," Sheqoa said, sounding confused. "Earlier, when I was giving the others their instructions."

"If I'd called him in, he'd be helping," Villachor snarled, glaring at the newcomer. "Who are you?"

"My name is Dygrig," the other's filtered voice came. "His Excellency Master Qazadi ordered me to come and observe."

Villachor threw a look at Barbas and Narkan. The whole anteroom was starting to stink of Black Sun vigo. "Did he tell you to suit up in *my* armor for the occasion?"

"You already said there might be trouble inside the vault," Dygrig reminded him. "His Excellency thought it would be a good idea if someone else came prepared."

Villachor took a deep breath, his entire blood system feeling as if it were about to explode. For Qazadi to send one of *his* guards, fitted out in one of *Villachor's* armored suits . . . "Very thoughtful of His Excellency," he replied, fighting viciously for self-control. Going berserk in front of witnesses would be all the excuse Qazadi would need to throw him out and put someone else in his place. "As long as you're here, you can give my men a hand."

"I was told to stand ready for whatever we found inside," Dygrig demurred calmly. "My orders didn't say anything about helping with the preliminaries."

No, of course Qazadi wouldn't want his men to get their hands dirty. "Uzior?"

"We'll have the area clear in eight minutes," Uzior promised.

"I could call more men," Sheqoa offered.

"Have the search teams found the intruder?"

Sheqoa winced. "No, sir."

"Then we'll make do," Villachor said. He shot a glare at Dygrig, who was now watching with the same condescending detachment as Barbas and Narkan. If he survived this challenge, Villachor promised himself darkly, he would find a way to make Qazadi pay for his heavy-handedness, vigo or not. "Have the nearest search team go to the ready room," he ordered Sheqoa. "If Qazadi has more of his people up there helping themselves to our equipment, I want to know about it."

Rachele's comlink twittered. "Report," she said.

"Trouble," Han said, his voice so low she could hardly hear it. "Zerba, how hard did you lock the ready room after I left?"

"As hard as the lock that was there," Zerba said. "We didn't weld it or anything, if that's what you're asking. Why?"

"Villachor's sending someone up there," Han said. "The minute they see the hole, it'll be all over. They'll have ten guys down in the vault before Villachor stops screaming."

"And that'll be it for Zerba and Kell," Rachele said grimly. "So we blow it now?"

"We can't," Han said. "Villachor hasn't got the vault door open yet."

"You sure we *need* it open?" Kell asked. "The magseal didn't stop the lightsaber."

"You're not using a lightsaber this time," Rachele reminded him. "I don't know what the magseal will do, but I'd really rather not risk it."

"If you don't, *we* sure don't," Zerba agreed. "I vote we go ahead and turn Chewie and Lando loose."

"Hold on," Bink cut in. "They can't go yet—I'm not in position."

"You've got two minutes to *get* in position," Han told her tartly. "Uzior says the vault will be open in eight. We need something to distract the guards from this part of the mansion, and Chewie and Lando are it."

"Can you do it, Bink?" Kell asked.

"Do I have a choice?" Bink bit out. "Fine—go ahead. But if anything happens to Tavia, it'll be on your head. And I mean that literally."

"I know," Han said. "Two minutes, Rachele."

"Got it." Rachele braced herself as she switched over to Chewbacca's more secure comlink frequency. "Chewie, Eanjer: two minutes."

Over the years, Bink had accumulated an extensive collection of words that were appropriate to this kind of situation. On her way to the top of the dumbwaiter shaft, she ran through the entire list of them.

Two minutes. She was still half a mansion away from where Tavia was being held, and Han was giving her two measly kriffing minutes to get there.

There was no way she could make it there via the between-floors gap. Her grip-clamp techniques were perfect for this kind of surreptitious travel, but the very nature of their operation put a cap on speed. And that top speed wouldn't be enough.

Which left her only one option. An option that, like

the dumbwaiter itself, the mansion's original designers had given her.

The horizontal conduits were right at the top of the shaft, heading off in opposite directions: one each to the southeast wing and the northeast wing. With a fully enclosed conduit, even one as cozy as this, there would be no need for grip clamps. Her standard nonslip friction gloves were the only tools she needed, and she could easily cover the distance in half the time the between-floors route would take. Maybe even within the two-minute window Han had allotted her.

The problem was that the between-floors route allowed her to choose where she came out at the other end. With the food delivery conduit, unfortunately, there was exactly one exit. If Qazadi or his guards happened to be looking the wrong way at the wrong time, she'd never even see the shot coming.

But she had to try. It was Tavia. It was her sister.

She twisted her body around the bend at the top of the dumbwaiter shaft and worked her way into the conduit, angling her shoulders along the diagonal to take best advantage of the limited space. Pulling at the metal sides with her gloves, starting again at the top of her list of curses, she headed into the darkness.

Kastoni was starting to get dangerously impatient, and Lando was down to his second-to-last stalling technique, when the whole wing seemed to explode in a cacophony of shattered ceramic, wood, and stone.

And as he and Kastoni spun toward the door, an airspeeder roared past down the corridor, bouncing back and forth into the walls on either side. Kastoni had just enough time to bark a startled curse before a second vehicle went shooting past behind it.

And right behind the vehicles, running for all they were worth, were Chewbacca and Eanjer.

Lando puffed out a sigh of relief. Finally. "What in the name of—" he began. He broke off as the racket of the bouncing airspeeders was replaced by the bellowing of alarms.

"Emergency!" Kastoni shouted into his comlink clip as he snatched out his blaster. "Garage has been breached. Two airspeeders are running loose in the north wing heading for central—I say again, two airspeeders are moving through the north wing headed for central."

He got an acknowledgment and headed for the door.

"What can I do?" Lando asked, coming up behind him.

"You can get your rear back outside," Kastoni snarled. "You're done here." He stopped at the doorway, eased his head out for a quick look—

And crumpled to the floor as Lando rammed his fist directly behind Kastoni's left ear.

Shaking the sudden throbbing out of his hand, Lando dropped to one knee beside the unconscious man and scooped up his blaster. For a moment he considered checking in with Rachele, decided he didn't have the time, and headed off after Chewbacca.

He'd assumed earlier that the interior of the mansion was essentially deserted except for the kitchen staff crafting the refreshments for the Festival visitors outside. Certainly most of the security force had been outside, riding herd on the crowd and trying to chase down the last of the out-of-control droids. But as he followed in the wake of Chewbacca, Eanjer, and the airspeeders, he found a surprising number of people peering fearfully, cautiously, or disbelievingly through the various doorways. Most of them seemed to be techs of some sort, which wasn't surprising this close to the garage and droid repair facilities.

A couple of them helpfully pointed the way to the uniformed police sergeant charging after the intruders. None of them made any move to stop or challenge him.

He'd left the north wing and was heading up the wide staircase leading to the central section and the northeast wing beyond when he heard the first sounds of blasterfire.

The comlink built into Han's armor was locked into the Marblewood security channel, which meant he got the news about the rampaging airspeeders at the same time as Sheqoa, and a few seconds before Villachor.

He'd expected Villachor to go ballistic with the report of something else going wrong. But instead of dissolving into fire, the crime lord's attitude turned into ice. "Inform His Excellency that he may have intruders on the way," he told Sheqoa evenly. He gestured to Barbas and Narkan. "You might want to go assist in your master's defense," he added.

The two men exchanged looks. Barbas nodded silently, and they headed at a fast jog across the anteroom and out the north door.

Han grimaced. Hopefully, Chewbacca and Lando would know to watch for trouble coming up from behind.

"You can go with them," Villachor added.

Han blinked away his tactical visualizations. Villachor was gazing at him, the same deadly ice in his eyes. "I was ordered here," Han said. "I'll leave if and when I receive new orders."

"You'll leave when *I* order you to leave," Villachor said calmly. "This is still my territory. *My* word is the law here, not Master Qazadi's."

"I understand, Master Villachor," Han said, trying for the right mix of respect and arrogance that so many midlevel Fleet officers had mastered. "And I have no intention of violating that command. But—"

"Alert!" a taut voice came suddenly over the suit's comlink. "The vault has been breached from above. Repeat, the vault has been breached."

"Sir, the vault's been breached," Sheqoa relayed urgently to Villachor. "Sounds like they got in through the ready room."

For a heartbeat Villachor just stared at him. Then he spun around to the men straining at the frozen Zeds. "Get that door open *now*!" he snarled.

He jabbed a finger at Han. "And put that man under arrest."

CHAPTER TWENTY-THREE

The blasterfire was getting louder and more intense, Lando noted uneasily as he charged up the stairs three at a time. So far he hadn't spotted any of Villachor's guards coming up from behind. But that was bound to change soon.

Ideally, the blasterfire should have been over by the time he reached the fourth floor of the northeast wing. Halfway down the hallway was the reason it hadn't. One of the two airspeeders had ground to a halt in the center of the floor, blocking the one behind it. Chewbacca and Eanjer were crouched behind the rear vehicle, Chewbacca working the remote as he tried to get it past the damaged one. At the far end of the hall, a Falleen and a pair of human guards were crouched behind an F-Web repeating blaster that was sending a continual spray of fire at the airspeeders, while a second Falleen lay prone beside them sniping with what looked like a knockoff version of a BlasTech T-21.

Lando skidded to a halt beside Eanjer. "What's the holdup?" he shouted over the scream of the blasterfire.

"Got in a lucky shot," Eanjer shouted back. "Chewie thinks he can fix it, but it'll take some time, and we need to get the other one past it if we want to keep pressure on the gunners down the hall."

"Why can't you—" Lando strangled off the question.

Of course Eanjer couldn't do that for him. The remote pad took two hands, and Eanjer's medsealed right hand was useless. "Chewie, give it to me," he told the Wookiee. "I'll get it around. You get the other one fixed."

Chewbacca rumbled and thrust the controller into Lando's hands, then dropped to the floor and crawled toward the downed airspeeder.

With a normal airspeeder, Lando could have simply rammed the second one over the top of the first, crushing or shattering the first vehicle's canopy and creating whatever room he needed. But Villachor's airspeeders were too heavily reinforced and armored for that, which not coincidentally was also the reason they hadn't already been cut to ribbons by the blasterfire from the other end of the hall. Chewie's efforts had already smashed away part of the ceiling; unfortunately, the between-floors gap hadn't given him quite enough extra space to get the airspeeder past.

But he hadn't yet tried ramming the walls. If they were thin enough, and if there was enough room along the hallway's sides, that might do the trick.

Backing up the hovering airspeeder a few meters, Lando angled it toward the wall and prepared to ram.

The end of the dumbwaiter conduit was no more than twenty meters ahead when the hallway to Bink's left erupted in the sound of muffled blasterfire.

She swore again, trying to get a little more speed out of her sideways crawl. Lando and Chewie had started their assault, and Tavia's time was rapidly running out. Even a Black Sun vigo could put two and two together, and an assault on Qazadi's suite while he was hosting a prisoner was too obvious a connection to miss.

The war outside had settled down into a steady rhythm, with at least one heavy repeating blaster in operation, by the time she reached the end of the conduit. Stripping off the friction gloves, she drew her hold-out blaster. Setting her teeth, she put her other hand on the conduit door and pushed.

She'd worried that it would be locked and that she would have to waste precious seconds working a probe around the rubber seals to trip the catch. But there was no lock and no catch. She eased the door the rest of the way open, listening as best she could over the noise for any indication that the amazing self-opening door had been spotted.

Nothing. Getting a grip on the edge, she pulled herself the rest of the way through.

She found herself in probably the most gorgeous dining room she'd ever seen. There were two doors leading out of it, one of which was ajar. Moving silently across to the half-open door, she peeked through the gap.

And felt her stomach tighten. Tavia was there all right, seated on a low-backed couch with her back to Bink's door. Bink couldn't see her face, but she could see the tension in her sister's shoulders. Seated in a high-backed chair across from her was a Falleen in full intimidating royal-type garb. Qazadi, without a doubt. His eyes were on the hallway door to his right, his expression cool and calculating, a hint of a macabre smile about his lips.

Between him and the door, facing the muffled blasterfire with their own weapons drawn and ready, were two Falleen bodyguards.

Bink was a ghost burglar, not a soldier, assassin, or even a smuggler. She normally carried a blaster on the job, but only because it was an occasionally useful tool. She'd fired at another living being exactly twice in her life, and in both instances her full intent had been to keep the person pinned down so she could make her getaway. As far as she knew, none of those shots had even connected, let alone caused any actual damage.

Now she was going to have to shoot two Falleen. In the back.

To kill.

But there was no other way. Not if she was going to get herself and Tavia out of this alive. With her throat so tight it felt like she was strangling, she got a two-handed grip on her blaster, lined up the muzzle on the first guard, and squeezed the trigger.

He jerked as if he'd been slapped across the face, his legs collapsing and dropping him without a sound to the floor. The second guard was starting into a sort of spinning sideways leap when her second shot blew a small cloud of vaporized cloth and skin from his torso. He landed full-length on the floor, hitting hard enough to make Bink wince in sympathetic pain. Shoving the door the rest of the way open with her foot, she swiveled the blaster to point at Qazadi. "Don't move," she warned.

"I wouldn't think of it," the Falleen said coolly. He and Tavia were both looking at Bink now, Qazadi from the depths of his chair, Tavia over the low back of her couch. Qazadi was openly smiling, his eyes flicking between Bink and Tavia. Tavia's expression, in contrast, was tense and frightened. "Now at last we have the solution to the puzzle," Qazadi continued. "Very clever." He held out a hand to Bink. "You, I take it, are the thief with the tracking dye on her hands?"

"Just don't move," Bink ordered. The adrenaline rush of the brief battle was fading, and as her brain started working again, she realized she had no idea what she was going to do next. Obviously she and Tavia couldn't leave the same way Bink had arrived—all Qazadi had to do was saunter into the dining room, fire a few shots down the conduit, and call it a day.

But with the noisy war going on in the hallway, that way wouldn't be an especially healthy direction to run either.

Unless the two women brought along a hostage. "On your feet," she ordered Qazadi, stepping all the way into the room. The Falleen's smile was positively radiant, she noted suddenly. Odd that she hadn't picked up on that before. "You're going out that door . . ."

She trailed off. The smile wasn't just radiant—it was borderline saintly. Saintly, forgiving, loving—

And then, abruptly, she understood.

But it was too late. It was far too late.

Cursed kriffing Falleen pheromones.

"Please," Qazadi invited, gesturing to the couch beside Tavia. "We have so very much to talk about. Master Villachor, Lord Aziel, and this." He nodded toward a side table, where Winter's fake cryodex was prominently displayed.

Bink looked at Tavia's strained face. There was no hope there—her sister was as deep into Qazadi's chemical spell as she was. Probably even deeper.

Bink had a blaster, ready in her hand. She'd already used it twice. Surely she could use it again.

Only she couldn't. Even as her brain ordered her hand to raise the weapon and fire, her heart was ordering the hand to remain at her side.

And for once her heart was stronger.

Which meant it was over. She and Tavia were finished. So, probably, were the rest of Han's team.

And as she sank down onto the couch beside her sister, it occurred to her that she'd just killed two living beings. For nothing.

There were still two Zeds frozen in front of the vault door, but the path was finally clear enough for Villachor to get to the keypad. He folded it out from the wall and punched in the access code, jabbing the keys so hard that Han found it slightly amazing that his fingers didn't punch all the way through the pad. The door swung open, and Han craned his neck to look.

The safe had stopped near the center of the vault, the platform that normally carried it around the room now hovering motionlessly. The fold-down segment of the sphere that opened up into the Hijarna-stone cabinet in the middle was hanging wide open, and Han didn't need his helmet's audio enhancements to hear Villachor's vicious curse as he saw that his safe had been breached. Right at the edge of Han's vision, two security men were sliding down the syntherope line that Bink had left dangling, their blasters ready as they scanned the room. "Careful, sir," one of them called toward the door. "Give us a moment to make sure it's clear."

Villachor ignored them. He gestured three of the armored guards forward, and as they strode into the vault, he pointed the other two back to Han, just in case they'd forgotten he was supposed to be taken into custody. Spinning back around, Villachor strode into the vault behind the three guards, Sheqoa and Villachor's two usual bodyguards close beside him.

The two guards clumped toward Han, their massive hands resting warningly on their holstered blasters. Han reached his hands up to his head, just to show that he knew proper prisoner procedure.

And as his hand passed the helmet's right cheek flange, he slipped a finger around to Bink's trigger and gently pushed it forward.

With a final lunge and a crash of wood and stone, the airspeeder bashed out enough of the hallway's side wall to open a path past the stalled vehicle. Giving the control a final shove, Lando bounced the vehicle through one last half meter of wall surface and got it in front of its downed partner.

And with that, they were finally ready to take on the other end of the target range. F-Webs came with built-in shield generators, but he would bet heavily that a shield designed to deflect small-arms fire wouldn't do a bit of good against an armored airspeeder rocketing in on it at a hundred kilometers an hour.

He had started the airspeeder on its way, and the fire from the F-Web had suddenly intensified as Qazadi's guards saw the armored black death coming at them, when Eanjer abruptly leapt up and charged after the roaring vehicle.

"Eanjer!" Lando shouted after him. "Get back here!"

But it was too late. Eanjer was off and running, his legs pumping with a strength and speed Lando wouldn't have guessed the man had in him, pounding after the airspeeder like an Imperial Center bureaucrat trying to catch an airbus.

Lando hissed out a curse. He'd planned to keep the airspeeder right at the ceiling until the last second, presenting as much of the armored underside to the blasterfire as he could in hopes of protecting it from the same kind of lucky shot that had taken out the first one. But with Eanjer running like a maniac straight into the line of fire, that was no longer an option. Scowling, he dropped the vehicle nearly to the floor, moving its bulk into position to provide Eanjer with as much cover as possible.

And, of course, leaving the airspeeder more vulnerable to attack. If the guards nailed it before he could flip it up on its side and sweep both them and the F-Web out of action, as he was hoping to do, he and Chewbacca might just have to use Eanjer himself as their shield when they stormed Qazadi's suite.

With a suddenness that strongly implied to Dayja that it had been prearranged, Marblewood's massive fireworks display kicked off in all its full, brilliant glory. Not just the lower-flying rockets he'd seen being fired earlier, but also the high, elaborate, all-but military-grade explosives.

The problem was that the umbrella shield was still in place. And as the rockets hit the invisible energy field, bursting prematurely and showering fire onto the ground, the crowd below finally hit the breaking point. With shouts, curses, and a scattering of hysterical screams, the whole mass dissolved into chaos.

A piece of flaming debris crashed to the roof barely five meters from Dayja's chimney spire. He twitched back from it, grabbing his comlink. Enough was finally enough. Whether this was Eanjer's doing or just an accident, he couldn't sit by and watch any longer.

Another misfire burst against the shield, raining fragments down on the crowd, and with a sense of resignation Dayja put away the comlink. It was too late. The panic had started, and there was nothing he, the police, or any of Iltarr City's other emergency services could do about it now.

All he could do now was watch.

Han had warned Kell that the whole thing had to go quickly. The kid had taken him at his word.

The detonite beneath the floating platform went first, a set of deceptively small charges that knocked out the power lines to all the repulsorlifts on the forward half. The platform held position for maybe half a second, and then the front edge dropped to the floor with a booming crash. Almost buried in the thunderous echo was an even deeper creaking as the lightsaber-weakened connecting pillar bent and distorted under the sudden and unexpected stress. Another half second, and Kell's final charges went off, blowing away chunks of duracrete from the rear of the safe and triggering a pair of ear-numbingly powerful shaped-charge explosions from booby traps that had been buried just beneath the surface.

Looking like a miniature Death Star on afterburners, with a rumble that seemed to shake the whole mansion, the safe broke loose from its pillar, rolled down the slanted platform, and headed across the floor.

For a frozen second, Villachor and his men stared in disbelief at the six-meter sphere bearing down on them. Then, in almost perfect unison, they scrambled madly to get out of the way.

Villachor and his two bodyguards made it. Sheqoa and the three other guards didn't.

Even before they disappeared beneath the sphere, Han was in motion, stepping forward and planting himself between the two guards now gaping at the drama going on inside the vault. He put a hand on each of their chests and shoved as hard as he could to either side.

The suits were heavy, but Han's strength enhancements were more than up to the job. The two guards flew backward a good three meters each before sprawling onto the floor—maybe far enough to be out of the way of the approaching sphere, but Han really didn't care that much one way or the other.

Right now he was far more concerned with the lives of the hundreds of citizens who could be unknowingly walking or standing directly in the path of the rolling juggernaut about to crash through the mansion wall. The fireworks triggers Kell and Zerba had set up earlier should have most of the crowd moving toward the exits, but there were always a few who were too brave, too casual, or too stupid to know when it was time to get out.

For those people, the rolling safe was likely to be the last miscalculation they ever made.

The safe was nearly to the armored vault wall. Spinning around, Han raced for the anteroom side door, emptying his borrowed Caliban blaster into the wall around it as he ran. The weapon ran dry; tossing it aside, Han threw himself at the door, hoping his armor was as tough as it looked.

It was. He crashed through the door with barely a jolt, a large section of wall coming down with him. The nearest exit to the outside was thirty meters away to the south; recovering his balance, he angled toward it, hoping fervently that he could beat the sphere outside. Behind him, he heard the violent grinding crunch as the sphere ground its way through the vault's armor plating—

And then he was through the door, out into the courtyard, and angling back toward the sphere's path.

He'd been right about the crowd. Most of them were already far in the distance, racing for the gates as fireworks continued to splash spectacularly against the umbrella shield above them. But a few dozen of them were still hanging around, watching the misfires with studied casualness or bravado.

Han rolled his eyes. Even he knew enough to come in out of the rain, especially when the rain consisted of live coals. Still, if random overhead explosions weren't enough to get these last stubborn few moving, maybe something closer and more personal would.

Grabbing the neuronic whip from his belt, he activated it and whirled it high over his head.

Most of the loiterers had already spotted Han in his gleaming armor. *All* of them spotted the whip's crackling blue-white sizzle. "Go!" Han bellowed, spinning the whip over his head. "Get away from here—now!"

They were finally on the move, running like frightened Toong, when the sphere crashed through the mansion's outer wall and rolled across the courtyard, crushing the flagstones beneath it as it went. Ten meters ahead of it, where the flagstones gave way to textured grass, the spike-ring fence slashed its way upward out of the ground, encircling the mansion in a six-meter-tall crackling forest of electrified death.

The safe rolled through it without even slowing down.

Ducking through the still sizzling gap, pushing his armor's speed and power enhancements to the limit, Han sprinted around past the safe and got in front of it. Again thrashing the whip wildly above his head, he charged.

It was about as crazy a stunt as he'd ever pulled. But it was working. In the darkness, with the distraction of the fireworks, a lot of the people in the sphere's path probably would never have seen the danger until it was way too late. But an armored figure with a glowing blue whip was impossible to miss. They scattered in front of him, most taking the hint and heading for the exits, the others dashing in all directions except the vector Han and the safe were on.

He kept going, watching the safe in his rear display, hoping he could stay ahead of it until it finally ran out of steam. Hoping, too, that it wouldn't catch up with the rear of the main crowd heading for the exits, mow a wide swath of death through them, then shatter the outer wall and roll out into the heavy Iltarr City traffic.

He really, *really* hoped that didn't happen.

From out in the hallway came a horrendous crash, accompanied by the kind of piercing, metal-on-duracrete scraping that Bink had sometimes heard when a wrecked airspeeder hit a landing platform and skidded along it.

And as the scraping sound faded away, she realized the blasterfire had also ceased.

She looked at Qazadi. His eyes were on the door, his expression hard and cold. "Be silent," he told the two women. "No noise." His hand dipped into his robe and emerged with a blaster. "Sit quietly and watch your friends die."

Bink swallowed hard, fighting against the unreasonable calm and even more unreasonable sense of love and contentment flowing through her. Those were her teammates out there. She couldn't let them simply walk into the fire from Qazadi's blaster. She had to do something to stop him.

Only she couldn't. She couldn't even get her voice to work, let alone her hand.

Her hand. She looked down at her lap, at the hold-out blaster lying there. Qazadi had permitted her to keep the weapon, knowing she would be unable to use it against him.

And he'd been right. She willed her hand to move, willed it with all the strength she had in her. But her hand stayed where it was. The blaster would sit there uselessly, and she would sit here uselessly and watch her teammates come through that door and die.

"There's one thing you're forgetting, Master Qazadi," Tavia said.

Bink jerked her head, staring in disbelief at her sister. Tavia's face was pinched and strained, so much so that it was hardly recognizable. Her voice was low and hesitant, the words sounding like they'd been ground out individually from beneath a grain farmer's millstone.

Qazadi had ordered her not to speak. And yet she was speaking. Out of the corner of her eye Bink saw Qazadi turn to look, apparently as surprised as she was. "I told you to be silent," he said.

"You're forgetting," Tavia ground out, all but panting with the incredible mental exertion, "that we didn't come here alone. You're forgetting . . . that they *are* our friends."

"I said *be silent*!" he snarled. He swung his blaster to point at her.

With a violent shattering of wood and stone, the hallway door blew inward.

Qazadi was caught by surprise, his arm jerking with impacting debris as he tried to bring his blaster back on target. Through the cloud of smoke, Bink saw a figure step calmly into the room.

She caught her breath. She'd assumed it would be Chewbacca or Lando who would be risking his life to save them. But it wasn't either of them.

It was Eanjer.

His hands were stretched out in front of him as if he were surrendering, his misshapen right hand wrapped in its medseal, his left hand open and empty. "I bring you an offer, Your Excellency," he called over the muffled clatter of door shards hitting the floor and furniture.

"I don't make deals," Qazadi snarled. He got his blaster lined up on the intruder—

Green fire erupted from Eanjer's distorted right hand, flashing across the room squarely into the center of Qazadi's face.

And with the defiant snarl still in place, the Falleen slumped in his chair.

Dead.

Bink looked at Eanjer, her eyes dropping to the smoking hole in his medsealed hand. The hand hadn't looked the way it did because it was mangled, she realized now, or even because it had been replaced by some strange alien prosthetic.

It had looked that way because it was a normal, fully functional human hand curled around a hold-out blaster.

She looked up at Eanjer's good eye. "You—"

"It was him or us," he said calmly. "You two okay?"

"We're fine," Tavia assured him. Her voice still sounded ragged, but Bink could hear it starting to recover.

As was Bink's own brain. Without the pheromones, she could feel the fog rapidly lifting. "What's the plan?" she asked, grabbing her blaster from her lap and standing up.

"To get out of here," Eanjer said, nodding toward the ragged hole behind him. "Lando and Chewie are waiting beside the other airspeeder. Move."

Bink nodded, taking her sister's arm and helping her to her feet. "What about you?" she asked as she guided Tavia over the debris.

"I want to get the cryodex," Eanjer said. His half mouth half smiled. "Might as well leave them wondering. Go on—go."

Bink got her sister to the hallway, noting peripherally the half-crushed airspeeder to their right and the mangled F-Web blaster poking out from underneath it. To their left, Lando and Chewbacca were crouched behind a hovering airspeeder, their eyes and blasters focused the other way down the hall. She turned Tavia in that direction. As they headed away from the suite, she paused for a final look at Qazadi, wondering how her mind could ever have been fooled into thinking he was good and kind and loving.

And because she was looking in that direction, she saw Eanjer standing over the Falleen's body.

She couldn't be sure, not with the single quick glance she had. But it looked very much like he was taking holos . . .

It was like something out of an insane holodrama, Dayja thought numbly as he watched the scene unfold below him. An armored figure cracking a neuronic whip over the last remnants of the evening's crowd, driving them out of the path of the giant sphere rolling inexorably across the Marblewood grounds.

He'd expected Eanjer's team to steal the contents of Villachor's safe. He'd never dreamed they might try to steal the safe itself.

He'd also never dreamed that when the theft went down, he would be stuck on the mansion roof half a kilometer from the action.

So much for getting in and grabbing the blackmail files before the thieves made their getaway.

Still, it wasn't over yet. Eanjer had promised him the files, and Eanjer surely was still on the scene. Somewhere.

The safe was mostly invisible now as it rolled beyond the range of the lights from the mansion and the shimmering crackle of the spike-ring fence. But the distinctive glow of the neuronic whip more than made up for that, and the safe itself was sporadically visible in the brief flare-ups from the fireworks.

Picking up his electrobinoculars, Dayja began a careful scan of the area. If Eanjer was out there, he was going to find him.

It was, Han thought more than once, like something out of a crazy holodrama.

He'd expected the safe to roll in a nice, neat straight line. It didn't. The open sphere segment occasionally caught on the ground, sometimes slowing its forward momentum, other times drastically changing its direction. Han had to keep a close eye on his helmet's rear display to keep from losing the thing entirely, all the while continuing to play the berserk-droid role as he scattered people out of harm's way.

A couple of times he thought he spotted some of Villachor's security men, but they were gaping as hard as the visitors. None of them made any effort to stop him. About halfway across the grounds the dangling segment finally hit the dirt hard enough to break off. After that, the sphere's path was a lot more predictable.

For a few bad moments Han thought his earlier concern would be borne out, that the sphere would indeed crash through the wall and out into the city. But for once the worst-case scenario didn't happen. The sphere slowed and finally came to rest about fifty meters from the wall. Shutting off the whip, Han turned and headed back to it.

He was peering down the tunnel at the Hijarna-stone cabinet when the door swung open and Zerba and Kell crawled unsteadily out. "You all right?" Han asked.

"Just great," Kell said, sounding and looking drunk. "Remind me to never do that again."

"Still beats walking," Zerba offered. "Especially when there are people shooting at you."

"As long as your door doesn't end up at the bottom," Han said as he helped them out of the tunnel onto the ground.

"Not a chance," Zerba assured him. "The cabinet was off-center, and Hijarna stone is a lot denser than duracrete. Same principle as loaded chance cubes."

"I'll take your word for it," Han said. A stutter of muffled explosions came from the direction of the mansion, and he turned to see a multipassenger speeder truck zoom through the gap the safe had made in the spike-ring fence and head across the grounds toward them.

Behind it, a barrage of fireworks was pelting the mansion walls.

"Nice," Zerba said approvingly. "No chance they'll burn the place down, I suppose."

"Probably not," Han said. "But it ought to keep what's left of security inside, where they won't bother us."

"Unless that's some of them now," Kell warned, pointing a still unsteady finger toward the incoming vehicle.

"That's just Chewie," Han assured him.

"You sure?" Kell asked.

Han nodded. "I know his flying style."

Just the same, it wouldn't hurt to check. Keying in his suit's telescopics, he zoomed in on the speeder truck. It was Chewbacca, all right, with Lando and the twins riding behind him.

There was no sign of Eanjer.

Frowning, he keyed for more enhancement, in case he'd missed Eanjer sitting in the shadows in one of the rear seats. But the man wasn't there. Frowning a little harder, Han shifted his attention to the grounds behind the speeder truck, then to the mansion. Still no sign of Eanjer.

He was checking the mansion's windows to see if the other might be trapped inside when something above the windows caught his eye.

There was a man sitting on the roof.

Han bumped his telescopics up a bit. Not only was the man sitting calmly up there, but he had a set of electrobinoculars pressed to his eyes. Some kind of observer?

But those weren't ordinary electrobinoculars, Han realized as he focused on them. They were small and compact, the kind a person could stick in a side pocket without them even being noticed. The expensive kind that a senior Imperial officer might use.

A senior officer, or an Imperial agent.

Casually, Han looked away. Dozer had speculated earlier that Eanjer's contact might be an Imperial. It looked like he'd been right. "You get everything?" he asked Zerba, pulling off his helmet and popping the catches on his torso armor.

"Right here," Zerba confirmed, patting the hip pouch around his waist. "Blackmail files, a few other assorted data cards, and all of Eanjer's credit tabs."

"Good," Han said, dropping the arm and torso armor onto the ground. "Let me have it. Kell, give me a hand getting out of this thing, will you?"

In the reflected light he saw Zerba frown. But the other merely unfastened the pouch and handed it over.

The armor was off and Han was rummaging through the pouch when the speeder truck braked to a halt beside them. The door popped open and Chewbacca growled.

"Yeah, almost," Han said. "Where's Eanjer?"

"He stayed behind to turn a few more of the fireworks launchers toward the mansion," Lando said, climbing out the other side and striding over to Han. "He said he'd get to the rendezvous on his own." He held out his hand. "If you don't mind, I'll take my share now."

Han winced. He'd guessed that Lando would pull this stunt. "How about we wait until we're all at the rendezvous?" he suggested.

"How about you give it to me now?" Lando countered. "Then I can skip the rendezvous and get on with life."

"What's he talking about?" Zerba asked.

"He wants to trade his share of the credits for the blackmail files," Han said.

"Can he *do* that?" Kell asked, frowning.

"Yes, he can," Lando said firmly. "We've already agreed. And no offense, Han, but you've got a bad habit of losing the take to other people. So let's have it."

There was no way around it. "Fine," Han said with a sigh. Pulling out the blackmail file box, he handed it over.

"Thanks," Lando said, sliding it inside his police tunic. "Now, if you'll kindly drop me at my airspeeder, I'll be on my way. The rest of you, it's been fun."

A moment later they were inside the speeder truck and Chewbacca was heading toward one of the exits. There were probably still security guards on duty, but Han wasn't expecting them to make trouble. Not with one of Villachor's own vehicles.

He was more worried about Lando, and what Lando would say.

And what Lando might do.

"About one point seven-five meters, dark hair, dark skin, number-three-type mustache," Dayja said hurriedly into his comlink as the airspeeder drove through the gate and out into the bustling city traffic. "He's got the blackmail files, and if he has any sense, he'll be taking them off Wukkar as soon as he hits the spaceport."

"I don't suppose you have a name," d'Ashewl said. "There are a lot of ships on the ground right now."

"I don't know any names except Eanjer's," Dayja said. "But I think we can narrow it down. His ship will probably be something small and one-man—I got the feeling that he showed up a little later than the others and alone. From his grooming style, he's probably the sort who loves the better things in life but can't quite afford them, so look for a ship that was once high on the snob list but currently looks a little threadbare. Arrival time will be nine days ago, with probably a twelve-hour window on either side."

"Got it," d'Ashewl said. "What's he wearing?"

"This'll kill you," Dayja said, ducking back as one of the fireworks pelting the mansion splashed fire up onto the roof nearby. "He's in an Iltarr City police uniform. But I doubt he'll try to get through the spaceport that way."

"I would hope not," d'Ashewl agreed. "Anything else?"

"He'll be in a hurry," Dayja said. "In fact . . ." He paused, running the numbers through his head. Taking the stolen speeder truck to where a proper escape vehicle was undoubtedly parked, transferring to that other vehicle, driving to the spaceport, getting to his docking bay, firing up his engines . . . "He should be calling for a lift slot in either thirty-two or fifty-five minutes, depending on whether he comes in with an airspeeder or a landspeeder."

"Okay," d'Ashewl said. If he was surprised or skeptical at Dayja's estimates, he kept it to himself. "You want him picked up on the ground?"

"Better not," Dayja said. "I don't know what shape Villachor and his organization are in right now, but we can't risk one of his people at the spaceport getting in on this before we have him secured. Have the *Dominator* grab him after he passes orbit."

"I'll call Captain Worhven right away," d'Ashewl said. "I'm sure he'll be delighted to be handed yet another unexplained task."

"Part of his job," Dayja said. "Anything new on Aziel?"

"Unfortunately, we had to let him go," d'Ashewl said. "Prince Xizor was kind enough to provide him with diplomatic credentials. But there was just enough evidence that the cryodex was originally stolen that I was able to hold on to it as evidence."

"Perfect," Dayja said. "If we can grab the blackmail files, we'll have the lock *and* the key. The Director will be pleased."

"Never mind the Director," d'Ashewl said with a grunt. "Lord Vader will be pleased. *He's* the Empire's future."

"Maybe," Dayja said cautiously. The last thing he wanted right now was to get embroiled in yet another political discussion. "Get a tap into the spaceport tower feed and put the *Dominator* on alert. I'll be there as soon as I can grab an airspeeder from Villachor's garage."

"I assume you'll want to be in on the interrogation yourself?"

Dayja smiled tightly. "You just pick him up," he said. "I'll handle the rest."

Eanjer had expected to come though the job alive. He hadn't been nearly so sure about the rest of the team.

He was also more than a little surprised that the scheme had actually worked.

The docking bay was quiet as he slipped through the door. He'd worried that Han and Chewbacca might get here ahead of him, despite the fact they had to drop the others off at the vehicle switch point. But the *Falcon* was sitting silently in the backwash glow from the nearby city, its lights and systems dark and cold.

Briefly he wondered what the others would think when both he and Han failed to show up at the rendezvous. They'd probably conclude that the two of them had cooked this whole thing up between them, with no intention of ever sharing the millions in those credit tabs with anyone else. They would be furious, vow revenge, and do all the other things people did in those situations.

And they would talk. They would certainly talk. With luck, whatever was left of Han's blotchy reputation would never recover.

Not that Han would be needing that reputation. Not anymore.

He found a spot where he could sit comfortably and watch the entire section of open ground between the docking bay entrance and the *Falcon*'s ramp. Resting his hold-out blaster in his lap, he settled in to wait.

The last of the others had been dropped off, Han had ditched the borrowed speeder truck, and he and Chewbacca were finally ready to hit the spaceport themselves.

Chewbacca rumbled. "I know, I know," Han said irritably. Chewbacca had been giving him the same disapproving look for the past hour. "It'll be all right. Trust me."

Chewbacca rumbled a final comment and then went silent.

Han sighed. He was right, of course. Lando was going to be furious. Or worse.

But there'd been nothing else he could do. Not with that Imperial on the roof watching the whole thing. "He'll get over it," he told Chewbacca firmly. "They're not going to do anything to him. Not without any evidence."

Chewbacca growled the obvious.

"Sure, except that he's not just going to leave the box sitting out in the open," Han explained patiently. "Look, it'll be okay. Lando and me go back a long way. He'll get over it."

Chewbacca didn't answer.

There were two approaches when dealing with a sudden and overwhelming Imperial presence, Lando thought distantly. One was to continue along in calm and perfect innocence, an ordinary citizen of the Empire with nothing to hide. The other was to throw power to the sublight engines and make a run for it.

In retrospect, he should have made a run for it.

"I don't understand any of this," he insisted to the two hard-faced Fleet troopers standing between him and the door of his ship's lounge. "I don't even know what I'm supposed to have done. Can you at least tell me what the charge is?"

The troopers didn't answer. But then, aside from ordering him to open his hatch after he'd been tractored into the Star Destroyer's hangar bay, and then further ordering him into the lounge, neither of his guards had said a word.

With a sigh, Lando gave up this latest effort at communication. Clearly, they were all waiting for someone, and nothing was going to happen until that someone arrived.

It was going to be a long, long night.

Across the docking bay, the door latch clicked open. Eanjer raised his blaster, sighting along it with his good eye.

And lowered it again as a cleaning droid shuffled into the bay, its four arms scrubbing industriously at the walls and floor.

He checked his watch, frowning. Han was late.

The lounge door opened, and to Lando's surprise a masked, hooded, and cloaked figure stepped into the room. "Good evening," he said, stopping between the two troopers. "I apologize for the delay. I trust you've been comfortable?"

"Quite," Lando said, feeling his heart sink. No uniform, no badge, his face shrouded, and walking freely around a Star Destroyer. Some kind of special agent, then—Intelligence, Ubiqtorate, maybe even Imperial Security Bureau.

"Good." The man gestured to the troopers. "Wait outside."

"Yes, sir," one of them said. Together they left the room.

The man waited until the door had closed behind them. Then he pushed back his hood and cloak and pulled off his mask. "So much for that," he said briskly as he rubbed his forehead. "Sorry about the theatrics, but for reasons I won't go into I can't show my face aboard this ship."

"I understand," Lando said, his heart sinking even further. The man facing him was young. Far younger than he'd expected. Terrifyingly young.

Because the young were always ambitious. And in the murky universe where these people operated, there was only one way for young agents to climb up the ladder: by bringing in trophies to present to their superiors.

Enemies of the Empire. Real ones, or merely plausible ones.

This just got worse and worse.

"Now, then," the young man said, dropping his mask on the side table and settling into the chair facing Lando. "Let's start with introductions. I'm Dayja, and you're—well, let's just call you Lando, shall we?"

"Whatever you want," Lando said, stifling a grimace. So much for the carefully constructed false identity and ship's ID he'd flown in under.

"Good," Dayja said. "Well. It's late, we've both had a very busy day, and I'm sure you're at least as tired as I am. So what do you say we make this quick and easy, and you just give me the box."

"Box?"

"The box of Black Sun blackmail files," Dayja said patiently. "The ones you stole this evening from Avrak Villachor's safe. Magnificent work, by the way. I'm very impressed."

"We're glad you liked it," Lando said, his brain spinning with possibilities. There seemed little point in denying that Han had given him the files. Dayja obviously knew that somehow.

But if he played his cards right, maybe there was still some bargaining room. "If I give you the box—"

"If?" Dayja interrupted, looking puzzled. "Oh, no,

you misunderstand. Not *if*. *When* you give me the box. *Then* we'll see about making a deal."

"Sounds more like an ultimatum than a deal."

"I suppose it does," Dayja agreed, looking around the room. "Tell you what. To save time, how about I just get the box myself?" He stood up and walked over to the engineering monitor station on the side wall.

And to Lando's horrified disbelief, he gave the corner of the ventilation monitor display a quick push and release, and as the hidden catch popped, he swung the monitor open to reveal the concealed storage compartment behind it.

"Sorry," he said, giving Lando a tight smile. "Unfortunately for you, this little gem stash has been a standard feature on the G 50 series for quite some time."

Lando sighed. "I was told it was a custom refitting."

"And were charged extra for it, no doubt. Some people have no scruples at all." Reaching into the opening, Dayja carefully removed the box. He sent Lando an unreadable look, then almost reverently worked the catch and raised the lid.

His expression changed. For another moment he held the pose, then raised his eyes again to Lando. "Cute," he said, his voice suddenly brittle. "Where are they?"

"Where are what?" Lando asked, a nasty sense of doom rushing in on him. No—Han *hadn't*.

Dayja turned the empty box to face him. "Where are the data cards?"

Lando sighed. Yes, Han had. "Still on Wukkar, I assume," he said. "Actually, they're probably somewhere in hyperspace by now."

"Where were they going?"

"There's a rendezvous point on Xorth," Lando said. "But I doubt they'll stay there long. In fact, since they were obviously expecting you to pick me up, they probably won't go there at all."

For a long minute Dayja stared at him. Then, carefully, he closed the box. "You play sabacc, Lando?" he asked.

"Yes," Lando said, feeling a frown crease his forehead.

"Yes, of course you do," Dayja said, walking back over to the chair but remaining standing. "And I'll bet you rely heavily on your ability to bluff."

"I prefer having the actual cards."

"So do I," Dayja said. "But sometimes we have to be creative with the hand we've been dealt." He pulled out his comlink. "Captain Worhven? I'm finished. Have your men prepare my shuttle." He gave Lando an oddly wry smile. "As soon as I'm gone, our guest and his ship will be free to leave." He got an acknowledgment and put the comlink away.

"Really?" Lando asked cautiously.

"Really," Dayja assured him. Reaching down to the chair, he picked up his mask. "Fortunately for you, it's now in my best interest to make it look as if we had a deal, transacted our business, and then parted company." He cocked his head. "Unless you *wanted* to stay aboard?"

"No, no, not at all," Lando said hastily.

"You're not to tell your friends about this, of course," Dayja continued. "What happened here will remain our little secret."

"Don't worry," Lando growled. "I doubt I'll be seeing any of them again. Not for a long time."

"Good." Dayja put on his mask and readjusted his cloak and hood. "A good night to you, and a safe voyage. And one more thing."

He leveled a finger at Lando's face. "You owe me," he said. "Someday I'll be back to collect."

Tucking the box into a pocket of his cloak, he turned and left the lounge.

Lando waited for a minute. The troopers didn't come back. He waited another minute, then one more, and finally opened the lounge door.

The troopers were gone. So was Dayja. Lando went to the hatch, made sure it was properly sealed, then headed to the cockpit.

He was in the pilot's seat, gazing at the men moving around inside the flight control station across the hangar, when he was given his release order.

It took all the way to hyperspace, though, before he started breathing normally again.

The sound of fireworks from around the city had long ceased. So had the mass of traffic as the people of Iltarr City left the various Festival venues and headed for home. And Han still hadn't shown up.

Finally, belatedly, Eanjer got it.

It was an excellent copy, he had to admit as he walked beneath the ship, playing his glow rod over the hull. A vintage YT-1300 freighter, roughly the proper age and condition, even with some of the same modifications.

But only some. Others, like the concussion missile bay and the Ground Buzzer blaster cannon, were missing.

It wasn't the *Millennium Falcon.* It was a decoy, swapped out in the landing bay sometime during the past nine days.

Han wasn't coming. In fact, he was undoubtedly long gone.

Eanjer smiled a brittle smile into the darkness. Dozer, of course. It had to be. All that time he'd spent away from the suite during those first days of preparation, supposedly running errands and buying equipment for all the others.

He would have to find some way to pay the ship thief back.

Still, there would be other opportunities. He could wait.

Leaving the bay, he headed across the spaceport to where his own ship was docked. He didn't look back.

The crowds had long since gone, and the rogue fireworks had long since spent themselves.

And Villachor's life was over.

He stood at the railing of his balcony, gazing across the grounds at the massive, impenetrable safe sitting out there for all the universe to see. The impenetrable safe that had been breached.

Prince Xizor's blackmail files were gone. Aziel had gotten free from the Imperials but had lost the cryodex and was looking furiously for someone to blame.

And Qazadi was dead. Murdered.

In Villachor's own house.

Behind him, the suite's secure comm station warbled. Briefly Villachor considered ignoring it. But there really was no point. When Black Sun decided to track him down, there wouldn't be anything he could do about it. Giving his beloved, devastated estate a final look, he turned and went inside.

He'd expected it to be Aziel, possibly Prince Xizor himself. But it was neither.

"Master Villachor," Lord d'Ashewl said, smiling genially out of the display screen. "I trust I'm not calling too late?"

"Not at all," Villachor said. "What can I do for you?"

"I was thinking about our conversation of a couple of days ago," d'Ashewl said, "and I thought you'd be interested in something that's just come into my possession." Reaching down, he lifted the Black Sun file box into view. "I presume I don't need to tell you what this means," he added, opening the box to show Villachor the five black data cards nestled neatly inside.

"No, you don't," Villachor agreed wearily. "Did you call me to gloat?"

"Not at all," d'Ashewl assured him. "I called to see if you were still interested in a deal."

Villachor frowned, trying to read past that round, ruddy face. "You have the files and you have the cryodex. What do you need me for?"

D'Ashewl shrugged. "You know a great deal about Black Sun. You could be very valuable to us."

"And you would protect me, of course?" Villachor growled sarcastically.

"We're quite good at such things, actually," d'Ashewl said, all traces of levity gone from his face and voice. "Lord Vader is even better. I rather think that under the circumstances he could be persuaded to take a personal interest in this."

It was a long shot, Villachor knew. Black Sun had people and agents everywhere. His life was still probably measured in days or even hours.

But even a long shot was better than no shot at all.

"Very well," he said. He braced himself. All his life, all his efforts, all his amassed power and wealth . . . "You have a deal."

CHAPTER TWENTY-FOUR

"And still no sign of Eanjer?" Dozer asked, for probably the tenth time since he'd arrived.

"No," Han said, dropping tiredly onto the couch. The suite wasn't as large or fancy as the one on Iltarr City, and the furniture wasn't nearly as comfortable. But under the circumstances it was much safer.

And safe was good right now. Safe was very good. "And there won't be," he added. "Rachele just found—"

"Wait a second," Zerba cut in incredulously. "Are you telling us he just *bailed*?"

"More likely he missed the note at the rendezvous," Bink put in. "Maybe one of us should go back and see if he's still waiting there."

"He's not." Han waved at Rachele, seated behind her computer, a pinched look on her face. "You want to tell them, Rachele? Or should I?"

"I will," Rachele said, her voice somber. "I just picked up a report from the Iltarr City police. They've found Eanjer's body."

"Oh, no," Tavia breathed, looking stricken. "Oh, Rachele."

"Don't get too mushy," Han growled. "Tell them the rest."

"They found his body," Rachele repeated, "where he'd

apparently been dumped and left to bleed out." Her throat worked. "Six weeks ago."

For a long moment no one spoke. Han looked around the room, watching their expressions of surprise or confusion turn to horrified understanding. "You mean . . . *before* he even talked to Han?" Kell demanded. His eyes darted to Han. "Or—"

"Or whoever it was," Dozer said, sounding like he wasn't sure whether to be stunned or outraged. "But then—"

"What did he want?" Han shook his head. "I haven't the faintest idea."

"I do," Bink said in a low voice. "He came to kill Qazadi."

Chewbacca rumbled.

"That's for sure," Winter agreed soberly. "And we all fell for it."

"But you at least suspected something, didn't you, Han?" Rachele asked. "That conversation you had with him after we got Lando and Zerba back."

"I knew *something* was funny with the guy," Han said. "He seemed more interested in getting inside the mansion than he did in us getting his credits out. But I figured that was just the revenge part talking. The rest of it—" He shook his head. "I didn't have a clue."

"So he used us," Kell murmured. "He brought us in to do all the heavy lifting, get him inside, and take out Qazadi's guards. Son of a bantha."

"And for nothing," Zerba growled, tossing the credit tab he'd been fiddling with back into the stack on the table. "Without Eanjer—the *real* Eanjer—these things are worthless."

"Not completely," Rachele said. "I know some slicers. We should be able to get—I'd say about eight hundred fifteen thousand."

"My mistake," Zerba said sarcastically. "It's still closer to zero than it is to the hundred sixty-three million we signed up for. If I ever catch up with that guy—"

"You won't," Bink said. "Whoever he was, he was a professional."

"Or an Imperial," Dozer growled.

"Or an Imperial," Bink agreed. "My point was that we don't even know what he really looks like. Not with all that medseal plastered across his face. Wherever he disappeared to, he's gone for good."

"So what now?" Kell asked.

"We salvage what we can," Han said, trying hard to keep his own crushing disappointment out of his voice. So much for his dream of being free of Jabba. So much for *all* his dreams. "Rachele's said she can get eight hundred fifteen out of the tabs. That's eighty-one five each. Still not bad for a couple weeks' work."

"Eighty-one five?" Zerba asked, frowning. "I make it ninety plus change."

"Ten of us makes eighty-one five each," Kell reminded him.

"I only see nine people in this room."

"Lando still gets his share," Han said firmly.

"I thought his share was the blackmail files," Zerba said, scowling.

"Which he didn't get," Han said. "So he gets a tenth of the credits like he signed up for."

"Which you're going to deliver in person?" Zerba snorted. "*That* I'd pay to watch."

"We'll get it to him," Han said, eyeing the collection of loot on the table. The rest of the data cards had turned out to be worthless—details of Villachor's smuggling operations that would be interesting to a prosecutor's office but not to a bunch of freelance scoundrels.

But there were still the five blackmail cards. Like the

other data cards, they were worthless to everyone in the room.

But maybe not useless to everyone. From what Han had seen of the Yavin base, the Rebel Alliance had all sorts of strange stuff squirreled away. If they could dig up a cryodex somewhere, maybe they could put the blackmail files to some use.

And if so, maybe he could hit up Dodonna for some more reward. Probably not enough for a lifetime of leisure, like this job was supposed to have provided, but maybe enough to at least give him and Chewbacca a little breathing space.

He did a quick mental calculation. If he kept back enough to pay off his debt to Jabba . . . "Let me sweeten the pot a little," he offered. "I'll buy out your shares of the blackmail files for eighteen five each. That'll bring you all up to an even hundred grand."

Chewbacca rumbled a question.

"Well, yeah, I'm dipping into your share," Han confirmed. "How else did you think I was going to get to eighteen five each?"

"So first Lando wants the cards, and now you want them?" Zerba asked suspiciously. "Is there something you're not telling the rest of us?"

"Not really," Han said. "I just figured you could all use the extra credits. And it's not like Chewie and me are going anywhere."

"You could pay off your debt to Jabba," Bink pointed out.

"We'll have enough left to do that," Han assured her.

"Actually—" Rachele broke off. "Never mind."

"So is it a deal?" Han asked.

The others looked at each other. "Fine with me," Kell said.

"Me too," Dozer seconded.

"Sure, why not?" Zerba growled. "It's not like I can use them in my act or anything."

"Okay," Han said. "Leave your contact info with Rachele and she'll send you your splits after she gets the tabs sliced."

"And we never talk about this again," Rachele added. "To anyone."

"No problem," Kell said. "For starters, who'd believe us?"

"Only the people who'd kill us for having done it," Zerba said, standing up. "Well. So long, everyone. Happy flights."

"It was great not meeting like this," Tavia said wryly.

"For whatever it's worth, Han, it's been fun," Bink said as she also stood up. "Call us next time you've got a job."

Five minutes and a round of farewells later, all of them except Chewbacca, Rachele, and Winter had left. "Did you want something?" Han asked Winter.

"In a minute," Winter said. "First I'd like to hear what Rachele was starting to say earlier."

Chewbacca growled agreement.

"That makes it unanimous, Rachele," Han said. "Go ahead."

Rachele sighed. "It was something I picked up on the back channel earlier," she said. "Before we found out about Eanjer." She took a deep breath. "Jabba's raised your debt marker, Han. Raised it to half a million."

Han stared at her. "Half a *million*?"

"He's blaming you for Black Sun finding out about Morg Nar on Bespin," Rachele said miserably. "I'm so sorry. I figured it wouldn't really matter, since you were about to pull in almost fifteen million, and I didn't want to ruin the moment for you. But then we found out about Eanjer, and . . ." She trailed off.

"It's okay," Han said, feeling the weight of the entire universe crashing down on him. He hadn't expected word about Nar to get back to Jabba so fast. Even if it had, he wouldn't have figured Jabba would be able to pin it on him. He certainly wouldn't have expected Jabba to take the loss of his Bespin operation personally.

So instead of getting Jabba off his back for good, he was in even deeper.

Chewbacca grunted.

"Yeah, maybe," Han agreed doubtfully. "But he sure isn't going to cool down for a while. That Bespin operation wasn't bringing in much, but for some reason he really liked it."

"If you need somewhere to stay, I'm sure I can find you a place," Rachele offered.

"Or," Winter said quietly, "you could go back to your other friends."

Han frowned. "What other friends?"

"The people you work with," Winter said. "The people I assume you're going to give the blackmail files to." She raised her eyebrows slightly. "The people who just might be able to track down another cryodex."

Han shot a look at Chewbacca. How in space had she been able to figure *that* out? "I don't know what you're talking about."

"Yes, you do," Winter said. "You see, I work procurement for them . . . and that escape pod you fired into the factory was part of a lot I smuggled to them seven months ago."

"Of course it was," Han said in disgust. He should never, ever have let Her Worshipfulness talk him into letting her replace the escape pods he'd dumped during that Death Star thing. "Look, I didn't steal them, if that's what you think. She insisted we take them."

It was as if someone had flipped on a searchlight

behind Winter's eyes. *"She?"* she echoed, abruptly sitting straighter in her chair. "Which *she* are we talking about?"

Han stared at her, that bitter-edged confession she'd made suddenly coming back to mind. *I was connected with the royal palace on Alderaan* . . . "The Princess," he said. "Leia."

"You've seen her?" Winter asked, her voice shaking a little. "Since Alderaan, I mean?"

"Sure," he said. "In fact, I was with her at Yavin, where the—" He shot a look at Rachele.

"It's okay," Rachele said. "We know about Yavin and the Death Star."

"She got away from there just fine," Han said. "Far as I know, she's still fine." *And stuck-up and insufferable,* he thought about adding. Still, if Winter knew the Princess, she probably already knew all that.

"Thank you," Winter said quietly. "I've been . . . we hadn't heard the details."

"Well, you'll have to get the rest from someone else," Han said, standing up. "If Jabba's jumped my debt, he's probably jumped the bounty, too. We need to find someplace to lie low for a while."

"Leia will take you in," Winter promised.

"We'll see." Han eyed her. "By the way, that thing about never mentioning this to anyone? That goes double for Her Highness."

Winter smiled. "Absolutely," she promised. "Take care, Han."

"He will," Rachele said with a smile of her own. "He always does."

They were back in the *Falcon* and waiting for their lift slot when Chewbacca finally asked the obvious question.

"I don't know yet," Han said. "We'll go back when it's time, I guess."

Chewbacca considered, then rumbled again.

"Of course she likes me," Han said dryly. "Doesn't everybody?"

"Master?" the protocol droid called hesitantly from the doorway. "It's time."

"Time for what?" Eanjer asked, focusing on the mirror in front of him as he eased the last of the medseal strips off his face.

"His High Exaltedness awaits your presence," the droid said, sounding even more nervous than usual.

Not surprising, really. "Tell His Exaltedness I'll be there when I'm ready."

"Yes, sir." The droid hesitated. "If it's all the same to you, sir, I'd rather wait here until you're ready."

"Fine," Eanjer said. "Suit yourself."

Gently he prodded his cheek where the medseal had covered it. He hadn't realized what three weeks of being wrapped up like that would do to the skin. It was red and puffy, was mottled in places, and itched like deep-core chaos. His right hand and arm looked nearly as bad.

Still, the symptoms were temporary. They would fade away soon.

What wouldn't fade so quickly was the annoyance of a job only half done.

Any group of thieves or mercenaries could have gotten him into Villachor's mansion and over, around, or through all the guards while still leaving enough of Qazadi to be identifiable. The only reason for him to have lured Solo to Wukkar in the first place, and then manipulated him into taking the job, was so that the casually arrogant smuggler would be where Eanjer could nail him when it was all over. Planting that fake message with Rachele so that he could bring Calrissian into the crosshairs was another planned perk that had sputtered away into nothing.

So maybe he should consider the job only a third successful?

Still, what was past was past. All the annoyance and regrets couldn't change that.

And if only a third had been successful, it was nevertheless the biggest and most rewarding third. The bounty for Qazadi's death would more than make the whole operation worthwhile.

There would be other opportunities to catch up with Solo and Calrissian. Patience, as always, was the key.

"Master?"

"I heard you." Standing up, he picked up the battered Mandalorian helmet and set it on his head. "Jabba had just better have my credits ready."

"I am sure he does, Master," the droid assured him hastily.

"Good." Boba Fett gestured. "Lead the way."

Read on for

STAR WARS:
Winner Lose All

by Timothy Zahn

the thrilling prequel to *Star Wars: Scoundrels*!

Every sabacc tournament, Lando Calrissian had learned over the years, had its own special flavor and texture. Games on the upper levels of Imperial Center and other Core worlds were elegant and refined. Games run by other gamblers were more intense, populated by players acutely aware that the winners would go home rich while the losers might not eat for a few days. Games run by Hutts or Hutt clients usually involved blasters at least once before the final hand.

But it wasn't until he walked through the doors of the High Card Casino in Danteel City that Lando had felt an atmosphere he could truly label as electric.

Small wonder. Veilred Jydor, master gambler, financier, and the High Card's owner, was giving away his Tchine.

Lando actually hadn't even heard of the Tchines when the tournament was announced two standard weeks earlier. But it hadn't taken long to get up to speed. The Tchines were a set of sculptures sometimes called the Seven Sisters: slender, thirty-centimeter-tall figurines, delicately humanoid, created from a unique and incredibly tough gray stone by an unknown and certainly ancient artisan. Even more mysterious was the fact that all seven figurines were identical.

Lando hadn't believed that part at first. But as he

sifted through the HoloNet and read the reports, he was forced to the same conclusion that all the rest of the researchers over the years had been forced to. However impossibly it had been done, the sculptures were indeed perfectly and precisely identical.

There were many strange things throughout the galaxy, and Lando had learned to take them in philosophical stride. What raised the Tchines above the level of mere academic interest was the fact that each one was valued at between forty and fifty million credits. And Jydor was offering his as the tournament's prize. Winner take all.

A pair of Rodians shoved their way past Lando, nearly knocking him over. He caught his balance and forced back his reflexive annoyance. He'd never seen those particular Rodians before, but with an incredibly valuable art object up for grabs he expected to see a lot of unfamiliar faces before this was over. Speculation was rampant as to the reason Jydor had suddenly decided to part with one of his collectible treasures, the most popular theory being that he'd made some bad investments and needed to raise a stack of credits fast.

If so, he'd found the perfect way to do it. There were eight seats at the tournament table, with six of them going for ten million credits each. All six had been instantly snatched up, which meant that before the game even started Jydor was up ten to twenty million over where he'd have been if he'd simply sold or auctioned off the statuette. And that didn't take into account the extra visitors the game was drawing to his casino and the attached hotel.

Just to add to the excitement—and to swell the ranks of the crowd—he'd announced that the final two places at the table would be going to the winners of a preliminary wild-card tournament.

Lando meant to win one of those seats.

Ahead, in the direction the crowd flow was taking him, he could see a floating holo marking the sign-up table. Keeping an eye out for familiar faces, especially familiar faces who might be carrying grudges, Lando headed toward it.

"Well, well," Tavia Kitik murmured from across the dining table in the tapcaf overlooking the High Card's grand entryway.

Bink Kitik looked up from the delectable shrimpi cup she was currently eating her way around to find her twin sister gazing out at the crowd of hopefuls headed toward the registration table. "Well, well, what?" she asked.

"Another familiar face," Tavia said with a microscopic nod. "Lando Calrissian."

At the third corner of the table, Zerba Cher'dak stirred. "I've heard that name before," he murmured.

"Probably," Bink agreed. "Possibly from us."

"We've run into Lando on and off over the years," Tavia added. "A pleasant, relatively cultured sort."

"Only because we're cute," Bink said drily. Casually turning her head, she followed Tavia's eye line into the crowd of players, would-be players, and soon-to-be spectators.

It was Lando, all right. He was weaving his way upstream through the crowd, a blue data card in his hand and an intent but satisfied expression on his face. "Looks like he's got a spot on the blue track," she added. "Roving eye or not, the man does aim high."

"So he's here to play," Zerba muttered. "Wonderful."

"Relax," Bink said. "He's on the blue track; you're on the red. Who knows? Maybe you'll both win seats at the big table."

"I don't plan on hanging around long enough to find

out," Zerba countered. "I'm more wondering if he'll spot one of you and give the whole game away."

"Don't worry, Lando's smarter than that," Tavia assured him. "He's seen us work, and he knows better than to address us by name in public."

"At least not until he knows what our current names are," Bink added. "He's heard half a dozen of them over the years."

"Wait a minute," Zerba said. He leaned forward, as if better proximity to the two women would give the antenepalps concealed in his lacquered hair better access to their thoughts or emotions, or whatever it was Balosars were currently claiming their antenepalps could do. "He's seen you work? He knows you're a ghost thief?"

"Yes, and yes," Bink said. "And Tavia's right. He's not going to turn us in."

Zerba gave a little snort. "Anyone can be bought, Bink," he said. "It's just a question of price. Maybe I should switch to the blue track and make sure he gets bounced before he sees you."

"No," Tavia said firmly. "Lando hasn't done anything to deserve that." She looked at Bink. "Besides, he looks hungry. I'm guessing he needs a score."

"When hasn't he?" Bink agreed. "Not likely to happen here, though, not with the big names Jydor's already got at the table. Relax, Zerba. Whatever happens, he's not going to be a problem."

"Whatever you say," Zerba said, still not looking convinced. "Just remember, if you get caught I have no idea where you got that fancy dress and keycard." With that, he returned his attention to his plate.

Bink looked across the table at Tavia. Her sister had also resumed eating her dinner, but there was a stiffness in her shoulders that hadn't been there earlier.

Probably she was just ramping up her concern level as

the timer ticked down toward the job. Tavia hated the whole ghost-thief business and would be worried from the moment Bink headed up to Jydor's hundredth-floor penthouse until the moment she returned with whatever loot she was able to grab from his art display room.

Or maybe she was worried about Lando, and Zerba's all-too-true reminder that anyone could indeed be bought.

The moment had arrived, and Jydor was playing it like a true showman.

Not that it was easy to see from the table against the far wall where Lando had been seated for his first game. The double line of guards crossing the High Card's grand ballroom was little more than a stately procession of big, heavily armed men. Jydor was just another figure in the middle of the bunch, though he was far more elegantly dressed, in a mid-length layered tunic with a blue plume-feather upswept collar that contrasted nicely with his red-frosted white hair. The Tchine statue, which he carried in front of him in a protective transparisteel pyramid as if it were the royal Alderaanian crown or something, was visible only as a small, slender, gray lump.

Still, Lando counted himself lucky that he was in the ballroom at all. A lot of the players who'd made the cut had landed in various outlying rooms, where they would be refereed by the casino's game judges and watched over via unobtrusive cam droids hovering close to the high ceilings.

The procession ended at the round sabacc table that had been set up on the top level of a two-tier platform in the center of the ballroom. As the guards formed themselves into protective circles on the floor and the lower tier, Jydor climbed to the upper tier and carefully set the pyramid and figurine in the center of the table. "Herewith is the prize," he intoned, his voice booming through the ballroom's speakers. "Winner take all."

He stepped back, seated himself in the chair usually reserved for the game judge, and raised a dramatic hand. "Let the games begin."

With a deep breath, Lando turned his attention back to his table. The player who'd been chosen by lot to deal this first hand, a smooth man with a permanent half smile plastered across his face, was already shuffling the cards.

I can do this, Lando thought firmly. Flexing his fingers in anticipation, watching closely to make sure the dealer wasn't playing fast and loose with the cards, he prepared his mind for the game.

"Well?" Bink asked quietly.

"I count twenty guards." Tavia's equally quiet voice came from the comlink clip on Bink's shoulder. "Four appear to be newcomers, probably brought in from one of Jydor's other properties. The others are all from his penthouse rotation."

Which meant the art display room three hundred meters above their heads was effectively deserted. With a forty-million-credit art object on public display, Jydor's security setup had been rearranged exactly as she'd anticipated. "Keep an eye on them," she said. "I'm going in."

The hotel's main turbolifts were arranged in three banks just outside the ballroom. An open car was waiting as she arrived, with half a dozen people filing in. Bink slipped in among them and punched for the ninety-ninth floor, the one directly beneath Jydor's penthouse. It would have been more convenient to ride all the way to the top, but none of the public turbolifts went to that floor, and Jydor hadn't been careless enough to pull the guards off his private turbolifts to add to the ballroom contingent.

Fingering her small, clutch-type handbag, she watched the indicator and waited for the car to clear out.

The last person finally exited on the eightieth floor. As the car doors closed again, Bink slipped a small egg-shaped device from a fold of her dress and cupped it in the palm of her right hand, then turned her handbag on its side and balanced it on her left palm. The turbolift passed the ninety-eighth floor, and as it slowed to a halt, she activated the egg's hidden trigger.

Her thin silk dress vanished instantly, ripped along its tear-away seams, the pieces pulled into the egg by the nearly invisible attaching threads to reveal the demure white-trimmed black uniform that had been hidden beneath it. Opening her handbag, she pulled out the pair of compressed hand towels that had been squeezed inside, quickly fluffed and refolded them, then slipped the handbag and egg into concealment between them.

When the turbolift doors opened, it wasn't an elegantly dressed guest who stepped out into the corridor, merely one of the casino's maids on her way to deliver some towels.

She headed down the corridor, taking on the quiet, unassuming posture and expression she'd noted on all of the casino's service staff. On any other floor this masquerade wouldn't have been necessary—after all, few overnight visitors knew who else was sharing a floor with them, or whose room was whose. And even a rookie ghost thief would know that hotel staff were normally forbidden to use the guest turbolifts.

But there was a subtle trap in play here on the ninety-ninth floor, one that same rookie ghost thief might have walked straight into. Fortunately for Bink, Tavia had done her homework. The rooms up here were a special group, a mixture of VIP guests, the casino's upper managers, and off-duty bodyguards. On this floor, and really on this floor alone, there was a good chance that everyone had at least a passing acquaintance with everyone else. A total stranger, no matter how elegantly dressed, would likely raise enough suspicion for a closer look.

But not even managers noticed the service staff. As long as Bink made it off the turbolift without anyone witnessing that policy violation, she should be fine.

She had a chance to prove that theory twice on the way down the hallway as well-dressed visitors strode past her without even breaking stride. Reaching her target room, she knocked discreetly on the door and then pulled out her keycard and slid it into the slot. The keycard, unlike the uniform, was genuine casino-issue, lifted two hours earlier from a maid who was heading off-duty. The card Zerba had left in its place was an exact copy, though of course without any of the access coding. Since even the best keycards occasionally suffered scratch degradation, the maid would most likely never even realize it had been switched. The first time she tried to use it, which probably wouldn't be until tomorrow, she would almost certainly simply go to the housekeeping supervisor and get it reprogrammed.

The room was deserted, as Bink had known it would be, given that its occupant was one of the men currently guarding Jydor's Tchine. Going to the refresher, she tucked her towel bundle into a corner and added her maid outfit to the stack, leaving herself dressed in her usual working catsuit. Tavia's research had shown a narrow access crawl space between the ninety-ninth and hundredth floors that contained some of the emergency systems, and access panels into such spaces were often hidden in refresher linen closets.

There was no such panel in this one. But three minutes' work with her mono-edge wheel cutter and she'd made one of her own. Pushing the disconnected slab of ceiling ceramic out of the way into the crawl space, she pulled herself up.

If her calculations were correct, she was now directly beneath Jydor's art display room. The next step was to see what kind of internal security the room had. Pulling out her microdrill, she got to work.

The penthouse flooring was considerably tougher than the closet ceiling had been. But the drill was heavy-duty, and within another five minutes she had a pinhole punched through. Swapping out the drill for her optic line viewer, she worked it through the opening and adjusted the eyepiece over her eye.

Now to figure out how hard it would be to get through the display room's heavy, vault-class door. Turning the optic line in that direction, she keyed for light and full magnification.

She'd expected Jydor to be the type to trade extra security for convenience, and she was right. The door was an open-back design, where the mechanism was visible through a protective layer of transparisteel. That sort of setup made it easier for the owner to change the combination; it also made it easier for someone other than the owner to see straight into the coding bars and figure out the sequence. A couple of minutes' study, and she had it.

Of course, getting into the suite and to the door presented its own set of challenges. But it should be easy enough. An exit from the window of the room below her, a quick climb up the wall using her syntherope dispenser and some rock putty anchors, a popped catch on the ventilation aperture at the top of the window—after disabling the alarms, of course—a twitched noose through the aperture to trip the catch on the main window, and she would be in. Nothing to it.

And now came the fun part: figuring out what would be worth stealing.

Turning the optic line again, she began a slow sweep of the room. It was every bit as lovely a sight as she'd hoped it would be. The Tchine might be Jydor's priciest art object, but there were plenty of lesser artifacts in the display room that should keep her and Tavia in food and shelter for a couple of months. There was a Vomfrey sculpture on one of the nearest display pillars that would probably bring a few thousand credits. The antique Bocohn medtext hardbook would be trickier to fence, but would be worth a lot more if she could find someone who would take it. On another pillar on the far side of the Bocohn, hidden from the room's entrance by a half-draped black cloth, was a square transparisteel case.

Bink felt her whole body stiffen. Inside the case was a Tchine figurine.

For a long moment she just gazed at it. Then, reaching to her collar, she keyed her comlink clip. "Tav?"

"Yes?" her sister's voice came instantly.

"Is Jydor's Tchine still in the ballroom?"

There was a short pause. "Yes, of course."

"You can see it?"

"Of course. Is something wrong?"

Bink took a careful breath. Jydor had one Tchine. Just one. Every data list agreed on that. So if Jydor's Tchine was here, what was on the table in the ballroom?

"Bink?"

"I'm coming down," Bink said, pulling the optic line from the pinhole and packing it and the eyepiece away. "Meet me in the lounge. Any idea when Zerba will be free?"

"There's supposed to be a quarter-hour break every three hours," Tavia said. "You're not going in?"

"Not yet," Bink said as she started working her way back down through the opening she'd cut. "We may have just changed targets."

"No," Zerba said firmly. "All Seven Sisters are accounted for."

"You're sure?" Bink asked.

"Three on Imperial Center," Zerba said, lifting fingers. "One on Rendili, one on Corellia, one across town with that Devaronian noble—whatever her name is—"

"Lady Carisica Vanq," Tavia murmured.

"Right—Lady Vanq," Zerba said. "And one with Jydor. That's seven."

"You're sure there couldn't be an eighth?" Bink asked hesitantly, wondering if the question would sound stupid.

From the look on Zerba's face, it apparently did. "The Sisters were discovered three hundred standard years ago," he said. "They've been bought, sold, and traded among the elite for two hundred ninety-nine and a half of those years. Trust me, if someone had found an eighth, we'd have heard about it."

"Ditto if another collector had sold his to Jydor," Tavia added. "Big sales and trades are covered by the upscale news feeds, and I've been watching all of them lately." She looked at Zerba. "Which leaves just one possibility."

"Jydor's built himself a fake," Zerba said heavily. "Question is, which one is which?" Bink gazed off across the lounge, crowded with players rushing to get food and drink during the brief time-out. "He wouldn't bring the fake down here," she said, trying to work it through. "Someone might spot that."

"But then how would he make the switch at the end?"

Zerba objected. "I assume he *is* planning to foist off the fake as the genuine article."

"The tournament's going to last at least a couple more days," Tavia pointed out. "I doubt he'll leave the Tchine here overnight. It could be he's got the real one there right now, and plans to switch it for the fake at the beginning of the final day."

"On the other hand, why not just bring in the fake at the beginning and be done with it?" Zerba countered. "It has to be good enough to pass eventual inspection, after all." He gestured toward the ballroom. "Besides, the people in there are gamblers, not art experts. I doubt any of them has ever gotten closer to a Tchine than a holo on a data list."

Tavia stirred. "Except maybe Lando," she murmured.

"True," Bink said, frowning as she thought back to the incident Tavia was referring to.

How close had Lando been to the Tchine? She couldn't remember.

"Wait a second," Zerba said. "You're talking about the Lando who's in the game? When did he see a Tchine?"

"He was at Qarshan's game a few years back when Nintellor made that famous bet where he put half his collection on the table," Tavia said. "Nintellor's Tchine was part of that bet."

"Nintellor won it back, but the Tchine *was* right there in the open," Bink added. "I wonder if we should bring Lando in and see what he knows."

"Why?" Zerba asked. "I mean, why do we even care?"

"Because it would be embarrassing for me to grab the wrong one," Bink told him.

Zerba's eyes widened. "Whoa—back up, back up. What do you mean, grab the wrong one? We're not going after the Tchine."

"We *weren't* going after the Tchine," Bink corrected.

"But that was before we had an actual possible shot at it."

"You're joking," Zerba breathed, his eyes going even wider. "Please tell me you're joking."

"Look, Jydor is running some sort of scam," Bink said. "If part of that scam requires him to leave his most precious art object unguarded, we owe it to the galaxy to teach him a proper lesson."

Zerba stared at her another moment, then turned to her sister. "Tavia?" he pleaded.

Tavia sighed. "I'm on your side," she said. "But I've seen her in this mood. She's not going to back down."

"Hey, *you're* the one who always says you should set your sights high," Bink reminded her. "That's all I'm doing."

"That isn't what I meant," Tavia said with that patient look Bink had seen on her so many times over the years. "But you know that. How do you suggest we start?"

"Like I said: we bring in Lando."

"You're insane," Zerba insisted. "Both of you. Completely insane."

"Oh, come on, Zerba," Bink said, mock-severely. "Where's your sense of adventure?"

"Cowering behind my sense of self-preservation," Zerba retorted. "Look, Bink, whatever game Jydor's playing, it has to be for huge stakes. Can't we please just grab something he won't care about and get out of here?"

"Let's at least talk to Lando," Bink said. "If we decide the Tchine's too risky, we'll go back to the original plan."

Zerba eyed her. "You promise?"

"I promise."

He sighed. "You're the boss. But I still don't like it."

"Noted," Bink said. "Tav? You want to do the honors?"

There was a warning hoot from the ballroom's speakers. "Sure," Tavia said. "Next break's in three hours?"

"Yes," Zerba said, standing up. "Unless he loses before then."

"Then we'll meet here in three hours," Tavia said. She raised her eyebrows. "*All* of us."

"Sure," Zerba said sourly. "Wouldn't miss it for anything." He headed back toward the ballroom.

"You really think Lando can help us?" Tavia asked.

Bink shrugged. "He couldn't hurt. He's also smart and he knows gamblers better than we do." She cocked an eyebrow. "Besides, you think he's cute."

"*You* think he's cute," Tavia said stiffly. "Not me."

Bink suppressed a smile. "Right."

As far back as he could remember, Lando had always had an eye for the ladies. Even in the midst of a sabacc game, occasionally even when the other players were standing over him with drawn blasters, a passing beauty would still trip a switch in some back corner of his brain.

Fortunately, most of the time those distractions didn't rise to the level of potentially lethal. Nonetheless, the ladies passing through his life always caught his attention.

Which was probably why, even while facing an uphill climb in a tournament with stakes as immensely high as this one, he still managed to spot the twins Bink and Tavia at the far end of the ballroom.

Not that they looked like twins at the moment. Even at this distance he could see that they were using their usual tricks of makeup, hairstyle, and carefully positioned hats to create the illusion that their faces were merely similar instead of identical. There were times when Bink's schemes relied heavily on that accident of nature; even when that wasn't a part of her plan, there was no reason to advertise the fact that they were twins.

Under normal circumstances, Lando would have known not to approach them or even acknowledge that he knew them. But the circumstances here were hardly normal. The women were undoubtedly up to something—he'd never heard of them going anywhere just for their health—and he had no intention of letting them derail the tournament. Not without at least knowing what they were planning. Certainly not while he still had a chance of winning.

Which meant he was going to have to confront them. The question was how to do so without potentially ruining things for himself or them.

The next break had been called, and he was still working on the problem as he headed toward the bar with the rest of the players when one of the twins sidled up beside him and took his arm. "Hello, Lando," she murmured in his ear. "Thirsty?"

"Always," Lando assured her. "You have a table?"

"Right over there," she said. "Bink's already ordered your favorite cognac."

"Great," Lando said. So it was Tavia hanging on to his arm, not Bink. Good thing mental bets didn't count against the tournament's single-elimination. "Lead the way."

They found Bink seated at a small corner table at the rear of the lounge along with a dour-faced human male. Bink did the introductions as Lando and Tavia sat down. "Lando; Zerba." The crisp professionalism in her voice ended Lando's last lingering hope that this was a social gathering. "Zerba; Lando."

"Zerba," Lando said, nodding. The other wasn't actually human, he realized now, but a near-human, probably a Balosar. "What's up?"

"Fasten your restraints," Bink advised. "There's a hell of a ride ahead."

Lando listened with a growing mixture of fascination and disbelief as she described her probe into Jydor's display room and what she'd seen there. "So what do you think?" she asked when she'd finished.

"I think Jydor's angling for an early grave," Lando said, looking around the lounge. "There are some big players here, and their patrons aren't going to be happy if he tries to pass off a fake."

"I didn't know gamblers had patrons," Bink said.

"They do on this one," Lando told her. "None of them could have managed a ten-million-credit buy-in on their own. I'm guessing the six players already in the game have been hired and funded by individual collectors to play on their behalf."

"Makes sense," Zerba commented. "It gives the collectors a better chance of winning than if they played themselves. It also masks their identities, which can be handy."

"Like sending a ringer to an auction," Bink agreed. "So what's Jydor's game?"

"No idea," Lando said. "Unless one of the players is secretly working for Jydor. If he can win the Tchine back . . . but then why bother with a fake in the first place?"

"Well, whatever the plan, the first thing we have to do is figure out which figurine is which," Bink said. "Any chance we could get a little closer to the one down here? Preferably with a small scanner in hand?"

Zerba gave a snort. "Sure," he said. "All we need to do is win one of the wild-card seats. Then we'll be right up there with it."

"Or win both seats," Bink suggested. "You two are on different tracks, you know."

Lando eyed Zerba. "What's your ranking?" he asked.

"Don't have one," Zerba said. "Don't need one, either." He smiled tightly. "I cheat."

Lando swallowed. A lot of sabacc players cheated. Few of them admitted it. "Really."

"Really," Zerba confirmed.

"He's quite good at it, too," Bink added. "Sleight of hand, reshuffles, skifters—you name it, he can do it."

"I've got a couple of spare skifters, if you want one," Zerba offered.

"No, thanks," Lando said. The last thing he wanted was to get caught with an adjustable card in his possession. "I trust you know what happens if you get caught."

"I do," Zerba assured him. "And I won't."

"Right." Lando picked up his glass and drained the last of his cognac. "In that case, I guess things are on hold until we see if we can win one of the wild-card spots. Or both of them," he added, inclining his head to Bink.

"May I make a suggestion?" Tavia spoke up.

Lando looked at her, feeling a mild flicker of surprise. She'd been so quiet since they sat down that he'd almost forgotten she was there. "Sure."

"You've seen a real Tchine close up," she reminded Lando. "But none of the rest of us has. More important, we really don't know how one shows up on a scan."

"Isn't that data on file?" Lando asked.

"Some of it is," Tavia said. "But not all of it. Probably deliberately."

"So that no one knows all of the readings that would have to be faked to make a copy," Lando said, nodding. "Makes sense."

"So we don't have complete sensor data," Zerba said. "So what?"

"So there's another Tchine right across town," Tavia said. "Lady Carisica Vanq's. If we could persuade her to let us take some readings, we'd have a head start on identifying the fake."

"I'm guessing that'll take a lot of persuasion," Lando murmured.

"Maybe not," Bink said thoughtfully. "Depends on how much security she has." Tavia gave her sister a look of strained patience. "Bink—"

She broke off as the warning hoot sounded. "You two sort it out," Lando said, standing up. "Zerba and I need to get back to the tables."

"How soon before you find out if you've made it to the main game?" Bink asked.

"I don't know," Lando said, running a quick calculation. "Not before tonight, though."

"Probably not until sometime tomorrow," Zerba said. "Depending on how late in the day the session runs, Jydor may postpone the beginning of the big game until the day after that."

"So you've got until then to break into Lady Vanq's house," Lando concluded. "Have fun."

He headed back toward the ballroom, wondering if there was any reason for him not to simply turn around and walk out of the casino. If he was going through all this for a fake . . .

He smiled tightly. No, of course he was going to keep going. There were a lot of big players here, and if he could help expose a scam before one of them was taken in, he would have bought himself a fistful of goodwill and possible future favors. In his line of business, both could mean the difference between success and failure.

Sometimes even between life and death.

"Thank you," Tavia said quietly as she and Bink reached the end of the long hedge-lined walkway of Lady Carisica Vanq's estate and came within sight of the main house. "I appreciate you trying it this way first."

"You're welcome," Bink said.

Tavia winced. Bink was trying hard to make it sound like she meant it, but Tavia knew her sister's moods and body language, and she could tell that Bink thought this was a waste of time. Worse, she probably thought that asking politely and straightforwardly for a scan would alert Lady Vanq to the more clandestine approach Bink obviously expected they would eventually have to use.

On one level, Tavia had to agree. Still, it seemed only right to try the polite approach first.

They reached the door, and Tavia rang the chime.

There was a moment's pause, and then the door swung ponderously open to reveal an LOM protocol droid. "Yes?" it asked stiffly.

"Lady Pounceable and Lady Michelle to see Lady Vanq," Bink said in that condescending, high-snoot-value voice she'd spent years perfecting.

"Lady Vanq is not at home," the droid said.

"Do you expect her back soon?" Bink asked.

"I cannot say," the droid said. "She has gone on a long journey."

Out of the corner of her eye, Tavia saw Bink cock her head slightly. Probably wondering whether they should give the LOM a high-power jolt into its motivator from her concealed sparker and simply walk in right now.

Fortunately, Bink was smarter than that. "Very well," she said. "We'll call another time."

"Yes," the droid said. Taking a step back, it closed the door.

"Now what?" Tavia asked. Her sister, she noted, was giving the house and windows a casually penetrating visual examination. "Plan B?"

"Actually, it was always Plan A," Bink said. She finished her survey and turned away from the house. "Let's get back to the casino."

"We're not hitting it tonight, are we?"

"No," Bink assured her. "First I need to dig up everything we can on the old—what is she?"

Tavia suppressed a sigh. For Bink, objects and targets were everything. People were just what you had to deal with along the way. "Devaronian."

"Right—the old Devaronian," Bink said. "We'll want her house schematics, her alarm setup, and any servant or droid information we can get. We'll work out a plan tonight and go in tomorrow."

Tavia thought back on the timing Lando and Zerba had laid out. "I hope that won't be too late," she warned. "If the wild-card rounds finish tonight, the main game will begin tomorrow."

"Not a chance," Bink said flatly. "With every game the field's average talent goes up a notch, which means the last few games will be long and brutal. No, the final table isn't going to start until the day after tomorrow at the earliest."

"I suppose," Tavia murmured. "I wonder if Zerba or Lando will make it through."

"That's their problem." Bink nodded back over her shoulder at the house. "This is ours. Come on—we've got work to do."

Lando had known going in that his chances of making it all the way to the big table were extremely slim. There were a lot of players who'd swarmed in for the tournament, and many of them were as good as or better than he was.

But for once, Lady Luck seemed to be solidly at his side. Often the better players drew positions where they were competing at other tables and more often than not ended up taking one another out. On the occasions when he faced someone whose skills were superior to his own, the cards invariably ran in Lando's favor.

In a normal tournament, that kind of luck wouldn't gain him more than a temporary reprieve. In the long run, the whims of fortune would even out, and the better player would eventually emerge triumphant. But Jydor had set up the wild-card games to be single-elimination, which meant Lando only had to hold off his equals and betters for a single game each.

As the afternoon turned to evening and then to night, he slowly but steadily made his way from the edge of the ballroom inward toward the elevated table. By the time the games were called for the night, he was more than halfway toward his goal. Exhausted but with a deep satisfaction he hadn't felt in a long time, he watched as the bodyguards formed their protective curtain around Jydor and the Tchine and they all marched from the ballroom and disappeared into the private turbolifts.

He hadn't seen Bink or Tavia since that one meeting, but he caught a glimpse of Zerba as the players filed out and began dispersing to their own rooms. Apparently, the Balosar had also survived the night's combat.

It was a good sign, he decided as he settled tiredly into bed in his own modest room. He could only hope Bink and Tavia were making similar progress.

The games downstairs were still going strong when Bink finally conceded defeat to her drooping eyelids and said her good nights. Tavia muttered a distracted good night in return, the bulk of her attention clearly still on the array of four datapads laid out in front of her.

Bink ran quickly through her pre-bedtime routine, wondering yet again at the complicated dance that must go on inside her sister's head. For someone who hated the whole idea of stealing from people, Tavia nevertheless threw her whole heart, mind, and strength into the prep work that went into each job. Obviously, she was trying to make sure Bink made it through without getting caught; but the whole thing was still an interesting and no doubt tension-filled compromise between ethics and sisterly love.

Or maybe it was the challenge of the hunt that intrigued Tavia, the art and science of digging through floor plans and alarm zones as she searched for weaknesses and opportunities.

In some ways, Bink knew, the two of them really weren't all that different.

By the time Bink awoke the next morning, the entry plan was finished and laid out on her datapad. Moving quietly so as not to wake her sleeping sister, she got herself a cup of caf and settled down to study the plan.

She was halfway through her second cup by the time she finished her examination. It would work, she decided as she gazed thoughtfully out the window at the city stretching toward the horizon. A nighttime sortie; and by the time the games once again broke for the night, she and Tavia should have a complete sensor scan of Carisica Vanq's Tchine. All they would need then would be close access to the figurine Jydor had on display in the ballroom.

Hopefully, Lando and Zerba would make that happen.

"I just heard from Zerba." Tavia's voice came softly over Bink's comlink clip. "He and Lando are both still in the game."

"Glad to hear it," Bink murmured back, studying the bedroom window as she hung in midair half a meter from the glass. The defenses at the edge of Lady Vanq's grounds had been easy enough to penetrate, and she'd avoided the lower wall sensors by the simple expedient of using her syntherope dispenser to travel from hedge top to roof and then come down to her target window from the eaves. Now, as she swung gently back and forth in the warm night air, the last barrier lay before her.

As barriers went, it wasn't much. Satisfying herself that she'd spotted all the alarms and sensors, she pulled out her mono-edge wheel cutter and got to work. Five minutes later, with the glass cut, the alarm disabled, and the window open, she eased herself carefully inside.

Most collectors Bink had gone after over the years had situated their vaults or display rooms near their offices or, if they enjoyed showing off their collections, near the conversation room or some other public area. Lady Carisica Vanq's vault, in contrast, was right off her bedroom.

That wasn't entirely unheard of—Bink had known of other, mostly elderly, art hoarders who liked to look over their lifetimes' accomplishments every night before retiring. But it wasn't very common. It was rare enough, in fact, that Tavia had speculated that the vault had actually started life as a safe room and only been retasked after Lady Vanq decided that life in Danteel City was safe enough not to require a place of instant refuge.

Breaking into someone's bedroom always made Bink a little nervous. The house droid had said Lady Vanq was out, but for all their electronic memories, droids occasionally got things wrong.

The room was dark, the only illumination coming from the muted city light leaking in through the drapes across the row of windows. Bink moved carefully across the floor, noting the shadowy shapes of chairs and lounge tables and wondering idly what sort of furnishings a wealthy Devaronian noble would indulge in. The bed was a little too big for her taste, with tall posts at each corner rising nearly to the ceiling and lifting the main part of the bed about half a meter off the floor. Probably an airflow thing, she decided, for nights when the temperature outside was uncomfortably high—

She froze, her breath catching in her throat.

The house droid had indeed gotten it wrong. Lady Vanq wasn't gone. She was right there, lying beneath the blankets in the middle of the bed.

Bink stood motionless, her heart thudding, silently cursing her carelessness as she tried to figure out what to do. If the Devaronian was asleep, there might still be a chance to backtrack and escape.

And then, as Bink's mind began to catch up with her, a fresh shiver ran up her back. Something was very wrong here. The figure in the bed was way too still.

She took a careful breath. "Tav?" she murmured. "What is it?"

"Hang on." Steeling herself, she headed toward the bed. The figure still didn't move, and as Bink drew closer she realized with a sinking feeling that she couldn't see any rise and fall of blankets across the figure's chest.

Lady Carisica Vanq was dead.

Bink took another careful breath. This time she caught a hint of a spicy-sweet aroma. "Tavia?"

"Bink, what's wrong?" Tavia's anxious voice came back. "If you need to get out—"

"There's no hurry," Bink said, the words aching through a suddenly burning throat.

"She's dead."

"Who's dead?"

"The lady of the house." A ripple of half-hysterical laughter bubbled through the acid taste in Bink's mouth. Sternly, she choked it back down. "The droid said she was on a long journey. I guess he was right, after all."

"I don't understand," Tavia said, her voice starting to

shake. "You mean she died of—I don't even know what kind of diseases Devaronians can die quickly of."

"In this case, the same thing a lot of other people in the Empire die from these days," Bink said, gingerly lifting the edge of the blanket from the body. One look was all she needed. "She was shot."

"She—*what*?"

"Single blaster bolt to the upper torso," Bink said. "Close range."

There was a muffled gasp from the comlink clip. "Bink, get out of there. Get out of there *now.*"

"There's no hurry," Bink said, gently laying the blanket back and looking around. "From the smell of biosuppressant around the body, I'm guessing she's been dead for a while. Several days at least."

"Or maybe two weeks?"

An eerie feeling seemed to flow across the room with the wind drifting through the open window. Was Tavia suggesting what Bink thought she was suggesting? "Stay with me," she said, heading toward the massive door at the far side. "I'm going to check out the safe."

Tavia hissed out a breath. "Be careful."

Safes of this class usually took ten to fifteen minutes to crack. This one took less than two. Clearly, someone had already made it through the barriers. "I'm in," she murmured as she pulled the door open and stepped inside.

"And?"

Bink played her glow rod around the room. The late Lady Vanq's collection was even more eclectic than Jydor's, with art objects ranging from fist-sized flutterines to Wookiee-sized flat sculpts, their vintages stretching from the days of the ancient Rakatan Empire all the way up to modern oddments with no intrinsic value that Bink could see. Off to one side was an empty display pedestal.

The Devaronian's Tchine was gone.

"You're right," Bink said. "Jydor's second Tchine must be Lady Vanq's—" Behind her, the bedroom door opened.

Bink froze, her head half turned toward the doorway. It was a cleaning droid, running a vacuum attachment across the threshold to the hallway and a meter or so inside the room. It finished its job, and its head rose and swiveled slowly around. Bink tensed . . .

The mechanical eyes passed the open safe door without any reaction that Bink could detect. Its gaze likewise swept without pause across the dead body in the bed. Backing out of the room, it closed the door behind it.

Bink took a careful breath. "Still there?" she murmured.

"Of course," Tavia said. "What's happening?"

"Oh, it's pretty much bad news all around," Bink said. She stepped out of the safe and closed the door behind her. "Any idea when the players' next break is?"

"Actually, they're finished," Tavia said. "I don't suppose it matters now, but Lando and Zerba both won their tracks."

"No, it probably doesn't," Bink agreed, sitting down on the windowsill and reattaching her harness to the syntherope. "Go find them and get them to our room. We all need to have a serious conversation."

Zerba's eyes widened, the top part of his lacquered hair undulating like a small animal as the hidden antenepalps beneath it twitched. "She's *dead*?"

"Take it easy," Lando said, keeping his voice and face under rigid control. So neither of Jydor's Tchines was fake . . . and one of them was in his possession because of theft and murder. The fake–Tchine thing had been bad enough, throwing an unpleasant pall over the whole tournament. With this new revelation, the situation had risen to an entirely new level of nastiness. "This is no time to panic."

"Do be good enough to let me know when that moment comes," Zerba retorted acidly. "Are you *insane*?"

"Lando's right," Bink said firmly. "Yes, it's bad. But it could be a whole lot worse."

"Bink, you were *seen* in there," Zerba bit out. "Seen *and* recorded in a droid memory. The fact that you saw the body and didn't immediately report it automatically makes you an accessory after the fact." He snorted. "In fact, given that we all now know about it, we're *all* accessories after the fact."

"Two points," Bink said. "First of all, Danteel law on these things allows for reporting delays based on certain mitigating factors."

"Such as?"

"Such as it's acceptable to hold off if you think that reporting it will put your life in danger."

Lando grimaced. "With Jydor involved, that's a pretty safe bet."

"And second," Bink continued, "I'm pretty sure I *wasn't* seen. Not really."

"You said the droid looked right at you," Zerba reminded her.

"It looked, but it didn't see," Bink said. "The fact that none of the droids has apparently even noticed their mistress is dead implies that someone's fiddled with the house's overall programming matrix. They're not being allowed to see anyone inside the house, alive or dead."

Zerba snorted. "Call me stupid," he said. "But this makes no sense at all."

"It does if you're a thief and murderer," Lando pointed out.

"I meant it makes no sense from Jydor's point of

view," Zerba said. "Why in the galaxy would you kill someone for something as easily traced as a Tchine?"

"Why not?" Lando countered. "There are plenty of collectors who keep their prizes hidden away for their own private viewing. A lot of them probably wouldn't much care if an item or two in their vault happened to have been stolen from someone else."

"Or it might have been the other classic motive for murder," Bink said. "Tavia's been digging into Jydor's money deals, and it looks like Lady Vanq suckered him out of a big contract and a *lot* of money a few months ago."

"How much money?" Lando asked.

"It's rumored to be in the neighborhood of fifty to sixty million credits," Tavia said. "Which is the same amount he's just made back by selling those first six tournament seats," Bink added. "Takes a creative man to combine revenge *and* profit into the same murder."

"But it's *stolen,*" Zerba persisted. "Sooner or later, someone's going to notice that Lady Vanq is dead and that her Tchine is missing. The minute they find that Jydor still has one, it'll be obvious what happened."

"Except that there's a cute little glitch in Danteel law," Bink said. "Possession of stolen property is a major crime on Danteel. But the Tchines are identical. Once Jydor's gotten rid of one of them, unless the police can figure out which is which, they can't touch him for that."

"But they'll know he *had* both of them at one point."

"But they won't have any proof that he was the one who stole it," Bink said. "Without that, and without proof that the one in his display room is the hot one, they'll have no grounds to dig any deeper." She shrugged. "Like I said, it's a glitch."

Zerba shook his head. "Ridiculous. Who else could have stolen it?"

Bink's lip twitched. "Yes, well, that's the other problem," she said reluctantly. "Aside from bringing in enough credits to make up his loss, this tournament has the side benefit of attracting a whole bunch of thieves to Danteel City. Which means that when the balloon goes up, there will be a lot of people Jydor can point fingers at."

Lando winced. "People like you," he said. "And since you've actually been in Lady Vanq's home . . ."

". . . the finger-pointing will likely start with me," Bink agreed heavily. "Especially since, depending on what the thief did to the matrix programming, I may also have been recorded as having come to the front door yesterday afternoon."

Zerba muttered something under his breath. "That's it, then," he said. "Nice seeing you again—nice meeting you, Lando—and I hope we run into each other under happier circumstances." He started to get up.

"Wait a second," Lando said, grabbing for the Balosar's shoulder and missing. "Didn't you hear her? She's on the hook for this."

"Which is why we need to scatter to the wind," Zerba countered. "What else are we going to do?"

Lando looked at Bink. She was tempted, he could see. Tempted to run, to change her name from whatever she was using today to whatever she'd been planning to use tomorrow, and hope she could hide herself in the shadows of the fringe until Lady Vanq's murder was forgotten. And really, given the state of justice in Palpatine's Empire, it probably would be the smartest move.

And then he looked at Tavia. At her composed but smoldering expression.

Tavia had no intention of letting Jydor get away with this. Unlike most fringers—unlike even Lando himself, on certain days—she hadn't totally given up on right and wrong.

Especially not when her sister was poised to take the fall for murder.

Lando squared his shoulders. A pity, really, that this wasn't one of those certain days. "Fine," he said to Zerba. "Go." Turning to Tavia, he raised his eyebrows. "So how do we nail him?"

Zerba, already two steps toward the door, came to a confused-looking halt. "What are you talking about?"

"I'm talking about nailing Jydor," Lando said. "Tavia?"

"The reprogramming of Lady Vanq's house is the key," Tavia said, her eyes narrowed in thought. "If I can figure out what he did, I might be able to backtrack to the programmer. Then we'd have some proof."

"At which point, we can sic the police on him," Bink said, eyeing her sister. She was still not sure running wouldn't be the best option, Lando decided. "If he's smart, he'll make a deal that fingers his boss."

"It's a start," Lando said. "What do you need?"

"Right now, I mostly need time," Tavia said. "If Bink's right about the droids, we should be able to get back into the house without trouble. But it'll take time for me to slice into the system."

"Too bad Rachele Ree isn't here," Bink murmured. "She could slice it in nothing flat."

"Well, she's not," Tavia said, a little crossly. "We'll just need to figure out a way to stall the tournament."

"We could call in a bomb threat," Bink suggested. "Plenty of people don't like Jydor. Or we could finger the Rebellion—that would stir up every Imperial in the hemisphere."

"Don't be ridiculous," Zerba growled, coming back to his chair and sitting down. "The way to stall a game is to make sure no one wins for a while."

Lando eyed him. "You mean throw our hands?"

"Or cheat a little on behalf of whoever's losing." Zerba

gave a theatrical sigh. "And since I doubt you can cheat worth anything—no offense—I guess that'll be my job."

Bink reached over and laid a hand on the Balosar's forearm. "Thanks, Zerba," she said quietly.

"Yeah, yeah, you're welcome," Zerba said sourly. "The main game starts at five tomorrow evening. I don't suppose there's any chance you'll be in by then?"

Tavia shook her head. "I first need to find a datapad with the right programming hardwired into it."

"I know a couple of places to look," Bink said. "But it'll probably take most of tomorrow, and I don't want to risk going back to the house until it's dark. That'll be about an hour after you start."

"Can you stall the game that long?" Tavia asked.

"No problem," Zerba assured her.

"In fact, given the caliber of the players we've got, it'll probably drag out at least six hours without any finagling at all on our part," Lando added. "Sounds like we've got a plan."

"Right," Zerba muttered. "Lucky, lucky us."

The players assembled at the table precisely at five, after Jydor had once again made his grand entrance and placed the Tchine in the center of the table. After looking at it for two days from across the ballroom, Lando decided the thing didn't look all that impressive close up.

Maybe it was because he couldn't look at it anymore without seeing a sheen of blood on it. Or maybe it was because the double ring of Jydor's guards now encircled him as well as the figurine.

Still, at least all the guards were facing away from him. That was worth something.

Jydor gave the standard best-of-luck speech that tournament hosts always made, resumed his seat in the game judge chair, and the game began.

As Lando had already noted, the assembled players were some of the best in the galaxy. Most of the main six were far better than he was, and they certainly knew it. More than once he caught a side look from one of them directed at him or Zerba that clearly carried the unspoken question of what such rank amateurs were doing in their company. It was just as well, he thought, that he was no longer trying to win.

But all the rest of them were, and the play was every bit as cutthroat as he'd expected. It was going back and forth so much, in fact, that they were two hours into the game before he noticed something odd.

One of the players, a craggy-faced Rodian named Mensant, had settled into a pattern of winning every few hands. Every eight hands, in fact, plus a handful of others.

The logical suspicion was that the guy was cheating. The problem was that he wasn't winning the hands he himself was dealing. Instead, it was the hands being dealt by a blank-eyed man named Phramp.

Lando gave it another dozen rounds, just to be sure. Then, during one of the deals, he casually looked over at Zerba and gave a microscopic nod toward Phramp.

Zerba's lip twitched, and he gave an equally small nod in response. So he'd caught it, too. An hour later, Jydor called for a break. Heading toward the bar, carefully avoiding getting anywhere near Zerba, Lando pulled out his comlink and keyed for Bink. "We need a conference," he said when she answered. "Can you add in Zerba?"

"Sure." There was a short pause.

"Yes?" came Zerba's voice.

"What do you think?" Lando asked.

"I was wondering why Jydor had set it up so that the players took turns dealing instead of having one of his own people do it," Zerba said. "Looks to me like he's got Phramp trying to throw the game to Mensant."

"He's throwing the *game*?" Bink echoed. "What in chaos for?"

"I don't know," Lando said. "Before you told us about Lady Vanq I would have said Mensant and Phramp were working for Jydor and that he was trying to scam the Tchine back into his collection."

"But now it looks more like he's trying to unload the stolen one onto someone in particular," Zerba said.

"Let's see if we can find out who Mensant is fronting for," Bink said. "I'll see if Tavia can track that down after she finishes the coding search."

"Good," Lando said. "How's that going?"

"Slow," Bink said. "But she's making progress." There was an indistinct voice in the background. "She says it's creepy in here."

"You're in the *bedroom*?" Zerba asked.

"It's the only place we're absolutely sure the droids can't see anyone," Bink pointed out. "Talk to you later."

She clicked off. Grimacing to himself, Lando put away his comlink—

"Excuse me," a voice behind him said.

Before Lando could even start to turn, a large man appeared beside him. "Master Chumu's compliments," the man continued. "He'd like a word with you."

"And Master Chumu is . . ." Lando prompted, edging away.

"Master Jydor's business manager," the man said, staying right with him.

"Maybe later," Lando said. "I've got a game to get back to."

"I'm afraid I have to insist," the man said. "Don't worry about the game—it won't resume for at least twenty minutes."

"How do you know?"

"Because Master Jydor's gone to the private dining room for a snack," the man said. "He always has crab rotoven, and it always takes him twenty to thirty minutes to eat it."

Lando frowned. "And how do you know *that*?"

"Because I'm one of his household guards," the man said tightly. "Call me Rovi." He gestured in the direction of the private turbolifts. "And I really *must* insist."

"Did you see where he took him?" Bink asked, gripping her comlink tightly.

"Straight to one of Jydor's private turbolifts," Zerba said, his voice strained. "And the guards there obviously knew the guy."

"They probably play cards together after hours," Bink said, staring at the body lying on the bed. She'd known this charade couldn't last. But she hadn't expected it to fall apart this fast. "But you're still free?"

"Free and clear, as far as I can tell."

"Then it must have been something he said that was overheard," she concluded, trying to remember Lando's exact words. He'd said Lady Vanq's name, she remembered. That might have been all it took, especially if that particular guard knew the old Devaronian had been murdered.

Even if they didn't know the details, Jydor certainly did. Lando was in it, all right, all the way up to his neck.

Unless Bink could manufacture another interpretation for his comment . . .

"Okay," she said, crossing over to Lady Vanq's safe. "I'll handle this. Stay put and pretend you don't know anything. That means rejoining the game if and when it starts up again."

"I know what it means," Zerba growled. "I hope you know what you're doing." "Me, too," Bink said. "Let me know if anything interesting happens."

"What are we going to do?" Tavia asked tightly.

"*You're* going to keep on the programming patch," Bink said, setting to work opening the safe. "Where are you right now?"

"I've got the patch itself figured out," Tavia said. "But I haven't been able to backtrack it yet. There's something funny in one section of the coding, too."

"What kind of funny?"

"The confusing kind," Tavia said. "It reads like encrypted text. I'm trying to clear it so I can see if it's something we should be worried about."

"But you *could* cut out the patch and let the droids see what's happened in here?"

"Anytime you want," Tavia confirmed. "I'd like to decrypt that text first, though."

"Go ahead and give it a shot," Bink said. "But if we run out of time, we'll just have to pop the patch and hope the text isn't a problem."

The safe lock snicked open. Pulling on the door with one hand, she keyed Lando's comlink with the other. "Here goes nothing."

Darim Chumu was a middle-aged human with the look and feel of a born huckster. From his casual body language as he sat comfortably in one of the chairs in the penthouse entryway lounge, to the deep smile lines in his face, it was clear that he was a man who'd closed countless deals over the years.

But that face wasn't smiling now. And the languid posture carried the same underlying tension of a gambler trying to read an opponent's hand. "I apologize for the abruptness of my invitation," he said after the somewhat strained introductions had been made and Lando had been seated across from him. "But you mentioned Lady Vanq, and that name is not to be spoken casually in the High Card Casino."

"I'll make a note," Lando said, striving to match his host's tone. "Was there anything else?"

Chumu's eyes narrowed microscopically. "I don't think you fully understand, Master Calrissian," he said. "Lady Vanq cheated Master Jydor out of a great deal of money a few months ago. Friends of hers aren't welcome here."

"I'm hardly a friend," Lando protested mildly. So Chumu was probing to see just how close Lando and the murdered Devaronian had been. "More a business acquaintance."

"I didn't know she did business with gamblers," Chumu said. "Do you own a casino or gambling pit?"

"Actually, it was regarding one of my other professions," Lando said. "It's rather confidential, I'm afraid."

Chumu's eyes narrowed a little more. "I'm afraid I must insist on an answer."

"I don't know if I can—" Lando broke off as his comlink twittered.

"Go ahead and answer that," Chumu said.

"They'll call back," Lando said, leaving the comlink where it was. Odds were that it was Zerba calling to chat, and cheating, scams, and murder were the absolute last topics of conversation he wanted brought up right now.

"Answer it," Chumu said, his tone making it clear it was an order. "Or Rovi will." With a grimace, Lando pulled out the comlink. As he did so, Rovi reached over his shoulder and closed a massive hand around Lando's. "On wide-focus, if you please," Chumu added.

There was nothing for it but to comply. Mentally crossing his fingers, Lando clicked it on. "Lando."

"It's Michelle," Bink's voice came. "Listen, do you know where Lady Vanq is? I've tried all the comlink numbers I have, but I can't get ahold of her."

"I don't have any numbers you don't," Lando said, trying to hide his relief. Bink calling—and using a pseudonym—meant that she was on to the problem. Probably Zerba had spotted the grab and alerted her.

Of course, he had no idea where she was going with this. But whatever it was, it would probably beat anything he could come up with on the fly. "Is it important?"

"Of course it's important," Bink said stiffly. "She still owes me the last payment on that Tchine copy."

And with that, Lando was suddenly up to speed. "She hasn't paid yet?" he asked, feigning surprise.

"*And* she's late on the initial for the Caffreni flutterine," Bink said. "You told me she could be trusted to pay on time."

"That's her reputation," Lando agreed. "I'll see if I can get hold of her."

"You do that," Bink said. "When you do, tell her the Jam'arn circlet's also done. That one I'm not so worried about—it was a lot easier than the others. Don't tell *her* that, of course."

"I won't," Lando promised. "I'll get back to you."

He clicked off. "I suppose there's no point in being coy now," he said to Chumu. "I also act as intermediary on small art jobs."

"You mean *forgeries*?" Chumu growled.

"They're not forgeries," Lando countered. "Forgery implies intent to deceive, and there's no such intent here. Collectors are well within their rights to have decoys fabricated to throw off potential thieves."

"Perhaps," Chumu said. His expression was still under control, Lando noted, but his face seemed a couple of shades whiter than it had been.

Small wonder. He clearly was in this with Jydor, and was now facing the horrible possibility that they might have committed murder for nothing more valuable than a high-quality forgery.

"Trust me," Lando said. "I always check out the legal issues before I accept a job of this sort."

"I'll take your word for it," Chumu said. "Interesting you should happen to pop up here. Master Jydor was just wondering a few days ago whether we should do something similar for a few of the pieces in his own collection. But he was never convinced that anyone could make copies good enough to fool a knowledgeable thief."

"Michelle can," Lando said. "I've brokered quite a few of these deals, and I've never seen anyone better than she is."

"I'd like to meet her," Chumu said. "Do you think she'd be willing to drop by?"

"I'm sure I could set something up," Lando said. "Right now, though, I have a game I need to get back to."

"Of course," Chumu said. "Just call and set up a meeting, will you? Then Rovi will take you back down."

Lando sighed. "Fine," he said, pulling out his comlink again.

"And ask her to bring samples of her work," Chumu added. "I'd like to see them."

Bink finished her conversation and clicked off. "I'm in," she announced. "Any progress on that text?"

"Not yet," Tavia said, frowning at her datapad. "How much time do I have?"

"I can stall him for at least a day," Bink said. "That should give you plenty of time." Her eyes flicked to the body in the bed. "That is, if you don't mind staying here overnight."

"I'm not staying any longer than you do," Tavia declared with a shiver. "I've got a recording. I can work on it from our room."

"Good enough," Bink said. She wrapped the Caffreni and Jam'arn carefully and slipped them into her hip pouch. Just borrowing them, she thought with a twinge of guilt toward the dead Devaronian. "Grab your gear, and let's go."

Chumu was impressed by Bink. He was even more impressed by the Caffreni and Jam'arn she'd brought. "These are really forgeries?" he asked, peering closely at each of them in turn.

"They're copies," Bink corrected. "Forgery implies intent to deceive. A copy is intended only for whatever legal purpose the owner wishes to put it to."

"You sound like your friend Calrissian."

"He's a colleague, not a friend," Bink again corrected.

"My mistake."

Casually, Bink looked around. Chumu had brought her deeper into the penthouse than Lando had been, right into the main conversation room. Presumably because there was more privacy here, along with more comfortable chairs.

The view was certainly better. Directly behind Chumu was the massive but artistically decorated door to Jydor's art display room. "Let's cut to the core," she said. "What do you want copied?"

"Not so fast," Chumu admonished. "I'm still not convinced your copies can stand up to a sensor scan. How close a match is one of these to the real thing?"

Bink suppressed a smile. "It'll pass any test a normal thief could run on it," she said. "You'd need a special sensor array to tell the difference."

"How special?"

"Special enough that I doubt there's anyone in the sector except me who knows how to put one together."

"Interesting," Chumu murmured. "I'd like to see one." Bink cocked her head. "Why?"

Chumu's lip twisted. "There were some rumors going around at the time Master Jydor bought his Tchine figurine," he said with just the right mix of reluctance and embarrassment. "Hints that the statue might be a forgery. Naturally, we had it checked out, and it came through clean." He set the other two art objects onto the conversation room's low center table. "But at the time we had no idea that a special sensor was needed."

"Hold on," Bink said, frowning. "You're saying the big prize on display downstairs might be a *fake*?"

"I think the likelihood of that is extremely small," Chumu assured her hastily. "But if there's even a chance that it is, we need to know about it before the tournament ends."

"Oh, absolutely," Bink agreed, peering thoughtfully off into space. "I can certainly put a sensor together and take a look. Unfortunately, I can't do so until tomorrow."

"Not tonight?"

"There are some special components I need to get." Bink smiled faintly. "Components I can't simply carry around with me, for various legal reasons. You may also need time to collect the necessary money."

"What money?"

"*My* money," Bink said. "The fee for the test will be ten thousand."

Chumu didn't even bat an eye. "That will be satisfactory," he said. Standing up, he pulled out a data card. "Here's my contact information," he said, handing it to her. "Call me when you're ready."

"I will." Tucking the data card away, Bink returned the two art objects to her bag. "I'll see you tomorrow. Have my fee ready."

As best as Lando could tell, Phramp was the only player at the table doing any serious cheating, and he was still cheating toward Mensant.

Or at least he was the only one until Zerba got going.

Lando had seen plenty of cheating over his years at the gaming tables. He'd seen it done well and badly, adroitly and so incompetently that he wondered how the perpetrator avoided getting blasted on the spot.

Zerba was an artist.

His eyes never betrayed his moves. His hands never fumbled or twitched. His tells, which Lando suspected had been carefully designed to give the other players the illusion that they knew everything they needed to about him, never wavered.

And slowly, Mensant's steady climb toward victory began to falter.

Zerba didn't throw the hands to himself or Lando, of course. That would have been too obvious, not to mention dangerous. Instead, he threw his deals to the other players around the table, never falling into a pattern, chipping away methodically at Mensant's lead.

Naturally, Mensant himself didn't seem bothered. He was a professional gambler, well accustomed to the ebbs and flows of fortune.

Far more interesting was Phramp's reaction.

It came gradually, as gradually as the reversal of fortune itself. But Lando could see his change from confusion to suspicion to certainty as he realized someone else at the table was playing his game straight back at him.

Only he wasn't quite as good at spotting cheaters as he was at being one. Lando watched in dark amusement as Phramp's eyes darted back and forth around the table, trying to tag his unknown opponent. But as far as Lando could tell he never completely narrowed it down.

Of course, the task was made harder by the fact that Zerba wasn't operating alone. Lando didn't dare risk any actual cheating, not with this crowd, certainly not with the cam droids hovering at the ceiling showing the hand-by-hand action to the spectators spread out around the ballroom. But that didn't mean he couldn't judiciously throw a hand whenever it would help one of Mensant's rivals.

And as the game progressed through the late-night hours into those of early morning, he wondered what Jydor was going to say when Phramp warned him that someone was messing with his plan.

What he would say, and what he would do.

"The game's certainly getting interesting," Bink reported, her tone giving Tavia a quick mental image of her sister's smugly satisfied expression. "Hard to tell from back here, but it looks like Phramp's about to burst a blood vessel."

"That's nice," Tavia said mechanically, only a fraction of her attention on Bink's running commentary. She almost had the encryption solved now. The right nudge, in the right direction, and it should shatter, leaving the mysterious text clear and open.

She took a deep breath, feeling a surge of satisfaction. This kind of computer slicing wasn't really her forte—her strengths ran more to the hardware side of the electronics spectrum. To have gotten this far this quickly was highly gratifying.

Of course, the person who'd created the patch didn't seem to be all that skilled at such things, either. But that was okay. An achievement was an achievement, and there was no point in muddying it up with ifs, ands, buts, and qualifiers. She gave it one final tweak—

And the encryption was gone. Smiling, Tavia ran her eyes down the mysterious text. Her smile faded, the glow of satisfaction vanished into something cold and unpleasant.

She read the note three times, her sense of bewilderment growing deeper with each pass.

Distantly, she became aware that Bink was still chattering cheerfully. Reading through the text one final time, she groped for the comlink. "Bink?"

"What's wrong?" Bink asked, all levity gone from her voice. She knew Tavia's verbal cues as intimately as Tavia knew hers.

"Something very strange," Tavia said. "And very wrong."

"I'm on my way," Bink said. "Looks like the boys will be going on for a while. Do you need them, too?"

"There's no rush," Tavia said. "Actually, the longer they're in the game, the longer we'll have to figure out what's going on. And I'm thinking we're going to need every bit of that time."

"No," Zerba said firmly, his eyes narrowed, his hair again doing that rippling thing Lando had noticed once before. "I don't buy it."

"It's right there," Bink said, gesturing toward Tavia's datapad.

"But it's ridiculous," Zerba said. "Who leaves a murder note?"

"Lady Vanq, apparently," Lando murmured, his eyes tracking down the text:

To the Danteel City police authorities:
If I am found dead by violence, be advised that my killer is Master Veilred Jydor. He has been a business rival for many years, and currently holds me responsible for his failed bid for the Lockyern account. He is a violent and vindictive human, and I have no doubt that he will soon make a deadly move against me for pride's sake.

I have arranged for this note to be transmitted upon news of my death. I beg from the dark beyond that you will bring justice to my fate.

Lady Carisica Vanq, Danteel City, Danteel

"It can't be legit," Zerba insisted. "The only way it could work is if the programming patch was in place before the murder, *and* Lady Vanq somehow managed to intertwine a message into it, *and* that she did it while dying of a massive blaster burn."

"*And* that it didn't occur to her to simply call the police directly instead of doing all that," Lando added.

"Exactly," Zerba said, nodding. "That sort of thing only happens in badly written mystery holodramas."

"Agreed," Bink said. "And you're right about the patch having been created before the murder—otherwise, the droids would have seen the killer come in. As you also said, the message had to have been intertwined at the same time." She seemed to brace herself. "And since the message implicates Jydor, that means he's *not* the murderer."

Lando looked at Tavia. She'd always been the less talkative of the pair, though she was perfectly capable of relaxing and having fun if the circumstances and company were right. But at the moment her usual reserve had descended into something dark and brooding. "If not Jydor, then who?" he asked. "Tavia?"

Reluctantly, she raised her eyes from her contemplation of the floor. "There's only one person that makes sense," she said. "Jydor's business manager, Chumu."

"*Chumu?*" Zerba echoed, his eyes widening briefly. "No—that's ridiculous. He's a businessman. An accountant and deal maker. They're not the murdering type."

"That guard, Rovi, is probably in it with him," Bink pointed out. "From what I saw, he could definitely be the murdering type."

"But—" Zerba began.

"Look at the facts," Bink interrupted. "Or rather, look at the situation if this all goes down the way it looks like it was supposed to. Lady Vanq, a serious business rival, is now gone. Her supposed warning note will be enough to launch an investigation, and under Danteel law Jydor will be barred from running his business until the probe is complete. That leaves Chumu in charge."

"There's more," Tavia said. "I've done a correlation analysis with HoloNet communications and credit transfers, and I'm pretty sure Mensant is playing the tournament on behalf of another of Jydor's business rivals, a Twi'lek named Arvakke. If Phramp can throw a charge of cheating against Mensant, and make it stick, that'll wash up against Arvakke under Danteel's agent–principal felony linkage laws."

"Meaning that Arvakke won't be able to run *his* business, either, until the charges are cleared up," Bink said. "With two major rivals out of the way—three if you count Jydor himself—Chumu is in the perfect position to move in and take over."

Zerba gave a little snort. "Winner take all, just like Jydor said."

"Except it's not the winner he had in mind," Bink agreed tightly. "The question is what we do about it."

Zerba shrugged. "I'm still good with running, especially if Chumu's targeting Jydor. With a fish that big on the hook, he's not going to bother hunting minnows."

"Only if the big fish stays on the hook," Tavia said. "If he wiggles free, I don't doubt Chumu would go back to pointing fingers in the most convenient direction."

"That direction being toward Bink?" Lando asked.

"Exactly," Bink said. "With the bio-suppressant masking the decay profiles and time-of-death readings, the cops won't know whether she died two weeks ago or yesterday until they do a complete layer-autopsy. There's no way Jydor or I or anyone else will be able to come up with an alibi for that long a window."

"And the whole thing will be triggered by the supposed murder note," Lando said. "I assume the encryption vanishes when the programming patch is taken off?"

"Basically," Tavia said. "And it doesn't just sit in her computer system, either. Like the note said, it's set to be transmitted straight to the police."

"So Bink's only way out is for us to prove that Chumu did it?"

"Basically," Bink said, eyeing him closely. "You have an idea?"

"I think so," Lando said. "Tavia, can you get into the text of that note? I mean far enough to change it and then put the encryption back on without that being obvious?"

"Probably," Tavia said. "But not from here. This is just a copy—I'd have to get back into Lady Vanq's house to do that."

"Good," Lando said. "One more question: can you also get into the casino's computer system?"

"How deep in do you need?"

"Not very," Lando assured her. "I just need access to low-level functions. Housekeeping, environmental functions—that sort of thing."

"She'll need a tap," Bink said. "But I can pop one in anytime and have it ready whenever she needs it."

"Good." Lando looked at Zerba. "Winner take all, you said? I think it's time we realigned Chumu's way of thinking."

The next evening's session was well under way when Bink arrived at Jydor's private turbolift and announced she was there to see Master Chumu. There was a short comlink conference, after which the guard allowed her passage.

Not surprisingly, Chumu was waiting when the turbolift doors opened. Also not surprisingly, he didn't look happy to see her. "What are you doing here?" he demanded.

"You said you wanted me to check out the Tchine downstairs," Bink reminded him.

"The operative word being *downstairs,*" he retorted. "I don't need you up here."

"You do if you want your readings," Bink said, slipping past him and heading for the lounge outside the art display room where the two of them had held their meeting the previous day.

"Wait a minute," Chumu said, hurrying to catch up. "Where are you going?"

"I can't exactly wander the streets with an illegal sensor," Bink said over her shoulder. "I have to assemble it, and for that I need privacy." She reached the lounge and sat down in the chair directly in front of the security holocam.

"You might be more comfortable at the kitchen counter," Chumu said, dithering uncertainly in the doorway as she opened her bag and started laying out the collection of electronic components she and Tavia had thrown together. "There's more space and considerably more privacy."

"This is fine," Bink assured him. "If you really want privacy, you can shut off that holocam behind me. Or feel free to leave it on—I'm sure you'll be able to explain my presence somehow."

Chumu threw a hooded look at the holocam. "You're here to take some acoustical readings for a possible new entertainment system," he said. "There's no sound on that holocam, so you don't have to worry about what we say."

"Fine," Bink said. "Incidentally, you're welcome to watch. But I promise you won't see anything."

For a moment she continued laying out her gear in silence. Chumu looked at the security holocam again, then crossed reluctantly to one of the other chairs around the table. Pulling out a datapad, he settled down to read.

Bink finished laying out the components. As she started putting them together, she surreptitiously checked her chrono. Her timing, as usual, was perfect.

Any minute now . . .

Theoretically, Tavia knew, the maid outfit Bink had worn a couple of days ago should fit her just as well as it had her sister. But where Bink had worn it with casual ease, Tavia could feel the clothing pressing against her torso and arms, the effect hovering on the edge of claustrophobia. The stack of towels she'd collected from their room as camouflage felt as heavy as an Imperial cruiser balanced across her forearms. The plush carpet and carved ceiling and walls of the ninety-ninth-floor hallway seemed to stare accusingly at the intruder even as they echoed her heartbeat back at her.

She hated this. She really, truly hated this. "You! Stop!"

Tavia's breath froze in her lungs, her muscles fortunately stiffening instead of betraying her by jerking with obvious guilt. Sternly ordering her body to behave, reminding herself that by all appearances it was perfectly reasonable for her to be here, she turned around. "Yes?" she asked diffidently.

An elegantly dressed Togruta was striding down the hallway toward her, his striped upper horns gleaming as if freshly polished, the dark eyes in the red-and-gray-patterned face staring at and through her.

"Yes?" Tavia repeated, this time hearing a slight shaking in her voice.

The Togruta reached her and, without a word, plucked the top towel off the stack in her arms, then turned and walked away.

For a moment Tavia watched as he headed back to his room, her heart slowly calming down. He could have just asked. He *should* have just asked.

But she was simply a maid, a human doing a droid's work, here for no better reason than that Jydor thought living servants made for a more elegant background than mechanical ones. Why *shouldn't* one of the guests treat her as if she were nothing?

She turned back around and continued on her way. She really, truly, *passionately* hated this.

But it was Bink's life on the line. What else could she do?

The suite Bink had specified was, thankfully, unoccupied. Locking the door behind her, Tavia crossed to the window and set down her small pile of towels on a nearby chair. She pulled out Bink's ghost-burglar sensor and the rest of the equipment that had been hidden in the middle of the stack, and set to work.

Her first task was to find and neutralize whatever alarms had been set up on the windows. Fortunately, there was only one, which the sensor quickly spotted. Bink, Tavia knew, could probably have disarmed it in five seconds or less. It took Tavia two nerve-racking minutes.

Most hotels in Danteel City employed the standard opaquing window glass common throughout the galaxy. But true luxury places still used curtains or drapes, especially in their finest suites, and Jydor was clearly determined that his ninety-ninth floor be as elegant as the best of them. The window had two sets of curtains: one set gauzy, with a half-twist weave that turned stars and city lights into individual spinning galaxies, the other set a much heavier and more luxurious material that would block the morning sunlight from late sleepers.

The gauzy ones would be faster and easier to work with, she decided. Pulling down one of them and its support rods, she arranged the curtain and rods in a square on the floor. Two minutes later, she had the curtain stretched across the rods like a wind sail, all of it glued solidly together with dabs of rock putty. She fastened two more curtain rods to the far end of the square, angling them back and upward.

Now came the tricky part. Opening the window, she eased the net outside, setting it horizontally just beneath the window and gluing the near end to the wall. Two more daubs of putty on the ends of the support struts, likewise anchoring them to the wall, and it was ready.

For a moment she gazed out at her handiwork. Bink had assured her this would work, and Bink was almost always right about these things. Tavia could only hope she was right about this one, too.

She checked her chrono. Any minute now . . .

It started subtly, with Zerba muttering under his breath as he gazed hard at the Tchine sitting in its display pyramid in the center of the table. But it didn't stay subtle for long. Gradually, his volume increased until the whole table could hear him.

"I'm telling you, there's something wrong with it," the Balosar insisted. "I saw another Tchine up close once. There's just something wrong with this one."

Lando looked around the table. The current dealer—Mensant, as it happened—was still shuffling, either oblivious to Zerba's monologue or simply ignoring it. The other players, though, were paying attention, and some of them were now also staring hard at the figurine.

Time for Lando to put in his half credit's worth. "It's probably some kind of optical illusion," he told Zerba. "I saw one once, too, and I agree it looks odd. It's probably just some kind of reflection off the transparisteel."

"Maybe," Zerba said darkly. He half turned into his seat and gestured to Jydor. "How about letting us see it without its fancy dress?"

"I think not," Jydor said, his tone polite but with an edge to it. "I owe it to the eventual victor to keep his prize safe."

"Besides, I'm sure he has a certificate of authenticity," Lando said. "He would hardly have bought it without one."

"Maybe he could show that to us," Zerba suggested, still gazing suspiciously at Jydor.

"I'm sure Master Jydor is trustworthy," Lando said. "As I said before—"

"A trick of the light," Zerba growled. "Yes, we all heard you. I'd still like to see the certificate."

Across the table, Phramp cleared his throat. "With all due respect, Master Jydor, it wouldn't take long, and we're about due for a break anyway."

Jydor hesitated, then gave a reluctant nod. "If it'll put an end to this nonsense, fine," he said. He pulled out his comlink.

Right on schedule, Chumu stirred and pulled out his comlink. "Yes?"

There was a moment of silence as the person at the other end spoke. Watching out of the corner of her eye, Bink saw Chumu's lip twitch. "Yes, of course," he said. "I'll bring it down immediately."

He clicked off and stood up. "I have to go downstairs for a minute," he said, crossing the lounge in the direction of Jydor's private office.

"Take your time," Bink said, not raising her head from her work. "I'd just as soon not have an audience anyway."

Chumu reached the door and hesitated, and she saw his eyes again flick up to the security holocam. The reminder that she was under constant surveillance seemed to calm him a little. "There's a guard in the next room over," he added. He was trying to project a gruff forcefulness, but Bink could hear the tension and nervousness beneath the words. Clearly, he wasn't happy with all these changes that were interfering with his neat little frame-up. "If you need anything, just call. If he asks, don't forget—"

"I'm taking acoustical readings," Bink cut in. "Yes, I've got it."

Chumu hesitated another second, then finally left, closing the door behind him. Bink gave him thirty seconds more, just to make sure he wouldn't pop back in unexpectedly. Then, making a final minute adjustment to the angle of the projector she'd set up under Chumu's nose, she turned it on.

And with the projector sending the video she and Tavia had created straight into the surveillance holocam, whatever guard or droid was watching the feed would see nothing except her working industriously at the table.

For the next two minutes, she was invisible.

She'd been able to read the vault door's coding sequence during her earlier soft probe through the display room floor, but there was always the chance that Jydor might have changed it during the past couple of days. But luck was with her. She punched in the sequence, and the door popped. Pulling it open just far enough to slip through, she headed inside.

The Tchine was right where she'd last seen it, hidden away in the corner of the room. She pulled off the cloth covering it, grabbed another similar-sized object, and put it in the Tchine's place with the cloth again draped over it. Then, with her prize in hand, she slipped back out to the lounge. She closed and sealed the door, and headed over to the line of windows.

Hopefully, Tavia was ready. Even more hopefully, she'd gotten the correct room and the correct window.

Bink opened the ventilation aperture at the top of the window, maneuvered the Tchine through the narrow gap, and let it fall.

When it finally happened, it came almost as an anticlimax. One minute the net was empty, the curtain material fluttering in the wind flowing across the city. The next minute there was a muffled thud, and a priceless art object lay within Tavia's reach, bobbing gently in the breeze.

Three minutes later, with the curtains and rods back in place and the window alarm reset, she walked back through the door and the relative safety of the hallway, the Tchine concealed inside her stack of towels. On one level, she always expected Bink's plans to work. On another level, she was always terrified they would fail.

So far, this one seemed to be working. So far.

Bink gave her sister five minutes to complete her part of the operation, then another three just to be sure. Then, putting three final pieces into the ridiculous-looking device she'd been building, she called for the guard.

"I'm ready to go," she said, stuffing everything back into her bag. "Master Chumu said I should meet him downstairs."

"All right," the guard said, stepping forward and taking a quick look into her pouch. Apparently satisfied that she hadn't somehow teleported the fancy tableware out of the dining room cabinet, he escorted her to the turbolift and gestured her in.

Twice on the trip down she almost called Tavia to see if everything had gone according to the plan. Both times she left her comlink in her belt.

Tavia was good at this, far better than Tavia herself realized. Besides, if you couldn't trust your own sister to come through for you, who *could* you trust?

Lando took his time examining the Tchine certificate Chumu had brought down from the penthouse. The other players were equally thorough. By the time they finished, nearly fifteen minutes had passed, and Chumu was clearly starting to sweat.

"Satisfied?" Jydor asked as the last player handed back the datapad.

"Absolutely," Phramp said, apparently having decided that he was authorized to speak for the entire table. "Thank you, Master Jydor."

Jydor looked at Zerba. "Satisfied?" he repeated.

"I suppose," Zerba muttered.

"Then I suggest we continue with the game," Jydor said, settling back in his chair and handing the datapad to Chumu. "Take it back upstairs," he ordered.

"Yes, sir," Chumu said. Tucking the datapad under his arm, he climbed down from the double platform, eased between the guards, and headed across the ballroom.

Lando watched him go, then turned back to the table. Bink had said ten minutes should be enough, and he and Zerba had given her fifteen. They should be good to go.

Mensant finished his fresh shuffle and began dealing the cards. Smoothing out his mustache, Lando prepared his mind for the game.

Tavia had expected Chumu to spot her in the restaurant on his way out of the ballroom. But he apparently wasn't expecting things to have moved this quickly and bypassed the restaurant in favor of heading straight to the private turbolift. Tavia thought about chasing him down, decided it wasn't something Michelle the professional art forger would do, and remained seated at her table. Sipping the nonalcoholic drink she'd ordered, she nurtured her patience.

Three minutes later he was back. This time he spotted her and hurried over.

"*There* you are," he growled as he dropped into the seat across from her. "What are you doing here?"

"My job," Tavia said, trying for the sardonic-edged professional tone that Bink had said she'd used on the man earlier. "What kept you?"

"What kept—" He broke off, glaring a little harder. "How long have you been down here?"

"Almost as long as you have," Tavia told him.

Which wasn't quite true, of course. In actual fact, she'd arrived at the table barely a minute before he'd left the ballroom, after her quick exchange of clothing and equipment with Bink in the ladies' refresher. "You need to pay better attention to your surroundings," she added.

"Don't be cute," he bit out. "How are you planning to do this?"

"No planning needed," Tavia said. "It's done."

He seemed taken aback. "What do you mean?"

"I mean I took the readings." Tavia gestured toward the ballroom. "You were right. It's a copy."

"Wait a minute," he growled. "How could you have taken the readings? I didn't see you in there."

"You weren't supposed to," Tavia said, adding some strained patience to her voice. That one was easy—it was a tone she used with Bink a lot. "Did you hear what I just said? Master Jydor's Tchine is a copy."

Chumu's face stiffened, then seemed to close in on itself as the words finally penetrated. His eyes shifted to her equipment bag, resting on the chair beside her, then to the ballroom entrance, then back to her face. "You're sure?"

"Positive," Tavia said. "It's a very good copy, actually. The artist used the same techniques and materials I do."

Chumu swallowed visibly. "No way to tell who that artist is, I suppose?"

"Not without a closer look." Tavia wiggled her fingers. "You have my ten thousand?"

Chumu looked back into the ballroom. "Yes, of course," he said, pulling a credit tab from his pocket and sliding it across the table to her. "You said you made a similar copy for Lady Vanq?"

"I did," Tavia said sourly. "Though if I don't get paid soon I'll be taking it back."

"Assuming you can even find it."

"Oh, it's probably in her vault with the real one," Tavia said, peering at the credit tab. Ten thousand as agreed, nonencrypted, ready for her to simply take somewhere and deposit or cash. "She was talking about taking it to Devaron with her, and according to the spaceport records her ship's still here," she continued, tucking the credit tab into a pocket. "So what are you going to do about your little tournament problem?"

"That'll be up to Master Jydor," Chumu murmured, his mind clearly elsewhere. "I'll let him know and we'll go from there. Thank you for your assistance. I'll be in touch."

Tavia frowned. "About . . ."

"About making copies of some of Master Jydor's other artwork."

Tavia felt her stomach tighten. With the end of her masquerade in sight, she'd briefly forgotten that that had been Bink's entry vector into this whole thing.

Luckily, Chumu seemed too preoccupied to notice her slip. "Of course," she said, standing up and looping the strap of her bag over her shoulder. "Good luck."

She headed across the restaurant, her shoulder blades itching with the vivid image of a blaster bolt flashing across the open space and burning between them.

But the shot didn't come. Chumu had apparently bought the story. Now if only he would react the way Bink and Lando hoped.

From that last lingering look he'd sent toward the ballroom, Tavia rather thought he would.

It was late evening when Jydor finally called for a dinner break.

It had been a good few hours, Lando decided as he eased himself out of his chair, wincing as unused muscles were suddenly recalled to duty. Mensant was still ahead of the pack, but his once commanding lead had been whittled down to nearly nothing. The other players had noticed and were brimming with fresh confidence as they realized it was once again a wide-open game.

Phramp, unsurprisingly, was fit to be tied.

So, apparently, was Chumu, though for entirely different reasons. As Lando and the other players and spectators filed out of the ballroom, he caught a glimpse of the business manager pushing his way upstream against the crowd, making for the platform where Jydor was still sitting, studying something on his datapad.

Pulling out his comlink, Lando keyed for Zerba.

"Yeah, I saw him," the Balosar said after Lando gave him the news. "He's worried, all right."

"The question is whether he's worried enough," Lando said. "You want to watch him, or should I?"

"No need," Tavia's voice cut in. "I've got electrobinoculars and a clear view. You two go get some food. I'll let you know what happens."

Tavia's first report came as Lando was ordering a light meal: Chumu was telling Jydor of rumors that a professional armed robbery team was in the city, and that he was concerned the Tchine might be their target. Jydor seemed unimpressed, but Chumu was pressing his point and urging that the figurine be returned to the safety of the penthouse display room.

Jydor didn't seem inclined to bow to pressure, especially not pressure from a gang of robbers. But Chumu kept at him, and as Jydor headed to his private dining room for his own meal he finally gave in. As Jydor disappeared into the dining room, Chumu collected the Tchine and the guards, and they marched together out of the ballroom and into the turbolift.

Tavia's second report, midway through Lando's meal, was that the guard Rovi had emerged alone from the turbolift, a carrybag looped securely over his shoulder, and was heading for the exit.

"Better warn Bink that company's on the way," Lando said, though he doubted Tavia needed any such nudging.

She didn't. "Already done," she said. "By the time the game resumes, it should all be over."

Lando made a face as he put away his comlink. Their part of it would be over, certainly.

But his wouldn't.

Though it could be. Things were far enough along that even if he left right now Chumu's grand scheme would still lie in ruins. Jydor would be in the clear; and while Chumu might not get all the punishment he deserved, Lando had long ago recognized that it wasn't a perfect universe.

He scowled. On the other hand, if he bailed Bink wouldn't be pleased. And Bink not pleased wasn't something he was ready to face right now. Probably not ever.

With a sigh, he turned back to his meal. Not exactly what he'd signed up for when he first arrived on Danteel. But he'd come this far. He might as well see it through.

Tavia, Bink knew, hated the rare situations where she had to impersonate her ghost-thief sister. But even hating it, she still did a good job of it.

Unfortunately, the same couldn't be said in reverse.

"You finished?" Tavia's anxious voice came over Bink's comlink clip.

"Almost," Bink growled, glaring at her datapad and Tavia's supposedly simple, step-by-step instructions on how to break into the encryption.

Step-by-step, maybe. Simple, absolutely not.

"You mean you *aren't*? Come on, Bink—he'll be there any minute."

"Then shut up and let me work," Bink shot back, irritably swiping at a lock of hair that had fallen down in front of her eyes. She could do this. She *had* to do this.

And then, from somewhere outside, she heard the unmistakable sound of a closing door. "He's here," she whispered urgently. "I'll call you back." She keyed off the comlink clip and looked quickly around the bedroom. Even with half a dozen chairs and wide lounge tables scattered around, there was really only one place she could reasonably hope to hide.

She was under the bed, as far back as she could get, when the door opened and someone stepped into the darkened room. From what she could see of his boots, it was almost certainly Rovi.

Bink held her breath, wondering if he would take a

moment to clear the room before he got down to business. Most thieves made that a habit, and she suspected thieves who also dabbled in murder would be even more likely to do so. She had a small hold-out blaster, but it was buried beneath her in a belly holster. If he decided to look under the bed, she was finished.

But for once he missed a bet. Closing the door, he headed directly across the room to Lady Vanq's safe. Bink heard the faint sound of clicking code bars, and with a soft thud the door unlocked. The heavy panel swung open, and Rovi disappeared inside.

Keeping one eye on the door, Bink keyed her datapad again. With cracks starting to show at the edges of Chumu's plan, she had little doubt that Rovi's orders were to dissolve the computer patch as soon as he'd replaced the supposedly fake Tchine with the real one and was safely out of the house. Bink had until then to break in and change the text of the murder note. She finished the last two steps in Tavia's instructions . . .

And with gratifying and about-time speed, she was in.

She'd hidden the Tchine she'd gotten from Jydor's display room just well enough to make it plausible that Rovi could have missed it on his first pass through the safe after the murder. Barely a minute later he'd done the switch and emerged from the safe, closing it behind him and retracing his steps across the room.

But that minute had been all Bink needed. She'd altered the text, put the encryption back in place, and extricated herself from the house computer system.

She waited thirty seconds after Rovi closed the bedroom door behind him. Then, slipping out from beneath the bed, she hurried to the window and the harness tucked out of sight there. Rovi would be returning to the High Card, no doubt wanting to be present when the police swooped in on his soon-to-be-former boss.

Bink had no intention of letting the show start without her.

The hand had just been dealt when Lando spotted Chumu making his way through the crowd of observers to the base of the platform. Apparently all was set, and he'd come to watch firsthand the culmination of his plan.

Lando looked at his cards. It wasn't a bad hand, but it certainly wasn't a great one. Even with the shifting-card system that was part of sabacc, it wasn't likely to get much better.

He set down his cards and took a deep breath. This was going to hurt. "All in," he announced, pushing his small stack of chips into the center of the table.

The other players looked at him, their expressions ranging from disbelief to contempt to suspicion.

Lando agreed pretty much with all of them, especially the contemptuous ones. Unfortunately, he needed to be away from the table when the police arrived, and this was the fastest way to make that happen.

The bidding began, with some fresh spirit infusing the proceedings as the others saw a chance of eliminating one of their number. A few minutes later, after equally spirited play, the hand came to an end.

To no one's surprise, Lando lost.

He stood up, offered the traditional gracious thanks to the other players and to their host, then headed down the steps to the floor below. Choosing a seat where he was in Chumu's line of sight, he sat down and waited.

The wait wasn't long. Phramp had dealt the next hand and the bidding was under way when a sudden surprised murmur rippled across the floor from the ballroom entrance. Lando craned his neck to look just as half a dozen men and women in the uniforms of Danteel City Police strode into the room and headed toward the double platform.

Lando looked at Jydor. The man was still just sitting there, his face unreadable as he watched the officers' approach. The players, concentrating on the game, seemed largely oblivious.

"Good evening, Lieutenant Stenberk," Jydor called courteously as the group reached the platform and came to a stop outside the lower guard ring. "May I ask what brings you to the High Card at this hour?"

"I'm afraid I have some unpleasant news, Master Jydor," Stenberk said. His tone was also courteous, but it had a grimly official edge beneath it. "I suggest we continue our conversation in your office."

"What kind of unpleasant news is it?" Phramp asked before Jydor could reply. The players had finally become aware of the looming drama, their cards forgotten in their hands as they stared at the police. "Is it something that might affect the tournament? If so, we deserve to know what it is."

"I'm sure it has nothing to do with any of you," Chumu soothed.

"How can you possibly know that?" Phramp retorted scornfully. "No, on behalf of all of us players, I formally request that this be handled out in the open where we can hear what's going on."

"Master Phramp—" Chumu began.

"In fact, I'll go further," Phramp cut in. "Having paid ten million credits for a seat at this table, I insist that what Lieutenant Stenberk has to say be said right here and now."

Chumu looked up at Jydor and held his hands out helplessly, as if the whole scene hadn't been carefully scripted between him and Phramp. "Master Jydor?" he asked.

"I have nothing to hide," Jydor said, his voice steady but his eyes narrowed. "You may proceed, Lieutenant."

"As you wish," Stenberk said. "I regret to inform you, sir, that Lady Carisica Vanq has been found dead in her home."

Jydor sat up a bit straighter. "She's *dead*? How?"

Lando shifted his attention to Chumu. There was just the hint of a satisfied smile playing at the corners of the manager's lips.

"It was suicide, sir," Stenberk said. "She shot herself with a blaster."

The smile on Chumu's face vanished. "*Suicide*?" he gasped. "But . . . how do you know?"

"She left a note," Stenberk said, turning to face him. "More precisely, she had it transmitted to us."

"There was a—" Chumu clamped his mouth shut. "I mean . . ."

"The reason we're here, sir," Stenberk continued, looking back up at Jydor, "is that Lady Vanq also possessed a Tchine statue like yours. Under the circumstances—I'm sure you understand."

"Of course," Jydor said. "I'll have Master Chumu get my certificate of purchase and authenticity."

"That would be very helpful, sir," Stenberk said. "We'll also want—a moment, please," he interrupted himself, pulling out his comlink. "Stenberk."

There was a moment of silence as he listened. "Understood," he said. "Thank you, Sergeant."

He put the comlink away. "It turns out the certificate won't be necessary after all," he told Jydor. "We've now been allowed into Lady Vanq's safe, and her Tchine is there."

Chumu's eyes were bulging now, his breath quick and shallow, his face tight with utter bewilderment. "Are you sure it isn't—" He broke off. "I understand some collectors make copies of their artworks," he continued, his voice strained, his words obviously being chosen very carefully. "Are you sure the Tchine you found isn't something like that?"

"Quite sure," Stenberk said, eyeing Chumu thoughtfully. "The sensor profile precisely matches that of a genuine Tchine." He looked at Jydor again. "I'm sorry to have bothered you, sir." He started to turn away.

"Hold it!" Zerba snapped, jabbing a finger at Phramp. "What the—that's a skifter. You've got a skifter!"

"What are you talking about?" Phramp demanded, frowning at his cards. "I don't use skifters."

"Like hell you don't." Zerba gestured emphatically at Stenberk. "You—Lieutenant. Come up here. I want a witness."

"Master Jydor?" Stenberk asked.

"Of course," Jydor said, gesturing to the lieutenant as he stared hard at Phramp. "Let's have a look."

He stepped over behind Phramp as Stenberk climbed the steps. Lando looked at Chumu again, to see that the manager's earlier bewilderment had turned to frozen horror.

Stenberk stepped behind Phramp and plucked the cards from his hand. He touched each corner in turn— "He's right," he told Jydor, offering the other one of the cards. "It's a skifter."

"That's impossible," Phramp protested. "It must have been planted on me."

"How?" Jydor asked. "You dealt that hand."

"I—" Phramp sputtered, looking around the table in bewilderment. "I don't know. But it must have been."

"Get out of here," Jydor said, his voice deadly soft. "I don't ever want to see you in the High Card again."

Silently, his face a mass of confusion and anger, Phramp stood up and headed down the steps, moving like a man in a bad dream.

"Do you want me to arrest him?" Stenberk asked.

"Don't bother," Jydor said, watching Phramp as he

moved through the crowd toward the exit. "Someone paid ten million credits to get him into the game. I doubt the punishment he'll receive from his patron for his failure will be easier than the legal penalty for cheating at sabacc."

"You're probably right," Stenberk agreed. "Speaking of sabacc, I'd best let you get on with your tournament. Sorry to have interrupted."

"Not a problem," Jydor said, his eyes still on Phramp. Lando turned to look at Chumu again.

This time, Chumu was looking back at him. And there was murder in those eyes.

Time for Lando to make himself scarce. Standing up, he turned his back on Chumu and headed across the ballroom.

But not toward the main entrance, the direction Phramp had gone. For the next few minutes, that area might not be healthy for Lando to be in.

Fortunately, there was another option. The previous night at this time, he'd noticed that one of the large side chambers separated from the main ballroom by a high archway had been closed for cleaning. Cleaning schedules being the rigid things they often were, there was a good chance it would be closed now, as well.

It was. Slipping past the simple rope barrier that had been set up between the chamber and the ballroom, he picked up his pace, making for the emergency exit at the far end.

"Stop."

Lando allowed himself two more steps before coming to a halt. Keeping his hands visible, he turned around.

Chumu was striding toward him, his face thunderous, a small hold-out blaster gripped in his hand.

"I'd think you'd have better things to do right now," Lando suggested. "Finding a way to clean up your mes[illegible] for starters."

"The mess is yours, not mine," Chumu retorted, [illegible]

ping three paces away and leveling the gun at Lando's stomach. "Who are you? Who are you working for?"

"My name's on the tournament application," Lando said. "And I'm not working for anyone."

"No, of course you're not," Chumu ground out sarcastically. "You just *happened* to stumble on my plans and decide to spit on them?"

"Actually, that's pretty much exactly what happened," Lando conceded. "Though I suppose in your place I wouldn't believe it, either." He nodded toward the blaster. "You're not seriously thinking about going the revenge route, are you? I doubt the police will believe two blaster suicides in the same day."

"Oh, and that was *especially* cute," Chumu growled. "What did you do, slice into Rovi's droid-block programming and change the message?"

"Basically," Lando said. "It was a great plan, though. Really. Freezing Jydor out of his own operation while simultaneously taking down his two biggest competitors was sheer genius. Winner take all, just as Jydor announced at the beginning." He considered. "Though now, I suppose, it's more like winner lose all."

Chumu snorted. "What makes you think I've lost?"

"Please," Lando said disdainfully. "What are you going to do, find another of Jydor's rivals you can kill and frame him for? Police *do* know how to look for patterns, you know."

"What pattern?" Chumu countered. "There's no pattern here. Thanks to you, Vanq's death will go into the data list as a suicide." He raised the blaster a little higher. "And you're right about two suicides looking suspicious. I guess we'll have to kill you in self-defense."

"*We* meaning you and Rovi?" Lando asked. "Or do ›u just mean Rovi? Generally, you mastermind types ı't handle any of the actual killing yourselves."

ˈlot normally, no," Chumu agreed. "But in your case,

I think I'll make an exception." With his free hand he pulled out another hold-out blaster and tossed it onto the floor at Lando's feet. "Pick it up."

"I don't think so," Lando said, making no move toward the weapon. "I'd hate there to be any misunderstandings when the police arrive."

Chumu shook his head. "Nice try, but the police all went in the other direction."

"They'll be back," Lando assured him. "Right now, they're probably just enjoying the show."

Chumu frowned. "What show?"

"That one." Smiling, Lando raised his hand and pointed upward . . .

. . . at the cam droid that Tavia had retasked with the job of following Lando around. "Winner lose all," Lando said quietly. "And my friend is right. You really *do* need to pay better attention to your surroundings."

Chumu was standing motionless, apparently with nothing left to say, when Stenberk and his men arrived.

"So how does it feel?" Tavia asked as the police escorted Chumu through the murmuring crowd and out through the ballroom exit. "Doing the right thing, I mean?"

A flip, slightly sarcastic answer popped into Lando's mind. But Tavia deserved better than that. "It feels good," he admitted. He looked back at the platform where the tournament was already in progress again. "It also feels expensive."

"You wouldn't have won," Bink reminded him. "You know that, right?"

"Maybe," Lando said. "Probably." He exhaled a sigh. "You know the worst thing about being a gambler? It' all the wondering about what might have been. How different play—a different card—a different hand m have made all the difference in the universe."

Bink gave a little snort. "I've got news for you, Lando. That's not a gambler's problem. That's life, for everyone."

"She's right," Tavia said soberly. "Once you make a decision, you can never go back and change it. Sometimes, farther down the line, you have a chance to alter its effects. But the original decision is there forever."

"And we all have those wonderings and regrets," Bink agreed. "There's really only one way to soothe them."

"Time?"

She smiled. "Money." Taking his hand, she pressed something into it. "Here's the ten thousand credits Chumu paid me to tell him the Tchine was a fake."

Lando frowned. "For me? Shouldn't we split it four ways?"

"We should," Bink agreed. "But we aren't going to."

"After all, we dragged you into this," Tavia reminded him. "It's not like winning a forty-million-credit figurine, but it should at least get you off the planet and someplace more promising."

"But—"

"And don't worry about us," Bink admonished, closing Lando's fingers firmly over the credit tab. "If I know Zerba, he's off looking for another job as we speak."

"Or going through other people's pockets," Tavia said disapprovingly.

"Either way, we'll be fine," Bink said. "So go. Shoo."

Lando made a face. But there was a time to object, and a time to simply accept something with thanks.

And it wasn't like he hadn't earned it. "You two take care," he said. Scooping up their right hands, he lifted them to his lips for a quick kiss each.

"We will," Tavia said.

"Until the next job," Bink added with a roguish smile.

"Which will probably be a long time coming," Lando ned.

k shrugged. "Maybe. But you never know."

Look for these thrilling new *Star Wars* novels, featuring classic characters

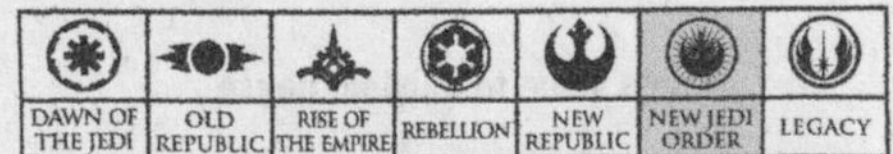